Dear Reader,

Many years ago, when I was a kid, my father said to me, "Bill, it doesn't really matter what you do in life. What's important is to be the *best* William Johnstone you can be."

I've never forgotten those words. And now, many years and almost 200 books later, I like to think that I am still trying to be the best William Johnstone I can be. Whether it's Ben Raines in the Ashes series, or Frank Morgan, the last gunfighter, or Smoke Jensen, our intrepid mountain man, or John Barrone and his hard-working crew keeping America safe from terrorist low-lifes in the Code Name series, I want to make each new book better than the last and deliver powerful storytelling.

Equally important, I try to create the kinds of believable characters that we can all identify with, real people who face tough challenges. When one of my creations blasts an enemy into the middle of next week, you can be damn sure he had a good reason.

As a storyteller, my job is to entertain you, my readers, and to make sure that you get plenty of enjoyment from my books for your hard-earned money. This is not a job I take lightly. And I greatly appreciate your feedback—you are my gold, and your opinions *do* count. So please keep the letters and e-mails coming.

Respectfully yours,

William Johnstone

Dear Readers,

Respectfully yours,

WILLIAM W. JOHNSTONE

PURSUIT OF THE MOUNTAIN MAN

THE FIRST MOUNTAIN MAN: BLOOD ON THE DIVIDE

PINNACLE BOOKS
Kensington Publishing Corp.
http://www.kensingtonbooks.com

PINNACLE BOOKS are published by

Kensington Publishing Corp.
850 Third Avenue
New York, NY 10022

All Kensington Titles, Imprints, and Distributed Lines are
available at special quantity discounts for bulk purchases for
sales promotions, premiums, fund-raising, and educational or
institutional use. Special book excerpts or customized printings
can also be created to fit specific needs. For details, write or
phone the office of the Kensington special sales manager: Kensington Publishing Corp., 850 Third Avenue, New York, NY
10022, attn: Special Sales Department, Phone: 1-800-221-2647.

Pinnacle and the P logo Reg. U.S. Pat. & TM Off.
ISBN-13: 978-0-7860-1899-4
ISBN-10: 0-7860-1899-2

First Pinnacle Books Printing: May 2007

10 9 8 7 6 5 4 3 2 1

Printed in the United States of America

PURSUIT OF THE MOUNTAIN MAN

I never forget a face, but in your case I'll make an exception.

G. Marx

1

The young man had been eyeballing the quiet stranger for several minutes. The young man stood at the bar, sipping whiskey. The quiet stranger sat at a table, his back to a wall, slowly eating his supper and sipping coffee. The young man couldn't understand why the stranger didn't take offense to his staring; couldn't understand why the tough-looking stranger wearing two guns didn't reply to his silent insults.

He just sat there, eating his supper and drinking coffee. The young man concluded the stranger was yellow.

"Kid," the barkeep finally said, "I'd leave that man alone. He's got bad stamped all over him."

"You know him?"

"Nope. But I know the type. Leave him be."

"He don't look like nothin' special to me."

"Your funeral," the barkeep said, and moved to the other end of the bar.

Jack Lynch looked at the barkeep and snorted in disgust. Jack had four notches cut into his gun and was considered by some—in this part of the country—to be very quick on the shoot. He was considered by others to be a loud-mouthed punk who was going to drag iron on the wrong man one day.

That day had come.

Late winter in Utah. The stoves in the saloon glowed red and the winds were cold as they buffeted the building. Four men sat playing a quiet game of penny-ante poker, a few others stood at the long bar, talking and sipping beer or whiskey or, in a couple of cases, both. A gambler sat alone at another table, playing a game of solitaire, waiting for a sucker to come in. One man was passed out, his head on the table, snoring softly.

And the stranger sat alone, finishing his supper.

Jack Lynch turned and put his back to the bar. Now he openly stared at the stranger, a sneer on his face. "You don't have much to say, do you, mister?" he called.

The stranger did not look up. He poured another cup of coffee from the pot and sugared it, slowly stirring the strong brew. Then he started in on his fresh-baked dried apple pie. It had been a long day and he wanted no more than to eat his meal in peace and get a good night's sleep at the small hotel in this Northern Utah town, not many miles from the Wyoming border.

But if this loudmouth kept pushing him . . .

"Hey! I asked you a question, man," Jack raised his voice.

The stranger chewed his pie, swallowed, and took a sip of coffee. He lifted his eyes to the loudmouth. The stranger's eyes were brown and cold-looking, no emotion in them. His shoulders were wide and his arms heavily muscled, his wrists thick. His hands were big and flat-knuckled, scarred from many fights. He was a ruggedly handsome man, well over six feet tall. He wore two guns, one tied low on his right side, the other worn high and butt forward on his left side. A long-bladed knife was in a sheath behind his right-hand gun.

"Since the question was probably very forgettable, I've already forgotten it," the stranger said in a soft voice. "Is it worth repeating?"

"Huh?" Jack said.

"See? You've already forgotten it. So how important can it be?" The stranger returned to his pie and coffee.

The gambler smiled. He thought he knew the stranger's name. And if he was correct, this loudmouth was standing very close to death.

"I don't think I like you very much," Jack said.

"You're at the end of a very long list," the stranger replied. He tapped the coffeepot and looked at the barkeep. "It's empty. Would you bring another pot, please?"

"My, don't he talk *po*-lite, though?" Jack sneered the words. "Like a sissy."

"Jack," one of the cardplayers said. "Why don't you shut your damn mouth and leave the man alone? He ain't bothered no one."

"You want to make me?" Jack challenged the man. "Come on. Make me shut up."

"Oh, go to hell, Jack," another cardplayer said.

Another pot of coffee was placed on the stranger's table and the barkeep backed quickly away. The stranger poured and sugared and stirred and then carefully rolled a cigarette, lighting up.

"My name's Jack Lynch," the young man called to the stranger.

"Everybody should know their name."

The cardplayers laughed at that. The gambler smiled and riffled the cards.

"What do you mean by that?" Jack asked.

"Boy," the stranger said, "do you push all strangers like the way you're proddin' me?"

"Just the ones who think they're tough. I usually prove they ain't."

"And how do you do that, Jack?"

"By stretchin' 'em out on the floor!"

"Did you ever stop to think that one of these days it might well be you that's stretched out on the floor?"

"That don't ever enter my mind," Jack said.

"It should."

"You think you're the man who can do that?"

"Yes," the stranger said softly.

Jack flushed deeply, the color rising to his cheeks. The only reason he hadn't called them old coots at the card table out after they laughed at him was that none of them was wearing a gun. "Stand up!" Jack shouted.

The stranger pushed back his chair and stood up.

"Big," a cardplayer said.

Jack Lynch stood with his legs spread, his hand by his gun.

The front door opened and a blast of cold air swept the saloon. The town marshal stepped in and sized up the situation in about two seconds. "Back off, Jack," he barked the words. "And I mean right now, boy."

"Marshal, I . . ."

"Shut up, Jack!" the marshal hollered. "Put that hammer thong back in place and do it slow. Ahh. That's better. Now settle down." He looked at the stranger. "Been a long time."

"Five years ago. Your horse threw a shoe and you stopped in town. You're looking well."

"Feel fine."

"I recommend the apple pie," the stranger said. "It was delicious." He picked up his hat and settled it on his head.

"I'll sure have me a wedge. And some coffee, Ralph," he said to the barkeep.

"Comin' right up, Marshal."

"See you around," the stranger said.

"See you."

The front door opened and closed and the stranger was gone, walking across the still frozen street to the hotel.

"Sorry, Marshal," Jack said. "I didn't know he was a friend of yours."

The marshal sipped his coffee. "Jack, do you have any idea at all who that was?"

"Some yeller-bellied tinhorn," Jack replied.

The gambler smiled.

The marshal's eyes were bleak as he turned his head to look at the young man. "Jack, you've done some dumb things in the years that I've known you. But today took the cake. That was Smoke Jensen."

Jack swayed for a moment, grabbing at the bar for support. The gambler kicked a chair across the floor and the marshal placed it upright for Jack to sit in. Jack Lynch's eyes were dull and his face was pale. A bit of spittle oozed out of one corner of his mouth.

"I knew it was him as soon as he stood up and I seen that left-hand gun in a cross-draw," the gambler said.

"And . . . you didn't say nothin' to me?" Jack mumbled the words.

"Why should I? It was your mouth that got you into it. You're a loudmouth, pushy kid. It would have served you right if Jensen had drilled you clean through."

Jack recovered his bluster and now he was embarrassed. He stood up from the chair. His legs were still a little shaky and he backed up to the bar and leaned against it. "You can't talk to me like that, gambler."

The marshal was more than a little miffed at Jack's attitude. He'd pulled him out of one situation; be damned if he'd interfere in this one. He walked over to a table and sat down.

Across the street, in his room, Smoke had taken pen and paper and was writing to his wife, Sally.

"Don't push me, kid," the gambler said. "I've lived too long for me to take much crap from the likes of you. Jensen just didn't want to kill you. He's tired of it. I haven't reached that point yet."

"You son of a . . ." Jack grabbed for iron.

The gambler shook his right arm and a derringer slipped into his hand. He fired both barrels of the .41. Jack coughed and sat down on the floor.

Smoke thought he heard gunshots and paused in his writing. When no more shots were heard, he dipped the nib into an ink well and began writing.

Dear Sally,

How are you? I miss you very much but hope you are having a good time visiting family and friends back east . . .

The gambler broke open the .41 derringer and reloaded. Jack's eyes were on him. The front of Jack's white shirt was spreading crimson.

"I don't want to die!" Jack cried.

"You should have thought about that before you strapped on that iron, boy," the marshal told him.

"It hurts!"

"I 'spect it does."

. . . Nothing seems to change here, Sally. The only place where I am reasonably assured of being left alone is on the Sugarloaf. But you know the urge to see the land is strong within me, and I shall not be tied down like a vicious yard dog. This evening, while I was having supper, another young punk tried to goad me into drawing . . .

"I want you out of town on the next stage, gambler," the marshal told the man.

"Would you have told Jensen that?" the gambler asked.

The marshal met his eyes. "Yes."

The gambler nodded his head. "Yes, I think you would have. All right, marshal. I'll leave in the morning."

"Fair enough."

. . . I must go still further, up into Wyoming, then maybe across into Idaho, to find the bulls I'm looking for, Sally. If it were just a little bit warmer, I would sleep under the stars and not even enter towns except for provisions. But I fear this married man has grown too accustomed to comforters, feather ticks, and rugs on the floor on cold mornings. And, I must add, the nearness of you . . .

"Put on my headstone that I was a gunfighter, will you, Marshal?" Jack said, his voice growing weak.

"If that's what you want, Jack."

"It don't hurt no more."

"That's good, Jack."

"I can't hear you, Marshal. Speak up. They's a roarin' in my ears. I'm a-feared, Marshal Brackton! Is there really a hell, you reckon?"

. . . I'm in a little town just south of the Uinta Mountains, Sally. I know the marshal here, and he intervened this evening and saved a young man from death, at least at my hands. I'm going into the high country tomorrow, Sally. Where there are no towns and hopefully, no young hellions looking to make a reputation. I shall build a lean-to for my shelter and think good thoughts of you and the children . . .

"Marshal!" Jack cried. "I can't see! I'm blind. Oh, God, where's that Holy Roller. I thought he'd done come in to comfort me."

"I'm right here, son. Are you a Saint?"

"I ain't nothing," Jack whispered.

. . . I send all my love over the miles, Sally, and pray that I shall see you soon.

Your loving and faithful husband, Smoke.

The barkeep leaned over and looked at Jack Lynch. "Yeah. He's something, all right. He's dead!"

2

Smoke posted his letter to Sally at the hotel and left before dawn the next morning, amid a light falling of snow. The big Appaloosa he rode was rough and shaggy-looking, with his winter coat still on. His packhorse was tough and had been patiently trained by Smoke.

Smoke rode for five miles before dismounting and building a small fire to prepare the coffee and bacon he'd resupplied back in the town. After he ate the bacon he sopped chunks of bread into the grease and finished off his meal with another cup of hot, strong coffee.

He camped for the night close to a little river, with snow-capped Marsh Peak to his east. The morning dawned pristine white, with several inches of new snow on the ground.

The country he was riding through was wild and high and beautiful, but already being touched by the hand of man. Smoke remembered when he rode through this country as a boy, years back, with the legendary mountain man, Preacher. The two of them could ride for days, sometimes weeks, without ever seeing a white man. No more.

For the most part, the Indians no longer posed any threat.

Only occasionally would a few young bucks bust loose from some reservation and cause trouble. The west was slowly being tamed. The outlaw Jesse James had been killed, shot in the back by a man he'd called friend, so Smoke had heard. Jesse had given Smoke a pistol back during the war, when Smoke was just a boy, trying to hold on to a hard-scrabble farm back in Missouri, while his daddy was off in the fighting. John Wesley Hardin was still in prison down in Texas. Earp had killed Curly Bill Brocius just last year. Sam Bass was rotting in the grave, as was Clay Allison. Mysterious Dave was still around, but Smoke had no quarrel with him. As far as he knew, Mysterious Dave was still down in Dodge City.

But someone had been sticking close to his backtrail for two days now, and Smoke was getting a little curious as to who he, or they, might be.

He thought he was in Wyoming, but he wasn't sure. If he was, what was left of Fort Bridger would be off to the west some few miles. Smoke didn't know if there was anything left of the old post and wasn't that interested in checking it out.

But he would like to know who was trailing him. And why.

He was heading up toward the Green, to a little valley where a friend of his raised cattle, good cattle, and he'd written Smoke, telling him of the bulls he had for sale. The railroads had tracks all over the country now—well, almost—and getting the bulls back to his ranch would be no problem; a short drive on either end of a rail trip. Smoke could have taken the train most of the way, but with Sally gone back East to visit her family, the kids in school in Europe, Smoke had felt that old faithful tug of the High Lonesome and decided to saddle up and ride the distance.

He began seeing familiar landmarks and knew he was in the Cedar Mountains. In a couple of days, barring any difficulties, he'd cross the Blacks Fork and then pick up the Green River and follow it all the way to his friend's ranch.

He found a little spring bubbling out of the earth, a spot of graze for the horses around it, and made an early camp. It was still cold, but the snow was gone—at least for the present— and Smoke had killed a couple of rabbits and needed to get them on a spit, cooking.

He stripped saddle and pack from the horses and watched them roll and snort and kick and shake, then settle down for a bit of grazing. Smoke gathered up twigs to get his fire going, then laid on heavier wood and made himself a spit. He got the rabbits cooking, filled his coffeepot with cold springwater right at the mouth and fixed his coffee in the blackened old pot.

The horses abruptly stopped grazing and lifted their heads, ears pricked up. Smoke picked up his rifle and eared the hammer back.

He heard the sounds of hooves, coming from the north. Then the call. "Halloo the fire! I'm friendly and I got my own grub so's I won't be eatin' none of yourn. The twilight gets lonesome without conversation. All right to come in?"

"Come on," Smoke called.

The man looked to be in his sixties—late sixties—but he was spry and Smoke figured him to be a man of the mountains. Just a tad too young to have been a part of the heyday of mountain men, but nevertheless a man who'd probably spent his life in the High Lonesome. Smoke had been halfway raised by mountain men, and he knew the mark it left on a man. He had it himself.

"Light and sit," Smoke told him.

"Obliged. Let me tend to my animals and then I'll join you by the fire. My good horse here got hisself all tangled up in some of that goddamned barbed wire a couple of days ago. I got to put some salve on the cuts. The devil's own doin's, that's what that stuff is."

A lot of cowboys called barbed wire the devil's hatband. It was used, but many despised it.

"Name's Lute," the old man said.

"Pleased," Smoke said.

Lute looked under his horse at him and smiled when Smoke did not offer his name. "I got to call you somethin', boy."

"I'll answer to just about anything."

Lute chuckled and carefully rubbed salve on the healing cuts inflicted by the devil's hatband. "I come in from the west. Smelled your fire and cut north. I didn't want you to think I was part of that bunch that's comin' up behind you."

"I knew I was being followed."

"I'm sure you did. You appear to be a mighty careful man. You got the mark on you, son. I think you've spent some time in the high country."

"For a fact."

"Thought so. Brands a man deep. The burn don't never come out. I come into the Lonesome back in '39. Me and old Preacher was partners for years."

"I knew him. He still alive?"

"Yep. Gettin' fat and sassy in his old age. Him and a bunch of other old mountain men got 'em a place up in the mountains. Them old coots just sit and rock and tell lies all the damn day. Mountain men and old gunfighters. I might go there myself some day. When all the fire gets burned out in me and there ain't nothin' but ashes left."

"This bunch that's on my trail: how many?"

" 'Pears to be a goodly bunch, boy. I bellied down on a rise and watched 'em. They ridin' like men with a mission. Hardcases, I'd say. You wanted by the law?"

"Not that I know of." Smoke rummaged around and found another cup. He poured the scalding coffee and passed a cup to Lute, who had finished doctoring his horse and had sat down by the fire.

"Much obliged to you, boy." He warmed his hands on the hot tin cup, waiting a moment for the coffee to become drinkable. His eyes took in Smoke's guns. "Don't see a rig like yourn too often," he remarked.

"Not often. But it suits me." Smoke turned the rabbits to even the cooking.

"Jensen," Lute said the words softly. "I knowed it would come to me. Smoke Jensen."

"That's right."

"Ol' Preacher sort of jerked you up after your pa died back in '66 or '67."

"That he did. But he never mentioned anyone named Lute. I find that odd."

"Had to change my name after I killed a man down in civilization back in '55. I hate towns . . . hate the people in towns. They fearful people, afraid to go it alone. Bullies live in towns, too. It was a bully I opened up with my good knife."

Smoke smiled at Lute's words. He didn't agree with the man in the main, but part of what he said held some truth to it.

"They comin' after you, boy," Lute said. "Has to be you. Someone has hired them to kill you. I know you got enemies."

"Then why don't they come on and try to do the job?"

"Don't know. You and me, we'll ambush 'em in the mornin'. How 'bout it?"

Smoke shook his head. "Lute, they may or may not be after me. I don't know that for sure and neither do you. I'm tired of killing. I just want to live in peace."

The mountain man snorted. "Right nice thought, but it ain't never gonna happen. As long as you're alive, they's them that'll be wantin' to try you. I shouldn't have to be tellin' you this." He stood up. "I'll get my grub. Told you I wouldn't eat yourn."

The fire burned down to coals several times and each time one of the men would rouse from his blankets to place wood on the coals. The stars began to fade when Lute rolled out of his blankets and disappeared into the brush outside of camp to do his morning business. Smoke took the other side of the camp, then came back and put coffee on to boil and lay slices of bacon in the frying pan.

Lute called, "You wanna see this?"

Smoke climbed up the small hill and stood by the old mountain man. About five miles away, below where they stood, Smoke could see a half dozen fires twinkling in the darkness. He took off his hat and scratched his head.

"It makes no sense. It's as if they want me to see them; they want me to know they're after me."

"Maybe they do, boy. You seen bear-baitin', ain't you?"

"Yes. It's a cruel sport. What about it?"

"Maybe they do want you to know, boy. Maybe it's a game to them."

Smoke thought about that. "A game? Lute, what do you know that you're not telling me. And don't hand me any more crap about you just happening up on my camp yesterday afternoon."

"Let's get some coffee and bacon. I'll level with you."

They ate and drank their coffee. Eating was serious business and they wouldn't talk until the food was gone and they'd settled back for a pipe or a hand-rolled and a cup of coffee.

"I come up on a buddy of mine about two weeks ago over yonder-ways on Badwater Crick. He'd just ridden the steam engine as fer as he could from Dodge City. Whilst he was in Dodge he overheard some talk about this German Count or Baron or something like that, name of Frederick von Hausen. He's some sort of world traveler and adventure seeker. He was in some saloon there and askin' who was the meanest, toughest man in the west. Somebody piped up and said Smoke Jensen."

He paused to stuff and light his pipe and Smoke said, "You've been looking for me since then?"

"I owe Preacher," was Lute's response.

"You knew who I was all along, then?"

"I was pretty sure it was you. Anyways, this Baron—whatever the hell that means—said he wanted to mount a party and come lookin' for you. He said it would be great sport to hunt you down and see just how tough you really was."

Smoke's coffee was cold in the cup and forgotten. He set the cup down and rolled a cigarette. Finally he said, "Lute, you can't hunt a man down for sport like some animal!"

" 'Pears he's doin' it, boy."

"Didn't the law try to stop him?"

"The law ain't got nothin' to do with it, Smoke. And them men with him ain't talkin' 'bout it. He's payin' 'em big money."

Smoke had never heard of such a thing, and his face mirrored his inner confusion. "It's got to be a joke, Lute."

"No joke, boy. They aim to hunt you down, run you until you can't go no further and then kill you."

Smoke lit his cigarette and inhaled. "Well . . . I have no option but to go to the law with this."

Lute smiled. "And tell them what, boy? You ain't got no proof that anybody's doin' anything wrong. Think about it."

Smoke took his hand-rolled down to the butt and tossed it into the fire before he spoke. He had been hunted before, certainly, by men who were after him in the heat of anger or for promise of a false bounty, but never for sport. Smoke was genuinely tired of all the killing. The west was being tamed; why in the hell didn't people leave him alone and let him live in peace?

"I'll not play their game, Lute. I'll head for the High Lonesome; I know places there where not even you could find me. He can't keep these men on the payroll forever."

"He's worth millions, Smoke. And his family's worth more millions. He ain't never worked. He's a so-called professional adventurer; whatever the hell that means. And yeah, he can keep these randy ol' boys on the payroll forever,

I reckon. Son, the more you run, the more excitin' the hunt is for them."

"That's the reason you suggested we ambush them."

"That's right. Might as well get the unpleasantness done with."

Despite the situation facing him, Smoke had to chuckle at the old man's coldness. Preacher had been the same way; mountain men were not known for their kind, loving attitudes toward anyone who might be planning to do them harm.

Smoke sighed. "I just can't do it, Lute. I just can't ambush a group of people who, so far, at least, have done me no harm. Don't you see that?"

Lute refilled his own cup, tossed the cold out of Smoke's, and filled it up. "No, I don't. But I ain't settled like you, neither. Tell me, would you have acted this way ten years ago? Or even last year?"

Smoke shook his head. "Probably not. Lute, the most famous gunfighters in all the West have killed no more than twenty or thirty men—at the most. Do you have any idea of the number of graves I've got on my backtrail?"

"I 'magine it's a right large number."

"Enough to populate a fair-sized town, and then some. And I'm tired of all the blood. I'm tired of all the killing. I'm tired of the looks people give me. I'm tired of being the most notorious gun in all the so-called Wild West. Now, I haven't turned over a whole new leaf; I'll fight if I'm pushed to it, Lute." He told him of the young man back in the saloon. "I didn't want to draw on that kid, Lute. But I saw that he was working himself up into a frenzy to drag iron on me. And I wasn't going to die so that he could live. I just wish to God that people would leave me and Sally alone and let us raise our kids and our cattle and our horses. Goddamnit!" Smoke cursed and threw his tin cup of hot coffee and all against a boulder. "Is that too much to ask of people?"

Old Lute smiled a sad moving of the lips. "You'll do what

you have to do when the time comes to do it, boy. I see that writ all over you."

Smoke said nothing.

"And them down yonder by the fires," the old mountain man said. "They think that you're the fox and they's the hounds. Oh, they'll run you, boy. I can see that, too. You're gonna give them a long, hard run for their money. But I know something that they don't: you ain't no fox. You're half great gray timber wolf and half puma. With some grizzly bar tossed in for spice. And when you get your fill of runnin', and turn to face them, you gonna chill 'em to the bone when you throw back your head and howl to the mountains."

3

He was a man who had never failed at anything. No matter what the cost, no matter the misery caused or the price in human life, he always succeeded.

Frederick von Hausen had so much money not even he knew the total of his wealth. The money he was paying the men who rode with him on this quest was an enormous sum to them, to von Hausen it didn't even amount to petty cash.

He was a handsome man; not even his constant sneer could take away from that. Tall and blond and muscular, he was highly educated at all the right schools in Europe. He was an expert swordsman, an expert shot with rifle or pistol. He wore a dueling scar on his cheek like a badge of honor.

Frederick stood by the fire on this cold morning and looked toward the north. This Smoke Jensen person was up there, not more than four or five miles away. Hausen smiled. All that claptrap and big scene back in that saloon in Dodge City had been staged for the benefit of others. Hausen had been planning this hunt for months. He had a small fortune in bets riding on his ability to hunt down and kill Jensen. He rubbed his hands together. He was looking forward to this.

Frederick von Hausen looked for his companions; they were just now rising stiffly from their blankets and moving around in their tents. The cook had been the first one up and was now preparing breakfast, having first made coffee, a strong bitter brew that was not to von Hansen's liking. But the twenty-odd men he'd hired along the way seemed to enjoy the black poisonous brew.

The first to leave their tent was von Hausen's traveling companion, Marlene Ulbrich. Just as haughty and almost as rich as von Hausen, Marlene was blonde and beautiful and just as bloodthirsty as von Hausen. Gunter Balke and his fiancée, Maria Guhl, were the next ones up and moving about. They were followed by Hans Brodermann and his wife, Andrea. All reasonably young, in their early thirties, and all enormously wealthy, they all shared something else in common: they were easily bored, spoiled to the core, and considered everyone else on the face of the earth to be their inferior.

They had slaughtered the earth's animals in every country that would allow them entry—and that was most. If a day's hunt proved unproductive, they would shoot dogs or cats or people, if they felt they could get away with the latter bloodletting. And they always had before.

They were all dressed properly for the hunt and carried the most expensive weapons that could be handmade for them. And they all had spent weeks gathering the scum of the earth around them.

The twenty-odd men—odd in more ways than one—gathered in a quiet circle around the big fire, staying away from the aristocracy, as they had been instructed to do.

"How long do they figure on stretchin' this thing out?" Al Hayre asked, after noisily slurping at his coffee.

"They plan on makin' a springtime event of it," Leo Grant told him.

"I ain't yet figured out just what it is we're supposed to do," Utah Bob said.

"Prod Jensen 'til he makes a fight of it," Larry Kelly told

him. "But we'll stay back, out of range, if we can, 'til we push him clear into the Rockies."

"These people, do they not know Smoke's reputation?" Angel Cortez asked in soft tones.

"Jensen's reputation don't spell crap to them or to me," Tom Ritter said. "I don't believe nothin' I ever heard about that man. I think most of it is lies."

Pat Gilman looked across the dancing flames at Tom. "There ain't none of it lies, Tom. Smoke Jensen's a he-coon from way back. I seen some of his graveyards; and they's plenty more that I ain't seen."

Tom Ritter said a very ugly word.

John T. Matthey smiled. "You boys is all from Texas and Kansas and Arizona and New Mexico way. Me, I'm from Montana, like Montana Jess there. Pat there is from Colorado. He knows about Jensen, just like Utah Red do. Let me tell you this: they's gonna be some of us ain't gonna come back from this foolishness. Maybe a lot of us ain't comin' back. Them uppity, high-falutin' folk over yonder, them barons and counts and princes and their snooty women think this is gonna be a real fun game. It ain't gonna be no such of a thing. Right now Jensen is tryin' to figure out why we're trackin' him close. Today, tomorrow, the next day, he'll try to lose us. When we keep on comin', he's gonna turn mean. And boys, that is one man who was born with the bark on. That man has faced six, eight, ten men eyeball to eyeball and tooken lead and kept on his boots. When the gunsmoke cleared, Smoke Jensen was still standin'. Now, I ain't got no use for him; he's kilt several of my pards. But I got respect for him. And you boys better have some respect for him, too."

Von Hausen had been listening. He said, "Are you afraid of this penny-ante gunslinger, Mr. Matthey?"

"There ain't nothin' penny-ante about Jensen, Mr. Hausen. Wild Bill Hickok said Smoke Jensen was the fastest gun in all the West. Earp said he'd sooner be locked in a room full of mountain lions than face Jensen. Sam Bass was a pard of mine. He was offered thousands of dollars to kill Jensen. He threw the money back in the man's face. Billy the Kid said Smoke Jensen was like a God. I could go on and on namin' gunfighters who had better sense than brace Smoke Jensen. You don't know the man . . . I do. I've seen him work . . . you haven't. Now, you payin' us top wages to track and corner him. And I tooken your money and when I do that I ride for the brand. But don't none of you low-rate Jensen. That would be a fatal mistake."

"You say you know him," Hans said, strolling up. "What are his weak spots?"

"Mister, Smoke Jensen ain't got no weak spots. He's about two hundred and thirty pounds of pure poison when he's riled up. Got arms on him 'bout the size of an average man's upper leg. He fist-fought men that stood six-eight and outweighed him seventy-five-eighty pounds and stomped them into a bloody pulp. He'll fight you with guns, knives, or fists or clubs. It don't make a damn to Smoke Jensen. He's a man that don't bother nobody 'til you start messin' with him. Then he's gonna come at you lookin' like nine kinds of Hell. He was raised by mountain men during the day and suckled in the den by she-wolves at night. Don't never sell Smoke Jensen short."

"What an intriguing description," Marlene said, stepping closer to the fire. "You make him sound like something out of mythology."

"I don't know what that means, your ladyship," John T. Matthey said.

"Well, let me put it like this," Marlene said. "You make it sound as though this Smoke Jensen person cannot be killed."

"Oh, he can be killed, ma'am. He's a human bein'. But I know for a fact that he's been shot a half a dozen times with rifles and pistols and just kept on comin'. That ain't hearsay, ma'am. That's fact."

Marlene clapped her expensively gloved hands together.

"Oh, I just love it, Frederick! This is going to be such an exciting hunt."

"Quite, my dear," von Hausen said. "Come, let's have some breakfast."

Lute had pulled out shortly after Smoke had told him to go on about his business. He wasn't going to ambush the crowd supposedly chasing him—not yet, anyway—they'd have to open fire on him. But he was going to try to lose them.

"I'll be around, boy," the old man had told him. "You might need some help further on up the trail."

"I'm going up north to buy bulls, Lute."

Lute grinned; what few teeth he had left were tobacco stained. "Shore you are, boy. I believe that. But them down yonder just might put a kink in your plans. See you, Smoke."

Smoke broke camp and headed north toward the Green. He smiled as he settled into the saddle. These folks wanted to see some country. He'd show them some country. He decided to leave his friend up in Central Wyoming out of this.

Lute had told him that von Hausen had been on his trail for over a month, able to move much faster because of the trains. He had so much wealth that if the train was full, he'd just order up several more cars and hook on.

Smoke thought about that as he rode. Rock Springs was on the Union Pacific's transcontinental line. He wondered if von Hausen would have supplies waiting for him there? Smoke bet he would. Either there or at the town of Green River just to the west of Rock Springs. Smoke's smile toughened as he changed direction, heading southwest, into very tough country. He'd lose them in that area and then head for the little settlement he thought was still there at the old Fort Bridger site—if the Mormons hadn't burned it down again like they burned it and Fort Supply back in '57 or '58 during the Mormon War.

He lost the party trailing him by setting a grueling pace, once he discovered they had several women with them, all riding sidesaddle. Smoke couldn't imagine the mentality of any woman who would have anything to do with something this foolish and bloodthirsty.

"He's got to be headin' toward Fort Bridger," Montana Jess told von Hausen.

"The terrain?" the German asked impatiently.

"It ain't high country, but it's rough country. And the army's still got a garrison there."

"They most certainly do not!" Hans said. "It was abandoned several years ago. I have information to that effect."

Montana shifted his chew and spat, looking at the man. "Your information is wrong. And here's something else: you call me a liar again, Brodermann, and I'll kill you!"

Gunter stepped between the gunfighter and the prince. Hans really was a prince from some German family who had more princes and princesses than they knew what to do with. "We are not accustomed to your ways and methods in the Wild West, Mister Jess. Be patient with us."

Montana nodded his head. "Yeah," he said, then walked away.

Hans said, "I'll have to give that fellow a good thrashing before this expedition is through."

"He is certainly deserving of one," Hans' wife, Andrea said.

"And he smells bad, too," Marlene pointed out.

"The fort was reopened a couple of years back," John T. told them. "What about the supplies up in Green River?"

"We can always resupply," Frederick said. "Let's pick up this man's trail and press on."

"What if he tells the army about us?" Marlene asked. "That man that our scout saw riding away from Smoke's camp the other morning might have told him about us?"

"It's possible," von Hausen admitted. "But we have done no wrong. Besides, all of us are in this country under diplomatic papers. We have immunity from any type of prosecution."

"Has that been tested in the Wild West?" Gunter asked.

"You're forgetting I was trained in international law. It's been law in the United States since 1790," von Hausen replied. "Mount up."

"It's a pleasure to meet you, sir," the commanding officer at Fort Bridger said, adding with a smile, "I think. Have you eaten?"

"No. I've been pushing hard getting here."

"Trouble?"

"More than my share of it, I'm afraid."

"We'll discuss it over some food. Perhaps I can help."

"Von Hausen," the Colonel said, after the meal was over and they had settled back over coffee and cigars. "Damn little I can do—even if this rather . . . bizarre story is true. Not that I'm doubting your word, Mister Jensen," he was very quick to add. "But have the people following you actually done anything?"

"Not one hostile move, Colonel."

The colonel leaned forward. "Von Hausen is not an unknown name in Washington, Smoke. The von Hausen family have long been in diplomatic service. I'm sure the younger von Hausen is protected under international law."

"You want to explain that to me?"

The colonel spoke for several minutes. When he finished, Smoke sat his chair and stared at him.

"Do you mean that somebody protected under this dumb law can cold bloodedly kill anybody they like and there isn't a damn thing any lawman can do to them?"

"They can be expelled from the country."

Smoke shook his head in disbelief.

"But it works both ways, Smoke. The same law protects our diplomats in their country."

"That doesn't give a whole lot of comfort to a man in the grave, now, does it?"

The colonel smiled. "No. I'm afraid it doesn't. What will you do, Smoke?"

"Keep on traveling north. They'll get to see some wild country if they hang on my tracks."

"I remember you from fifteen years ago, Smoke. When you were no more than a boy who was quick with a gun. You would have handled this quite differently back then."

"I hope I never have to pull a gun in anger again, Colonel. But I'll only be pushed so far. No man will talk down to me, and no man will threaten the life of my wife or children, or me, and expect to live. And I don't give one tinker's damn about this so-called diplomatic immunity."

"Just between you and me, Smoke, this Frederick von Hausen has been expelled from several countries and told not to come back. He calls himself an international sportsman—as some have taken to using the word—but he's no sportsman. He's a cold-blooded killer. You haven't said anything about those with him, but I expect they're pretty much of the same caliber he is. Male and female. Did this old man tell you any of the names of those riding with von Hausen?"

"He knew some of them. J. T. Matthey, Tom Ritter, Utah Red, Cat Brown."

The colonel shook his head. "Bad ones. I've heard of them all. Guns for hire. After hearing those names I have to conclude that the old man just might be right. Von Hausen is certainly up to something."

"He had to have planned this, Colonel. This isn't something von Hausen just came up with on the spur of the moment. And if that is the case, he's studied me."

"I would think so. Yes."

"So he can make a sport of tracking me down, hunting me, cornering me, and then killing me like some wild beast."

Smoke smiled, but the colonel noticed very quickly that it

was not a pleasant curving of the lips. The colonel sat silently, waiting.

"I'm going to give this baron or count or whatever he is a chance to break off this hunt, Colonel. I might even take a few shots in my direction—providing they don't come too close. I'm going to do this because I'm tired of all the bloodletting. I'm going to let these people see some country, and some mighty rugged country too. But when I've had enough, I'll stand and fight. And when I decide to do that, Colonel, I won't be taking any prisoners for trial."

"You're telling me that you are going to commit murder," the colonel said stiffly.

"Call it anything you like. I'm a man who set out to visit a friend and fellow rancher to buy some bulls. That's all. Then I find myself being dogged by some European aristocrat and his friends who have hired about twenty-five of the most mangy bunch of men who ever sat a saddle. I am warned that this bunch plans to make a sport out of tracking and hunting and cornering and then killing me. I go to the army for help. The army tells me there is nothing that can be done because of some law that I never even heard of. Put yourself in my place, Colonel."

The army officer sat for a moment without speaking. He toyed with his coffee cup, then said, "Off the record, Smoke?"

Smoke nodded.

The colonel's eyes were bleak as he said, "When it comes time for you to make your stand, don't just wound anybody."

4

Smoke resupplied at the fort and pulled out early the next morning, telling the boys at the livery he was heading for a little town just north of the mouth of Hams Fork. He left the post and headed straight north, riding north until he came to Muddy Creek. He rode in the riverbed for several miles, then left it and headed northwest, toward the Bear River Divide.

This was a land not for the fainthearted, even in the early 1880's. Between Fort Bridger and north to Trapper's Point, as the mountain men used to call it, there were no towns and few settlers. The northern branch of Muddy Creek forked almost in the center of Bear River Divide. When Smoke reached the southernmost branch of the fork, with Medicine Butte far to the south of him, he made a lonely camp, cooked his supper, then carefully hid all traces of his fire and rode north for several more miles before making his night camp amid a jumble of rocks that gave him a good lookout and a secure site.

He was on the trail before dawn, picking his way north, utilizing all of his skills in making his way, leaving as few tracks as possible.

He tried to put himself inside the head of von Hausen. What would he do in a situation like this? For one thing he would not accept that his prey had gone north toward Hams Creek as Smoke had told the boys at the stable; that would be a deliberate ruse. Von Hausen had some good trackers with him. The gunslingers might be no more than human trash, with little values and no morals, but some of them could track a snake across a rock. Von Hausen had enough salty ol' boys with him to split his forces. Yeah. He'd do that. He'd send men racing toward the north, then start working them south, from the old stage road at Hams Fork over to the Utah line.

"Good, Smoke," he muttered. "Very good move on your part. Now you've got people coming at you from two directions. Preacher would not be happy with this move."

Then he chuckled and turned his horse's head due east. When he came to the stagecoach road, he turned north and headed for what was called the Sublette Cutoff. The cutoff was developed as part of the Oregon Trail—a faster way to get to Oregon country.

As Smoke approached the little town at the cutoff, he circled and came around from the east. He stabled his horses at the livery and stood for a moment in the darkness of the huge barn, studying the horses at the hitch rail in front of the saloon.

"Those two horses over yonder," he asked the boy. "They local brands?"

"Naw," the lad replied. "They come in this mornin'. From the south. Hard cases, they look to me. Askin' questions about any strangers in town. You look familiar, mister. Are you famous, or something?"

Smoke smiled. "In a way that I did not choose," he told the boy, then gave him a silver dollar. "That's for you. Rub my horses down good and give them grain. Watch that Appaloosa; he'll kick the snot out of you if you aggravate him."

"I seen you on the cover of a book!" the boy said. "You're

Smoke Jensen, the gunfighter. Jeepers! Smoke Jensen is standin' right here in front of me!"

"I'm Jensen. Does that little cafe over there serve up good meals?"

"Yes, sir. It's the best place in town to eat." He thought about that. "It's the *only* place in town to eat."

"Fine. I want me a meal, a bath, and a shave, and I can't do any of that until I get those two gunhands over there in the saloon off my back."

"Is there gonna be a shoot-out?" the boy asked excitedly.

"I hope not. But there might be a pretty good fistfight in a few minutes. Is there a back door to that saloon?"

"Yes, sir. You can duck around the side of this barn and come up from the north. That's a blind side."

"Fine. Now you keep still about me being in town for a few minutes. Then you can tell your friends. All right?"

"Anything you say, sir. Yes, sir."

"Where's the marshal?"

"Out of town chasin' a thief. Stole a horse and rode right through Mrs. MacKenney's wash. Took her drawers slap off the line. She ain't found 'em yet."

Smoke laughed at that. "Is there a jail?"

"Right over yonder." He pointed up the street. "Got four cells."

"I'll just need one. Do my horses right now, you hear?"

"Oh, yes, sir!"

Smoke stepped out the back of the livery and walked the alley to the edge of the small town. He crossed the street and cut back toward the saloon, taking the alley route. If his plan worked out, von Hausen was going to be plenty miffed. Smoke thought that might do the arrogant baron some good. Or count, or whatever he was. Smoke had a pretty good idea what he was, but that wasn't printable.

Smoke found the rear door to the saloon—easily done because of the mound of broken whiskey bottles and beer kegs—and slipped inside. He made his way through the gloom

and peeked through a hole in the wall. He could tell the regular patrons because they were staying well away from the
two trail-dusty, sweat-stained and unshaven men standing at
the bar.

Smoke opened the door and stepped inside the barroom.
He walked up to the bar and told the barkeep, "Beer."

Lou Kennedy and Pride Anderson glanced at each other.
Both of them wore very startled looks on their ugly faces.

The mug of beer was placed in front of Smoke and he
took a sip. Bootsteps sounded on the short boardwalk in
front of the saloon. A young man hurried inside, sat down at
a table, and whispered something to the men seated there.
The men all took a quick glance at Smoke, their eyes wide.

The barkeep waddled over to the table and listened. He
looked at Smoke and at the two men standing at the bar.
"Bar's closed," he announced, and sat down at the table.

Smoke dropped his right hand down to the butt of his
gun. "Before I kill a man, or in this case, two men, I like to
know their names."

"Oh, Lord!" a farmer-type said. "Somebody call the law!"

"Shut up," a cowboy seated across the room said. "Remember me, Mister Smoke?" he asked. "I rode for you down
on the Sugarloaf two, three years ago. Dusty Hill."

"Dusty. Sure. But you stay out of this. They got any friends
in town?"

"I don't think so. I'll watch your back, Mr. Smoke."

"Good enough." Smoke moved closer to the pair of gunslingers.

"I'm Pride Anderson and this here's Lou Kennedy. And
we ain't huntin' no trouble, Jensen."

"Then why have you and the rest of that pack of rabid
coyotes been crowdin' me for the past week?" He moved
still closer.

"It's a free country, Smoke," Lou said. "A man can ride
where he damn well pleases."

Smoke stepped well within swinging range. "A man can

get hurt crowdin' another man. But I'm not going to hurt either one of you—very much." Smoke hit Lou smack in the mouth with a big fist. As Lou was stumbling across the room, Smoke jerked Pride's gunbelt down, the rig falling around his ankles. A split second later, Smoke had busted him square on the nose. Pride hollered as the blood and snot flew as he fell down, all tangled up in his gunbelt.

Smoke met Lou coming at him and hit him a left and right that glazed Lou's eyes and further bloodied his mouth. Smoke turned and hit Pride twice in the belly just as he was getting up, the blows sounding like a man hitting a watermelon with the flat side of an axe. Smoke caught a blow to the side of his head that probably hurt Lou's hand more than it did Smoke's noggin. But it did sting. Smoke waded in, both fists swinging and connecting, the blow driving the man to his knees. Smoke turned and Pride hit him, bloodying his mouth. Smoke back-heeled him and sent the man crashing to the floor. Smoke stepped forward, and, grabbing the gunfighter by the back of the head, he brought a knee up into the man's face and Pride stretched out on the floor, his mouth a mess and his nose flattened.

Smoke turned just as Lou was getting up. He measured his blow and put one hard right fist onto the side of Lou's jaw. Lou's eyes rolled back while he was falling, until only the whites were showing. He hit the floor, out cold.

Smoke walked back to the bar and drank his beer down. He turned to face the crowd. "These two are part of a gang that's been hunting me . . . for sport. I should have killed them both. But maybe this way is better. Maybe when the others come into town, the sight of these two will change some minds. Dusty, will you and some of these other good citizens drag these two over to the jail, lock them down, and bring the key to me?"

"We'll shore do it," Dusty said.

"I'll be registering at the hotel and then I'll be having me a bath and a shave."

"I'll find you," Dusty said.

Smoke walked out the front door.

"Shoot!" one citizen said. "I was wantin' to see a good gunfight."

"If there had of been," Dusty said, grabbing hold of Lou's ankles, "if you'd blinked you'd a missed it."

Smoke took the key to the cell holding Lou and Pride and dropped it down an old unused well. He had registered at the hotel and after disposing of the cell key, he walked to the barbershop and told the man to get some hot water ready for a bath. After his bath, he had himself a shave and a haircut. Then he went to the cafe for something to eat.

Smoke was eating roast beef and boiled potatoes and gravy when the marshal walked in, all dusty and tired-looking. The marshal paused in the door, gave the crowded cafe a once-over, spotted him, walked to the table, and sat down.

"Coffee, Pat," he called to the waiter. "And a plate of food. I'm so hungry I could eat a skunk." He cut his eyes. "You got to be Smoke Jensen."

"That's right."

"Did you put those two beat-up lookin' characters into my jail?"

Smoke chewed for a moment. "Nope."

The marshal waited for a moment. "Well, if it wouldn't be too much of a problem, would you mind telling me who did?"

"Some of your citizens. At my request."

"Both of them yahoos wants a doctor."

"I imagine they do. They were both in fairly poor condition the last time I saw them."

The marshal looked at him. "One of them tagged you at least one good lick."

"Yes, he did. The waiter said they had apple pie. Is it any good?"

"It's very good. I have it every day. It's the only kind of pie the damn cook knows how to bake. Mister Jensen, what the hell do you want me to do with those two gunslingers in my jail?" He lifted his coffee cup, blew, and took a sip.

"I imagine you'll be keeping them for awhile. I threw away the cell key."

The marshal choked on his coffee. "Damnit, man. I only had the one key for that cell."

"I know." Smoke smiled at him. "Don't worry. The man who'll be coming to get them has plenty of money. He'll pay for rebricking the rear wall, after you have someone jerk it out to set them loose."

Smoke was miles north of the settlement when Frederick von Hausen and his party arrived, looking for the two missing members. The German was not amused at what he found.

"I demand that you release those men immediately," he told the marshal.

"I ain't got no charges against either of them," the marshal replied.

"Well . . . turn them loose!"

"I surely wish I could. They're eating the town's treasury outta money. Never seen two men who could eat that much."

"Release them!"

"I can't."

"You are straining my patience," von Hausen told the man. "First you tell me there are no charges against either man, then you tell me that you cannot free them. This is all very confusing."

"I can't open the damn door," the marshal said. "Smoke Jensen threw away the only key."

Von Hausen cussed.

The marshal waited until the German had stopped swearing. "He said you probably wouldn't see the humor in it."

"Get us outta here!" Lou hollered.

"Where is the nearest locksmith?" von Hausen asked, getting a grip on his temper.

"Lord, I don't know," the marshal said, scratching his head. "Denver, I reckon."

"My good man," Hans stepped in. "We must free these men. It is an injustice to keep them locked up when they have done no wrong."

The marshal looked at him. "You got any ideas?"

"We could get some dynamite and blow the wall," John T. suggested.

"The hell you will!" Pride bellowed.

While the manhunters were arguing among themselves, the marshal opened a drawer of his desk and pulled out a pile of old wanted posters. Several of the gunslingers hit the saddle and left town.

"Just as well. Didn't want to fool with them anyway," the marshal muttered.

Smoke was a good twenty miles north of the town, camped along the banks of Fontenelle Creek, drinking coffee and cooking his supper before a team of mules was found and a chain hooked to the bars of the cell.

Frederick von Hausen had to count out the money for jail repairs and put it in the marshal's hand before the townspeople would allow the wall to be pulled down.

"Now will you release my men?" the German asked.

"Take it down," the marshal said.

The big Missouri Reds strained but the wall would not budge.

"Damnit, do something!" von Hausen yelled.

"You wanna get out there and get in harness with them mules?" the marshal asked him.

"You are a very impudent fellow," von Hausen told him.

"And you're beginnin' to annoy me," the marshal replied. "And when I get annoyed, I tend to get testy. The second best thing you could do is shut your mouth. The first best thing you could do is go back to wherever the hell it is you come from."

"Pull, babies!" the mule's owner yelled and the wall finally came down in a cloud of dust.

Lou and Pride staggered out, both of them looking as though they had picked a fight with a tornado.

They told their stories to an incredulous von Hausen.

"He whipped both of you?" the German said.

"Incredible," Gunter said.

"I warned you about Jensen," John T. reminded them.

While the back of the jail was being demolished, the ladies in the group had been enjoying hot baths and the boys in the town had been enjoying them a whole lot more by peeking through holes in the fence at the back of the barber shop.

By the time the men had been released, it was late in the day and pointless to continue. Von Hausen and his party stayed at the small hotel while the gunslingers slept wherever they could.

When the morning dawned and the European community and their scummy entourage finally got underway, Smoke was riding along the Fontenelle, with Commissary Ridge to the west.

He'd had his fun, and now the game would turn serious, he guessed. He had insulted his majesty and his lordship, and the prince and their ladies, and the Germans would not take it lightly.

But Smoke was still not going to start tossing lead at this point. He just could not accept that this was going to turn lethal. He just couldn't. Those following him were going to have to show that they really intended to kill him before he turned and made his stand.

He hoped von Hausen would call it off.

Deep inside him, he knew the German would not.

5

"He's stopped tryin' to hide his trail," Gil Webb said. "That makes me wonder what he's up to."

Nat Reed nodded his head in agreement. He took off his hat and ran his fingers through his shaggy hair. "What you gonna do with all the money them crazy people is payin' us, Gil?"

"Spend it on women and booze," the man-hunter said, simply and honestly.

They were waiting for the main party to catch up, taking a few minutes to rest.

"That's a lot of damn money to spend on women and whiskey."

"So what are you gonna do with your pay?"

Nat grinned. "Spend it on women and whiskey."

The men laughed.

"You ever been up in this part of the country, Nat?"

"Nope. I'm a plains and desert man myself. That map we looked at the other day showed some hellacious mountains just a few miles north of here."

"Yeah. John T. and Utah and them other high-country boys

is gonna have to take the point from here on out. I ain't got no idea where we are."

John T. sat his saddle and looked down at the clear tracks Smoke was leaving. His smile held no humor. "He's leadin' us straight into the wilderness. I got a hunch he's gonna take us into the big canyon country."

"What is that?" Gunter asked.

"A damn good place to stay out of," John T. told him. "Smoke was raised by mountain men, so he'll know the High Lonesome mighty well."

"The what?" Andrea asked.

"A place where it's hotter than hell and colder than ice. Where the winds blow all the time and they don't never blow. Places were you can crawl to the edge and look down for more 'un five thousand feet—straight down." (Only a slight exaggeration). "Wild lost rivers that don't go nowhere." (Actually they do). "They's still Injuns in there that ain't never seen a white man." (Probably true). "Unless it was a mountain man. Like Smoke Jensen."

"Has it been explored?" Gunter asked.

"Rivers been traveled on some. Mountain men and Injuns know it. And Smoke Jensen."

"How big is this place?" von Hausen asked.

"Don't nobody know for sure. If that's where Jensen is takin' us, he'll find a good spot to stash his horses and start to give us pure-dee hell. Jim Bridger country. It's wild, people, and it gets wilder the further north you go. Any of you ever seen a lightnin' storm in the high-up? They're terrible. You claim to have studied him, von Hausen, but I bet you got most of your information from gossip and from them damn Penny Dreadful books. The same with you boys from the plains and the flats. So I'll tell you what Jensen is and ain't.

"He's a mountain man. He knows 'em, he ain't scared of 'em, and he can climb 'em. He's at home in the mountains. And when he makes his stand, it'll be in the mountains."

John T. paused to roll a cigarette and light up. "You see,

people, this is just a game to him right now. He's havin' fun with us. If he was takin' this serious, why they'd be some of us layin' back yonder on the trail, dead from ambush. You real sure you want to go on with this so-called sporting e-vent, von Hausen?"

"Of course, I do!"

"Just checkin'."

"Mount up and let's go," von Hausen said.

Smoke crossed and recrossed the Fontenelle several times, knowing that would slow up those behind him. He could have taken a much easier route, but he didn't want to make things easy for his pursuers. He was hoping—knowing it was a slim chance—that if he took them over the roughest terrain he could find, they might decide to call off the chase.

Maybe.

He was going to ride straight north, up through the Salt River Range, have some fun with them up in Jim Bridger country—maybe get them good and lost for a time—and then head up the Snake Range, through the Teton Range, and then over the Divide. If they were still after him, and had proved hostile, there he would make his stand.

He had considered talking to the German, but decided that probably wouldn't do a bit of good. He had thought about leaving them a note, stuck to a tree, warning them off. But von Hausen might decide that was a challenge and really put on the pressure. Smoke had never been in any situation quite like this one and didn't really know how to handle it.

His rancher friend was not expecting him—Smoke had told him he'd be up sometime in the spring or summer—so his friend would not be worried about him.

"Hell of a mess," Smoke muttered, and headed north.

"This is the goddamnest country I ever seen in my life," Marty Boswell griped. "The sun's out now and it's warm;

tonight it'll be so damned cold a body's gotta jump up and down to keep his feet from freezin'."

"At least Jensen's just as cold," Paul Melham said.

"No, he ain't," John T. corrected. "He's used to it and come prepared. He can build him a lean-to and a soft bed outta sweet smellin' boughs near 'bouts as fast as you boys can unsaddle your horse."

"Why do you constantly try to discourage the men?" Marlene asked him.

"I ain't tryin' to discourage 'em. I just want the soft ones to quit and get long gone away from me 'fore we tangle with Jensen. I don't want nobody but hard cases with me when that hombre decides to fight."

"Am I a hard case, John T.?" she asked teasingly.

"You all are payin' the bulldog, your ladyship. I just don't want no little puppy dogs around me when push comes to shove."

"What do you have against Smoke Jensen, John T.?"

"I don't like him. He's too damn high and mighty to suit me. Somebody needs to slap him down a time or two."

"And you think you're that man?"

"I might be. I do think that all of us—if we get real lucky and work real careful—can put an end to Smoke Jensen."

"Oh, I assure you, John T., that we are going to most definitely do that. Frederick has never failed—*never*."

He ain't never run up on the likes of Smoke Jensen, neither, John T. thought, but didn't put it into words.

Smoke figured he was at least two full days ahead of his hunters, and perhaps even three. He was going to have to resupply and discard some gear while adding things more practical if this game turned deadly, as he feared it would.

He knew of a tiny town located on the west side of the Salt River Range, not more than three or four miles from the

Idaho border. He'd head there, but he'd do so carefully, and try to lose his pursuers—at least for a time.

Smoke headed out and put Salt River Pass behind him, then he cut west and stayed on the east side of the Salt River, leaving plenty of tracks. He rode across a rocky flat, then stopped and tore a blanket up and tied squares of cloth over his horses' hooves so they would not scar the rock, then doubled back to the river and stayed in it, as best he could, for several miles. He found another rocky flat and exited the river there.

He swung down from the saddle and spent some time working out his tracks. Satisfied, he mounted up and headed for the settlement. He had probably gained another day; if he was lucky, maybe two days.

He spent a night in a cold camp, not wanting to chance a fire, on the off chance his hunters had gained on him, and Smoke was in no mood for nonsense when he rode into the tiny town the next day, at mid-morning.

He told the man at the livery to rub his horses down good and give them all the grain they wanted to eat.

"Payable in advance," the man said sourly.

Smoke looked at him for a moment through the coldest, most dangerous eyes the man had ever seen.

"It's for ever'body, mister," he spoke gently. "Boss's orders. I just work here."

Smoke smiled and handed the man some coins, including a little extra. "Have yourself a drink on me at day's end."

"I'll do it," the man said with a returning smile. "Thanks. They's beds over at the saloon or you're welcome to bed down here. Beth's is our only cafe, and she serves up some pretty good grub."

"I'll check it out. Much obliged."

"Ain't I seen you before, mister?"

"Never been here before in my life."

"Shore looks familiar," the man muttered, when Smoke

had walked away. Then he stood still as a post as recognition struck him. "Good God!" he said. "And I got lippy with *him?*"

Smoke checked out the rooms over the saloon, saw fleas and various other crawling and hopping creatures on the dirty sheets, and decided he would sleep in the loft of the barn. He'd always liked the smell of hay.

"You mighty goddamn particular," the combination bar-keep and desk clerk told him.

That did it. Smoke grabbed the man by the shirt, picked him up about a foot off the floor, and pinned him to the wall. "Would it too much of a problem for you to be civil?"

"You better put me down, mister. Tom Lilly runs this town, and he's a personal friend of mine."

"And you'll run to tell him about this little incident and he'll do your fighting for you, right?"

"Something like that. And he'll clean your plow, drifter."

Smoke dragged him to the landing and threw him down the stairs. "Then go tell him, you weasel. I'll be having a drink at the bar. From the good bottle."

The man scrambled to his feet and ran out the front door. Smoke walked down the steps, rummaged around behind the bar until he found the good bottle of whiskey, and poured himself a drink. Although not much of a drinking man, the whiskey was smooth and felt good going down.

He fixed himself a sandwich from the freshly laid out lunch selection and poured a cup of coffee, then walked to a table in the back of the room. He took off his coat and sat down. Slipping the hammer-thong from his Colts was some-thing he did the instant his boots touched ground out of the stirrups.

The front door opened and the lippy barkeep entered, fol-lowed by a huge bear of a man.

"There he is," the barkeep said, pointing Smoke out. Then he ran back behind the bar. "And that'll be fifty cents for that drink of good whiskey."

"Money's on the bar," Smoke told him.

The man lumbered over, stopping a few feet from the table. The floor had trembled as he moved. Smoke figured him to be about six feet six inches tall and weighing maybe two hundred and seventy-five pounds.

"My name's Tom Lilly," the big man rumbled.

Smoke took a bite from his sandwich and said nothing.

"Are you deaf?!" Lilly hollered.

"I will be if you keep shouting," Smoke told him. "Quiet down, will you?"

The man looked shocked. "You really tellin' me what to do, cowboy?"

"Yes, as a matter of fact, I am. And you smell bad, too. Step back, before your breath contaminates the cheese."

Tom was so shocked he was momentarily speechless. Nobody ever spoke to him in such a manner. A few had challenged him, years back, and he had broken their heads, their backs, or just simply and quickly stomped them to death. He had run this town with an iron hand—or fist—for several years; now this drifter shows up and starts with the mouth.

Finally Tom found his voice. "You better enjoy that sandwich, drifter. 'Cause it's gonna be the last thing you'll ever eat except my fist."

Smoke shoved the square table with all his strength, one sharp corner catching Tom in the thigh and pushing through the cloth of the big man's trousers, tearing a gouge in his leg. Tom screamed in pain and grabbed at his bleeding leg just as Smoke came around the table, picking up a sturdy chair during his brief journey. Smoke brought the chair down on Tom's head, driving the man to his knees and destroying the chair. Using what was left of the chair back as a club, Smoke proceeded to rain blows on the bully, the wood ringing like a blacksmith's hammer as Smoke bounced it against Tom's head.

A crowd began to gather, both inside the saloon and on the boardwalk in front.

When Smoke had beaten the man unconscious, he tossed

the club to the floor and dragged Tom Lilly across the floor
and to the now open door. He dragged him across the boardwalk and dumped him in the street.

The citizens, male and female, stood and applauded Smoke
as he walked back inside the saloon. The barkeep stood rooted
behind the bar, disbelief and fear in his eyes. "Don't kill
me!" he finally squalled.

"He's been Tom Lilly's biggest supporter," a tired-looking
man said. "But he's nothing. As soon as Tom's men come
back from making their collections around the area, you're
gonna be in real trouble, mister."

"Collections?" Smoke asked.

"They claim to be protecting us," a woman said, standing
outside the saloon and speaking through the open door. No
way a good woman would enter a saloon. "They showed up
here about three years ago. Next thing we knew, our part-
time marshal was dead and Tom and his bunch were running
things."

"Several tried to intervene," a man said. "They come up
dead or missing."

"How many in Tom's gang?" Smoke asked, knowing he
had gotten himself into another situation.

"It varies. Anywhere from six to ten. Scum just seem to
gather around the likes of Tom Lilly."

"Oh, my Lord!" a woman cried. "Tom's gettin' to his feet."

Smoke stepped out onto the boardwalk. By now, all had
noticed the unusual way he wore his guns and pegged him as
a gunfighter. The man from the livery stood on the fringe of
the crowd and said nothing. But there was a big grin on his
face.

With blood running down his face from the savage beating he'd just taken from Smoke, Tom Lilly staggered to his
feet and swayed for a moment. "No man does this to me and
lives," Tom snarled the words. Then he grabbed for his gun.

6

Smoke's draw was faster than the blink of an eye. He put a .44 slug into Tom's arm, the slug breaking the bully's elbow and rendering the arm useless. Tom screamed as the gun dropped back into leather. Smoke's draw had been so fast Tom had been unable to clear his holster.

"Jesus," a man said. He cut his eyes to Smoke. "Who in hell are you, mister?"

"A man who doesn't like bullies," Smoke told him.

"My arm's ruint!" Tom bellowed. "You done crippled me."

"You people do with him as you see fit," Smoke told the crowd. The whole town had turned out—about a hundred people, including the dogs and cats.

"My boys'll burn this damn town to the ground," Tom yelled. "They'll have their way with the women and kill the men. You people better wise up and run this drifter outta town and get me some medical help."

"We'll help you," a man said, uncoiling a length of rope he'd taken from his saddle.

"I'll be down the street at the cafe," Smoke said. He walked back into the saloon and got his coat and hat. He looked at the barkeep. "If you have any sense at all, you'd better take to the air and don't look back. The townspeople are gettin' ready to hang Tom Lilly and they just might decide to string you up, too."

"Who are you?" he stammered, his face sweat-shiny from fear.

"Smoke Jensen."

The barkeep gulped a couple of times, then hit the back door at a run. Seconds later, the sounds of a galloping horse filled the cool air.

"Now wait a minute!" Tom Lilly yelled. "You people can't do this to me."

"Shut up, Tom," a woman told him. "Your days of bullying and killing are over."

Smoke walked over to Beth's Cafe and stepped inside.

"Get him up on that horse!" a man yelled, just as Smoke was closing the door. "Take him down to the hangin' tree."

"Goddamn you all to hellfire!" Tom screamed.

Smoke sat down by a front window and smiled at the lady behind the counter. "Coffee and a plate lunch," he said. "Or would you rather go down and see the hanging first?"

"Just as long as Tom Lilly does get hanged," she said. "He's got about seven pretty bad ol' boys due back in town right around noon. What are you going to do about them?"

"I'm not going to do anything," Smoke told her. "Unless they crowd me. I think the townspeople will handle them."

She brought him coffee. Smoke watched through the window as men armed with rifles began stationing themselves on rooftops.

"He ran the town through fear and intimidation," Beth said from the kitchen. "He threatened to do terrible things to the kids. He would take a child's pet and kill it with his bare hands, right in front of the child. He's raped more than one woman. Tom Lilly is a horrible man."

"Was," Smoke said, as he watched the crowd of people

come walking back up the wide street, leading a riderless horse. "Tom Lilly is swinging in the wind now."

Beth placed his plate of food in front of him. "Got puddin' for dessert."

"Sounds good." Smoke ate slowly of the thick stew and hot, fresh-baked bread laden with sweet butter. When he had finished, Beth brought him a big bowl of pudding and he topped that off with more coffee.

Riders galloped into town just as Smoke was sugaring his coffee. He rolled a cigarette and watched the men rein up in front of the saloon.

"Lilly's men?" he asked.

"Yes. And a scummier bunch never sat a saddle."

"I don't think they'll ever sit another saddle," Smoke told her.

The words had hardly left his mouth before a dozen rifles smashed the mid-day air and seven bodies lay crumpled in the street, their blood staining the dirt.

"Town's yours again," Smoke said.

Smoke made his purchases that afternoon, and although the owner of the general store was curious about what the stranger bought, he asked no questions.

Smoke bought several hundred feet of rope, dynamite, caps, and fuses. He bought a rifle and several hundred rounds of .44's, then bought a sawed-off shotgun and several boxes of shells. He carried his purchases back to the livery and packed it very carefully.

"Thanks for not spreading my name around town," he told the liveryman.

"I figured you wanted it that way. You got people on your backtrail, Smoke?"

"Yes. A big bunch of them."

"They must be fools," the man said.

"I haven't figured out exactly what they are, to tell the

truth. I'm trying to avoid a fight, and they just keep on coming at me."

"I think," the liveryman said drily, after seeing Smoke's
purchases, "them folks comin' up behind you are gonna be
awful sorry when they do catch up with you."

Smoke had a long, hot bath—figuring this might be the
last chance he'd have to take one for some time—and then a
shave. He ate an early supper at the cafe but heard no mention of Tom Lilly nor his gang among the townspeople. It
was a closed chapter in their lives and probably would never
be discussed outside the home. There are an awful lot of
people buried in unmarked graves throughout the west.

Smoke went to bed shortly after dark and was up long before dawn. The liveryman had his quarters in the big barn
and had coffee boiling when Smoke climbed down from the
loft.

"I ain't fitten for nothin' 'til I have my coffee," the liveryman said. "Some folks say I'm plumb grouchy. I figured you
for a coffee-drinkin' man, too."

"You figured right. What's between here and the Montana
line?"

"Damn little. Couple of old tradin' posts is all."

"That's what I thought." Smoke sipped his coffee and
took a bite of the cold biscuit with a piece of salt meat in it
the liveryman had offered. That meant that von Hausen
would have to carry a lot of supplies with him, for once they
passed this little settlement, there was nothing for a lot of
long hard miles.

"You got a wicked look in your eyes," the liveryman said.

"I got wicked thoughts in my head," Smoke replied with a
smile.

The liveryman went off to get the coffee pot and Smoke
took that quiet time to think. The Tetons had been explored a
half dozen times by the government, the last one being only
a couple of years back. Settlers were now coming into that
area, entering by way of the Gros Ventre River and Teton

Pass. What the liveryman didn't know was that two little villages were already established in that area; there might be more but if so, Smoke hadn't heard of them. But once past the junction of the two narrow roads, just south of Pacific Creek, there was nothing except wilderness until you got up into Montana. And Smoke doubted that von Hausen and company had ever seen wilderness like where he was leading them.

"Tell the people in this town that while they might think they owe me, don't refuse any type of service to this bunch that'll be coming along the next day or two. They're a bad bunch, so don't cross them."

"I understand, Smoke."

"Be sure you do." He shook hands with the man and saddled up. "See you around, partner," he said from the saddle.

"See you around, Smoke."

Smoke rode out into the cold early morning air and headed north.

Angel Cortez picked up Smoke's trail on the west side of Salt River. Some rocks had been disturbed and that was enough to put the Mexican on the trail. Satisfied he had the right trail, Angel rode back to the main party and told them the news.

"Excellent!" von Hausen said.

"I know where he's goin', now," John T. said. "Little settlement just a few miles north of here. Tom Lilly's town, so I been told."

Utah Red spat a stream of tobacco juice. "I bet it ain't if Jensen rode through there."

"No bets there," John T. said, picking up the reins. "We'll soon find out."

The townspeople heeded Smoke's warning, but they didn't like it and made that very clear by having every man and woman in the town armed when von Hausen and party rode in. It made for quite a show of force.

"He's been here," John T. said glumly. "Don't nobody make any quick moves or act hostile. Smoke's done shoved some steel up these folks' backbone and they gonna be quick on the shoot. You boys understand all that?"

They understood, and so did von Hausen and his party of adventurers.

"We'll have us a bite to eat, conduct our business quietly, and we shall be gone in one hour," von Hausen instructed.

"Probably be gone sooner than that," Leo Grant told him. "They's a closed sign in the cafe winder." He looked at the abundance of sawed-off shotguns in the hands of grim-faced men and shuddered. He'd seen men cut in two with those things. Sickenin' sight.

"Saloon's closed, too," Nat Reed observed. "I think that we'd just better tend to our business as quickly as possible and ride on."

"I concur," Gunter Balke said. "What say you Frederick?"

"Yes. From the looks of things, this Tom Lilly, and would assume his men too, are no longer around."

"Oh, they're around," John T. said. "Six feet under."

"Yonder's the hangin' tree," Cosgrove said softly. "With the rope still on it."

"Makes my throat hurt just lookin' at it," Paul Melham said. "I got an idea: why don't the most of us just ride on through and we'll be waitin' for y'all outside of town. This is a stacked deck if I ever seen one. They's men on rooftops with rifles, too."

"Boss?" John T. looked at von Hausen.

"Yes. Good idea. Ride on. You men leading the pack animals stay to help load."

Von Hausen's stomach muscles knotted up when he led his group into the general store. There were men all around the store, all armed with sawed-off shotguns.

"We mean no harm to anyone," Gunter said. "We just want to resupply and we'll be gone within the hour."

"Fine," the owner of the general store said. "But you gonna find this mighty expensive shoppin'."

Marlene looked at a freshly printed sign and smiled. Beans: $4.00 a lb. Taters: $6.00 a lb. Sugar: $15.00 a lb. Coffee: $20.00 a lb. And so on.

Von Hausen found the whole thing humorous and laughed when she pointed out the sign to him. "Obviously a depressed area, my dear. Let them have their fun. Spread our wealth among the colonials, so to speak. It's good public relations, you know."

They bought their supplies, paid for them, and were gone in thirty minutes. At the edge of town, Bob Hogan pointed out a row of fresh-dug graves, the mounds still muddy. "Smoke Jensen came through," was all he had to say.

Frederick glanced at Hans and arched an eyebrow. "Formidable opponent," he said, and rode on.

Ol' Preacher talked about this country and took Smoke through it when he was just a boy. The old mountain man told Smoke all about the rendezvous he'd attended in the Snake River country back in the early '30's. The event was held close to where three Wyoming rivers meet: the Snake, Greys, and Salt.

Smoke rode deeper into the High Lonesome, memories of Ol' Preacher all around him. It seemed to Smoke that his friend and mentor was guiding him on.

After leaving the settlement, Smoke had angled over, crossed the Salt River Range, and followed the Greys up. He was not far from where the old mountain man, William Sublette, had reached a particularly beautiful and lonesome place and named it Jackson Hole, after another mountain man and close friend, David Jackson. Preacher had told him that was back in '29, long before the damn settlers started coming in and civilizing everything they touched.

Five decades later, there were still damn few settlers in the area, but those hardy ones who had come, had stayed. The valley where Smoke was heading was approximately forty-eight miles long and about six to eight miles wide, with mountains pushing thousands of feet into the sky all around it and in it.

Smoke was going to test those following him. He was going to give them a little taste of what was in store for them if they persisted in hunting him clear up into the High Lonesome of northwest Wyoming, where the peaks pushed two-and-a-half miles into the sky and one misstep meant death.

Here in the hole is where he'd find out if those on his backtrail really meant to kill him. For if that was true, he would leave some of them to be buried among the Aspen, Englemann spruce, Douglas fir and lodgepole pine. And where the mountain men used to join the wolves in their howling, lending their voices to the ever-sighing winds of the High Lonesome.

7

"Magnificent country," Gunter said, riding in a valley between the towering mountains.

"Some of us will enjoy it for eternity, I think," Angel said.

The words had hardly left his mouth when John T. called for a halt. Frederick rode up to the point. "What's the matter?" the German asked.

John T. pointed to a strange design of rocks in the middle of the trail. "That's the matter."

"What does it mean?"

"That's the Blackfoot sign for warning. Tellin' us not to come any further."

"Oh!" Marlene said, riding up. "Will we get to shoot some red wild Indians?"

"No Injun put that there, your ladyship," John T. told her. "Smoke Jensen done that."

"How do you know that?" Hans asked.

"See that little squirmly lookin' thing off to one side? That's the sign for smoke. He's tellin' us that from here on, the game is over."

"Good, good!" Frederick said. "He's throwing down the

glove." He dismounted and with his boots, kicked the strange assemblage of rocks apart.

"How will Smoke know we've picked up his challenge?" Gunter asked.

" 'Cause he's watchin' us right now," John T. said. "Bet on it."

The howl of a wolf touched them, the quivering call echoing all around them.

Montana Jess looked at John T. "And there he is."

"Yep. And there he is," John T. said.

Frederick looked all around him. The silence of the deep timber was all he could feel and see. "Jensen!" he called. "Smoke Jensen! Your time has come to die. Not by a faster gun, but by a man who is much more intelligent than you. You'll see, Jensen. You'll see."

Jerry Watkins glanced at Mike Hunt. The two gunmen from West Texas shrugged their shoulders. They'd heard brags before.

Von Hausen took his rifle from his specially-made saddle boot. "Well, come on!" he said impatiently. "Our quarry is challenging us to hunt him. So, let's hunt him."

John T. looked down from his saddle. "You want us in on this?"

"No," von Hausen said. "We're just going to toy with him a bit this time."

"Uh-huh," John T. said. He swung down from the saddle and led his horse away.

Von Hausen and the others loaded up and took the caps from the telescopic sights. Von Hausen grinned. "We'll have some fun with him now." He levered in a round and started blasting at the quiet of the woods.

The others in his party followed suit and between the six of them put about eighty rounds into the woods, the slugs howling off rocks, scaring the birds, scarring the trees, and ruining the peacefulness of the hole.

"All right," Smoke said, and lifted his Winchester .44-.40

he'd bought back at the settlement. "Now we know." His first round tore the saddle horn off of von Hausen's horse and sent the animal bucking and snorting in fear. His second slug tore up the earth at von Hausen's feet and put the German nobleman on the ground. His third slug howled wickedly off a boulder and just missed—as was his intention—Gunter's head. He hit the ground and hugged it.

The women—who had never been under fire—shrieked and ran for cover.

Hans gallantly stood his ground. He raised his rifle to fire at the puffs of gunsmoke coming from above him and Smoke put a round between the man's boots, showering and stinging his ankles with rocks. Hans hit the ground and sprawled out quite unaristocratically.

Smoke shifted positions immediately, vanishing silently as a great gray wolf back into the thick timber.

John T., cold-blooded killer that he was, had taken cover— just like the rest of his crew—before the echo of the first shot had died away. John T. had the general location of Smoke spotted, but damned if he was going to expose himself to Smoke's deadly fire. Not yet. They had plenty of time.

"Swine!" von Hausen said, getting to his knees and brushing himself off. He shook both his fists at the wilderness. *"Arschloch!"*

"Wonder what that means?" Ford asked his buddy Cosgrove.

"I don't know. But it sure sounds nasty."

"Are you ladies all right?" Gunter called to the women, huddling behind a huge boulder.

"Yes. We're quite all right," Andrea returned the call. "That man really must be of terribly low quality to fire on women, don't you think?"

The fact that she fired first at Smoke apparently never entered her mind.

Cat Brown and Paul Melham exchanged glances, Cat saying, "That's a strange way of lookin' at it."

"Ain't it the truth. Women start shootin' at me, I'm damn sure gonna return the fire."

"Break up into groups," von Hausen ordered the gunfighters. "Five groups. The first group to corner Smoke Jensen and lead me to him gets an additional five thousand dollars. We start the hunt first thing in the morning. John T., find us a suitable place to make camp."

"We break up into groups of five," John T. said. "One group stays with the Germans and we'll switch around ever' day so's ever'body can get the same chance at the additional money." He rolled him a cigarette. "Damn sure beats the hell out of killin' homesteaders. I think," he added.

Smoke had worked his way back to his horses and was gone, vanishing back into the rugged wilderness. He rode through the harsh and unforgiving terrain with the ease of a man who was comfortable with the elements; at home with them. The mountains, the desert, the swamps . . . they are neither for nor against a man. They are neutral. But if one is to survive, that person must understand what he is up against and work with his surroundings, never against them.

Smoke understood that. Probably the men of the west riding with the Germans knew it, too. He doubted any of the others did. And eventually, he would use that lack of knowledge and their natural arrogance to work against them.

He could have easily killed von Hausen and the others a few moments ago. But he did not want to kill anymore. He wanted to dissuade them from this stupid hunt.

He wondered if that was possible?

He didn't think so, but he had to try.

Briscoe killed a deer and the meat was cooking as the night began closing in around the hunting party in the Tetons. The hunters were very quiet, each with their own thoughts in this harsh land. Miles away from them, in a very carefully selected spot, Smoke sat before his own small fire—which he would soon extinguish for safety's sake—and cooked his supper and boiled his coffee. It had been years since he'd been in this country, but all the trails and creeks and rushing mountain streams and cul-de-sacs were mapped in his mind.

He was camped between Hunt Mountain and Prospectors Mountain. To the west lay Fossil Mountain, the east, Phelps Lake. Below him were the hunters. He could actually see their fires, when he stepped out of the rocks which concealed his camp.

"Vain, silly people," Smoke muttered to the night. "Leading others to their death if they keep this up."

A wolf howled in the night, and Smoke smiled. He could commiserate with the wolf; he knew just how the animal felt. Knew how it felt to be hunted for no real reason. He knew the wolf posed no real threat to mankind; never had and never would, if people would just give it room to hunt and exist. But Smoke knew that much of humankind was timid and selfish; much of what was left were just like those hunting him: the types of people who wanted to kill for the sake of bloodletting alone, enjoying seeing their prey suffer. Smoke had no use for those types. None at all.

Ol' Preacher had told him, long ago, that if God hadn't wanted all the critters of the forests and plains and swamps and deserts to exist side by side with man, the Almighty wouldn't have put them here. Preacher had said that if given the chance, nearly all the critters would leave man alone, if man would just take the time to understand them. Indians felt the same way. But most men were too impatient and would not take the time to really understand the value of those who share the earth.

Smoke recalled ol' Preacher's words: "One of these days, boy, after we're dead and gone and has become a part of the wind and the sky and earth, man is gonna look around him and say: I wonder what happened to the wolf, the puma, the bear, the deer, the beaver, the jaybird, and the eagle. I miss them. What happened? And most will be too gawddamn stupid to understand that *they* was what happened. Bloodthirsty for the kill. Arrogant and unfeelin' for God's lesser creatures. Sometimes I wonder just who is God's lesser creatures. Us, or the animals. Animals don't kill for sport, just man. Animals don't kill 'ceptin' for food to eat or to protect young'uns or territory. Hell's fire, Smoke, I've personal seen babies that wandered off from their tipis that was taken in by wolves and kept alive until they was found. And that's the truth. You'll see it yourself as we travel this land, you and me. I have to laugh when I hear folks say wolves is savage creatures. Not unless you mess with 'em they ain't. But don't we humans turn savage if somebody messes with us? We damn shore do. It's a mighty strange and hypocritical world we live in, boy. We humans expect more out of animals than we do out of our own kind. And that's stupid, boy. Stupid and arrogant."

The wolf howled again. Its voice was beautiful in the night. Somewhere close to the wolf, a puma coughed a warning to stay out of its territory. An owl hunted in the darkness.

"Stay with us," Smoke muttered as he put out the fire. "Stay with us. We need you a lot more than you need us."

Smoke put out his fire and wrapped up in his blankets; but sleep was elusive on this night. He wrestled with his thoughts. He knew he should take the fight to those hunting him. Knew that with just one night's deadly work he could so demoralize those man-hunters that many of those left would pull out, their hearts and minds numbed with fear.

So why didn't he?

Because he was tired of the killing. He didn't want to spill any more blood. It was just that simple. He wished he could shout to the world: Smoke Jensen wants no more.

Wants no more?

When did he ever want the killings? Sure, he had taken the fight to many people over the years. But only after they had done harm to him or those he loved.

So what made this situation any different from any of the

others? What had he done to any of those people hunting him?

The answer was that he had done nothing to any of them.

So why all the reluctance on his part?

He tried to convince himself as he turned in his blankets that it was because of the women with the group.

But he knew that held little truth. From what he had seen so far the women were just as savage and bloodthirsty as their male counterparts. They certainly hadn't shown any hesitation to fire their weapons. He had seen that evidenced this afternoon.

The bottom line was that he was sick of all the killing. But there was an addendum to that.

Those hunting Smoke seemed determined to kill him.

So where did that leave him? What options did he have? Sleep finally took him as he was thinking: No options.

Al Hayre and his group looked at the silent timber and the towering mountains that loomed all around them. They could feel eyes on them; sensed that Jensen was watching them. It was an uncomfortable feeling knowing that he could see them but they couldn't see him.

"I don't like this," a bounty hunter known only as Gary said.

"You got any better ideas on how to flush him out?" Utah Red asked.

Gary sat his saddle and shut his mouth, a glum expression on his face.

"That's what I figured," Utah said. He looked around him. "Where the hell is Cosgrove?"

The wind sighed off the mountains and through the lushness of the unspoiled wilderness; the cold breeze teasing the men, as if to say: I know.

"Well, hell!" Al Hayre said, twisting in the saddle and

looking around him. "He was right behind me a minute ago."

"Somethin' movin' in the timber," Gary said, pointing. "Right over there."

The men dismounted and ground-reined their horses, taking their rifles from the saddle boots and fanning out, moving toward the timber.

Cosgrove's horse walked out of the timber, dragging its reins and trying to graze.

"Rope's gone from the saddle," Angel Cortez said.

"What the hell does that mean?" Gary asked.

No one replied. No one knew.

As the men drew nearer, muffled sounds came from the gloom of the timber and the thick underbrush.

"Somethin' kickin' in there," Utah said. "High up, 'bout twenty foot off the ground. See it?"

"Si," Angel said. "But I don't know what it is—it does not look human."

Utah was the first to enter the timber from the valley. He pulled up short. "Hell, it's Cosgrove. He's all trussed up and hangin' from a limb. Cosgrove," Utah yelled, "what in the hell are you doin' up there?"

But Cosgrove couldn't answer. One of his socks was stuck in his mouth and tied in place with Cosgrove's own bandana. He was swinging from his own rope. His guns were missing from their holsters.

The man-hunter was lowered to the ground. The dirty sock was pulled from his mouth. Cosgrove coughed and spat and cussed for a full minute.

"Son of a bitch trussed me up like a side of beef," Cosgrove said. "He was sittin' on a tree limb and jerked me off like I wasn't no more than a baby. I didn't get to holler or nothin' 'fore he whapped me up side the head with a club. I wasn't out no more'un a couple of minutes. He's got to be close. Took my guns, too. Damn!"

"Don't bet on him being close," Utah said. "He's probably cleared out of this area and huntin' some of the others."

He was wrong. Smoke was less than fifty yards away, flat on his belly under some brush, listening and watching.

"The man must move like a ghost," Angel said, nervously looking around him.

"Knock off that ghost business," Utah said. "He puts his pants on the same way we all do. He just got lucky, that's all." But Utah didn't sound too convincing.

"He gave me a message to tell y'all," Cosgrove said. "He said he was tired of this business and to leave him alone. If we keep pushin', he's gonna start killin'. And when he starts, he's gonna do it right; that there wasn't none of us gonna leave the High Lonesome alive. He said that no amount of money was worth our lives. And to think about that."

"Jensen had you and didn't kill you," Utah said, thinking: That ain't like him. If what I'm thinkin' is true? . . .

Angel looked around him, at the silent timber and the towering mountains, thrusting their snowcapped peaks into the skies. The clouds were low this day, the hint of rain or snow in the air. "I do not like this place," the Mexican gunfighter said.

"This place is just a place," Utah said. "The place ain't what we got to worry about. It's Smoke Jensen we got to watch out for."

"Smoke Jensen is this place," Angel said. "He is of the mountains." Angel sniffed a couple of times.

"You smell somethin'?" Gary asked.

"Yes. Death."

8

Marlene Ulbrich sat her horse and stared at the dark timber. Her horse had just pricked up its ears and she was instantly alert. She was an excellent horsewoman and knew to trust her animal's instincts. She saw something move. It looked like a man. She lifted her rifle and fired. The others in her team were at her side within seconds.

"What did you see?" Hans asked.

"A man. Right there by that lightning-marked tree."

Smoke had hit the ground the instant he saw the woman lift her rifle. The slug had missed him by several feet; but the act had confirmed his suspicions that the women in the group were just as dangerous as the men. Maybe more so. He had rolled back into the timber, leaped to his now-moccasined feet, and made his way deeper into the thickness of nature.

With a sinking feeling in his stomach, he now knew he had no choice in the matter. He was not going to run and run and run in the hopes they would give up; that would do nothing except delay the inevitable. Those hunting him were set on killing him, so he had to fight with the same callousness they were exhibiting.

He would let the man he'd strung up give his warning to the others. If they still chased him after hearing that . . . Smoke would do what a man had to do, and let the chips fall.

"Anybody want to leave?" von Hausen faced the group. No one spoke or moved.

"Very well," von Hausen said. "We shall commence the search at first light. John T., put out guards. Jensen will surely attack the encampment in some fashion this night. We've got to be ready for him."

"Yes, sir. You men get your slickers. It's gonna rain," John T. told them, after looking up at the leaden skies. And the advantage is gonna be Jensen's, he thought, but did not say it aloud.

"I am sure I hit him," Marlene said. "You know, I seldom miss a shot."

"Perhaps he's wounded," Gunter said.

"There was no sign of blood," Hans said. "And I inspected the area carefully. If he is wounded, it's slight."

"Jensen'd pay no more attention to a flesh wound than he would a mosquito bite," John T. muttered to Utah.

"You goin' all the way with this, John?" Utah asked.

"Until either me or Smoke Jensen is dead," the gunfighter said. "It's personal."

"Thought it might be. He kill a friend of yourn?"

Utah grunted. "He's killed about a *dozen* friends of mine. And about a dozen friends of yours and a dozen friends of every man here. But I know something them royal folks over yonder don't, Utah, and you keep it to yourself, all right?"

"If you say so."

"I put it all together just this morning, after the news about Cosgrove. I had me a hunch all along, and that just sewed it up in my mind."

"What?" Utah moved closer. He had a hunch he knew.

"Jensen don't wanna kill no more, Utah. I think he's run out of nerve."

"But I been hearin' you tellin' them counts and dukes and such that . . ."

"I know what I been tellin' them. I been doin' that deliberate, tryin' to get them skittish. I want Jensen myself, Utah. I want him bad."

"I see what you mean. I had the same feelin' this mornin'."

"Think about it. Jensen's probably gonna slip into camp and scare the drawers offen them ladies. But he ain't gonna kill, Utah. He ain't got it in him no more. He's all burned out. If Tom Lilly had faced Jensen last year, Jensen would have shot him without blinkin'. That rummy from the town told us that Jensen shot Tom in the arm. In the arm! That ain't the Smoke Jensen I been hearin' songs sung about and books writ about and stories bein' told. You see what I mean?"

"You right, John T." He grinned in the lightly falling mist. "You gonna be famous, John T. I can see it now. The man who kilt Smoke Jensen."

"That's right. I want you boys to just stand back when we corner him. I want him, Utah. Me. Understood?"

"You got it, John T. He's all yourn."

Maria did not stir at the slight bumping sound in the night. The bumping sound was Smoke laying the butt of a .44 against Gunter's head. Hard. She did not even stir when the lightly falling rain and the cold winds entered through the slit in the back of their tent. What did get her full attention was when a hard hand clamped over her mouth and another hand grabbed her by her long blonde hair and jerked her halfway out of the blankets.

Her wide open and frightened eyes looked into the coldest, meanest eyes she thought she had ever seen in her life.

"I'm Jensen," the big man said in a whisper. "You didn't pull out after I roped and trussed-up and warned your hired skunk today, so I thought I'd pay you a visit and tell you personally. No, your man's not dead. I just conked him on the noggin. He'll have a headache, but nothing else when he wakes up. But if you continue to chase me, he will be dead. Do you understand that, lady?"

She nodded her head.

Outside, the sky rumbled darkly with deep thunder and the rain picked up.

Smoke looked through the very dim light at the badly frightened woman. Gunter snored in his Smoke-induced unconsciousness. "I want to be left alone, lady. That's all I want. You people leave these mountains now. Do it tomorrow . . . first thing. I don't want to see any of you women hurt. But if you keep on chasing me, odds are you'll get hurt. You understand?"

She nodded her head.

Smoke turned her head with the biggest and hardest and roughest hands she had ever felt in her life. She looked at his guns. He had two in holsters, and two stuck down in his gunbelt. "Now what you'll do, lady, is this: I'm leaving. You're going to count to one hundred and then you can squall and holler all you want to. But if you start screaming before that real slow hundred count is over, I'm going to turn around and fill this tent so full of lead there isn't a chance you won't catch at least one slug. Do you understand all that?"

Again, she nodded her head.

Smoke lowered her head back to the silk pillows and pulled the covers up to her eyes. "Goodbye, your ladyship. I really hope I never see you again."

Then he was gone, moving silently through the rainy night.

Maria lay in her warm blankets and dutifully counted to one hundred. Then she started bellowing like a lost calf in a hail storm.

The camp was filled with men in various stages of dress and undress.

"Smoke Jensen!" Maria screamed. "He was in my tent. He manhandled me and hit Gunter on the head." Then she lost all her expensive finishing school training. "Five thousand dollars to the man who kills that son of a bitch!"

The night erupted in gunfire, with nobody hitting anything except raindrops. But in the two minutes that Smoke had been gone, he had covered a lot of ground, far out of range of even the best rifle made. He had not heard Maria's offer for his head. An hour later, Smoke had dried off, changed clothes, and was snug in his lean-to.

He had built a hat-sized fire, boiled his coffee and fried some bacon, and then put out the fire. He leaned back amid the sweet-smelling boughs that lined the ground under his ground sheet and blankets.

He chuckled. If he hadn't been mistaken, Princess Maria had been so scared she had peed in her expensive drawers.

The morning brought with it a mountain downpour. There was no way anybody was leaving camp in all this fury. Gunter was nursing a headache to go with the lump on the side of his head and Maria was still cussing, furious because a damn commoner had dared put his filthy hands on her.

"You was right, John T.," Utah said. "Jensen could have kilt a dozen of us last night. He's lost it."

John T. nodded his head in agreement. "But it shore shook them noblepeople up, didn't it. Even ol' ramrod-up-the-butt von Hausen is lookin' at Jensen in a different light. We got it made, Utah. Got it made, man!"

But John T. was wrong about von Hausen's different attitude.

"Nothing that Jensen has done so far agrees with all the talk about him," von Hausen told his group. "The man could have demoralized the camp last night. He could have killed a dozen men. He didn't. Why?"

Gunter shook his head and grimaced at the pain.

Hans shrugged his shoulders.

Maria cussed.

"He hasn't lost his nerve, if that's what you're thinking," Marlene said. "That took a lot of cold nerve to come into an armed camp."

"Oh, no," Frederick said. "He still has plenty of courage. But he *can't kill anymore!*"

That got everybody's attention.

"Add it up. That chap we met on the trail several days back. He told us about that young hooligan in that saloon back south that braced Smoke. According to what the drifter heard, Smoke refused to be goaded into fighting him; actually walked away from the young hoodlum. A gambler killed the loudmouth moments later. And that thug, Tom Lilly. That old drunk said Smoke shot him in the *arm*. Smoke Jensen never shot anybody in the arm in his life. He fired at us the other day. But did he? I think not. He was shooting all around us. But not at us. He roped Cosgrove but didn't even hurt him. Smoke Jensen can no longer kill. The game now becomes ever so much more interesting."

"How do you mean, Frederick?" Marlene asked.

"We press him. Push him. Force him to stand and fight. And then we can all have a good laugh at his expense as we watch him stand helplessly, unable to kill. That will truly be a moment for posterity. The great legendary Smoke Jensen, unable to use his guns, reduced to tears." His laugh was triumphal.

"This calls for champagne," Hans said. "I believe we can safely open one of the few bottles we brought for this occasion.

"But of course!" von Hausen said, his voice full of good cheer. "But we must save at least one bottle to drink over Smoke Jensen's body while Hans takes pictures of the event. Your camera equipment is intact; it stood the journey well, Hans?"

"Oh, yes. We shall have our pictures, Frederick. I assure you of that."

Smoke took advantage of the furious storm to break camp and move north. He moved carefully, taking his time, and rode up to just south of Jenny Lake. It took him two days to make those few miles. The yellow arrowleaf balsamroot blossoms were just opening and, when he crossed the little valley, he seemed to be moving through a living sea of yellow and green. He made little effort to hide his tracks. He had heard the gunfire after he'd left the woman's tent, and knew his words had been wasted. And it had saddened him. Von Hausen and his people were not going to quit. They were going to continue pushing him, pressing him, until he would be forced to start shedding blood.

Their blood, not his.

Smoke caught his supper from the lake and after eating, moved his camp back into the rocks where he was protected from prying eyes, the wind, and bullets.

The next morning he found a secluded and well-protected place for his horses, with plenty of water and graze. He rigged a pack for himself and chose the weapons he would take that day—and they were formidable ones. He stuck a packet of crackers into his pack and set out, skirting the meadow he'd crossed and staying in the timber as much as possible as he back-tracked to the trail he'd used coming in.

There was no point in kidding himself any longer. He had run out of options; run out of ways to try to convince those chasing him to give it up. Those coming after him were not going to quit. This was going to be a fight to the finish so, he concluded, let us get on with it.

At the trail, he rigged a swing trap using a limber limb, a length of rope, and a stake set off the trail. Someone was going to have a very messed-up face when the horse triggered the rope placed close to the ground. Further on up the trail he rigged a deadfall employing the same methods. Then he carefully chose a defensive position and waited for the action to start.

Nick was at the point, riding slowly, scanning the terrain ahead of him. Jensen had left plenty of sign to follow, so there was a need to look at the ground only occasionally. His horse's hoof hit the rope and the limb sprang forward. Nick took the full force of the green limb in the face, slapping him out of the saddle, smashing his mouth and nose, and knocking him unconscious. He was still out, sprawled on the ground, when Pat Gilman found him.

"Hold it up!" Pat shouted, swinging down from the saddle. "John T. Up here, Nick's down."

"He ain't dead," John T. said, kneeling down beside the bloody Nick. "But his face is some messed up. Lost some teeth and busted his nose for sure." But Jensen isn't killing, he thought. We'll all take some bumps and bruises, but that's a damn sight better than taking a bullet.

"Oh, I say now," Hans said, riding up and looking at the bloody Nick, sitting up and bathing his face with a wet cloth. "This isn't playing fair at all. The man obviously is no sportsman."

John T. glanced up at the man, thinking: and none of you is playin' with a full deck, either. I never met no people like you in all my days. You're all nuts! If Jensen hadn't run his string out, you'd all see that this here ain't no damn game.

"Can he ride?" von Hausen asked.

"Yeah," John T. told him. "Just as soon as he comes to his senses. He took a pretty good lick in the face."

"I'll get the medical kit," Gunter said, waving to a man leading a packhorse.

"Scout on ahead," von Hausen told a gunfighter from Nevada. "And keep your eyes open for more booby traps."

The hired gun nodded and moved out. He was soon lost

from sight in the lush wilderness. The brush and timber and undergrowth were so thick a horses' hooves could not be heard more than a few yards away.

John T. stood up from his squat and met the eyes of Frederick von Hausen.

He knows, John T. thought.

He knows, Frederick von Hausen thought.

The man from Nevada accidentally missed the deadfall when he left the trail and rode for a few hundred yards in the timber. He was riding with his rifle across the saddle horn. He turned and got back on the trail. The trail wound around a jumble of huge boulders. The man from Nevada pulled up short and tight when he saw Smoke Jensen standing in the trail right in front of him, his right hand hovering near the butt of a pistol.

"I tried to warn you the best I could," Smoke said. "But none of you would listen."

The man from Nevada stared at Jensen. His mouth was cotton-dry.

"None of you can say I didn't try," Smoke said.

"Now what?" the man from Nevada managed get his tongue to working.

"Make your play, gunfighter."

"I ain't got a chance thisaway."

"That's your problem. You're chasing me, not the other way around."

The man from Nevada suddenly turned his horse, jerked up his rifle and eared the hammer back. Smoke let him get the hammer back before he drew. He shot the man one time, the slug striking the man from Nevada just under the armpit, right side, and blowing out the other side. The gunslinger tumbled from the saddle, dead before he hit the ground.

Smoke vanished back behind the boulders and picked up his rifle. "Come on," he muttered to the winds. "All bets are off now."

9

Everybody was in the saddle and moving as the sounds of the single shot filtered faintly to them. John T.'s horse triggered the deadfall and the logs came crashing down, blocking the trail behind him and putting several horses into a panic. They bucked and snorted and tossed Gunter to the ground, knocking the wind from the man. Briscoe's horse reared up and the gunfighter fought to regain control. His horse's hooves slammed against the flank of the horse Marlene was riding. Her horse jumped in fear and Marlene's butt hit the ground. She squalled in shock and sprawled quite unladylike in the hoof-churned mud. She said a lot of very ugly words, in several languages.

John. T. left the saddle in a flying dive when he spotted the body of the man from Nevada. A slug whined wickedly just as he left the saddle. If he had waited another second, his brains would have been splattered against a tree.

So much for Jensen losing his nerve, John T. thought, as he hugged the ground.

Smoke's second shot tore the saddle horn off and the horse bolted in fear. Leo Grant came riding up and Smoke sighted him in and fired just as Leo turned in the saddle, the .44-.40 slug taking him high in his left arm. Leo screamed in pain but managed to stay in the saddle and jump his horse into the timber.

Smoke had lost the element of surprise and knew it. He grabbed up his pack and ran into the timber behind the jumbled mass of boulders.

"Stay back!" John T. yelled down the trail. "Stay back and get down. Get off those horses and get into the timber."

"Oh, damn!" Leo moaned. "I think my wing's busted. Jesus, it hurts."

"Quit complainin'," John T. told him. "You'll live."

"Is Matt dead?" Utah called, crawling through the brush.

"Near as I can tell, he is," John T. returned the call. "Leastwise he ain't movin' and they's an awful lot of blood on the ground."

"Damn!" Utah said. "Guess we was both wrong about Jensen."

"Yeah. Von Hausen had the same idea, I'm thinkin'. We all misjudged Jensen."

Smoke had moved back into the timber for a ways, then cut south, making his way through the timber silently and coming up in back of the group.

Larry Kelly turned to glance nervously at his back trail and his eyes widened in shock and fear. Smoke Jensen was standing in the center of the trail.

"Oh, no," he said, just as Smoke lifted his rifle and pulled the trigger.

The slug took Larry dead center in his stomach with the same effects as a blow with a sledgehammer. The force of it doubled him over and dropped him to the trail, screaming as the pain surged through him, white-hot fingers that seemed to touch every nerve in the man.

Smoke jumped to the other side of the trail and vanished. But he didn't vanish for long.

A stick of dynamite, tied to a short length of broken off limb came sputtering through the air.

"Goddamn!" Valdes yelled. "That's *dynamite!*" Then he hit the ground and said a prayer. It was said very quickly.

The dynamite exploded and horses went running in blind panic in all directions. The pack animals ran into the timber, losing their packs and sending supplies scattering everywhere. Another stick of dynamite came hissing through the air and landed near Maria. When it blew, the concussion lifted her off the ground and sent her tumbling down the hill. She landed in a creek, banged her head on a rock, and came up sputtering and yelling.

Nat Reed tried to cross the trail to get a shot at Smoke and a bullet burned his face, taking a chunk of meat out of his cheek. Thinking he was more seriously wounded, Nat bellied down on the ground and started hollering that he was dying.

The wilderness became silent; no more dynamite was thrown, no more shots. But the people of the von Hausen party did not move from their cover for several minutes. With the exception of Maria. She had crawled from the icy waters of the creek to lay huddling, trembling, and sobbing behind a large rock.

"He's gone," John T. announced, his voice reaching those sprawled on the ground, crouched behind trees, and hiding in the bushes. John T. stood up and walked over to Larry Kelly who lay on the ground, his legs drawn up and both hands holding onto his .44-.40 punctured belly.

"Help me!" the gun-for-hire said.

"You know there ain't nothin' nobody can do," John T. told him. "We'll build a fire and make you comfortable, Larry. That's about it."

Larry started weeping.

Even von Hausen was shaken by the suddenness and the viciousness of the attack. He sat on a rock and willed himself to be calm.

Gunter slipped and slid and stumbled down the bank toward Maria. Halfway there he lost his footing and rolled the rest of the way, landing on his ass in the cold waters of the creek.

Gunter said a few very vulgar words.

"Assemble," von Hausen said. "Let's see how much damage was done."

"One dead, one dyin', and two wounded," John T. told him.

"I don't wanna die!" Kelly screamed.

"You shoulda thought of that 'fore you signed on," Utah told him. "That's the problem with you young squirts. You don't consider that a bullet might have your name on it."

"Go to hell!" Kelly yelled at him.

"I'll be right behind you, boy," the older gun-for-hire told him.

The cook, Walt, was walking around gathering up what supplies he could find and muttering to himself. An old gunfighter who had given it up years back, Walt no longer carried a gun on him.

"What the hell are you mumbling about?" Hans asked the man.

"You told me this was a huntin' trip," Walt snapped at him. "You didn't tell me 'til we was five hundred miles gone that it was a *man*-huntin' trip."

"You find that repugnant?" von Hausen asked from his seat on the rock.

"I don't know what that means," Walt replied, a sack of flour in his hands. "But I think you're all about half nuts—or better—chasin' after Smoke Jensen. If'n you'd asked me from the start I woulda told you Jensen is pure poison. You'd be better off stickin' your arm in a sackful of rattlers."

"Keep your opinions to yourself," Gunter panted the words, as he shoved Maria over the top of the bank. "Just cook."

"I'll do that," Walt said. He tossed the sack of flour to Gil Webb.

"What the hell do you want me to do with this?" Gil asked.

Walt suggested a couple of things.

Smoke left the trail and headed west, between Jenny Lake and Leigh Lake. Miles behind him, Larry Kelly and the man from Nevada were buried in shallow graves, the mounds covered with rocks to keep the scavengers from digging up and eating the bodies.

"Suggestions?" von Hausen said to John T.

"We ain't got nothin' to use as leverage to make him come to us," John T. said. "If you wanna go on, all we can do is keep chasin' him."

"I shall press on to the last man," von Hausen told him. "Will the men stay?"

"There ain't nobody talkin' about quittin'."

"Mount the men."

Marlene fell back to ride beside old Walt—when the trail permitted that. "Did you know this Preacher person who raised Smoke Jensen?"

"I knew of him." The cook didn't like the women any better than he liked Von Hausen, Gunter, or Hans. If anything, he liked them less. Women didn't have no business out here in the wilderness, shootin' and chasin' a human bein' like he was some kind of animal.

"What was he like—that you know of."

How could I tell you somethin' about him that I didn't know, you ninny? Walt thought. "Tough as rawhide and wild as the wind. He taught Smoke well. Give this hunt up, missy. You're headin' for grief if you don't. Smoke's done showed you how he fights. And if you think he'll spare you 'cause you're a woman, you're flat wrong. You start shootin' at him, he'll put lead in you just as fast as he would a man."

"Frederick will never quit," she said with a toss of her head. "This is the ultimate challenge for him, and for us."

"Well, you couldn't have picked a prettier place to be buried, Missy."

"You can't believe that Smoke Jensen is going to win this, do you? That is ludicrous!"

"I don't know what that means, Missy. But I do know this: Smoke cut down your party some yesterday. Tomorrow or the next day he'll whittle it down by two or three more, all the while leading us north, always north, higher and higher into the mountains. And I'll bet you a dollar that when we get to the north of this lake, Jensen will have cut west." He smiled.

"Why are you smiling and what significance does the direction have?"

"I'm smilin' 'cause Jensen is smarter than you folks; only the whole lot of you don't have enough sense to see it. You're all a bunch of arrogant fools. The direction means that if we follow his trail, we'll soon be out of food and the only tradin' post open to us is on the east side of Jackson Lake. Jensen will be on the west side, headin' straight north. That'll give him two, three days, at least, to get ready for us up yonder in the wilderness."

Marlene left the old cook's side, in a huff because of his words. "Arrogant, indeed!" she said. She rode straight to Von Hausen and told him what the cook had said.

"I know," von Hausen said. "I've been looking at maps—such as they are. He's right about that. What the old fool thinks of me, or us, is of no concern at all. And there is the head of the lake," he said, pointing. "We'll rest here for a time. I have to think."

Von Hausen walked back to the cook, gathering up a few men along the way. "Walt, you and these men take the pack horses and head up to the trading post on this little creek or river or whatever it is. We'll rendezvous here on the Snake." He looked at the old cook. "Marlene tells me you think we're all on a fool's mission."

"That's right, your lordship on high." There was no

backup in Walt. None. He'd lived too long and seen the
varmint too many times to back up from any man.

Von Hausen laughed at him. "And she also tells me that
you think we are all arrogant and not nearly as intelligent as
Smoke Jensen."

"Tattlin' little thing, ain't she? That's right. I shore said it.
And meant every word of it."

"Old man, if you were younger, I'd give you a thrashing
for saying those things about us."

Walt stared at him and smiled slowly. "No, you wouldn't,
Baron von Hausen. And you won't do it now, neither. But if
you want to test your mettle, Baron, you just let me get my
rig outta my pack and we'll have us a showdown right here
and now."

John T. had walked up, standing off to the side. He was
slowly shaking his head at von Hausen, warning him off.

Frederick smiled, then laughed. He patted Walt on the
shoulder. "Perhaps later, Walt. Not now. We need you to cook
for us." He walked away, John T. following him.

"Don't never take up no challenge on fast gunnin' out
here, Baron," John T. told him. "Walt Webster's no man to
fool with. That old man's still poison with a short gun. He's
laid men a-plenty in their graves over the years."

"Why . . . the man must be seventy years old!"

"That don't make no difference. Not out here. His daddy
was a mountain man. Come out here to Washington or Oregon Territory in 1810 or so. Married him a French lady that
had something to do with the North West Company. Walt
was raised by Injuns and mountain men and the like. He was
a fast gun before it become a household word. And he'll kill
you, Baron. Don't crowd that old man."

Smoke cooked his supper of fresh-caught fish and fried
potatoes, then he leaned back against his saddle and enjoyed
a pot of coffee just as the sun was going down. It had been

three days since he'd ambushed von Hausen's party and Smoke lay in a little valley just north of Ranger Peak. He was under no illusions; he knew that von Hausen was somewhere behind him, probably a day or day and a half. He'd climbed a high peak a couple of days back and picked them up through field glasses. Least he thought it was them. At that distance they were no more than dots, even magnified.

He'd follow the Snake into the Red Mountains and wait for his pursuers to come to him. There might be a few people up in that area, since Smoke had heard talk about the federal government making it some sort of park a few years back. Called it Yellowstone. But Smoke didn't figure there would be too many folks around. If there were some sightseers and gawkers, he'll tell them to get the hell out of the way, there was about to be a shooting war.

Smoke was letting his fire burn down to coals in the pit he'd dug. He'd wake up occasionally to add twigs and such to the coals, in order to keep it going through the cool night.

Smoke poured his pot empty and leaned back, trying to figure out what month it was. After some ruminations, the closest he could come was maybe the latter part of March or the first part of April.

He sipped the hot strong brew and frowned. Had it been that long? Yes. Von Hausen and his bunch had been on his backtrail for weeks, worrying at him, nipping at his heels like some small dog, and he was growing very weary of it. It was just a damned nuisance.

Smoke had stopped worrying about any moral aspects of his situation, as he had started calling it in his mind. He'd done everything he could to end it without killing. So much for good intentions.

He smiled as the face of his wife entered his mind. He wondered if Sally was enjoying her vacation back east. He sure hoped she was having more fun than he was.

10

The more Smoke thought about people being in the park area—although it was still early and the nights were cold— the more he decided against following the Snake into the area. He abruptly cut east, crossed a road that had not been here the last time Smoke was in the area, and headed for the Continental Divide. The point he was looking for was just east of Pacific Creek. He crossed the Divide and then cut due north when he reached the Yellowstone River.

One thing about it, Smoke thought with a faint smile, he was sure giving those behind him a chance to see some wild and beautiful country. Although he doubted that few, if any, among his pursuers would take the time or have the mental capability to appreciate the view.

Smoke made his camp in a long, narrow valley sandwiched by low hills, the high peaks behind them. He'd killed a deer before entering the park boundaries and spent a day jerking some meat. He wanted to have something in his pockets to eat on in case he got cut off from his horses and supplies.

He took a very quick bath in a creek, in waters that almost turned him blue. But he got most of the dirt and all the fleas off him by using strong soap. He was shaking with cold by the time he dried off and climbed into clean dry long-handles and dressed in brown shirt and jeans. He put his boots and spurs away and stayed with high-top moccasins, his britches tucked inside and laced up.

He caught some fish and broiled them over a low fire. He was out of beans and flour and lard; but, he thought, smiling, von Hausen's group had probably resupplied at the post down by Jackson Lake and they would have plenty. He'd have to see about stealing some of their supplies some night. And maybe doing some headhunting while he was at it.

He'd cross the Yellowstone tomorrow, and once he crossed Monument Creek, he'd be in the Big Lonesome once more. There he'd start the fireworks.

"He crossed the road," Montana Jess said, riding back to the main party. "He's headin' for the Divide."

"Why, for God's sake?" Hans blurted. "I thought he was going to take us into this park area?"

"He is," John T. told him. "But he don't want to get amongst a bunch of visitors when he opens this dance. He's probably waitin' for us 'tween the Beaverdam and the Monument. And it'll take us a good week to get over there."

Ol' Walt smiled with deadly humor. And he's runnin' you yahoos out of supplies, too, the cook thought. You folks just ain't yet figured out that you're up agin a professional.

Ol' Walt had given a lot of thought to just pullin' out some night and leavin' these blood-crazy people. But he wanted to stick it out and see the final outcome. He figured it was gonna be right interestin'.

"Take the point, Utah," John T. told the man. "Jensen ain't makin' any effort to hide his tracks."

That became very apparent the next day when Utah gave a whoop and the party came on a gallop.

"Those are *mine!*" Andrea shrieked, looking at a pair of bloomers hanging from a tree limb by the trail. "I lost them when the packhorses bolted and scattered the supplies." She snatched the bloomers from the limb and stuffed them in her saddlebags, her face crimson. "The nerve of that man," she fumed. "The gall of that . . . that . . . *heathen.*"

"Jensen has a very strange sense of humor," Gunter remarked. "Especially when one considers he does not have that much longer to live."

Walt shook his head at that remark. These people still hadn't got it through their noggins that Jensen wasn't plannin' on dyin'. Jensen was plannin' on killin' *them.*

Walt met the dark and serious eyes of Angel Cortez. The Mexican gunfighter knows, the cook thought. He knows just how deadly this business is. Of all of them here, Angel'll be the one to hold back and maybe come out of this alive. Angel had told him the only reason he came along was that he'd been buddyin' with Valdes and the outlaw had convinced him to come along. He had nothing against Smoke Jensen and had yet to fire upon the elusive Smoke.

Angel nodded his head and smiled at Walt. The two men reached a silent understanding.

They swung back into the saddle and pulled out, both of them hanging back at the rear of the column.

"These people," Angel said, "I think they are playing a fool's game."

"I know they are," Walt told him.

"I have tried to convince my compadre, Valdes, that what we are doing is the same as hunting a panther in his own territory while armed with no more than a stick. He does not see it that way. I think Valdes will die in this terrible wilderness."

"If his lordship up yonder don't call this fool thing off, they's gonna be a lot of people die up here," Walt said.

"Do you think Jensen would harm the women?"

"I don't know. I don't think so. No decent man wants to

harm a female. And Jensen is a decent man. I think he'll do everything in his power not to harm them. He might turn them female man-hunters over his knee and wallop the bejesus out of their backsides. Lord knows they sure need it."

Angel grinned. "Now to witness that would be worth the ride, I think."

Walt chuckled. "Shore would be some caterwaulin' goin' on, for a fact."

"Why can't the men we ride with see that Jensen is goading us on? He is deliberately leading us into another ambush. He is going to whittle us down one by one. You see it, I see it, why not the others?"

"Them blue-bloods up yonder is too damned arrogant to see anything past the end of their noses. The rest of these outlaws and gunslicks . . . well, all they can see is big money danglin' in front of them."

"And the reputation of being among the men who killed Smoke Jensen," Angel added.

"True. But what they're gonna get, Angel, is nothin' but a very cold and lonely grave."

"Is there such a thing as a grave that is not cold and lonely, senor?"

Smoke had laid down a trail that a one-eyed, city slicker could follow. And he was waiting for his pursuers. He had chosen his spot well, and only after careful scouting. He had a mountain pass at his back, a pass that he had found only after very carefully searching the area. Inside the pass, there was a small valley hollowed out by millions of years of winds and rains and slides. There was water for his horses and good graze for four or five days. He would move his horses into the green pocket when he spotted his hunters coming across a dusty plain some five miles in the distance. The area being chosen with just that thought in mind. Unless of course they moved through at night. But Smoke didn't think any of them would be willing to take that chance. He'd probably still be able to smell the dust. Unless it rained, he thought with a warrior's grim humor.

Now he was ready to get this show on the road. He had some bulls to buy before the summer was over and he was anxious to get back to the Sugarloaf . . . and Sally.

The gunfighters and man-hunters traveling with von Hausen and party knew this was too easy; they knew Smoke was setting them up. But none of them really knew this country. Only John T. and Utah had ever even been in this area, and maybe Montana Jess—except for Walt Webster, and the old cook had told only Angel about his knowledge of the wilderness. The two of them had become good friends on the long ride north. Valdes had begun to shun Angel, preferring instead the dubious company of the other gunslingers.

Angel had taken it philosophically with only a very Latin shrug of his shoulders. "He is a greedy man, that Valdes. And that is something I have told him to his face more times than once. It makes him very angry. But he knows better than to draw on me."

"You pretty good with that iron, huh, boy?" Walt asked.

"I am quick enough. But I have never started a fight in my life. Well . . . only one. A vaquero down in New Mexico Territory tried to take my girl from me one night. He called me many bad names. I invited him to step outside. He stepped. He called me more bad names and went for his pistol. I was faster. Now I can never go back to New Mexico Territory."

"And the girl?"

Angel smiled. "She married and now has two babies. I think she had forgotten about me before I had left the county."

Walt nodded. "Monument Crick is just ahead, Angel. 'Bout five more miles. We'll be off this plateau soon as we cross the crick."

"And? . . ."

"That's when Jensen will open this dance."

* * *

Mountains loomed up in front of the party. Von Hausen halted the parade and consulted a map. "Monument Creek," he said. He turned his head and looked at the mesa to his right. He started cussing.

The others followed his gaze. Scratched into the side of the million-year-old rock formation, in huge letters, was this message: STRAIGHT ACROSS THE CREEK, PEOPLE. The initials S.J. followed that.

"That arrogant *bastard!*" von Hausen said.

Walt and Angel exchanged glances.

John T. smiled as he took off his hat and scratched his head. They'd have to split up and ride cautious from here on in, riding with rifles across the saddle horn. Jensen was through playin' games. He moved his horse forward, reining in by the still cussing Baron von Hausen.

"You're doin' 'xactly what he wants you to do," John T. told the German. "Losin' your temper."

Von Hausen glared at the gunfighter for a long moment, then slowly began calming himself. He nodded his head in agreement. "You're right, of course. Absolutely correct. Now is not the time to lose one's composure. Not with the quarry so close. We'll camp here for the night, John T. Put out guards."

"Yes, sir."

Von Hausen walked to where Walt was setting up the cook tent. "How are the supplies holding out?"

"Somebody better start killin' some deer," Walt told him. "The larder is gettin' mighty low."

"Is the shooting of animals permitted in a national park?" von Hausen asked.

Walt looked at him and smiled. "Now that is a right interestin' question to ask, your nobleship. Here you done chased a man about five hundred miles tryin' to kill him for sport, and now here you stand, worryin' about whether it's against the law to shoot a deer in a park. You are the beatin'est fellow I believe I have ever seen."

"I see nothing unusual about it," von Hausen said stiffly. "Nothing unusual at all. I have always considered myself a law-abiding man."

Walt blinked a couple of times at that. He stared at the man to see if von Hausen was having fun with him. The German's face was serious. "Do tell?" he finally said. "Well, now, that's plumb admirable of you. Yes, sir. Shore is."

"Thank you," von Hausen said. He wheeled about and marched away.

"Angel," Walt said. "That feller can act as crazy as a damn lizard on a hot rock."

"Si," the Mexican said. "But really he is just as sane as you or I. He is a man who has always gotten his way, I think. And a man who has no regard for the lives of others . . . those who work for him, and those who he hunts."

Walt nodded his head. "Let's get the beans to cookin'. I'll make a good bait of biscuits, too. We'll feed 'em right tonight. For some of them, this just might be the last supper they ever get."

Von Hausen and his party rode all the next day. The only sign they saw of Smoke were the stone arrows he placed along the trail, so von Hausen would be sure to see them. The more miles they put behind them, the madder von Hausen got. Every time von Hausen saw another stone arrow it set him off into fits of cussing.

They stopped for the night at a spring near the base of a towering mountain. Pat Gilman brought von Hausen a note he'd found under a small rock near the spring. Then the gunfighter got out of the way.

THOUGHT YOU MIGHT CAMP HERE. WATER'S GOOD. HOW'S YOUR SUPPLIES HOLDING OUT, VON HAUSEN? It was signed S.J.

Von Hausen threw the note on the ground and jumped up and down on it, cussing and screaming like a madman. He stomped the note into muddy shreds.

Panting for breath, his chest heaving, von Hausen screamed, "Tomorrow, Jensen dies." He pointed a finger at Utah. "You find him, Utah. When you do, report back to me immediately. We will launch a frontal assault." He stomped off.

Briscoe said, "I ain't real sure what that means,"

Walt cut his eyes to the gunfighter. "It means that some of you won't be comin' back, Briscoe."

"Aw, shut up!" Briscoe told him. He looked at Angel. "What are you, now, the cook's helper?"

"Si," the Mexican said. "You have some objections to that?"

"Then I tell you now, your pay will be the same as the cook's," Gunter said.

"That is quite all right with me," Angel replied. "I will sleep much better at night." He took off his gunbelt and stowed it in his saddle bags.

Valdes walked over to his friend. "I cannot believe you are actually doing this, amigo. You are too good with a gun to make biscuits and stew."

"What we are doing is wrong, Valdes. Smoke Jensen does not deserve to be hunted down like a rabid animal. I say to you in friendship, give up this madness."

Valdes stared at him. "I never thought you would lose your nerve, Angel. You are a coward. You are no longer my friend. Go to hell!"

Valdes gave his friend an obscene gesture and walked away.

"Forget it," Walt said. "He wasn't never much of a friend to do something like that. Money's cloudin' his eyes. I tell you this for a fact, Angel: you and me'll 'bout be the only ones ridin' out of this mess."

Angel's good humor surfaced with a small smile. "But we will have callouses on our hands from all the grave digging, no?"

Walt chuckled. "But less cookin' and washin' up dishes, right?"

The rough humor was infectious and soon both men were laughing as they set up the cook tent.

"Sounds like a gaggle of old women. I think they both done lost their brains," Tom Ritter said, listening to the men crack jokes and laugh.

"Or found 'em," Leo Grant said, trying to ease his shot-up left arm into a less painful position in the sling.

"Now just what the hell does that mean?" Gary asked, a sour expression on his unshaved face. "Are you turnin' yellow on us, too?"

John T. stepped quickly between the two men, just as Leo was dropping his hand to the butt of his .45. "Stand easy, boys. Look at it this way: with Angel out of the picture, they's that much more money to be spread around. Think about that 'fore you start pluggin' each other."

Gary looked at the mountains looming around him, then nodded his head and returned his gaze to John T. "What the hell is a frontal assault, John T.?"

"Somethin' that we're not gonna do," the gunfighter told him. "Von Hausen will cool down by mornin'. He's just mad right now, that's all. You boys get you some coffee and settle down. We might just bring this hunt to a close by this time tomorrow."

"And when we do, we'll be pocket heavy with money, won't we?" Leo stated with a grin.

"Damn right! And Jensen will be *dead*."

11

Utah Red sensed more than heard movement behind him and to his right. He twisted in the saddle just as the rope settled around him and jerked him from his horse. Utah hit the ground hard, knocking the wind from him. He struggled to free himself of the loop and managed to slip loose and was reaching for his guns when a hard fist connected solidly against the side of his jaw. The blow knocked him sprawling. His guns fell from leather.

Cursing, Utah scrambled to his boots and swung a big fist at his attacker's head. Smoke ducked the blow and planted a left, then a right in Utah's gut. Gasping for breath, Utah stumbled away, trying to suck air back into his lungs. Smoke pressed him hard, with left's and right's that bloodied Utah's mouth and smashed his nose flat.

Utah made a dive for his guns, sliding belly down on the rocks and the dirt. Smoke gave him a foot in the face that slowed his slide and further bloodied his mouth.

Reaching down, Smoke jerked the man to his boots and walloped him on the side of his face with a big right fist. The clubbing blow knocked Utah to his knees. The last thing

Utah remembered before he lost consciousness was his daddy's warning that if the boy didn't straighten up, he'd never amount to a thing.

Pride Anderson and Lou Kennedy untied the ropes that held Utah belly-down across his saddle. They noticed that Utah's guns were gone, short guns and rifle. When they laid him on the ground, on his back, both of them grimaced at the mess that was once Utah's face.

"Jensen shore whupped the snot outta him," Walt said, walking up with a pan of water and a cloth. "He's out of it for a week, at least."

The party had stopped for their nooning and Utah had decided to scout on ahead for signs of Jensen. He found much more than he bargained for.

"Teeth knocked out, nose busted, both eyes swelled shut," Pride said. "I ain't seen but a couple of men whupped this bad in all my life."

Marlene stood away from the growing circle of men, a worried look on her face and in her eyes. Nothing was turning out the way they'd planned. This was supposed to had been a fun trip: hunt down and shoot a western gunslinger, celebrate with a bottle of champagne, and return to Europe to boast about it among their limited circle of friends.

But none of them had taken into consideration that the men of the American West—who had helped tame the country—didn't like to be hunted down. None of them had planned on their quarry fighting back so savagely. Marlene didn't think Smoke Jensen was really in the spirit of things; he certainly wasn't playing fair.

"I can't feel that he's got any ribs busted," Pride said, standing over the conscious and moaning Utah Red. "But he's sure out of it. I guess Jensen took his guns."

"I'll check his saddlebags," Bob Hogan said, walking to

Utah's horse. "I know he's got a bottle in there. He could use a drink, I reckon."

Seconds later Bob screamed out a shriek that chilled all in the camp. They whirled to look at the man. A rattlesnake was wound around his right arm, the big fanged mouth striking at his face again and again. Marlene and Maria and Andrea started screaming and the men stood around helplessly. There was nothing they could do. The big rattler presented no target with its writhing and striking.

Bob fell backward to the ground, his face blackened and swelling from the venom. His hands were clenched into fists of pain and his throat was too swollen to allow sound to push through. He kicked and jerked a couple of times and then lay still as the massive injection of poison killed him stone dead.

The women had turned away, weeping and sickened by the sight.

"What kind of man would think to do something like *that?*" Gunter questioned. His face was pale, his hands shaking, and he wanted to throw up.

"A man like Smoke Jensen," Walt said bluntly. "One of you boys kill that rattler and somebody get the shovels. Angel, get a blanket to wrap Bob up in. I'll go get the Good Book outta my gear."

Von Hausen's legs were trembling so badly he had to sit down on a log and try to regain his composure. He was in mild shock, sweating profusely. He clenched his hands into fists to still the trembling. He had never seen anything like this in all his years. He tried to put himself into the mind of Smoke Jensen. He could not. But it never occurred to him to call off the hunt.

Less than a half mile away, Smoke sat on the ground and ate jerky for his lunch while he thumbed the cartridges out of Utah's gunbelt and put them in a small sack.

Finding the rattlesnake and sticking it into Utah's saddlebags had been a nice touch, Smoke thought. He bet it sure got everyone's attention. He picked up his pack and rifle and moved out. He was smiling.

"Be interestin' to see what the Baron does now," Walt said to Angel.

"Yes. Utah is out for a good three or four days—his face is so swollen he can't open his eyes—and Bob is dead. That's three dead and two wounded and nobody has yet to get a clear shot at Jensen. A smart man would give this up."

"You don't see any of these man-hunters and so-called gunslingers pullin' out, do you?"

"No."

"That tells you how smart they are right there."

John T. walked over to von Hausen, who was sitting in a camp chair in front of his tent, drinking coffee. He looked up at John T. and shook his head.

"Barbaric act on Jensen's part."

"Yes, sir."

"I wonder how long he had that snake?"

"He probably just caught it and come up with the idea. The snake got away 'fore anyone could shoot it."

"Wonderful," von Hausen said sarcastically.

"Hole's dug and Bob's ready for plantin'. Walt's gonna read words over him."

"The ladies are still quite distraught. They won't be attending. Andrea had to take to her bed."

"Sorry to hear that, Baron."

"I'll get my jacket and be right with you. I'll join you at the services."

At the gravesite, John T. noticed that both Angel and Walt were wearing white handkerchiefs tied around their upper arm. "What the hell's all that about?"

"We want Jensen to know we ain't huntin' him," Walt told him. Just in case he decides to attend the services, he added silently.

John T. shook his head in disgust.

The entire camp—except for the ladies—gathered around the grave and Walt read from the Bible. The body was dumped in the hole and Walt closed his Bible. Just as two men picked up shovels and started covering Bob, a sputtering stick of dynamite landed in the center of the camp with a thud—about a hundred yards from the burial site.

"What was that?" Montana asked.

The dynamite blew and the horses tore loose their picket pins and went galloping in all directions. One of them ran behind Gunter and Maria's tent, a rope tangling around the horse's neck and bringing the tent down and taking it with him. Maria was in the middle of a sponge bath one second and standing smooth out in the open the next second, frozen in wide-eyed, open-mouthed shock for all to see. And she had a lot for the men to see.

It didn't take her long to find her voice and let out a shriek that probably echoed around the mountains for days. Then she fainted.

Smoke was busy setting the other big tents on fire. He touched the flame to a very short fuse and let another stick of dynamite fly just as the men—minus Walt and Angel who had the good sense to jump behind the mound of earth at the gravesite—came running toward the dust-swirled camp grounds.

"Get down!" John T. bellowed, seeing the dynamite come sputtering through the dust.

This stick of dynamite took out the cook tent, ruined the pot of beans and demolished the clutch oven.

"Crap!" Walt said. "I wish he hadn't a done that."

"Least he saved the coffeepot," Angel said.

No sooner had the words left his mouth before Smoke's .44-.40 barked twice and the coffeepot got punctured.

Andrea and Marlene came staggering out of what was left of their burning tents, in various stages of undress, both

of them coughing and choking, hair all disheveled and looking like sisters of Medusa.

Smoke couldn't see because of all the dust and billowing
smoke from the fires he'd started so he chose that time to
haul his ashes out of there. He hit the timber running and
slipped away. But he was very curious about the two men
he'd spotted at the gravesite with white handkerchiefs tied
around their arm. And neither one of them had been wearing
guns. One of them looked like the old gunfighter, Walt Webster, and the other was a Mexican. Maybe he had two allies
in camp?

The tents were gone and most of their contents went up
with them. The women had been hustled off—after Maria
was revived and a robe draped over her—and positioned
safely behind a jumble of rocks, under guard.

"One big coffeepot left," Walt said. "The cook pot's
busted. The oven's bent plumb outta shape and broke besides. The big skillet ain't got no handle. They's flour and
beans and lard all over the damn place."

Men were out looking for and rounding up their horses.
They never did find the horse that took Maria's tent with it,
but they did find what was left of the tent.

Von Hausen found his camp chair, sat down in it, and the
chair collapsed, sending the Baron sprawling on his butt in
the dirt. He picked himself up with as much dignity as he
could muster, and brushed off the dirt from his riding
breeches.

"How far are we from civilization?" he asked through
clenched teeth.

"There's a tradin' post up on the Shoshone," Montana
said. "That'd be north and east of us. As the crow flies, about
thirty miles or so."

"Could you get there?" Gunter asked.

"Oh, yeah. Best way to go would be to stay on the south
side of Eagle Peak, then cross the north end of the Absaroka

Range and hit either Eagle or Kitty Creek. Follow that on up to the Shoshone."

"And that would take how long?" Hans asked.

"Days. Some of that is mighty rough country."

Von Hausen tossed a small sack to the man. "There is more than ample funds to resupply and to hire more men—if you can find them. We're going to fall back to that plateau we crossed several miles back and set up a defensive position. That's where we'll be. Assign men to go with him, John T." He looked toward the north. "I shall not leave this wilderness until I have spat upon your grave, Smoke Jensen. I swear that."

Smoke didn't figure von Hausen would be sending anyone after him—if he could get anyone to come after him—so he returned to his camp and set about fixing supper. He wanted all fires out by dark, just in case.

He'd grabbed up a side of bacon and a sack of potatoes in the jumble of supplies he'd rooted through before getting down to business at the camp, and now planned on having a hot meal and a pot of coffee. But first he saw to his horses and found them looking fat and sleek and contented.

Smoke fixed his supper, drank a pot of coffee, and then rolled up in his blankets. He went to sleep with a smile on his face.

John T. assigned four guards to a shift, the shift to be changed every two hours so no one would get sleepy and let Jensen slip into this new camp. John T. still planned to kill Smoke, but he had to admit that his admiration for the man had grown over the long weeks of tracking him. Smoke Jensen was every bit the warrior rumors made him out to be. That was one hell of a daring move, coming into their camp in daylight and blowing things up and setting tents on fire.

Man could move like an Injun, for sure. But he had to have a weak spot. John T. would find it. He was sure of that.

"Keep a sharp eye out, boys," he called across the elevated flat to the guards. "And keep in mind that Jensen can move like a damn ghost."

At that moment, Frederick, Hans, and Gunter were making a pact that they would carry out this campaign down to the last man. Smoke Jensen would die, or they would all die trying.

"It's now a matter of honor," Gunter said. "If we fail in this hunt, we'll be ridiculed back home. I won't have that."

"Nor will I," Hans agreed.

Von Hausen nodded his head in agreement. "We may possess all the money in the world, but if we are stripped of our honor, we would have nothing. We must go on with this hunt. And we must be victorious."

"I have spoken with the women," Gunter said. "They are also in agreement that this sporting event must continue. They have been humiliated and they are very angry."

"The mood of the men?" von Hausen asked.

"John T. is testing the waters now, so to speak," Hans informed him.

"Work's hard enough to get for men like us," John T. said offhandedly to a small group of gunslingers. "Times are changin' all around us. I just can't see turnin' my back on no good-payin' job like this one."

"I ain't about to give up this here hunt," Pat Gilman said. "We stand to make more money doin' this than we could make in five years doin' anything else."

"Count me in." Ford said.

"And, me," Al Hayre echoed.

"Montana and them with him told me that they was in all the way," John T. said. "Lemme go talk with the others." Tom Ritter and Gil Webb and Marty Boswell were in. So were Pride Anderson, Lou Kennedy, Cat Brown, Paul Melham and Nat Reed. Utah Red mumbled that he'd done swore on his mother's tintype to kill Smoke Jensen; he wanted to torture him first. Make it last a long time. Ford, Jerry Watkins, Mike Hunt, and Nick were in all the way.

"They're in," John T. reported to his bosses. "For the money and because their pride's been hurt."

"Excellent," von Hausen said, and smiled for the first time since Smoke's attack that day. "Montana said he could probably round up three or four more men. He thought he knew where there was a long-range shooter. I wanted Mike Savage, but he's somewhere down in Arizona Territory at this time. Montana said the man he had in mind was better. We'll see."

"All this waitin' is just givin' Jensen more time to dig in and plan," John T. pointed out.

Von Hausen brushed that aside. "It can't be helped. We've got to be resupplied if this expedition is to continue with any hope of success. Look at it this way: There is no way Jensen can get to us up here on this flat. We have an excellent view in all directions and a fine field of fire. And the supplies will afford us some much-needed creature comforts. We have to keep the ladies in mind, John T."

John T. nodded. "Whatever you say, boss. I sent a couple of the men south to see if they could kill a deer or elk so we'll have a change from beans and hardtack."

"Excellent. I wish them a successful hunt."

After John T. had walked away from the group, von Hausen rubbed his hands together and smiled, a cruel glint in his eyes. "I feel better now. We've had our setbacks, but that is to be expected in any campaign. I feel that we've ironed out the kinks and learned some hard but valuable lessons. I think that from this point on, success is inevitable. Let's drink to it, gentlemen. To the death of Smoke Jensen!"

12

Smoke had watched the camp on the flats through long-lenses and decided that now was a dandy time to pull out. He returned to his own camp, packed up his gear, and pulled out, heading straight north. He crossed the Beaverdam, keeping on the west side of Atkins Peak. He spent a couple of days camped along the Columbine and then once more headed north. After crossing the Clear, he pointed his horse's nose northeast and headed up toward the northern end of the Absaroka Range, recalling a camp he and Preacher had made between the Lamar River and Miller Creek, up near Saddle Mountain. He spent a couple of days there then headed west, for the Mirror Plateau; from there, he'd take his followers into canyon country and see how they liked that. He had a strong hunch that some of them would spend eternity there.

Montana returned with the supplies and five new men. "This is all I could round up on short notice, boss," he told von Hausen. "But they're good boys and they'll stick it out to the end. Roy Drum, Mack Saxton, Ray Harvey, Tony Addison, and this here is Don Langston. If he can see it, he can hit it with a rifle."

Von Hausen was impatient. Smoke had had days to hide his trail. There had been no sign of him, so all concluded he had pulled out. He voiced that shared opinion with Montana and the new men.

"Don't fret none," Montana said. "Roy's the best tracker in this part of the country. We'll find Smoke. Roy's got a personal reason to find him."

"Oh?" von Hausen looked at the man.

"Killed my uncle 'bout ten year ago over in Utah. I hate Smoke Jensen."

"What did your uncle do to provoke Jensen?" Gunter asked.

"That don't make no never mind. Jensen killed him, and I'm gonna spit on Smoke Jensen's body. That's all that matters."

"Get packed up. We pull out at first light."

The trail was cold, but Roy knew his business. He found Smoke's trail and stayed on it. When Smoke crossed Cold Creek and turned more east than north, Roy pulled up and scratched his head. "This don't make no sense. I think he's leadin' us on a fool's chase."

"What do you mean?" Hans asked.

"He's just killin' time. Just wanderin' to wear us out. If I was gonna make me a stand up here, I'd do it in the canyon country. I think if we head north, we'll pick up his trail after he crosses the Lamar. He'll be headin' west, over the plateau. Bet on it."

"We'd save how many days if you're correct?" Gunter asked.

"Week, maybe more 'un that."

"John T.?" von Hausen asked.

"I'm with Roy. Let's try it."

"Lead the way, Roy," von Hausen ordered.

Smoke didn't know if his aimless wanderings would fool

those behind him for very long. It really didn't make much difference; the situation had to be settled sooner or later.

He had made an early camp after killing a deer. He had skinned it out and was roasting a steak when he heard a rider coming. He reached for his rifle.

"Hello, the camp!" came the shout. "We're government surveyors."

"Come on in," Smoke called through early twilight. "I've got food if you've got coffee."

"That we have, sir. My, but that venison does smell good."

There were four of them, all dressed like eastern dudes on an outing. But they were friendly and not heavily armed.

Smoke pointed to the meat on the spit. "Help yourselves. I've plenty more to cook when that is gone."

"Say, this is very kind of you. I thought we had provisioned ourselves adequately. But I'm afraid we stayed out a bit longer than we should have. By the way, I'm Charles Knudson. This is Harold Bailey, Morris Robertson, and Perry Willard."

"Pleased," Smoke said.

The men fell to eating and with a smile, Smoke cut another hefty chunk off the hanging deer and fitted it on a fresh spit.

"Haven't eaten since last evening," one of the government men said, coming up for air. "And would you believe that we haven't even seen so much as a rabbit this day?"

"I can believe it," Smoke said. "I've been there a time or two myself."

Charles took a break to rest his jaws and said, "Sightseeing, sir?"

"In a manner of speaking."

"Unusual arrangement of pistols, sir," Perry said. "I don't think I've ever seen a rig quite like yours."

"Not too many of them around. I like it for a crossdraw. You boys aren't from the West, are you?"

"Why . . . no. As a matter of fact, we're not," Charles replied. "What gave us away?"

"Nothing in particular. I just guessed."

Smoke let them eat in peace for a moment, then asked, "Not that it's any of my business, but what direction did you men come in from?"

"From the north," Harold said. "We've been working up near Tower Falls." He looked puzzled. "Why would it not be any of your business? It was a perfectly harmless thing to ask?"

"Out here, boys, it's sometimes not healthy to ask too many questions about a man's back trail."

"Ahhh!" Charles said. "I see. The person to whom the question is directed might be a road agent?"

"Something like that." Smoke fixed his plate and poured a cup of coffee.

"Would it offend you if I inquired as to your name, sir?" Morris asked.

Smoke smiled. The young men all looked to be about the same age. Early twenties at best. "My name is Jensen. People call me Smoke."

The young men stopped eating as if on command. They froze. Smoke went right on eating his supper and sipping his coffee. Finally he lifted his eyes and looked at them. "Eat, eat, boys. Your supper's getting cold." He smiled again. "I don't bite, boys, and I've never shot a man who wasn't trying to do me harm. So relax."

"I . . . ah . . . thought you would be a much older man," Harold said when he finally found his voice.

"We've read all the books about you and we saw the play about you in New York City our senior year in college," Morris said. "Did you really ride with Jesse James?"

"Nope. Only met the man one time. I was just a boy during the war when Jesse and his bunch stopped by the farm and I gave them a poke of food. He give me a pistol; Navy

.36 it was, and an extra cylinder. That's the only time I ever saw him."

"You've killed a . . . ah . . . uh . . ." Perry stopped, an embarrassed look on his face.

"A lot of men," Smoke finished it for him. "Yes. I have. First white men I killed was down in Rico, just west of the Needle Mountains. Back in '69 or '70. Me and a mountain man name of Preacher was riding over to Pagosa Springs to find the men who killed my father. A man by the name of Pike and a buddy of his—I never did know his name—braced me in the trading post. They were a little slow on the draw."

"You killed both of them?"

"Yes."

"And since then?" Charles asked softly.

"Long bloody years. I changed my name for several years. Married and had children. But trouble came my way and I faced it. I'm Smoke Jensen and if people don't like it they can go to hell."

"Mind another question, sir?" Harold asked.

"Go right ahead."

"I—we—heard that you were a successful rancher over in Colorado."

"That's correct. My wife and I own a spread we call the Sugarloaf."

"Yet . . . here you are in the middle of the wilderness. The first national park in America. There are no cattle here, Mister Jensen."

"No. But there is plenty of cover here, and no people to get hurt when the lead starts flying. I've got about twenty-five or thirty hardcases on my backtrail, led by a crazy European Baron name of Frederick von Hausen. They plan on killing me . . . for sport."

All four young men stared at Smoke, disbelief in their eyes. Morris broke the silence. "They plan on *killing* you, sir?"

"Yeah. It's a sporting event, according to them. Track me

down, corner me, kill me, and then go home and boast about it, I suppose."

"Have, uh, they found? . . ." He shook his head and frowned. "Well, it's quite obvious they haven't found you. You're still alive."

"Oh, they've found me a couple of times. I killed three or four of them, beat the crap out of one, and nicked two or three more. I blew up their camp last week. I suspect von Hausen has sent for more men. He seems to be a very determined man."

"You *killed* three or four, sir?" Charles said.

"Yeah. I could have killed them all when I Injuned into their camp one night and laid down a warning to one of the women in the bunch. But I didn't."

"They have *ladies* with them?" Perry was horrified at just the thought.

"I don't think they're ladies. That'd be stretching the point some. But they're definitely female."

"And this bunch of hooligans . . . they are here, in the park?"

"Oh, yeah. I blew their camp up down on the Monument, then hauled my ashes after I watched several men head out to resupply. Probably at that trading post up on the Shoshone. But they're coming after me. So you boys rest easy here tonight, and I'll fill you full of deer meat for breakfast and then you best be on your way 'fore the lead starts flying."

"But we can't have anything like that going on here!" Charles said. "Good heavens, sir. This is a national park. We have many visitors every year. Many come just to see Old Faithful erupt."

"Old what?" Smoke asked.

"Old Faithful. It's a geyser just north of Shoshone Basin. It was named by the Washburn-Langford-Doane expedition back in '70 because it spouts so faithfully."

"Valley of the Roaring Clouds," Smoke said. "That's what Preacher says the Indians called it. Sure. I know what you're talking about now." He smiled a very wicked smile. "That thing still go off regular?"

"Certainly does. Every 65 to 70 minutes."

"Do tell? That's interesting. A man could get badly burned if he got caught out in that stuff, now couldn't he?"

"Oh, yes, sir. Badly burned. That is extremely hot water coming out of the earth."

"Might work," Smoke muttered.

"I beg your pardon?" Perry asked.

"Nothing of importance," Smoke told him. "You boys getting enough to eat?"

"Oh, plenty, sir. Mister Jensen," Charles said, "I must report this deadly game to the superintendent. You understand my position?"

"Sure. Go right ahead. I imagine it'll take you boys three or four days to get to him—after you've resupplied at your base camp—then three of four days to get back here. But I'll be long gone by that time. Then what will you do?"

The young government surveyors looked at each other. "The important thing, I believe, Mister Jensen, is what will you do?"

"Survive," Smoke told him.

"There they are," Roy said, pointing to the now familiar tracks of Smoke's horses. "He's headin' for the canyons."

"Will there be many people there?" Hans asked. "Sightseers?"

Roy shook his head. "Doubtful. It's too early in the season. 'Sides, this place is about three thousand square miles. Take a lot of gawkers to fill that up. We'll find a place to corner and kill him." He lifted the reins and moved out.

"How long will Smoke keep this up, you wonder?" Angel questioned.

"He's kept it up longer than I thought he would," Walt replied. "I reckon he's hopin' they'll give it up and go on back home. When he does decide to make his stand, Angel, it's gonna be a terrible sight to behold."

"That rattlesnake business told me that," Angel said soberly. "I do not ever wish to see another sight like that."

"I 'spect Jensen's got tricks up his sleeve that'll equal it," the old gunfighter said, as the two men rode along, bringing up the rear of the column.

Angel shuddered. "What in God's name could be worse than that?"

"Jensen'll think of something. Bet your boots on it. He ain't even got mad yet."

"I have a brother in Chihuahua. He is a lawyer. I think I will visit him when this is over."

"Least you'll be able to visit, son. That's more'un them thirty-odd fools up ahead of us'll be able to do. And them three gettin' stiff in the ground behind us."

Smoke found the canyon area along the Yellowstone River completely void of human life. And he had never seen a more perfect place for an ambush.

He carefully scouted out the area where he'd chosen to raise some hell, locating a retreat route that wound down to the river, and selected a place in the narrow pass to plant dynamite. He'd light the fuse on his way out and block the pass, forcing those behind him to detour miles before being able to ford the river. By that time, he'd have chosen another place of ambush and would be lying in deadly wait.

He picketed his horses close to the narrow, torturously twisting pass, near water and graze, and moved into position just at dusk, about half a mile from the river and high above it. He awakened long before dawn and built a tiny fire to boil his coffee. He put out the fire as soon as he had warmed his hands and boiled his coffee. His breakfast was jerky and hardtack. He had already sighted in his .44-.40 for long-range shooting and fixed in his mind the landmarks he'd chosen for distance markers along his approach to the area. Now he waited.

Two riders appeared. Smoke lifted his field glasses and adjusted them for distance. He recognized one rider by his shirt and the horse. He did not think he'd ever seen the second man before. So that meant von Hausen had recruited more man-hunters. Smoke wondered where in the hell he'd found them up here and how many he'd hired?

He put those thoughts out of his head and concentrated on staying alive. The point men were still much too far away for any kind of accurate shooting when they reined up, obviously wary and suspecting an ambush. That told Smoke the men weren't entirely stupid. That left greedy and rather foolish.

More men rode up. Smoke lifted his binoculars and pulled in von Hausen and more men than he'd seen previously. "Come on," he muttered. "Come on. Let's get this going."

He was facing east, and the sun was bright. He did not want to risk any reflection from the lenses of the field glasses, so he cased them and settled back, rifle in hand, and waited. The point men rode closer. He saw one of them point to the ground, spotting Smoke's tracks. The other one twisted in the saddle, calling back to the others and pumping his clenched fist up and down in the military signal to come on.

"Yeah," Smoke muttered. "You do that."

The point men passed the first landmark Smoke had fixed in his mind. Smoke lifted the rifle and jacked back the hammer on the .44-.40, sighting one of the riders in. He took up slack on the trigger and the rifle boomed, jarring his shoulder. Cosgrove was knocked from his horse as the big slug struck him dead center in his chest.

Smoke levered in another round and squeezed the trigger. But he shot high and blew the second man's hat off. The winds caught the hat and sent it sailing. Smoke waited.

"Cosgrove's had it," Roy said, reaching the column. "Jensen shot him right through the heart."

"Goddamnit!" Ford cussed. "Me and Cos buddied all over the west together." Before anyone could stop him, Ford had spurred his horse and was racing up the trail. He shucked his rifle out of the boot just as he passed his ax-partner in crime, stone dead on the rocks beside the trail.

Smoke led the rider in the sights and let him come on. He could hear Ford cussing and hollering in his rage. "Come on," Smoke muttered. "I want you close enough so maybe your horse will come this way and I can see if you've got anything to eat in your saddlebags."

Ford was less than a hundred yards from Smoke's position when Smoke pulled the trigger. The bullet caught Ford in the center of his chest and Ford joined his buddy on the trail. He hit the ground and did not move. His horse kept right on going. Smoke jumped down into the rocks and grabbed the horse's trailing reins, talking to the spooked animal, calming it down.

He found some salt meat and biscuits wrapped in a clean cloth and nothing else of value. He stripped saddle and bridle from the animal and turned it loose. Then Smoke climbed back into position and had breakfast . . . compliments of Frederick von Hausen.

13

Von Hausen studied Smoke's position through binoculars, studying every angle carefully. Finally, with a curse and a shake of his head, he cased his field glasses and returned to where his group had gathered.

"Whatever else the man may be, he knows tactics," von Hausen said. "He could hold off an army from his position. It would take several days to get to one end or the other of this canyon then find a way through and work our way behind him. If we split our people and try to trap him in there, he'd know it because of the damned flats on both sides of us, and the high ground to our rear. To charge him would be suicide. It's a standoff." He looked around him. "Where is Langston?"

"Trying to work his way out to get a shot at Jensen," John T. told him.

Von Hausen had decided, several days back, that the sporting aspects of this hunt could go to hell. Just kill Jensen, he told his people.

"Where is he leading us?" von Hausen asked. "Or is he leading us anywhere? The man doesn't think like anyone I ever knew. He's unpredictable. In every war there are plans, tried and true, that are followed by both sides. This man is a . . . a savage. I can't work out what he is going to do from one day to the next."

"Do we make camp here?" Walt asked. "I gotta know so's I can start cookin'."

A single shot rang out. Von Hausen ran to the rocks, the others right behind him. Don Langston lay sprawled on his back below them, his fancy inlaid rifle shining in the sunlight, on the rocks some twenty feet from the body. Langston had been shot right between the eyes.

Walt shifted his chewing tobacco and spat. "I'd say he got a mite too close. I'll go put the beans on."

"Hey, Baron!" the shout came across the rocky flats. "How about you and me settling this?"

"What do you mean, Jensen?" von Hausen yelled.

"Just what I said. You and me, pretty-boy. Stand up, bareknuckle fight. The best man wins."

"Marquess of Queensberry rules?"

Smoke's laughter was taunting. "Anyway you want it, Baron. We'll hold it in Denver."

"Denver!" von Hausen shouted.

"That's right—Denver. In front of a crowd at a ring. I'm not going to take a chance out here on one of your rabid skunks shooting me after I beat your face in."

"I wouldn't recommend it," Utah Red said. He was now able to see out of both eyes, but his face was lumpy and still mottled with bruises.

"Oh, I could take him in a ring," von Hausen boasted. "It might be fun."

"How about it?" Smoke shouted.

"I think not, Jensen. You can't run forever."

"Hell, I'm not running now, von Horse-face. Why don't you come on across and get me."

Von Hausen's face reddened at the slur upon his name. "You, sir, are no gentleman."

Smoke told von Hausen what he thought about the German's ancestry.

Obviously, Walt concluded, he don't think much of it.

"You are a foul, stupid man, Jensen," von Hausen hurled the words.

"But I'm a better man than you, von Hose-nose," Smoke called. "I don't need an army to do my fighting."

Frederick touched his nose. *Hose-nose!* "Fill that area with lead!" he shouted.

The men fired, but it was done half-heartedly. The distance was just too great to hope for any damage.

After the firing had ceased, von Hausen called, "How about that, Jensen?"

Silence was his reply.

"You don't suppose we got him with a ricochet?" Cat Brown questioned.

"We wouldn't be that lucky," Pat Gilman said. "He's just playin' 'possum, hopin' one of us will go over there to check it out."

"Hold your positions," von Hausen said. "We've already lost three this day."

"Ford died 'cause he was stupid," Mike Hunt said. "You can't lose your control when fightin' a man like Jensen. Ford better be a lesson to us all."

"Agreed," von Hausen said.

The group waited, all bunched up, for almost half an hour. An explosion jarred the area, followed by a dust cloud drifting up out of the rocks.

"Now what the hell? . . ." Gary muttered.

"I betcha he blew the pass," John T. said. "And I betcha it's the only pass for miles, north or south. Time we work around over there it's gonna be another cold trail."

"I'll find it," Roy said. "I told you all: I aim to kill that man."

"Collect the bodies," von Hausen said wearily. "Get your Bible, Walt."

* * *

"Now let me get this straight," the superintendent of the park said to the four young surveyors. "Smoke Jensen—*the* Smoke Jensen, the most famous gunfighter in all the world—is here in this park?"

"That is correct, sir," Charles told him. "He shared his food with us."

"He was a very nice man, I thought," Morris said.

"Smoke Jensen . . . was a very nice man?"

"Yes, sir. Much younger than any of us thought. I would say he is in his mid-thirties."

"That's about right. And people are hunting him? To kill him. In *my* park?"

"Yes, sir. Quite a large gang, I understand. Led by someone named Baron Frederick von Hausen."

"Von Hausen. I'm not familiar with the name. A Baron, you say?"

"Yes, sir."

"Who are the men with him?"

"Bounty hunters, professional killers. Men of very low quality," Perry said.

"Quite," Charles added.

"Well, this cannot be allowed to continue," the superintendent said. "I'll get word to the Army. They'll do something about it. This is federal land, after all."

After crossing the Yellowstone, Smoke headed north, into the Washburn Range. He knew he had bought himself a day, maybe a day and a half; no more than that. He was out of supplies, except for a little coffee, and he was living off the land, just as he and Preacher had done during those early years. But Smoke, like most western men, was a coffee-drinking man, and he wasn't going to be out of coffee for very long. He could live off of fish and rabbits and berries, but damned if he was going to be denied coffee.

On the second day after fording the Yellowstone, he spotted a thin plume of smoke in the distance and headed for it. He rode up to the camp, stopping a respectable distance from it, and eyeballed those in the camp who were, by now, eyeballing him.

The three men and three women were dressed in some sort of safari clothes; Smoke thought that was the right description for it. The women dressed just like the men, in britches and high-top, lace-up boots. He'd never seen hats like they were wearing. Looked like a gourd hollowed out. Funniest looking things he'd ever seen.

"Hello, the camp," Smoke called. "I'll approach with your permission."

"Why, of course. Come right in, sir," a rather plump man returned the call.

Smoke rode in and dismounted. He loosened the cinch strap on the horses and picketed them on graze.

The men and women—none of whom were armed— quickly noticed Smoke's guns. One of the women thought the stranger moved like a great predator cat. And my, what a ruggedly handsome man. She fanned herself at his approach.

They were scientists, Smoke was told. Gilbert, Carol, Robert, Paula, Thomas, and Blanche. Anthropologists and some other names that sounded to Smoke like they were clearing their throats. He didn't have the foggiest idea what they meant.

"Share our lunch with us?" Robert asked.

"I'd be obliged. I ran out of supplies several days ago."

"You poor man!" Blanche said. "You must be starved."

"Oh, no," Smoke told her, "I've been living off the land." He smiled at her. My word, what a handsome man, she thought. "No reason for anybody to go hungry in this land of bounty, ma'am. You just have to know something about surviving out here. The only bad thing is running out of coffee."

"Well, we have plenty of that," Thomas said.

Something popped in the timber and suddenly the stranger was on his feet from his kneeling by the fire and he had a gun in his hand. His draw had been so smooth and so fast none of the scientists were aware of it. It just seemed to appear in his hand.

All did notice, however, how hard and tight his face had become, and how cold were his eyes.

"One of our mules," Paula said quickly.

Smoke nodded and walked to the edge of the small clearing. He could see mules and horses picketed. "Pull them in closer," he said, returning to the fire and the coffeepot. "You got your picket line too far away from camp. There are folks out here who'd steal from you. The West has tamed somewhat, but not that much. Move it right over there." He pointed. "You see anybody trying to steal your livestock, shoot 'em."

"*Shoot* them?" Gilbert said.

"Yes. You do have weapons, don't you?"

"We have a rifle and a shotgun," Thomas said. "And Robert has a sidearm."

"That's good. Keep them close by." He walked to his packhorse and returned with two gunbelts he'd taken from bounty hunters in von Hausen's party. "Here," he said, handing the guns and leather to Gilbert. "I'm gettin' loaded down with weapons. I'll give you folks a .44 carbine, too."

"This is very generous of you, sir," Gilbert said. "Let us pay you for these fine weapons. We're out here on a government grant."

Smoke shook his head. "The people I took them from don't need them any longer."

"You're a lawman?" Blanche asked.

"No, ma'am. Those guns belonged to some ol' boys who were chasing me. They caught up with me." He looked at her confused expression and smiled, transforming his entire face, taking years from him. "I'm not an outlaw, if that's what you're thinking. I'm a rancher from down in Colorado. My wife is the former Sally Reynolds of New Hampshire."

"How marvelous!" Paula said. "The banking family. Very old and respected name." She closed her mouth and looked at the others in her group. "Then you must be? . . . It was in all the newspapers . . . Some thought it was so scandalous . . . For her to marry a . . . Oh, my God!"

"Yes, ma'am. I'm Smoke Jensen."

The women got all flustered and the men got all nervous. Smoke sipped his coffee. Too weak for his taste. But he wasn't about to complain.

"I read in the newspapers before we left that Sally was home visiting friends and family," Carol said. "Her parents are still in Europe, are they not?"

"Yes, ma'am. With our children. Look here, what do you call those hats y'all are wearing?"

"Pith," Robert said.

Smoke almost spilled his coffee. He blurted, "I beg your pardon, sir?"

"Pith helmets," Paula said. "They're quite the rage for any type of expedition into the wilderness."

"If you say so," Smoke mumbled.

Thomas said, "These guns you just gave us . . . the men chasing you gave them up voluntarily?"

"They did after I shot them."

Blanche sat down on a log. "Were they severely wounded?"

"About as severe as you can get," Smoke said, spearing a piece of bacon from the skillet. "They sure weren't in any condition to complain about it."

"You turned the thugs over to the law?"

"No. Their buddies buried them."

Carol sat down beside Blanche and both women started fanning themselves vigorously.

"You . . . *killed* them?" Gilbert asked.

"I sure did." Then Smoke explained, in detail, about those

chasing him. While he was explaining, he spotted the coffee can and made a fresh pot of coffee. Stuff that was drinkable. Cowboy coffee. "I just can't seem to convince that crazy German to leave me alone. He's about to make me mad."

Robert poured a cup of the fresh brew and took a sip. His eyes bugged out as he bravely swallowed it. He sat the cup down.

"How . . . many men do you have chasing you?" Gilbert asked.

"Oh, I don't know. Twenty-five or thirty, I suppose. I killed three more the other day, over on the Yellowstone. They just keep coming at me and I just keep whittling them down. I'm goin' to have to make a stand of it somewhere, I reckon. But I don't want to see any innocent people get hurt."

"I don't think there is anyone else in the park this time of year," Thomas said. "We did see some young men a couple of weeks ago. Government surveyors."

"I ran into them. Nice bunch of boys. They said they were going to tell the superintendent about the men after me. But by the time he gets word out and the Army, or U.S. Marshals get in, this fracas will be over."

"You are very . . . well, *cavalier* about this matter, Mister Jensen," Carol said.

"No point in getting all worked up about it." Smoke nibbled on a biscuit. "I'll just handle it my way."

"But there are *thirty* gunmen chasing you!" Blanche said.

Smoke shrugged. "More or less. And I assure you it'll be less in a day or two. I faced eighteen men in the streets of a town on the Uncompahgre some years back. I was just out of my teens. I left all eighteen belly down in the dirt."

"Eighteen!" Robert said. "You killed eighteen men by yourself?"

"Sure did. They got lead in me, I won't deny that. Almost killed me. But I was still standing when the dust cleared . . . sort of. I was on my knees in the street but I was still alive."

"Where was the law?" Paula asked.

Smoke tapped the butt of a Colt. "Right there, ma'am. The law is good for handling lost horses and finding runaway kids and the like. It's good to see the law walking the street and tipping their hats to ladies. Makes everybody feel good. All secure and such as that. But there are some things that a man has to handle personal. If he's been pushed to the end of the line and can't get any relief and if he's capable and has the where-with-all. I'm capable and I damn sure have the where-with-all."

Smoke rolled a cigarette and poured another cup of coffee.

"Then you are a follower of Kropotkin?" Thomas asked.

"Who?"

"A Russian anarchist. A revolutionary."

"No, sir. I'm just a man who believes in saddling his own horses and stomping on his own snakes. I'm all for law and order. We have us a fine sheriff back home. I voted for him. But I also believe there are people out there in society who don't give a damn for anybody's rights or wishes or privileges. Now if the law is around when those types break the rules, that's fine; let the law handle it. But there are others in society who would have me run away from this situation with my tail tucked between my legs and go crying to the law about those chasing me. I don't believe in that. I believe that if a man can't or won't follow even the simplest rules of conduct, or abide by the simplest of moral codes . . . get rid of him. Sooner or later, somebody is going to have to do it. Why not now, before that person can bring more grief to innocents?"

"For the simple reason that as human beings they deserve a second chance; a chance to redeem themselves," Gilbert said.

"Fine. But do they deserve a tenth chance, or a twentieth?" Smoke countered. "When does society say that's enough and dispose of them? And how many more innocent, law-abiding people have to suffer all types of losses and indignities and injuries and even face death and die—sometimes horribly—before those criminals are either put away for life or hanged? Their victims often don't get a second chance at life. Why the hell should the criminal have more rights than the victim? That type of thinking doesn't make any sense to me."

The scientists looked at one another.

"I set out from my ranch to buy some bulls from a friend of mine in Central Wyoming," Smoke said. "That's all. Just a simple legal business transaction between two men. Suddenly I find myself being tracked and hunted by a gang of nuts. Then I learn that they plan on using me like some poor animal; cornered and killed for sport. I could have gone to the Army with it. I was told they couldn't do anything about it. Well, fine. But I can sure do something about it. I can kill every no-count scummy bastard—excuse my language, ladies—that's coming up the trail after me. And that is exactly what I intend to do."

14

The anthropologists resupplied Smoke and wished him well on his journey. Then they quickly packed up their equipment and beat it back to park headquarters as fast as they could lope their mules.

Smoke headed north, toward one of the strangest sights he had ever seen in all his life: the dead forest. Old Preacher used to tell a story about Jim Bridger, when someone asked him if it was true about the stone trees. Preacher said Bridger told the person, "That's peetrification. Head to the Yellowstone and you'll see peetrified trees a-growin', with peetrified birds on 'em a-singin' peetrified songs."

Preacher swore it was true. However, Preacher said he never could find them peetrified flowers a-bloomin' in colors of crystal that Bridger said he saw. "Bridger wasn't above tellin' a lie ever' now and then," Preacher admitted.

Smoke didn't make any effort to hide his tracks. The government—or somebody—had cut a nature trail through the park and he stayed on it. It was easier on his horses and on him. He crossed Tower Creek and followed the trail as it curved westward. Near as he could remember, the twenty-five or thirty square miles of stone trees were only a few miles further, most on a ridge.

The scientists in the pith helmets back yonder had told Smoke that the stone trees were millions of years old, buried alive by volcanic ash. Since Smoke had never seen a volcano—and really didn't want to see one, not up close—he really didn't have an opinion on it one way or the other.

He pulled up short this time, just as he had the other times he'd looked upon the strangeness of the stone forest. It was eerie, and very quiet. Many of the trees here had not fallen, but stood like silent sentinels over their fallen comrades.

Smoke did not enter the silent dead forest at this point. He rode on, staying with the trail for several miles. When he did decide to enter the stone forest, he made his trail clear for a time. Then he tied sacking around his horses' hooves and led them out of the stone forest to a small cul-de-sac with graze and water. He blocked the entrance with brush and logs and slipped back into the stillness of the stone forest, taking with him only what supplies he could comfortably carry in a small pack on his back.

He hiked back to Specimen Ridge and chose his site carefully; one that gave him a commanding view of all that lay in front of him. Since he had ridden up, no small feat for his horses, von Hausen and party would be coming up the same trail—he hoped. Smoke would be shooting downhill, so that would be tricky, but nothing that he couldn't overcome with the good sights on the .44-.40.

Now all he had to do was wait and hope that von Hausen and company took the bait.

Roy Drum halted the parade in the valley that Smoke overlooked from his spot on the small mountain that held the stone trees.

"What's the matter?" von Hausen asked.

"I don't like it," the tracker said. "Jensen went right up that big ridge yonder with them dead stone trees. It's like he wanted us to see his tracks."

"Hell, man!" John T. said. "He ain't tried to hide his tracks in a hundred miles."

"Well, that's a fact," Roy admitted.

Von Hausen began scanning the ridge with his long lenses. After several minutes of searching, he cased the binoculars, hung them on his saddle horn, and picked up the reins. "Let's go. The ridge is void of life."

"Gary, take the point," John T. said. "Might be a good idea if we walked our horses up. That's a steep climb. Wouldn't do to have a horse break a leg now."

"You're right," von Hausen said, and swung from the saddle to help the ladies down. A true gentleman.

Smoke lay flat on his belly behind a huge stone stump of what had been redwood, millions of years back. He had measured the distance between stone stumps and trees from where he now lay to the crest of the ridge. He had ample brush to help along the way and in addition, a cut in the earth several feet deep that led to the crest and curved with one wall facing those below him.

Gary paused to catch his breath and it was his last one. Smoke's .44-.40 boomed and Gary went down.

"Goddamnit!" Roy yelled, diving for cover. "I knowed it was a trap."

Al Hayre exposed part of his body from behind a stone and Smoke drilled him clean through the shoulder. Al dropped his rifle and began a fast roll down the ridge toward the valley below, hollering and yelling and cussing until his head hit a rock and shut him up.

Smoke slung his pack and rolled to another, better protected area, angling toward the cut. Pride Anderson stepped out from cover and dropped to one knee and fired, the slug howling off stone and sending chips into Smoke's face. Smoke wiped off the blood and moved to the other side of the huge fallen tree, slipping behind a mass of brush and stone. Pride made the mistake of trying for a second shot at Smoke. He would never get another shot at anything.

Smoke quick-sighted him in and pulled the trigger. Pride took the .44-.40 slug in the center of his forehead. The force of the bullet snapped his head back and Pride tumbled, rolling lifeless down the ridge.

Smoke sent several rawhide-bound sticks of dynamite down the ridge and everybody hit the earth. Everybody except Smoke. He scrambled for the cut and ran to the top of the ridge just as the dynamite blew. Once again, horses panicked and ran off down the hill.

Smoke found him a good spot behind a small stand of trees on the crest, punched more cartridges into his rifle then chewed on a biscuit and waited.

"A couple of you men work your way over to the timber in that direction," von Hausen ordered. "Two more to that side," He pointed. "Try to box him in."

"You'll never do it, your majesty," Walt said, safely behind a petrified log.

Smoke had pulled away from the ridge and worked his way some two hundred yards back from the crest. It put him that much closer to his horses and in better cover should von Hausen order men to attempt to flank him.

On the hill, Andrea and Marlene and Maria looked with horror and disgust in their eyes—more disgust than horror—at the smear of blood and hair and brains that Pride had left on the side of a stone stump.

"Al's stirring down there," Angel said, sitting beside Walt behind the huge log.

"If he's smart, he'll find his horse and get the hell gone from here."

"One arm's hanging limp by his side," Angel said. "He looks sort of confused."

"Busted his head on the way down. There's another

walkin' wounded for us to tend to. We're gonna look like a hospital 'fore this trip gets over."

Marty Boswell's daddy had always told him he had sawdust for brains. Marty got tired of listening to his daddy and shot him dead one day back in Nebraska. Smoke proved Marty's daddy wrong when Marty stuck his ugly face out from behind a large rock for a looksee. He had some brains. But they were now several feet behind the gunslinger, on the ground, due to the impacting of a .44-.40 slug with Marty's head.

Gil Webb wisely decided not to move from his position.

Smoke said to hell with it and made his way back to his horses. He was saddled up and riding out ten minutes later. Gil Webb left his hidey-hole only after long moments of silence had passed. He made his way carefully to Smoke's last position, checking out all possibilities along the way. He found where Smoke had left the ridge, his moccasin-clad feet digging into the soft earth, heading for the timber behind the ridge. Gil motioned for the two men on the other flank to check it out, then called down the ridge for the others to stay put. Of course, von Hausen and those in his immediate party ignored that.

The men scrambled up the ridge to squat panting beside a stone tree. "Marty?" von Hausen asked.

"Dead. Jensen put one right in the center of his forehead."

"That's three dead and one wounded," Hans said. "I don't know how badly wounded Hayre is."

"He's out of it," Cat Brown said, coming over the crest of the ridge. "Hit high and pretty hard. He wants his money and wants to get gone from this fight."

Von Hausen nodded his head. "Pay him off, Gunter. Wounded as he is he'd be of no further use to us. He'd only be a hindrance. Have Walt and Angel tend to his wounds and then send him on his way."

Gunter was gone back down the steep hill.

"He's gone," came the shout from the timber. "Headin' west."

Von Hausen paced the distance between Smoke's last defensive position over to where Marty lay dead, a hole in his head. Von Hausen reluctantly admitted—to himself—that Smoke was one of the best marksman he had ever seen.

"What type of weapon is he using?" he asked John T.

".44-.40. It's got an extra rear sight for better accuracy. Jensen's good," he grudgingly conceded.

The German looked at the gunfighter. "That's like saying trains run on tracks. I measured the distance. Smoke made this shot from two hundred and ten paces."

John T. whistled softly. "That's some shootin'."

"To say the least," von Hausen added very drily. "Have the men dig some graves, John T."

"Yes, sir. And have Walt fetch his Bible?"

"Yes. This is becoming a routine."

Smoke rode west. He put a few miles behind him, knowing that by the time von Hausen and party rounded up their horses, buried their dead, and tended to the wounded, it would be dark. There would be no further pursuit this day.

He stopped long enough to fix his supper and boil his coffee, then moved on another couple of miles before finding a good spot to spend the night. He was up and moving before dawn, pushing west. He was not all that familiar with this region. Years back, he and Preacher had cut north at the stone trees and headed up into Montana. Preacher had told him about the western part of this region, but Smoke had not personally seen it.

He cut southwest, heading for the Gallatin Range. As he rode, he added up how many people—approximately—von Hausen had left. As close as he could figure it, he still had about twenty-five people after him, including the women, and he damn sure wasn't going to discount them.

His horses began acting skittish, eyes all walled around and ears pricked up. Smoke reined up and listened. And he didn't like what he heard. This was grizzly country and it was spring, with the mother grizzlies out of the den with cubs. A big grizzly can be as much as seven feet tall and weigh close to a thousand pounds. Smoke heard the huffing sound of a grizzly, and the whining of cubs, and the sounds were close. And he also smelled fresh blood. That probably meant that the grizzly had killed a fresh-dropped elk calf and would be awfully irritated at anything that interrupted her meal.

Smoke left the trail and moved east for about a mile, getting away from the grizzly and her cubs—if any—and her meal. Smoke had enough to worry about without the added danger of a grizzly bear.

When his horses had calmed down, he cut west and once more picked up the trail. Although a bear steak would taste nice, there was no way Smoke would kill a mother with cubs. Preacher had instilled in Smoke a deep love and respect for the land and the animals that lived there. Should he kill a bear, there was no way he could come close to using the meat, and no one around to give it to. Smoke had never killed any type of animal for the so-called sport of killing, and never would. He had nothing but contempt for those who killed without need.

There was another reason that humans should be extremely careful in grizzly country: a grizzly can run up to thirty miles an hour; no way a human being could out-race one. But grizzlies, because of their bulk and long straight claws, seldom climb, even as cubs.

Ol' Preacher had told Smoke that there was only two kinds of trees in grizzly country: them that he could climb and them that he couldn't.

Smoke hoped that von Hausen and his party didn't run into a grizzly. Those stupid people would make no effort to avoid contact. They'd just shoot it.

Smoke rode for several days, sometimes making an effort to conceal his tracks, but oftentimes not. He crossed Panther Creek, Indian Creek, and made camp at the north end of Grizzly Lake. Roaring Mountain was somewhere off to his east, he believed, as was Obsidian Cliff, an outcrop of black volcanic glass that was used by various Indian tribes over the centuries for arrowpoints. Geyser Basin was to his south. Hot ground, Preacher had told him. Burn your feet, so said Preacher.

That afternoon, before the sun went down and Smoke could still see to write, he scoured the area until he found a large flat rock. Using a small rock, he scratched out a message. Before he left the next morning, he carefully placed the rock in the center of the trail. There was no way von Hausen could miss it if he came this way.

Then he left the trail and headed on over toward Solfatora Creek. He had another ambush to set up.

"Some of the men are grumbling," John T. informed von Hausen. " 'Bout half of them want to quit."

"We discussed this last evening, John T.," von Hausen said. "Among the six of us." He tossed the man a small leather sack filled with gold coins. "Several thousand dollars in there, John T. Spread that out among the men. That should make them happy. And tell them there will be a thousand dollar bonus for every man who finishes this."

"They'll stay after this," John T. said.

"The great unwashed," Gunter said after John T. had left. "They are the same all over the world." He opened a container of caviar and spread a bit on a cracker. He smiled, but there was a worried look in his eyes.

The next morning, Pat Gilman was riding point. He came up on the flat rock in the trail and read the words. He felt his guts churn and another part of his anatomy tighten up. He yelled for John T.

John T. sat his saddle and read the words scratched on the big flat rock.

I HAVE RUN OUT OF PATIENCE. FROM THIS POINT ON THERE WILL BE NO COMING BACK FOR ANY OF YOU IF YOU FOLLOW ME. THIS IS MY FINAL WARNING.

Von Hausen read the scratchings. He turned to the men. "Anybody want to quit?"

No one did. They all had big money in their eyes. It was easy to forget those men lying lonely in cold graves on the trail behind them when their pockets were jingling with gold coins and big money waiting at the end of the line. What they should have realized, but didn't, was that only death awaited them at the end of this line.

"How are the supplies holding out, Walt?" Hans asked.

"If we can kill a deer every other day or so we'll be all right. As far as eatin' goes. I 'spect if Jensen keeps thinnin' the culls out like he's been doin', we'll have plenty."

"I really wish you would stop that kind of talk," Gunter said.

"You wanna fire me and Angel? You say the word and we'll damn sure leave right now."

"Settle down, old man. You're entitled to your opinion. Relieve Pat at the point, Briscoe."

One minute off the trail, following the hoofprints of Smoke's horses, a shotgun roared.

"Down!" Hans shouted, as he left the saddle.

They all waited, crouched in the early summer foliage that grew thick and lush in the darkness of the timber. But no more shots were heard.

"Jensen!" von Hausen yelled. "Jensen!"

He received no reply.

"Smoke Jensen!" von Hausen tried again. "Stand and fight like a man, damn you!"

"He wouldn't be fightin' us with no shotgun," Montana Red said, after a moment of deep woods silence. "You 'mem-

ber we come up missin' the shotgun that night he attacked
the camp and figured it got burned up or blowed up. He
musta tooken it and rigged an ambush."

"Check it out, Nick," John T. ordered. "And goddamnit,
be careful."

The man with the busted mouth and nose—he wheezed
like a steam engine when he talked—was back in a few minutes. "Jensen's long gone. He rigged a booby trap with the
shotgun. You better come look at this." He cut his eyes to
von Hausen. "But not the wimmen, sir."

Smoke had secured the express gun in the fork of a tree,
about head high, then cocked the triggers, pulling the cord
taut, that was attached to a cord from the triggers to a trip
wire. The loads of buckshot had hit Briscoe in the neck and
face, completely blowing off his head. It was a very ugly
scene.

Hans took one look and barfed all over the place.

Walt strolled up, shifted his tobacco and spat. The old
gunfighter said, "I reckon we can scratch that one off the
supper list, Angel."

15

Briscoe was buried in the deep timber—minus his head. They couldn't find enough of it to bother with scooping up. The hunters rode on a few very careful miles before making camp for the evening. When they made camp, the bounty hunters and outlaws each sat apart from one another, saying little or nothing. Briscoe's death—more the way it happened than the thug's demise—had deeply affected them all.

All had heard the stories that when pushed to his limits, Smoke Jensen was a ruthless man, who would fight like a cornered puma, stopping at nothing. The events of earlier today had damn sure proved that gossip out.

Hans sat with Gunter. The women were in their tents. Von Hausen was talking with John T. and Roy Drum.

"Gunter," Hans said.

His friend cut his eyes.

"Is going on worth it?" Hans was the first among the three to say the words.

"By now, every gambler from Monte Carlo to New York City knows of this hunt and is taking bets," Gunter spoke softly. "If we left now, we would return home in disgrace.

Yes. I've been giving it some thought. We have to press on. As we discussed before, it is a matter of honor. Are you really having second thoughts?"

"Yes. My God, Gunter, how many dead men have we left behind us. Nine? Ten? Heaven forgive me, I can't even remember!"

Gunter chuckled and patted his friend on the arm. "Well, let's just hope that God has a sense of humor, Hans."

"*He* might. Smoke Jensen doesn't."

Smoke softly whistled part of a tune he'd once heard played at a concert he and Sally had attended in San Francisco. Pretty piece. Something by Brahms, he thought. Or maybe Wagner. Whatever. It was a pretty piece of music.

He was waiting in thick underbrush, behind a fallen tree, just off the bank of a fast-moving creek. He had angled down into the Central Plateau. Not too many large mountains in this part of the range, but plenty of hills and marshes and excellent ambush sites. Smoke was cold-minded now. He had issued his final warning. If von Hausen chose to ignore it—that was too bad for them. Smoke intended to empty every saddle he saw that he knew an outlaw sat in. Or a nutty European sportsman—so called.

It was almost a shame to do it, Smoke thought. None of those following him seemed to have any imagination; they just stayed on his trail and pushed blindly ahead. Smoke picked his ambush spots several days apart, having observed through binoculars that those behind him would be cautious for a day or so when approaching a likely spot but would become careless on the third or fourth day out.

They just never seemed to learn.

Like now, he thought, as he heard the sounds of riders approaching from the west. He eared back the hammer on his .44-.40, thinking: von Hausen and party damn sure made good time this trip. He wasn't expecting them until late that afternoon or the next day.

He gently let the hammer down when he saw that this bunch was not von Hausen's hunters. It was the Army. Smoke lay behind the log, in the brush, and listened to the men gripe.

"Top Soldier," a slick-sleeve private said to a sergeant major. "What are we gonna do with this von Hausen when we find him?"

"Order him from the park, MacBride."

"And Jensen?"

"He ain't done nothin'. Now, when we spot Jensen, just stand easy, men. Don't make any sudden moves. Don't do nothin' to rile him."

Smoke stood up. "Afternoon, troops," he called.

The Army patrol stopped in the creek. The top soldier forded on across and waved his men on. He reined up and dismounted. "Loosen 'em up and let 'em blow, men." He turned to face Smoke. "Would you be Smoke Jensen?"

"I am."

"I'm Sergeant Major Murphy. I got orders to say this, as silly as it sounds. Are you aware of a large group of men, and some ladies, following you with hostile intent?"

"I am quite aware of them, Top Soldier. I've emptied about ten or so saddles over the past month or so. I was waiting for them here."

"So I see. Well, the hunt is over, Mister Jensen. You are now under the protection of the United States Army."

"It's going to be interesting to hear what von Hausen has to say about that, Top."

"They will be escorted from the park and ordered to leave the country, Mister Jensen. Those American citizens with them will be placed under arrest—if you press charges."

"They'll just lie for one another and nothing will be accomplished by my doing that, Top. And you know it."

"That is probably very true, Mister Jensen. But I was under orders to inform you of that."

"I have so been informed. You men got here awful quick."

"We were here. We're an advance party checking out likely places to build the park headquarters."

"I killed a deer this morning, Top. It's strung up over there. Why don't you boys cut you a steak and we'll have an early supper."

"Music to my ears, Mister Jensen. Mighty pretty music."

"Just Smoke, Top Soldier. Just Smoke."

While the steaks were sizzling, being cooked in what skillets the six man patrol had and the rest on sticks held over a fire, MacBride asked, "How long has this crazy damn game been going on, Smoke?"

"Too long. As close as I can figure it—you know how you lose time out there—about two months."

"Two months!" a young soldier said. "How come you let it go on so long, Mister Jensen? I mean, with your reputation and all, why didn't you? . . ." He shut his mouth after a dirty look from Murphy.

"I didn't want to start the killing, and I didn't want it to go on. But they just kept pressing me, harder and harder. I finally knew that I had no choice in the matter. So I did what I felt I had to do."

"Nobody at all is blamin' you, Smoke," Top Soldier said. "Them people you run into all talked real nice about you. And you also got some powerful friends in government that jumped on this situation like a monkey to a banana."

Smoke nodded his head. He just didn't feel good with the situation. The six-man patrol could easily be shot to pieces by von Hausen and his men. Murphy was a grizzled old veteran of countless Indian wars—and probably the Civil War. But the rest were just kids. Murphy put his worries into words.

"You think they'd dare fire on the U.S. Army, Smoke?" the Top Soldier asked.

"Without hesitation, Top. Von Hausen has promised these

men all sorts of big money. They're not going to let it go without a fight."

Murphy lowered his voice. "Johnny over there, the single-striper, he's in his second hitch. He's a good one with more than enough battle experience. The rest . . ." He shrugged his shoulders. "They ain't been tested under fire."

"Yet," Smoke added.

"Somehow I knew you were gonna say that," Murphy said mournfully.

Montana Jess was riding point with the tracker, Roy Drum, when they reined up about two hundred yards from the fast-moving creek. They'd both been smelling wood smoke for about a mile, and were moving very cautiously. They dismounted and slipped through the timber to the west bank of the creek.

Montana Jess cussed under his breath. "Cavalry. And yonder's Smoke's horses. See 'em?"

"Yeah," Drum whispered. "I think we got us a problem, Montana. Let's get back to von Hausen."

"It might be a problem," the Baron admitted. The hunting party had stopped about two miles from the creek. "Does the U.S. Army have arrest powers?"

"They might in here," John T. said. "This bein' a national park and all."

"How big a patrol is it?" Leo Grant asked. His left arm was healing and he had limited use of it; he no longer had to use the sling.

"Six," Drum replied.

"What are you thinking, Leo?" von Hausen asked.

The gunfighter shrugged his shoulders. "Take 'em out," he said simply. "It sure wouldn't be no big deal. Injun up and blow 'em straight to hell."

"Now just wait a damned minute here!" Walt protested. "I ain't havin' no part of killin' government troops."

"Nor me," Angel said. "You boys better think about what you're about to do."

"Aw, shut your traps," Paul Melham said. "Who gives a damn about a bunch of soldier boys? I say we go for the money."

"I'm with you," Lou Kennedy said. "I ain't about to turn my back on more money than I could make in five years hasslin' homesteaders and the like."

"I'll stay," Gil Webb said. "I got warrants on me in half a dozen states and territories. I ain't about to ride in no army camp and let them arrest me."

The rest of the bounty hunters and gunslingers quickly fell in line. That left Walt and Angel looking down the muzzles of a dozen guns.

"You shoot us," Walt said, thinking very quickly, "you got no surprise left, 'cause them shots will carry to the soldier boys . . . and Jensen."

"Tie them up and leave them here," von Hausen ordered. "We'll dispose of them once we've killed the soldiers and hanged Jensen."

"Yeah. I like that idea. Hang 'im slow," Utah Red said. "I wanna see him die real slow and hard. We'll put his feet in the fire first. Make him scream."

"They'll be none of that!" von Hausen said sharply. "We'll hang him properly after we try him for the murders of those men we buried along the trail."

Walt shook his head in disgust.

"Now, I like that!" Tony Addison said. "Real legal-like. I wish somebody had brought some pitcher-takin' machinery. I'd like to have me a pitcher of Smoke Jensen swingin'."

Marlene smiled. "Oh, but we do have photographic equipment. The newest and very best. And it's packed very carefully."

The women had long miles back discarded their riding costumes and sidesaddles. They were all dressed in riding breeches and rode astride, and all of them carried side arms.

"Tie them up," von Hausen said, pointing to Walt and Angel. "Leave them here and picket the horses. We'll move out on foot as soon as this camp is secured. Take your spurs off and anything else that might make a noise."

Walt and Angel were trussed up and dumped on the ground. Cat Brown stood over Walt and grinned at the old gunfighter. "I'm gonna personal kill you, Webster. I been tired of your mouth for weeks. I'm gonna gut-shoot you and listen to you squall."

"That's about your speed, punk," Walt told him, defiance in his eyes.

Cat kicked the man in the belly and laughed at him.

"Move out," von Hausen ordered. "When we reach the creek, I'll go up to the bank alone and give the patrol a shout. When they stand up, open fire. Knock a leg out from under Jensen. We want him alive. Remember that. *Alive!*"

The hunting party was just out of sight when Angel said, "I am blessed with teeth that are ver' strong, Walt. If my brain was as strong as my teeth I would not be in this situation, I am thinking. Let me scoot around and I will go to work on your bonds."

"I'm glad one of us still has his choppers," Walt said. "I lost most of mine years back."

Smoke had led his horses to new graze, about two hundred and fifty yards from the camp, he picketed them behind a huge tangle of brush and thorns; it wasn't done deliberately, that was where the best graze was. He was walking back to the camp when he heard the shout. He recognized the voice and knew instantly that something was very wrong. Von Hausen wouldn't just walk up to an Army camp knowing by now that the word had spread about what he was doing.

Smoke ran toward the camp to warn the men when the first volley of shots thundered in the mid-morning air. A stray bullet whanged off a rock and slammed into his leg, knocking him sprawling. He grabbed his leg at the wound to keep any blood from leaking to the ground and crawled into a thicket. Inside the tangle, he turned and with a leafy branch on the ground brushed out any sign of his entry and re-arranged the brush at the opening. It might work, he thought. They would see his horses gone and just might assume that he'd never been in the camp, or had already departed.

If they didn't search too diligently, if they were anxious to get gone after the killing ambush of Army troops, if his horses didn't whinny and give away their position . . .

A lot of ifs.

"Finish him," von Hausen said, pointing to the top soldier, who was gut-shot and glaring at him through bright, pain-filled eyes.

Marlene coldly, and with a strange expression of excitement on her face, shot the sergeant major in the head.

"Help me," a young soldier pleaded.

"Why, certainly," von Hausen said. He lifted his pistol and shot him between the eyes.

"Damnit!" Roy Drum said. "Jensen's gone. Both of his horses is gone. He must have pulled out just after we seen them this morning."

"That's right," Montana Jess said. "Jensen's hoss was saddled. I 'member now."

"We'll pick up his trail," von Hausen said. "He can't have gone far. It's been no more than two hours. Scatter the supplies. The Army lives on hardtack. Leave it. I have no taste for that horrible ration."

"What about the bodies?" John T. asked.

"Leave them where they lie. The bears will have them eaten by this time tomorrow."

"Their horses?"

"Leave them. We don't want to be seen riding a horse wearing an Army brand. Let's get back to camp and get on Jensen's trail. Quickly, men. Move!"

When the last man had splashed across the creek, Smoke rolled out of his hiding place and limped to the death camp.

He quickly checked the bodies. They were all dead. Cussing under his breath, he tied a bandana around the wound on his leg and then grabbed as much of the scattered equipment as he dared take the time to do so. Then, gritting his teeth against the pain, he limped as quickly as he could to his horses. Ten minutes later he was in the saddle and gone, staying off the trail and weaving through the timber, heading for the high country. He would heat a knife point and dig the lead out later. Right now, he had to put some distance between himself and the death camp.

"Goddamnit!" von Hausen yelled, looking at the ropes on the ground. "They've escaped. I thought you said the men were tied securely?"

"They was!" John T. said. "I checked 'em personal. They was trussed up like pigs."

"Angel Cortez has teeth like a beaver," Valdes said. "He used to win bets in bars by bending coins between his teeth. But they cannot have gone far."

"John T.," von Hausen said. "Assign men to track down and kill Walt and Angel. Get in the saddle, men. We've got to get on Jensen's trail."

Marlene smiled. She had seen through von Hausen's plan. The men could not back off now. They had to kill Jensen if it meant dying to the last person. They would all—to a man— hang if caught for the killing of the troops. She trembled with excitement. There was no thrill on earth like that of killing a man. Nothing compared to it. Nothing.

She wondered how it would feel to slip the noose around Smoke Jensen's neck.

16

Smoke rode hard for several miles, then stopped to let his horses blow. He quickly built a small fire, ripped his jeans around the bullet wound, and took a look at it. The slug had lost some of its power when it struck the leg, but still had enough punch to tear a hole. He felt all around the wound and could feel the slug buried just beneath the skin. He took the hot sterilized blade and slipped the point under the skin, digging around and popping the slug out, his face dripping with sweat from the cauterization of the wound. That would have to do it. If the wound felt infected by morning, he'd cut it open, pour gunpowder in, and burn out the infection. He'd done it before, so he wasn't looking forward to a repeat performance. It wasn't pleasant, but it worked.

He swung back into the saddle and headed out. He was going to the temporary headquarters of the park superintendent. Von Hausen and his people could not afford to let anyone live. For their plans to succeed, anyone who knew they were in the park had to die. And Smoke was sure that by now, the surveyors, the scientists, and the superintendent and his staff knew about von Hausen. They had to be warned.

Smoke pointed his horse's nose toward the temporary headquarters of the superintendent. He had a hell of a ride ahead of him.

"You know where the home of the man who runs this place is located?" Angel asked.

"North. Up near the Montana line. And von Hausen knows it, too."

"I heard them talking, too, my friend."

The men had stopped to rest their horses and to make plans. "We for sure got men comin' after us, Angel," Walt said. "He can't afford to have us get free and bump our gums."

"We'll ride on until we find just the right spot," Angel said. "Then we will take some of the pressure off of Mister Smoke Jensen, si, amigo?"

Walt grinned. "Right, my friend."

The men swung into their saddles and headed north.

"We got to be careful with Ol' Walt and Angel," Mack Saxton said, when they had stopped to rest their horses. "That old man's a pistolero from way back."

"He ain't nothin'," Lou Kennedy said. "I used to think he was, 'til he started takin' Jensen's side in this. He's just a wore out old man is all he is."

"An old rattler'll kill you just as quick as a young one," Mack said. "And Angel ain't no one to fool with neither."

"He's just a damn greaser is all," Nat Reed said. "Full of beans and hot air. I'll take him."

Mack walked away to relieve himself in the bushes, thinking: Get us all killed is what you'll do. Angel Cortez is a bad man to fool with.

* * *

Smoke pushed his horses hard. He had the entire Washburn Plateau to travel before he reached the superintendent's quarters. And he knew he also had to deal with those behind him at some point along the way. He had to take some of the pressure off.

Smoke made a cold camp that night, not wanting to risk a fire, and was stiff and sore when he rolled out of his blankets the next morning. It was dark as a bat's cave so he couldn't look at his leg. He'd do that later; but when he touched the area around the wound, the leg was not hot with infection. He saddled up and headed north.

"He ain't makin' no effort to hide his tracks," Roy Drum said. "And he's headin' straight north."

"To the park headquarters," John T. said. "If he reaches there . . ." He let that trail off.

"It won't make any difference," von Hausen said. "We can leave no one behind. No one. Man, woman, or child who knows we were in the park." He looked at the men. "It has to be that way. We'll all hang if word gets out about the soldiers. Do it my way, and you'll all be rich men. I promise you that." He looked up at the leaden sky. "What is wrong with this wretched place? It's supposed to be summer, but the temperature seems to be falling and those clouds look like *snow* clouds."

"They probably are," Drum told him. "This is Yellowstone, Baron. Hell, it's liable to snow in July."

"But the vegetation is out and blooming," Hans said.

"It ain't gonna freeze hard enough to kill this stuff," Drum told him. "It's liable to be seventy-five degrees tomorrow. Let's go find Jensen today and finish this." He stepped into the saddle.

The temperature continued to drop during the day. Winter was not yet ready to completely lift its hand from the Yellowstone. It began to spit snow and the women began to complain (the men would have started it first but that was not the manly thing to do).

Von Hausen decided to stop for the night, although it was only mid-afternoon.

Smoke kept going, not pushing his horses as hard as the days behind him, but at a steady, mile-eating pace. He smelled the woodsmoke before he could see it through the snowfall. He dismounted and slipped through the foliage, strange now in green and white. He pulled up short with a smile on his lips. Then he went back to get his horses.

"Hello, the camp," he called.

"Mister Jensen!" Charles Knudson called. "My word, didn't the Army find you?"

"No. I found them." He dismounted and stripped his horses of their burden and rubbed them down before he thought to see to himself. Warming his hands by the fire, he explained what had happened.

"All . . . dead?" Gilbert the scientist asked. "The patrol has been murdered?"

"Yes." Smoke poured a cup of coffee and drank it down. It was the first he'd had in several days. It was still too damn weak. "Where is the superintendent?"

"Gone to Washington for a few weeks. My God!" Harold said, noticing the bloody bandana tied around Smoke's leg. "You've hurt yourself."

"They shot me. It's all right. I dug the bullet out and cauterized the wound. I just keep the bandana on to hold the bandage in place."

Paula stood up. "Please go over to the lean-to and sit down, Mister Jensen. Among other things, I am a trained nurse. Gilbert, get the first aid kit. And take off your pants, Mister Jensen."

Smoke stopped at that. "I got some extra jeans, ma'am. I'll just open the tear in this and let you . . ."

"Take off your damn pants!" she yelled.

"Yes, ma'am," Smoke said, and shucked out of his moccasins and jeans behind the blanket someone had rigged for privacy.

"I can see no sign of infection," Paula said, after applying some sort of medicine on the healing wound and rebandaging it. "But that knife must have been awfully hot. There are burn scars all around the entry point."

"Very hot, ma'am. But it still beat fillin' it up with gunpowder and burning out the infection."

She sighed. "I wish people would stop that practice. Gunpowder is not the most sanitary substance around."

"But it works," Smoke said.

Smoke gathered the group around him in the rapidly diminishing snowfall. It had dusted the land but would be gone shortly after sunup. "We've got problems, people. Big problems. Alone, I could shake those behind me and get out and tell the law about what happened to the Army patrol. But if I do that, you people will die. Von Hausen and his scummy bunch have to kill anybody that knows they were in the park. And that's all of you . . ."

"But the superintendent knows," Perry said.

"His word against twenty-five. Actually," Smoke continued, "von Hausen is playing a fool's game. I'm the only one who any defense lawyer would probably allow on the stand. You people have never seen him in here. But von Hausen and those with him are scared; they're not thinking rationally. So that means you're all in danger. Now I don't know whether von Hausen is still coming at me through this snow, or not. I'd guess not. But they will be at first light. Bet on it. And they're only about six or seven hours behind. We've got to come up with a plan for staying alive. And we don't have much time to do it."

"Run for it?" Charles suggested.

"We're not fighters, Mister Jensen," Gilbert said. "None of us here have ever fired a shot in anger at anything. None of us have combat experience. But if you say we stand and fight, we will."

Smoke thought about that for a moment, then shook his head. "No. You people have to get out. I've got to buy you some time to get clear and get to the Army. Are there any troops still in the park?"

"About half a dozen up at White Mountain. They're Army engineers. I don't even know whether they have guns."

"They're armed," Smoke said. "There are still hostiles in the area. I want you people up and ready to go at first light. Head for White Mountain. Connect with the Army, and get the hell gone for the nearest town that has wires. Get a telegram off to Washington and let them know what's happened in here and what is happening."

"Where will you make your stand?" Morris asked.

"Up the trail somewhere. I'll know it when I see it."

"More coffee, Mister Jensen?" Thomas asked.

"Only if I can make a fresh pot."

"I'll have tea," Gilbert said quickly.

"Their horses is gettin' tired," Mack said, looking down at the tracks left by Walt and Angel. "And them tracks is fresh. We're closin' in, boys."

"I want Ol' Walt," Lou said. "I want that old bastard lookin' at me when I drop him."

"This ain't gonna be no stand up and draw thing, Lou," Mack told him. "Our orders is to kill them both the best and quickest way we can."

"Hell with orders. I want to see what kind of stuff that old coot has."

"You do that," Mack said, "and he just might be the one standin' over you when it's done."

Lou sneered and cussed as he swung back into the saddle. "No way, Mack. No way. We got about an hour of daylight left. Let's go."

"Come up lame," Walt said, stripping the saddle and bridle from his horse and patting it on the rump. "I felt it when he hurt hisself back yonder on them rocks. Built a fire, Angel, let's have us some coffee and bacon. I 'spect them that's doggin' us will be along right shortly. I'll have me another horse right after dark."

Angel grinned and began gathering up firewood while Walt rigged a shelter-half for them in the timber. Walt had strapped on his guns and tied them down. He spun the cylinders, checking the loads.

Angel was thinking: I'd not want to mess with that old man. He knew Walt had given up gunfighting simply because he was tired of the killing, tired of the blood, tired of having to prove himself against every two-bit punk that came along. But he was still snake-quick and a dead shot. And now he was ready to go again. Walt Webster was a living legend. Not in Smoke's class, but close. Real close.

The two men drank their coffee and ate the bacon, then moved back into the timber, after building the fire up. It could not be missed by anyone coming up in the fading light.

"Lou Kennedy was always bragging about how he could take you any day, Walt," Angel said.

"He's a loudmouthed tinhorn," the old gunfighter said. "All bluster and no brains."

"What will you do if he calls you out?"

"Walk out and shoot him dead."

"I will have a rifle on the others should that be the way it happens."

"Obliged. Here they come."

"It's a trap," Mack said, spotting the fire. "One of the horses come up lame back yonder and they're sitting up there waitin' on us to ride in."

Before anyone could stop him, Lou Kennedy yelled, "Walt Webster! This is Lou Kennedy. Can you hear me, Walt?"

"I hear you, you big-mouth," Walt called. "You probably

scared all the little critters within half a mile flappin' your gums. What the hell do you want?"

"You and me, Walt. How about it?"

"With that scum with you backin' you up, Lou?"

"No. Just me and you, Walt."

"Damnit, Lou!" Mack said. "Back off now, you hear?"

"No way, Mack." Lou shook off the other man's hand. "I want him. If I gun Walt Webster down, I can write my own ticket, you know that."

"Then go on!" Mack said, anger and disgust in his voice. "Walt. Walt Webster. This is Mack. You can have him, Walt. I give you my word, we won't interfere. You got my word on it."

"How about the others with you?" Walt called, hoping they'd fall for the question.

They did. "Walt, this is Leo Grant. We're out of it, Walt. Me and Nat'll stand clear. And that's as good as gold, Walt. If you drop him, you can get on back to cover."

"Four of them," Angel said. "And the light's fading, amigo."

"Let it go." He raised his voice. "Let's get this done, Lou. We walk out on a five count. You count it down, Nat. Draw whenever you feel lucky, boy."

Leo looked at Lou with disgust in his eyes. "You're a fool," he said flatly. "Did you ever stop to think that old man just might get lucky and blow a hole in you?"

"He ain't even gonna clear leather. Start countin', Nat."

On five both men stepped out of the timber. Walt stayed close to the timber, forcing Lou to come to him. "How's it feel, Lou?" Walt called.

"How's what feel, you old fart?"

"Knowin' you're about to die."

Lou cussed him as he walked up the slope. Walt stood, a smile on his lips. Lou was a fool, playing right into Walt's plan. The slope was slippery, and by the time Lou got within shooting range, he'd be winded. Add to that he would have to shoot uphill—that is, should he be lucky enough to clear leather—and Walt didn't believe he had it in him to do that.

"Come on, you punk tinhorn," Walt called. "My coffee's gettin' cold."

Lou called him several very ugly names as he struggled to get up the slope.

"He's dead," Mack said. "Dead and he don't even know it. He'll be wore out time he gets into range. Ol' Walt planned it that way."

"Sure, he did," Lco said. "But I gave my word and I'm keepin' it."

"We all did," Nat said. "And we'll all keep it."

Lou stopped about sixty feet from Walt. The climb up the snow-slick slope had been hard and the much younger gunslick was winded. "You got any relatives you want me to notify, you old fart?"

Walt laughed. "When did you learn to write, you ignorant whelp?"

"Draw!" Lou yelled.

"After you, boy." Walt's words were calm.

"Drag iron, damn you!"

"Go ahead."

Lou hesitated. "You're yeller, Walt. You're scared of me, ain't you?"

"Not at all, you two-bit thief. Your momma shoulda dumped you in a sack when you was born and chucked you into the nearest river. Now pull iron, you cheap little son of a bitch!"

Lou's hand dropped to the butt of his .45. Walt's draw was smooth and deadly. His first slug hit Lou in the belly, the second one in the chest, right side, blowing through a lung. Lou managed to get his .45 out of leather and cock it. He fired once into the air before his legs buckled and he slumped to the ground.

Walt stepped back into the timber. "You want to come get him, boys, come on. We'll not fire on you."

" 'Preciate it, Walt," Nat said.

But they didn't have to climb the slope. Lou started slowly sliding down the slippery surface, losing his guns along the way. He was too weak to stop his slide. His hands did not have the strength to grasp anything. He rolled the rest of the way down. Leo reached out and pulled him into the copse of trees where they were hiding.

"Oh, Jesus," he blubbered the words, pink froth staining his lips. "I'm hard hit. Did I get him, boys?"

"Yeah," Nat lied. "Yeah, you got him, Lou."

"You boys pass the word," Lou said. "I kilt Walt Webster. You'll do that for me, won't you?"

"Yeah," Mack said, suddenly realizing that none of them were going to kill Ol' Walt. None of them were going to come out of this rich. None of them were going to come out of it with anything at all. Except dead. He looked down into the wide open and shuddered, seeing nothing but the eyes of Lou Kennedy.

17

Smoke raised his head and narrowed his eyes at the sound of the shots. "Close," he muttered, setting down his coffee cup. "No more than a mile. Probably less than that. Sound doesn't carry well in this kind of weather. Two shots."

"Does that mean something to you?" Gilbert asked.

"Sounded like pistol shots. Pistol's a poor choice of weapon to use in an ambush." He shook his head and stood up. "I don't know what it means." He picked up his rifle and checked it. "I'm heading over there to check it out. You people stay put and keep your heads down. Arm yourselves and be ready to use those weapons. And cut that fire back to coals to keep the smoke down." He was gone before any could say a word of protest.

Leo, Mack and Nat opened up on Walt and Angel, knowing that from their position, they weren't going to hit a thing. The body of Lou Kennedy lay on the cold ground behind them.

Smoke slipped through the timber, silently working his way toward the firing.

Walt and Angel lay on their bellies at the forest's edge,

not returning the fire; from their angle they would have about as much success hitting anything as those below them.

"We have, I think," Angel said, a twinkle in his eyes, "a Norte Americano standoff, hey, Walt?"

Walt smiled at the play-off of the expression. "You called it, partner."

Smoke slipped to within a few yards of the men. It was almost full dark now and he could not make out their features. He knelt down behind a tree and listened to them talk when the gunfire from below stopped.

"That loco German is going to kill everybody he thinks might know of his plan," Angel said. "Right, Walt?"

"That's right, partner," Walt replied. "That's the way I see it."

"But Al Hayre surely is out of the park and talking. So what is von Hausen's reasoning behind this madness?"

"He ain't reasonin', Angel. He's crazy. And so's them fools with him."

"I wonder if Jensen has put all this together?" Angel spoke softly.

"I 'magine he has. I just hope he can get clear and get any visitors out of this park. We've seen smoke from campfires from time to time. If von Hausen and that trash with him finds any campers . . ." He trailed that off.

"They will kill them."

"Yep. They shore will. Craziest mess I ever got myself mixed up in."

"Stand easy, boys," Smoke called softly. "I mean you no harm."

Walt grunted. Without turning his head, he said, "Jensen?"

"Yes."

"You're as good as the talk makes you out to be. Ain't nobody ever snuck up on me 'fore now. They's three pretty bad ol' boys down yonder . . ."

A burst of gunfire made him pause for a moment.

"Fools," Walt said when the firing had stopped. "They

can't hit us from their position. Leo Grant, Mack Saxton, and Nat Reed. Lou Kennedy was with them. I dropped him. You got to get clear, Jensen. You got to warn any in this park to get the hell gone."

"I know," Smoke told him. "I've got a bunch of park-people about a half mile from here right now. Are you Walt Webster?"

"Alive and still kickin'."

"Angel Cortez," the Mexican gunfighter said.

"You're the two who wore the white handkerchiefs on your arms."

"That's us."

"Stay where you are. Don't get out of position and don't fire in the outlaws' direction. You might hit me. I'm going down there."

"Well, if anybody can Injun up on them, you're the one to do it." He twisted around. "I . . ."

But he was talking to emptiness. Smoke was already gone, moving like a deadly ghost through the timber.

Angel had also turned around. He shook his head in the cold darkness. "That is a bad man, amigo. I thank God that I had enough sense to see through von Hausen's crazy game."

"You and me both, partner.'"

"Walt!" Mack called from below them. "Give it up, Walt. Join us and live. Von Hausen will take you back. You and Angel think about it. If you get out and talk, you're signin' our death warrants. Come on, men, what'd you say?"

"Let's keep them talking," Angel suggested. "That'll give away their positions to Smoke."

"No deal, Mack," Walt called. "You boys surrender to us and we'll see that you get a fair trial. You have my word on it."

"Surrender? Us?" Nat yelled. "You're crazy!"

Nat had moved to his right. He was trying to work his way up the other side of the slope. The timber side. Toward Smoke.

"Angel," Mack yelled. "Listen to me. You got good sense for a greaser . . ."

"What a compliment," Angel muttered.

". . . You don't wanna die no more than we do. Think about it and join us."

Nat ran into a long bladed knife that drove up to the hilt in his belly. Smoke jerked the blade upward with one hand while his other hand was covering Nat's mouth, to prevent any screaming. The blade tore into the gunslinger's heart and Nat Reed would hire out his gun no more. Smoke silently lowered the body to the cold earth, wiped his blade clean on Nat's jacket, and moved on toward the voices.

"We're just gonna outwait you, boys," Mack called. "We got food and blankets and coffee and time. You boys ain't got nothin'. You can't slip away. You got a lame horse. Think about it. Don't be fools and die for Smoke Jensen. He ain't never done a damn thing for either of you."

"What has von Hausen done for us?" Angel yelled. "What the hell have any of *you* done for us?"

"They ain't gonna give it up," Leo said. "We're gonna have to take 'em. Nat oughtta be in position about now. What'd you say, Mack?"

"He said he'd chunk a rock over this way when he got in place. I ain't heard no rocks, have you?"

"Naw."

"Will .44's do?" Smoke asked from behind the men.

They spun around, lifting their rifles. Smoke's twin .44's belched flame in the darkness. Mack was thrown backward, the slug tearing into his heart. Leo took his high in the chest, left side, and managed to lift his rifle. Smoke fired again, the slug lifting Leo off his boots and turning him around in a strange dance. He toppled over.

"That's it," Smoke called. He collected the rifles and gunbelts of the men and joined Walt and Angel on the crest of the small hill.

"I'll switch saddles and ride one of their horses," Walt

said. He took off his hat and ran his fingers through silver hair. "Mack had a decent streak in him at one time. I've knowed him for years. I don't know when he turned vicious."

"He can explain it to God," Smoke said.

"The ones that are left, Senor Jensen," Angel said. "They are vicious. All of them. Through and through. You heard us talking about von Hausen's plans?"

"Yes. We'll stop him. Bring the other horses along. We might need them. We're camped just over that ridge. Come on. I'll help you pack up."

When they got back to the camp Smoke checked over the short guns and the rifles taken from the outlaws. They were well supplied with ammo and Smoke divided that up and passed it around, then assigned the guns. Now everyone was armed, and well armed, for the four men who lay unburied on the cold ground a half mile away had each carried two six-guns tied down and each one had a rifle.

"What do we do now?" Carol asked, looking around her at the dark timber.

"Have something to eat and get some rest," Smoke said. "From here on in, it gets interesting."

The next day was clear and warm, the temperature climbing into the sixties before mid-morning. Roy Drum pointed to the carrion birds circling just ahead and to the west of the trail they were on. Von Hausen sent a man to check it out. He was back quickly.

"You best see this," he said, "all of you." He did not add: except for the women. The outlaw was well aware of how vicious these so-called ladies were. Especially that damned cold-actin' Marlene.

The flesh-eating birds had started their feasting and the men had to kick them away from the bodies. It was a gory sight.

"Took their guns and horses," John T. said. "I don't believe Walt and Angel done this."

"Found where a whole bunch of people camped last night," Cat Brown said, riding up. "And Smoke and Walt and Angel was among 'em.

"How many people?" Von Hausen asked.

"I'd say 'tween twelve and fifteen, countin' Smoke and Walt and Angel."

Gunter cussed and Hans looked worried. He wasn't liking any of this. It had turned too bloody, too savage. They had lost sight of the spirit of the hunt. It was out of control. It never occurred to him that it was out of control the instant they chose Smoke Jensen as the man they were to hunt.

"They're pilgrims," Cat said. "And they got some women with 'em.

"Interesting," von Hausen said.

"Frederick," Hans said. "I think . . ."

Von Hausen spat out rapid-fire German. Hans shut his mouth. Andrea came to him and took his arm. They walked away together

"This has got to stop, Andrea," Hans said, when they were out of earshot of von Hausen. "It's gone much too far."

"It can't stop, Hans. We have no choice but to hunt those people down and be rid of them."

"My God, Andrea! Listen to you. You sound like some bloodthirsty crazed person. How many deaths do you want? How much blood on our hands?"

"Have you lost your stomach for the hunt, Hans?" Her words were cold and borderline contemptuous.

"This isn't a hunt. What this is . . . I don't know what it is. But I do know that it is out of control."

"Hans," she said, touching his arm. "Listen to me. This is the American West. Not New York City. Despite our having diplomatic papers, do you think the western men out here—who tamed this country—would let us leave without punishment? Think about that. This is the Wild West, Hans. And it's still wild. Justice comes down very hard and fast out here. We wouldn't get ten miles before some vigilante group would have us hanged. And they do hang women out here, Hans."

Hans clenched his hands into fists. He took several deep breaths. "All right, Andrea. All right. You do make a presentable case. Let's just get this over with and get out of this dreadful place."

Hans went back to his horse and rode up to the trail to be alone. The sight of those disgusting birds tearing at dead human flesh was nauseating. He lifted his hands. They were trembling.

Von Hausen came to Andrea's side.

"He'll stay," she told him. "But this better end quickly, Frederick."

"He's that close to breaking?"

"He's very close, Frederick."

"I know you two care deeply for each other, Andrea— since childhood—but I will not let one man put all of us in prison. Do you understand that?"

"Perfectly. And I feel the same way about it."

"Good. We are of like mind."

Mountains loomed in front of them, miles away through rugged terrain. Smoke halted the parade north at a spring. While the surveyors and scientists were watering their horses and taking this time to rest from the saddle, Smoke waved Walt and Angel to him.

"We're not going to make it like this, boys. These folks are just not able to push it any harder. Von Hausen's party has got to be slowed up some. Walt, you and Angel stay with these folks . . ."

Walt opened his mouth to protest and Smoke waved him silent. "If von Hausen caught up with them, they wouldn't stand a chance. None of them have ever been in a gunfight. Probably a full third of them couldn't take a human life.

That's not a short-coming on their part; they just weren't raised out here and really don't understand the pickle they're in or the men they're up against. With you two along, they stand a chance."

"And you, Smoke?" Angel asked.

"I'm going to buy you people some time."

"Where?" Walt asked.

"West of here at the creek. Walt, get these people out of this country and over to the trail. It'll take you a few hours, but you'll more than make up for it once there."

The old gunfighter nodded his agreement. "Yeah, I been thinkin' on that myself."

"Rest them up and get gone. When you get to the headquarters, get with that small garrison of troops left and either make a stand or get the hell out of the park. That's up to you folks. But get word out."

The men shook hands. "Luck to you, boy," Walt told Smoke. "You damn shore got a passel of bad 'uns comin' up quick."

"Vaya con dios," Angel said, then walked to his horse.

Smoke stood as the men and women saddled up. Gilbert looked down at Smoke, standing in dirty, blood-splattered clothing, unshaven, and in need of a haircut. He was an awesome-looking figure of a man. "You are a very brave man, Smoke Jensen, and I speak for this entire group."

"Yes," Blanche said. "I know the President personally, Smoke. I shall see that you get a medal for this."

"That's good," Smoke told her. "But for now, just get any civilians out of this park. If you don't, there's going to be a blood-bath. I'm only buying you people a few hours; so don't waste any of it. Get out of here."

Charles Knudson saluted him and lifted the reins. The others did the same. Two minutes later, Smoke was alone. That was the way he liked it. Alone with and a part of the High Lonesome.

He knew he didn't stand a prayer of stopping the whole

group. Close as he could figure it, there was still about twenty or so coming up hard behind him. Maybe none of those he'd sent on before him would make it. But he had to try.

"Von Hausen," he muttered to the gentle breeze blowing over the land. "I've hated mighty few things in my life. But I definitely hate you."

He looked at the sky. Clear and blue and cloudless. High above him, an eagle soared on the winds, gliding gracefully toward the north. He remembered years back, after his first wife, Nicole, and their baby son had been murdered. He'd started to Idaho, to avenge them, and he'd seen an eagle, seeming to guide him. He smiled. Eagles lived a long time; might be the same one. He liked to think so.

He gathered up his reins, then paused, wondering what month it was. Summer, for sure, and Smoke was almighty weary of this hunt. With a sigh, he swung into the saddle and made his way after those who'd gone ahead of him, mixing his tracks in with theirs. Once, resting in the saddle on the crest of a hill, he could make out mounted figures, far below and behind him. They were closing in fast.

He knew he would never make the creek. Von Hausen and group were too close. He pushed on, his eyes constantly searching for a good ambush spot. He finally said to hell with it and swung down in a copse of trees on a rise that faced a meadow. The back of the hill touched a flat that offered him an escape route. He couldn't stay here any length of time, for he couldn't watch three sides for very long. But he might be able to empty a saddle or two and buy Walt and his bunch an hour or so.

He had handed the lead rope of his packhorse to Angel, so Smoke was traveling light. He picketed his horse and patted him on the rump.

"Stand easy, old boy. Relax. I'll be back soon. Right now, I got some work to do."

He got into position and checked his rifle. Full up. He levered a round into the .44-.40 just as the point man for von

Hausen's group entered the broad meadow, all bursting with new life under the warm sun.

Smoke had every intention of leaving some old life on the meadow. Forever.

The point man stopped and Smoke sighted him in through long lenses. He was still a good mile off. The scout raised his arm, and turned his head to another rider, his finger pointed toward the hill and the timber. Von Hausen rode up and joined the two outriders. He uncased his binoculars.

Smoke lowered his field glasses and hunkered down. "Come on, you crazy son of a bitch," Smoke muttered. "Be a big brave man and ride up with your scouts. If I can knock you out of the saddle, I'll have half the battle won."

When Smoke again lifted his binoculars, von Hausen's group was swinging down from their saddles to take a rest and to water their horses at the narrow little creek.

"Good enough," he said. "Take them north, Walt. Get them clear." Smoke took a sip of water from his canteen and chewed on a biscuit. He waited.

18

Someone among them smelled the ambush. Smoke knew it was going sour when the group split up into three's and four's and began skirting the meadow on two sides, staying well out of rifle range of the timber on the hill.

Smoke watched them for a moment, and then wormed his way back into the timber to his horse. "Not our day, fellow," he said, swinging into the saddle. "I'm not going to push you, boy. I know you're tired. So let's just lope for about a mile and see what we can come up with."

Von Hausen's group was right on his tail and the horse seemed to know it. If he was tired, he sure didn't act it when they hit the flats. That big Appaloosa stretched out and was flying like a young colt, his powerful legs eating up the distance.

Smoke grinned, even though the race was deadly. He loved to sit a saddle when the horse loved to run and was doing so. Enjoyed feeling the power of a horse that was doing what he loved to do. Smoke hung on as the 'paloosa scrambled up a ridge and leaped into the timber. Smoke cut left and weaved through the timber, smiling when he spotted the ravine that the north boundaries of the meadow ran into. Far in the distance, he could see riders entering the wide mouth of the ravine.

He heard a shout, but it was too faint for him to make out the words. If those coming up the ravine heard it, they did not seem to pay any attention to it.

Smoke grabbed his rifle and found adequate cover on the rim. He eased the hammer back and waited.

Paul Melham didn't like the looks of this ravine and told those behind him so, in blunt words. He ended with, "I'm tellin' y'all I heard a runnin' horse."

"Then how come none of the rest of us heard it, Paul?" Cat Brown challenged. "I'll tell you why: 'cause there wasn't no runnin' horse, that's why. If Jensen was in that timber back yonder, he wouldn't have come this way. That ambushin' bastard would have flanked us and picked us off. Relax, Paul. He's miles ahead of us."

"If you're so damn sure of that, then you come up here and take the point."

"Oh, hell, Paul!" Cat said. "If you're that skittish I might as well. You got fear sweat runnin' into your eyes. You wouldn't be able to see a grizzly if he reared up in front of you."

Smoke pulled the trigger and Paul was nearly knocked out of the saddle. He managed to hold on with his good right arm. His left arm dangled useless.

Smoke knew he'd shot off the mark. A fly had landed on the end of his nose just as he'd pulled the trigger. Probably shot the man-hunter in the shoulder by the way he acted.

But the ravine was void of man-hunters now, except for their horses, and Smoke wasn't about to shoot a horse. All in the group had left their saddles and found what protection they could in the rocks. Smoke smiled and started putting rounds close to the horses' hooves. That set the already panicked animals off and running. The last he saw of them they were running hot and hard out of the ravine.

Smoke ran back to his horse, swung into the saddle, and was gone.

Paul crawled back to Cat and Utah, pulling himself along with his good arm. He was cussing to beat sixty.

"Fall back!" Cat yelled. "Stay close to the sides and get back out of range. Somebody holler for von Hausen to get the medicine bag." He looked at Paul's shoulder. "You're lucky, Paul. Bullet punched right through. I don't think nothin's broken."

"When we catch up with that damn Jensen," Paul panted, his face shiny with pain. "I swear I'll skin him slow."

If any of us are left alive to catch up with him, Utah thought. That sudden thought startled him, for he'd never even considered quitting this bunch. He shook it out of his head. After killin' them soldiers, he couldn't quit. This was a race to the end—for all of them. Them who was runnin', and them who was chasin'.

"It's a painful wound, I'm sure," Gunter said, after cleaning out Paul's bullet-punctured shoulder. "But nothing appears to be broken and there is only the expected bleeding. Can you ride?"

"I can ride," Paul said grimly. "I want a shot at that damn Jensen."

No one among them, it seemed, could speak of Smoke in any other manner except 'that damn Jensen.'

"Let's find us a way around this ravine," von Hausen said. "He's probably still up there, waiting."

"He'll just move when we do," Hans pointed out. "He's got the high ground." That damn Jensen seemed to *always* have the high ground.

Von Hausen looked at Hans. The spirit seemed to have gone out of the man. He cut his eyes to Andrea. She was staring at Hans with a decidedly disgusted look in her eyes. "Round up the horses. We're riding until dusk."

Walt pushed his group as hard as he figured they could stand it. But by dusk, when he broke it off to make camp, he had a sinking sensation in the pit of his stomach that they were not going to make the park headquarters.

"They are worn out," Angel whispered to him, out of earshot of the others.

"I know. We're not going to make it, Angel."

"I could ride for the headquarters."

"And do what? Bring back six soldier boys who are engineers first and soldiers last. I ain't puttin' them down—they got a job to do like everybody else—but they ain't cavalry. We'll push on tomorrow and get as close to the park entrance as we can before we have to stand and fight."

"And then?"

"We'll just pick us the best spot we can find and show von Hausen and his boys and girls that we ain't gonna go down without one hell of a fight."

Gilbert walked up. "The ladies are exhausted, gentlemen," he said. He looked very tired. "And for that matter, so are the men in my party. The young surveyors seem to be holding up well."

"Yeah," Walt said. "We was just talkin' about that. The horses are tired, too. We'll push on at first light. When we find us a good spot to fort up—with water and graze and shelter—we'll make a stand of it."

"Might I make a suggestion?"

"Shore."

"We ride only a brief time tomorrow. There is a spot not too far from here that I know of—I've been in this park several times. It's almost a natural fort. We spend the rest of the day digging in. And I mean that literally."

Walt nodded his head. "That's fine with me, Gilbert. Angel?"

"Suits me. With us in front of them and Smoke coming up behind them, we could put them in a bad spot." "Yes," Gilbert said, obviously pleased that the two gunfighters approved of his plan. "That was my thinking."

"Let's have some coffee and get some rest," Walt said. "We'll see what the others have to say about this."

Walt and his group were about four miles north of Smoke. Smoke was camped only about five miles ahead of von Hausen's party. Neither had any way of knowing what the other was planning.

Smoke boiled his coffee in a small and beat-up coffeepot and chewed on jerky and hardtack for his supper. He was just about out of coffee. He'd have enough for in the morning, and then that was it. And when Smoke couldn't have his coffee, he turned short-tempered.

Smoke drank his coffee and then carefully cleaned and wiped down his guns in the dying light of the small fire. He tried not to think about Walt and his group and their desperate race for the park headquarters and the tiny garrison of army engineers stationed there. He tried not to think about Sergeant Major Murphy and his patrol, lying stiffened and ravaged by animals and carrion birds in the timber by the creek, shot down in the coldest of blood by von Hausen and those who followed him.

"You're scum, von Hausen," Smoke muttered. "Nothing but scum."

"I hate that damn Jensen," von Hausen said to Marlene. "The man has ruined a perfectly good hunt."

"He's a savage," Marlene said. "No class or breeding."

John T. was walking by the tent and heard that. He shook his head and walked on, wondering how in the hell he ever let himself get tied up with such a pack of fools. He walked over to the cook tent and poured a cup of coffee, carrying it over to his bedroll, close to the fire. He sat down, his back against his saddle, and looked at Montana Jess, sitting drinking coffee next to him. The man had a strange expression on his face.

"Time's runnin' out for us, John T.," Montana spoke the words softly.

"What do you mean?"

"I mean, them champagne-suckin', hoity-toity folks over yonder is takin' us to our deaths. That's what I mean. And you know it, John T."

"Spit it all out, Montana."

"We ain't got no choice left in the matter, John T. We can't come out of this unless'n we kill everybody in this park. Everybody."

"We've talked about that, Montana. What's left to talk about?"

"That ain't what I mean." He paused as others moved closer in. "We're not gonna get Jensen. You know it, I know it, and so do the rest of the boys. It's only them fools over yonder eatin' high off the hog that thinks we will. And if we do manage to kill them folks we're followin', and we don't kill Jensen—which we ain't gonna do—he'll spend the rest of his life trackin' us down. We'll have to change our names and get the hell gone to Vermont or Massesschewits or some damn other foreign place, and hope to God he don't find us."

John T. realized then that Montana, and the rest of the men, too, he supposed, were not talking about quitting and pulling out, but just letting off steam, with Montana being the spokesman.

That thought was dashed when Mike Hunt said, "Why don't we kill them princes and barons and whatnot over yonder, have some fun with them cold-actin' women, take their money and jewels, and just get gone from this place?"

"That thought entered my mind, too," Gil Webb said. "But that'd just make it worser."

Mike looked at him. "I don't see how."

"The German government would get involved in it then, and there'd really be an investigation."

Mike nodded his head. "I hadn't thought about that. You're right."

John T. did not enter into the conversation. Only when and if he was asked. Best to let the men hash it out among themselves, he concluded.

Paul Melham moaned in pain in his sleep.

"We best stick with what we planned," Nick spoke up. "With the money bein' paid us, we can disappear for a good long time if we're careful with it. This'll blow over after awhile. It always does, don't it?"

"Not no killin' like we done and like we're plannin', it don't," Utah Red said. "But I agree with Montana that we ain't got no hell of a lot of options left us. We just got to go on and do it, that's all."

Valdes tossed another stick on the fire. "I am more fortunate than most of you. I can head back into Mexico and vanish. And that is exactly what I plan on doing. With my money, I can buy a cantina and quit this business."

"You mighty quiet, John T.," Ray Harvey said.

"Just listenin' to you boys talk, that's all."

"Ain't you got no opinion a-tall?" Tony Addison asked.

"I reckon not, Tony. I'm goin' on, so there ain't much point in talkin' about what's behind us. We just do the deed we all agreed to do."

"Oh, I'm in, John T.," Tony was quick to say. "Don't worry 'bout that."

"I was wonderin', after listenin' to all this talk," John T. said, pulling out the makings and rolling a tight cigarette. "Just had me a little curious, that's all."

The men were all quick to speak up that John T. could count on them. Yes, sir. All the way.

"Good, boys, good." He smoked his cigarette down and tossed the butt into the fire. "I'm gonna turn in. I got a funny feelin' in my guts that tomorrow is gonna be a damn busy day."

"Why do you say that, John T.?" Valdes asked.

"Just got a hunch is all." He rolled his gunbelt and took off his boots. "I pay attention to my hunches, boys. They've saved my bacon more'n once."

"Good idea, John T.," Gil said. He got up and wandered off toward the bushes.

John T. Matthey went to sleep counting all the men they'd buried on their back trail. Thanks to that damn Jensen.

Smoke was up and drank the last of his coffee before dawn ever thought about opening its eyes. As he had done before rolling up in the blankets the night before, he climbed up on a ridge and looked to the south. Fires, and a lot of them. Von Hausen and his pack of hungry, rabid skunks were very close. He turned and looked to the north. Several small fires; that had to be Walt and his bunch.

He walked to his camp, made sure his fire was out, and then packed up, saddled up and pulled out. He had to find a place to make a stand this day. If he didn't, Walt's group wouldn't have any more days left to them.

Dawn was just breaking when Smoke rode out. He flirted with the idea of just picking a spot and make a stand to the death. But he didn't flirt with it for very long. The will to live was too strong in him. And just as strong was his will to win against seemingly insurmountable odds.

He'd have to admit he'd done a pretty fair job of doing just that so far.

No, Smoke would not make any stand-or-die move. No, what he would do is catch up with Walt and the others and then fight a rear guard action after seeing what kind of shape they were in.

They were going to win this fight, by God.

His horse sensed its rider's excitement and the big

'paloosa quickened its step. "That's right, boy," Smoke said. "You feel the same way, don't you?"

The Appaloosa snorted and swung his head. Smoke laughed.

Above him, an eagle soared.

19

Smoke put some distance between himself and von Hausen. Smoke's 'paloosa was a mountain horse and as sure-footed as a puma. Many times Smoke just gave him his head and let him go, so strong was the bond between horse and rider.

Smoke pulled up short when he heard voices and the sounds of an axe. "What the hell?" he muttered.

He urged his horse on, knowing that whoever was making all that noise wasn't setting up any ambush for him. When he climbed up the ridge and made the clearing, Smoke sat his saddle amazed at what he saw.

Just behind the dozen frantically working people, there was a falls, the water cascading down a sheer rock face. He could hear the sounds of running water close by. Then he saw the stream.

"Hello, Smoke Jensen!" Robert waved and called to him. "Come on into our fort."

Smoke returned the wave and muttered, "You damn sure got that right. It's a fort."

"You can put your horse right back there," the government scientist said, pointing. "It's a tiny valley that is accessible only from the front." He smiled. "Unless you know the back way in. And even Angel and Walt couldn't find that until Gilbert pointed it out."

"But . . ."

"You look tired. There is fresh coffee in the pot. Walt made it," he added.

"But . . ."

"And there is food being prepared now."

"But . . . what about . . ."

"They might dig us outta here, Smoke," Walt said, strolling up on his bowlegs, "but they'll have one hell of a battle on their hands doin' it." He waved to Charles Knudson. "Take his horse, will you, son? Thanks."

"Damnit!" Smoke yelled. "Von Hausen couldn't be more than two or three hours behind me. What the hell are you people doing? I thought . . ."

"The hosses couldn't go no more and neither could 'bout half the people," Walt said. "Gilbert knowed of this place, so here we are. Come on. I think you'll like what you see."

He did.

Montana got his hat blowed off when he rounded the bend in the trail. He left the saddle hollering for the others to lie back and get down.

From his position in the timber, Montana stared up in amazement at the sight on the ridge. It was a fort. A gawd-damned fort in the middle of the wilderness. And they had 'em a regular United States flag just a-flappin' in the breeze, all stuck up on a tall pole.

Von Hausen crept up to Montana's side and looked. And looked. Then he started cussing in several languages. He finally wound down and waved for John T. to join them.

John T. looked and shook his head and sighed mightily. "This ain't worth a damn, boss. This just ain't no good at all. I betcha there ain't but one way up there and we're lookin' at it. It'd be suicide."

"Yes," von Hausen agreed. "I'm afraid you're right. But there is one point in our favor. They can't get out." "True. But how long will it be 'fore the Army sends in troops lookin' for them soldier boys we killed?"

"Not long," von Hausen reluctantly said.

"Where'd you get the flag?" Smoke asked, belly down behind the ramparts on the ridge.

"We always carry a flag with us," Gilbert told him. "Anytime we're doing expeditionary work in the wilderness, whether it be in Africa or in the territories."

Smoke had agreed that the fort was solid and very nearly impregnable. While the men were busy fortifying the site, the women had busied themselves gathering up firewood, and not just for use as cooking. Both Walt and Jensen knew how to make smoke 'talk.' If they could hold out for a couple of days, the Army would, very probably, be sending patrols in to find out why the initial patrol had not returned and they would, hopefully, see the talking smoke.

Smoke had inspected the hidden opening at the rear of the falls. Nature had done her work very well. The entrance/exit had to be pointed out to him. Still, Smoke had insisted upon posting a guard near the entrance. If any of von Hausen's people found their way into the valley, those inside the natural fort would be in real trouble.

"Standoff," Smoke said to Gilbert. "At least for as long as there's light. They'll try to rush us as soon as it's dark." He thought for a moment. "Gather up any clothing you don't need and tear it into rags. We'll make torches. When they rush us, we'll light them and throw them over the side."

The stone ramparts were high and any openings between the huge rocks had been plugged with timber and dirt, gun slits added. Smoke walked the line of defenders, making certain all had plenty of ammo.

"Don't fire at shadows," he told each one. "We've plenty of ammunition, but not so much that we can afford to waste it. If you're not sure of a target, don't fire. We can wait them out. Tonight is going to be our biggest test of nerve. I want every other person to nap for a couple of hours. Then stand guard and let the others rest. Do that until dark."

Smoke walked to his blankets and laid down, a saddle for a pillow. He called, "If anything important happens, wake me up."

"There does not appear to be a nerve in his body," Blanche remarked.

Smoke awakened several times during the afternoon, when one of von Hausen's men would throw a shot at the fort on the ridge, the bullet thudding into wood or dirt or howling off a boulder. He would close his eyes and go back to sleep. As the shadows began to lengthen, Smoke rolled from his blankets, put on his hat, buckled his guns around his lean hips, and walked to the fire, pouring a cup of coffee.

"It's quiet," Angel told him. "But I think when the darkness comes so will they."

Smoke sipped his coffee. Hot and black and strong. "Yes. Von Hausen is fighting out of pure desperation now. But if we can beat back the first wave—and I see no reason why that can't be done—those gunslingers down yonder will have second thoughts about doing it again. Did you get some rest?"

"I napped off and on. I feel fine. I made sure the others got some sleep."

"Good. There damn sure won't be much sleeping come the night. Was the guard changed behind us?"

"Every two hours, to relieve the boredom."

Smoke drank his coffee and ate a biscuit. He checked his .44-.40. He shoved in a couple of rounds, then checked his .44's. He walked to the stone and timber walls. "How are you doing?" he asked Gilbert.

"Fine. Wonderful, in fact. The excitement is building among us, almost to a fever pitch. All of us here have gotten over our fright, for the most part. Now a sense of deep anger and resentment toward those below us has taken its place.

Our rights have been violated and we are all prepared to use force to get them returned."

Walt grinned. "In other words, y'all are ready to kick some butt."

"That sums it up rather well," Carol said.

Smoke looked at the woman anthropologist. He still wasn't all that sure what it was, exactly, that she did. And he was afraid to ask. He thought it had something to do with old bones. Carol wore a pistol in a military-style holster and held a long-barreled shotgun.

"I'm really quite good with the shotgun, Smoke Jensen," she said. "If I can hit a bird on the wing, I can certainly hit a man. And believe me when I speak for all of us here, sir: there will be no shirking among us. If those murderers down there come up that ridge, we will not hesitate to shoot."

There was a set to her chin and a determination in the woman's voice that gave Smoke no reason to doubt her. These gentle people had been pushed to their limits. Now they were going to do some pushing of their own.

Smoke smiled, patted her on the shoulder, and walked on. He stopped at Charles Knudson's position. Harold Bailey was a few yards from him, manning another post. The young surveyors smiled at him, Charles saying, "We're ready, Smoke."

"Good men," Smoke told him. He walked the interior of the fort which formed a crude half circle, stopping to talk for a moment with everybody. Paula and Thomas had left to guard the rear exit of the valley, relieving Robert at the lonely post. Two were sent so one could sleep while the other stayed awake during the long night. It might get so busy that they could not be relieved for many hours. And Walt had wanted the shift changed while there was still light to see.

He found Angel cleaning his rifle. "Senor Smoke," the Mexican gunfighter greeted him with a smile. "I think for some out there," he pointed toward the edge of the ridge, "this is going to be a good night to die."

"It might be a terrible thing to say, Angel; but I sure hope so."

"Not so terrible a thing when bad men chase good people," Angel said soberly.

"You do have a point, Angel." Smoke returned to his bedroll, slipped into a jacket, for the late afternoon was turning very cool, and filled his jacket pocket with cartridges. He poured another cup of coffee and then took the plate of food that was handed to him. He ate with a good appetite and rinsed out his plate in a pan and returned to the ramparts.

Walt had done a really bang-up job in securing the interior of the fort. The tents were set well back, too far back for anyone to throw a torch into them. A stray bullet might ricochet and scream off the rock of the sheer face behind them and hit someone, but that would be a long shot. All things considered, their position was a secure one.

"I have always heard that this was the hardest part of a battle," Gilbert said. "The waiting."

"You heard right," Smoke told him. "When the shootin' starts, a man doesn't have time to be scared. Scared-time is over. You don't have time to think about anything except staying alive."

"Would it make me sound callous if I said I believe I am actually looking forward to this fight?"

Smoke smiled. "No. It's like you said: you folks are feeling a lot of anger and resentment toward that pack of hyenas down the ridge. With good reason. You want to strike back at them. That's understandable. I do, too, believe that."

"Sometimes you speak like a very well-educated man, Mister Jensen."

"I married a schoolteacher," Smoke said with a smile. Gilbert chuckled as Smoke moved away, making yet another round inside the fort.

*   *   *

Roy Drum returned from his afternoon's circling around the mountain. He poured a cup of coffee and shook his head. "There ain't no other way in. If you want them folks, Baron, we got to go up that ridge and take 'em. And before you ask me if I'm shore about there bein' no other way in, yeah, I'm shore."

Von Hausen looked disdainfully at the man. "It isn't just a matter of me wanting them, Roy. It's you and all the rest of the men as well."

"Yeah," Roy said wearily. He sat down on the ground with a sigh. "I know that. But I ain't makin' no suicide charges up that ridge. And it would be suicide. I just ain't gonna do that, for nobody."

"If we done it durin' the day," John T. said," I'd agree with that. But they can't see no better at night than we can. We can look at the damn ridge and see there ain't no traps set for us. That's as plain as the nose on your ugly face."

"I'll concede the trap part," Roy said with a smile. "But they's some ladies who think I'm right cute."

"They must be blind," Montana Jess said.

Von Hausen stood quietly, letting the men banter back and forth. This was not something he could just flatly order them to do.

"It might work to our advantage to let them stew for one night," Gil Webb said.

John T. shook his head. "You're forgettin' about all them dead soldier boys back down the trail that probably was supposed to have reported back in a long time ago. Every hour we stall, means we're that much closer to a hangman's noose."

"I'll stick a gun in my mouth and pull the trigger 'fore I let myself be tooken in alive," Utah Red said. "I don't favor stretchin' no rope."

The men were unanimous in that.

"Well," John T. said. "Let's talk this thing out. We all know what we got to do, it's just when that's gotta be settled."

"I'll leave that up to you men," von Hausen said. He returned to his tent and closed the flap against the chill of the approaching night.

"Damn big of him," Cat Brown said.

Smoke had gone to where Angel had stacked his gear from the packhorse and dug out the sack of dynamite and caps and fuses. He prepared a dozen sticks and using thin strips of rawhide, tied them to nice-sized throwing lengths of branches he'd cut off. He gave three to Walt, three to Angel, and kept six for himself. He went to the pile of torches and passed them out.

"Put out the fire," he ordered. "That will give us better night vision."

"It'll be cold," Perry said.

"I'd rather be cold alive than cold dead," Smoke put a stopper in that kind of talk quickly.

Gilbert grinned at him in the waning light. "Very aptly put, Smoke."

Smoke watched as Carol broke open her double-barrel shotgun and checked the loads. She had a bandoleer of shotgun shells looped over one shoulder.

She was not a big woman and had elected not to use buckshot. She was afraid the charge might knock her down. But she was using a heavy load of birdshot that would make life miserable for anyone who caught a load of it.

Smoke smiled, thinking if she caught someone in the butt with that birdshot, they'd be damned uncomfortable sitting a saddle for some time.

He peered out through one of the gunslits. Night was gently closing in around them. Nothing moved below. That he could see. But they would come this night. He was sure of that. He'd bet on it.

They all were, with their lives.

20

Smoke caught a glimpse of a shadow moving near the base of the hill. He stared; there it was again. "Here they come," he whispered to Gilbert, manning a post a few yards away. "Pass the word."

The alert was quickly and quietly passed up and down the line of defenders.

"I can't see a thing," Gilbert whispered.

"They've probably blackened their faces with mud," Smoke returned the whisper. "For sure they've taken off their spurs and dressed in the darkest clothing they had with them. Those down there might be trash, but they're professionals, too."

"And desperate men," Blanche added. She was posted only a few yards to Smoke's left.

Smoke had not had to tell the women what would happen to them should the man-hunters breech the ramparts and get their hands on them. The women knew.

"I see something moving down there," Blanche whispered hoarsely.

"Let them get closer," Smoke said. "Make damn sure you've

got a target. The closer they are, the better your chances of a good hit."

A figure loomed close to the ramparts. Carol's shotgun roared twice. An outlaw screamed over and over in pain. The birdshot had taken him on the shoulders, neck, and the lower part of his face. He dropped his rifle and put both hands to his birdshot-peppered cheeks and jaw. He screamed again, lost his footing on the slope, and went rolling elbows over butt down the hill.

"One down," Carol muttered, and pulled out the smoking hulls, tossing them to the ground and reloading.

Smoke's lips moved in a warrior's smile. No doubts now as to how Carol would react.

"Good," Gilbert said. "Very good shot, Carol." He lifted his rifle and fired at a shadow. The bullet howled off a rock and the outlaw dropped belly down on the ground.

Angel found a target and drilled a man-hunter in the leg, the force of the bullet knocking the man down and sending him rolling and squalling down the hill.

"Back!" John T. called. "Back down the hill."

"Let them have it!" Smoke yelled, and the cool night air thundered with the sounds of rifle, pistol, and shotgun fire from the defenders on the hill.

Out of range, von Hausen stood tight-lipped, his face white with anger and his hands clenched into big fists, as John T. gave the orders to retreat. He watched impassively as Jerry Watkins came staggering in, the lower part of his face and his neck bleeding badly from the birdshot that had peppered him. The man was fortunate that the blast had not taken him a few inches higher and blinded him. Had that occurred, one of them would have had to shoot the man. Von Hausen was in no mood to waste any time with a blind person.

Tony Addison came hobbling in, his arm around the shoulders of Cat Brown. Tony's leg was bleeding from a .44

Winchester slug that had taken him in the thigh and his face was pale and tight against the pain.

John T. walked up. "No good, boss," he told von Hausen. "It looks like it's suicide day or night. They just flat stopped us cold. You can't get no footin' up that hill."

Frederick stared at him, then nodded his head curtly and walked away.

Utah grumbled, "Why don't he take his royal ass up that hill and try it one time?"

"'Cause that's what he's payin' us big money to do," John T. told him. "Or have you forgotten that?"

"Don't crowd me too hard, John T.," Utah warned the man.

The two skilled gunhandlers stood in the close darkness and stared at each other for a moment. A very tense moment since feelings were running high and the surging blood of each man was hot for killing.

"You boys cool down," Montana said. "Just back off. This ain't no time for us to start squabbling amongst ourselves."

"Montana's right," Pat said. "That's what them folks up on the hill want; for us to turn on each other. Now settle down. We got wounded to look after."

Utah nodded his head. "Sorry, John T."

"It's OK, Utah," John T. replied. "We're all on a short string this evenin'. Come on. Let's see about the boys and get us some coffee."

The defenders on the hill were quietly jubilant.

"Do you think we killed anybody?" Charles asked. No one had left their post.

"I know we put some out of action," Smoke said. "How hard they're hit I don't know. Good shooting, Carol."

"Thank you. Now if you all will excuse me, I have to throw up." She beat it to the bushes behind the camp.

"Natural reaction," Smoke said, punching out empties and reloading his six-guns. "I think I did the same thing first time I killed a man, back in '65 it was. In Kansas, I believe.

I was about thirteen or fourteen. Bunch of Pawnees jumped us. Me, my dad, and an old mountain man called Preacher. If I didn't upchuck, I damn sure wanted to. Nothing to be ashamed of."

"You think they'll be back this night, Smoke?" Blanche asked.

"It wouldn't surprise me."

"Let's get out of here and get out of America while we still can," Hans urged.

"Shut up, Hans," Gunter told him.

"No. No, I won't shut up," the man said. "I'll have my say and you all can be damned! We're not that far from a port in San Francisco. We can board ship and take the long way back. By that time most of the outcry will be over. What we're doing now is foolish. We won't be extradited out of Germany. So we take a few jokes at our expense; we're all grown people. We can endure that. Isn't that better than facing western justice? All I'm asking is that you give it some thought."

"What about the men?" Maria asked.

"Pay them off as agreed and let them go. They certainly aren't going to talk about this. They'd be putting a noose around their necks."

"Has the thought occurred to you, Hans," Marlene said, "that the men might not let us go?"

Hans looked startled. "What do you mean?"

"She means, Hans," von Hausen said, "that we have as much to lose as the men, and the men aren't going to just let us ride out of here and get away. If there is punishment to be had, it will be shared equally."

"The Americans have a phrase for it," Andrea said. "It's called being between a rock and a hard place."

Gunter laughed at that.

Hans shook his head. "There has to be a way out of this for us."

Von Hausen looked hard at the man he used to call his friend. If Hans kept this up, he thought, he knew of one way out for Hans Brodermann. He met the eyes of the others and knew they felt the same about it.

"Every other person try to catch some rest for a couple of hours," Smoke passed the word up and down the line. "If you feel yourself nodding off, wake up the person next to you. We've got to stay alert." He walked back to the coals—all that was left of the fire—and poured a cup of coffee. It was still hot and tasted good.

Smoke knelt by the fading coals and drank his coffee. Those below them had to try again this night. Time was not on the side of Baron von Hausen and those with him.

The defenders had scored two hits so far. But Smoke didn't think they were killing hits. That light load Carol was using would kill, but it would have to be at fairly close range. More than likely, the man she shot was very uncomfortable, but still able to fight, unless she blinded him. In that case, Smoke felt certain von Hausen would finish him off—or one of those coldhearted women with him.

Smoke tossed the coffee dregs to the ground, and walked back to the ramparts, rifle in hand. He stopped by Walt's position. "Anything moving down there?"

"Nothin' that I can see," the old gunslinger said. "And my eyes is about the only thing I got left that's workin' worth a damn."

"According to Angel, your gunhand still knows what to do."

"Hell, that comes natural to us, Smoke. You know that as well as me."

"I know it isn't a blessing."

"You shore got that right."

"What will they do next?" Smoke muttered. Walt didn't reply because he felt Smoke didn't expect any. "I don't think they have dynamite. Even if they did they have no way of delivering it up here. They might try to make bows and arrows and shoot fire up here. But they couldn't hit the tents using any bow that hasn't been cured out. And even if they did burn the tents, we won't be hurt."

"This was a good move on our part, I'm thinkin'," Walt said. "If we can hold out, we'll make it. Them down yonder knows they're runnin' out of time."

"And they just might get careless."

" 'Xactly."

"I got an idea," Smoke said. He explained it to Walt and to Gilbert, who had walked over.

"Let's try it," Gilbert said.

"You men down below!" Smoke shouted. "This is Smoke Jensen. Can you hear me?"

After a moment, a voice shouted, "Yeah, Jensen. We can hear you. What do you want?"

"I want you to listen to me. And when I'm finished, give some thoughts to my words. OK?"

"Let 'er bump, Jensen."

"That's John T. Matthey," Walt said.

"He's good," Smoke said. "I've heard a lot of talk about him."

"Yeah. He's good, and he's careful. Man don't get to his age without bein' careful. But they's several down there just about as good, or maybe as good as John T. Utah Red. Montana Jess. Cat Brown. I'd have to include Gil Webb in that bunch, too."

Smoke grunted. "Some rough ol' boys you just named, Walt. And fast. I've met John T. a time or two."

"So he said."

"All right, boys," Smoke shouted. "Here it is: way I got it figured, there can't be any more than fourteen or fifteen of you left . . ."

"He's close," Utah said. "They's fifteen of us still able to shoot, and three of them are wounded."

". . . Draw your money and pull out. I give you my word, and you all know that my word is my bond, I won't seek revenge. It ends right here. What the Army does is the Army's business. But I'll have no hand in it. None of the civilians up here know any of your names or faces. So they can't talk or be used as witnesses against you . . ."

"He's got a point," Tom Ritter said. "A damn good point."

"For a fact," Mike Hunt agreed.

"Damn him!" Marlene said.

"But Walt and Angel know us," Montana yelled. "What about them?"

"This here's Walt! I'm speakin' for both me and Angel. Haul your ashes outta here and we sudden got a loss of memory. And you got my word on that."

"But they're murderers!" Carol protested.

"They were murderers before this, ma'am," Walt told her. "And they'll be murderers after this. Right now, we're tryin' to save you folks' butts. Pardon my language."

"They'll meet their just end," Smoke told her. He raised his voice. "How about it, boys?"

"We'll think on it, Jensen," John T. called.

"Fine. You do that."

"Now what?" Robert asked from out of the darkness of the stone and wood enclosure.

"We wait."

"What do we do, Frederick?" Marlene asked.

"Do you have your checkbook with you?"

"Of course. One of them. It's the account we set up with Wells Fargo."

"Do you have thirty thousand dollars in that account?"

The look she gave him silently informed the baron that meager amount would be a mere drop in the bucket.

"Make it out payable to bearer, if you would, please."

When the ink had dried, von Hausen walked over to the group of gunslingers and handed John T. the check. "Let everyone see it, please, John."

John T.'s eyes bugged out. He carefully held the check up for all to see in the campfire light.

"That is, of course, in addition to the monies already paid you and is waiting for you in separate accounts back in Dodge City. And remember this, your share of that money has greatly increased over the past weeks due to the demise of several of your fellow hunters. The attorney handling that money knows to divide it equally among the survivors. Think about that. But one of my group has to give him the signal, in person, to do so." He smiled. "That was done in case any, or all of you, got it into your heads to kill us. With the addition of this thirty thousand, those of you who are left when this hunt is concluded, stand to walk away with a very large amount of money. Enough to retire on; buy a ranch or a business." He plucked the check from John T.'s fingers. "Think about it, gentlemen. Give it careful thought." Von Hausen carefully and with a lot of dramatic gestures, folded the check and put it in his pocket. He walked back to his tent.

"Any questions, boys?" John T. said.

Cat Brown picked up his rifle and punched in a couple of rounds. "I reckon it's time for us to go back to work, boys. I always did have a hankerin' to own me a whorehouse."

"Sit down," John. T. told him. "I got a plan that just might work. See what you boys think about this."

"It's been more'un an hour since you made your offer," Walt said. "They must be really talkin' it over."

"Or planning to hit us again," Smoke said.

"You cowardly sons of bitches!" the shouted voice of von Hausen drifted up the hill. "You agreed to stay on until the end. You have no honor. None of you!"

A lot of cussing followed that.

"What in thunder is going on down there?" Charles asked.

"Sounds phony to me," Walt grumbled.

"Both of us," Smoke said.

"Damn you all to hell! " a strongly accented voice shouted. More cussing.

"They're really putting on a good show, aren't they?" Smoke said with a smile.

"I thought you western men were brave?" a female voice was added. It was filled with contempt. "You're all cowards. Everyone of you."

"I think they're overdoing it a bit," Carol remarked.

More cussing.

"Smoke Jensen!" the shout cut the night.

"Right here," Smoke called.

"This is John T. We'll take your deal, Smoke. And to show you I mean what I say, you can watch us ride out at first light. Unless you want us to pull out now."

"That's good, John T.," Smoke called. "I think you made the right choice. No point in you boys losing a good night's sleep. You can pull out in the morning."

"That's fine with us, Jensen. Good night."

"Lying scum," Smoke said.

"We're all in agreement with that," Gilbert said. "That scenario was staged if I ever heard one."

"Von Hausen!" Smoke called.

"Right here, Jensen."

"You want to settle this right now, you and me?"

"I think not, gunfighter," his voice sprang out of the darkness. "But there will be another time and place for us, be assured of that."

"I imagine so, von Hausen." Smoke turned to his group. "This ought to be good." He raised his voice. "And your plans come the morning?"

"We'll be striking camp and pulling out, Jensen. I no longer have any appetite for the hunt."

"He's lyin', an' John T. is lyin'," Walt said. "So what the hell are they up to?"

"No good, and that's for sure," Charles Knudson said. "Now I'm getting worried."

"No need for that," Smoke told him. "I think we'll just let them outsmart themselves."

"What do you mean by that?" Carol asked.

But Smoke would only smile.

"Do you agree the hunt was a good one, Jensen?" von Hausen yelled.

"It was interesting, von Hausen," Smoke called.

"Oh, quite!" the man shouted. "Good night, Jensen. We'll all wave auf Wiedersehen in the morning."

"Yeah, you do that," Smoke muttered.

"Could it be they are actually leaving?" Perry asked.

"Oh, they'll pull out," Smoke said, "and set us up."

"And you have a plan to counter that?" Blanche asked.

"Oh, yes, ma'am," Smoke said. "I sure do."

21

"Oughta shoot 'em dead if they show themselves," Walt said. "And to hell with all their lies."

Silver was streaking the eastern sky. Those inside the fort stood by the ramparts, drinking coffee and waiting to see if von Hausen's party were really going to pull out.

"I know we should," Smoke agreed with him. "But there is that one chance in a million they're really going to leave."

"Of course, you don't believe that?" Gilbert asked.

"No. I sure don't."

"Yo, the fort!" came the shout.

"We're still right here," Smoke called.

"For reasons of security, none of us will step out into the open," von Hausen called. "You understand, of course?"

"Sure, von Hausen. I understand."

"You really have nothing to fear—any of you. After we've pulled out, and since you have the high ground you'll be able to see us cross the meadow to the south, and you will, of course, inspect the remnants of our camp. You will see that we are keeping our word. We'll have our coffee, and then we shall be gone. Goodbye, all."

"And good riddance," Walt muttered. "Even if you are lyin' through your teeth."

"They won't be going much further than those ridges past the meadow," Smoke said. "Just as soon as they enter the meadow, I'm gone out the back way, on foot. I'll carry some supplies with me in a pack. I'll stick to the timber on the ridges and make a half circle. You'll be able to hear the battle."

"You want some company?" Angel asked.

Smoke shook his head. "No. They started this. I'll finish it."

Smoke went to his supplies and packed a few items in a rucksack while breakfast was being cooked. He did not even look up when Robert called, "There they go."

Smoke checked his high-top moccasins. The soles were getting thin, but they'd hold out for this run. He tucked his jeans inside the leggins and wound the rawhide tight around his ankles and calves. Then he went over and had breakfast.

"Now listen to me, people," Smoke said, squatting down by the fire and fixing a biscuit and bacon sandwich. "You stay on the alert. Head's up at all times. Just as soon as von Hausen makes the timber on those ridges, he's going to send people back here, on foot, swinging wide through the timber to avoid being seen. They'll be getting into position and they'll have supplies to last a day or so, to wait you out. Stay behind these walls and don't expose yourselves. Just as soon as those he sends back here hear the shooting, they'll know it's gone sour for them. I don't know what they'll do. But I'll bet that von Hausen offered them big money to reject our proposal and to stick it out. Don't leave this fort after the shooting stops. For any reason. Don't leave the protection of these walls."

Smoke walked to the ramparts and looked down at the seemingly deserted timber.

"They're entering the meadow," Gilbert said, holding binoculars to his eyes.

"Count them."

"I count twenty-two."

"That's the whole bunch of them, then. OK, Gilbert. Keep the people behind these walls. I'm gone."

"You be careful out there, boy," Walt said.

"I'll do that. Take care of them in here."

"We'll do that," Angel said. "Vaya con dios, Smoke."

Smoke slipped into his pack, picked up his rifle, and left the fort, jogging across the tiny meadow and coming up to where Thomas and Paula were standing guard. Charles Knudson had visited them before dawn, telling them what was planned, so they were expecting Smoke.

They greeted him, wished him luck and Godspeed, and Smoke slipped through, being careful not to disturb the natural look of the exit.

He set out on a distance-eating lope, staying in the timber whenever possible, keeping low and moving swiftly when he had to cross short expanses of open terrain, using every bush and shrub for cover.

He had steeled his mind for this mission. He had offered them all safe passage last evening. If they were planning an ambush—and he had no doubts in his mind about that—there would be no mercy shown them. None. For any of them. Including the women if they turned hostile, and he was sure they would do just that. This was the most savage, cold-blooded, ruthless bunch of people he had ever encountered. He did not pretend to comprehend what went on in their demented minds.

As he neared the far ridges, Smoke slowed his approach. He slipped from tree to tree, his carefully placed feet making no noise when they touched the earth.

He stopped, still as a sturdy tree when he heard the first whisper of voices filtering through the lushness of untouched forest. He worked his way closer, moving only when someone was speaking. Von Hausen and party had stopped in a small clearing, well hidden from the eyes of those back at the fort.

Smoke counted those in the clearing. Six were missing. And he'd bet those six were the top guns in the bunch. So be it. He would deal with them later.

"How long you reckon it'll take the boys to get into position back yonder?" The question, or at least a part of it, reached Smoke.

He worked a few yards closer.

"Give 'em a good two hours," his question was answered.

"I don't 'spect Jensen and them will stick their noses out of the fort for several hours," another said. "Maybe longer than that."

"This is wrong!" a very accented voice reached Smoke. The words were almost a shout. "The man gave his word and we gave ours. What we are doing now is despicable!"

"Oh, stop your whining, Hans," a woman said. "I'm sick of it. We all are."

"This is a good plan," a man said. The words were just audible to Smoke.

So von Hausen and his immediate party were some distance away from the hired help. Figures, Smoke thought. Heaven forbid they should have to associate with the lower classes.

Smoke moved closer. He was very near the edge of the clearing now. He thumb-nailed a match into flames.

"Shut your goddamn mouth, Hans!" von Hausen said. "We're all tired of your silly whimpering. Now sit down over there and be quiet. Give us all a break. Those people back at that fort have to die. All of them. That's final, and it's settled."

Smoke stepped to the edge of the clearing, lit the fuse on a charge of dynamite and tossed it into the center of the men, sitting and squatting in a circle.

"Jesus H. Christ!" one bellowed.

"Run!" another squalled, and took off like his longhandles was on fire and he was in them.

Smoke laughed, threw back his head, and howled like a great gray timber wolf.

"What in the hell is that?" Marlene screamed.

Three sticks of dynamite blew. One man had been nodding off and was slow to move. The blast and concussion lifted him off the ground and moved him about thirty feet, one of his legs bent in an impossible angle.

Smoke started shooting, working the lever on his .44 carbine as fast as he could. Nick took a round in the belly that doubled him over. He fell to the shattered ground, screaming as the pain rode him down like a surging tidal wave.

Tom Ritter reached his frightened and rearing horse, got into the saddle, and Smoke put a slug in his shoulder as he was galloping off. He jerked in the saddle but stayed on.

Mike Hunt got to his boots, both hands filled with six-guns. Smoke shot him in the center of the chest just as Pat Gilman started throwing lead in Smoke's direction. Smoke dropped to his knees at the edge of the clearing and pulled the trigger. The slug was low and caught Pat in the hipbone, knocking him down. Pat hollered and began crawling for a horse, any horse.

Smoke dropped his carbine and jerked his six-guns. Tony Addison screamed obscenities at him and leveled his guns. Smoke sent him to Hell carrying two .44 slugs, one in his belly, the other one in his chest.

Smoke stepped back into the brush and squatted down. He could hear hard-running horses, the sounds of their hooves rapidly fading away. The little meadow was filled with flowers and gunsmoke and blood and death.

Smoke waited for several minutes, waiting for the dust to settle. He could see one man moving. He took that time to reload his carbine. He stood up, still in the timber and brush at meadow's edge, and surveyed the scene. He was startled to see the wounded man was dressed like he was on an

African safari. His stupid looking hat—what were they called, yeah, pith helmets—lay off to one side.

Smoke checked the dead. Two of them. Even the one who appeared to have a broken leg got away. But Smoke knew he'd put several out of action.

He walked over to the wounded man. The blood was dark as it oozed from his wound. Probably shot in the gizzard.

"I didn't shoot you," Smoke said. "A .44 round would have made a bigger hole than that."

"My . . . wife shot me. Andrea Brodermann."

"Your *wife* shot you?" Smoke knelt down beside the man.

"Yes. I'm . . . going to die, aren't I?"

"Probably. Looks like she drilled you through the liver. Small caliber pistol. Those small slugs tend to wander around in a person's innards; do all sorts of damage."

"You're Smoke Jensen?"

"That I am."

"Please accept my . . . apologies for this . . . insanity. Long days back I . . . tried to stop this. They would . . . have none of it." He closed his eyes and gritted his teeth against the pain. He sighed and said, "She shot me . . . just as the dynamite blew. I should have been . . . more careful."

Smoke started to tell him that when you run with hyenas, you shouldn't expect to get the best cuts of meat, but he decided against that. Man had enough troubles right now.

"I am a Prince," Hans said.

"Do tell?"

"Yes. The men left . . . alive. They will not give up, sir. They . . . have money deposited for them . . . and they will hunt you . . . down."

"Well, I shortened the odds some this day." Hans' face was deadly white. Smoke figured the man didn't have much longer. "You got family you want me to write, Prince?" He did not slur the title.

"In my wallet. My jacket . . . pocket. Inside. If you would be . . . so kind as to write my parents."

"Sure. I'll do it. You have my word."

Hans tried a smile. "With that tremendous dynamite . . . charge, you shouldn't have much of a . . . hole to dig."

Smoke returned the smile and wiped the sweat from the man's brow with a bandana. "I'll bury you better than that, partner. That's a promise."

"Be careful of the . . . women in our," he grimaced, "*that* group. They are vicious, sir. I think we have married too closely . . . over the years. It's beginning to . . . show."

Smoke said nothing. The man's time was running out. Let him talk until he shook hands with the devil.

"I have a considerable sum of greenbacks in . . . my wallet and . . . several small sacks of . . . gold coin in my saddlebags. That's my horse . . . over there. The . . . there is no word for it in my language." He cut his eyes. The horse was grazing not far away.

"Roan," Smoke said.

"Yes. That is it. I want to compensate you for all the misery we have caused you.

"There is no need for that."

"I want to."

"All right."

"Take it . . . now. Let me see you do it. Please. A final request."

Smoke walked to the horse, spoke to it, and opened the saddlebags, all the time keeping an eye on Hans. He took out three small but heavy leather sacks of gold coin. When he returned to Hans, the man was holding out a wallet.

"It will not make up for what . . . we have done to you and the others. But it is a step. I did not fire upon the soldiers."

Smoke believed him. He took the wallet.

"I told . . . Frederick last night it was a stupid plan. That you would . . . not fall for it. He slapped me. My wife . . . laughed. They are perverted people. Twisted. I . . ."

Prince Hans Brodermann died surrounded by the magnificence of Yellowstone. Smoke reached out and closed his eyes. He found a shovel on one of the packhorses that had wandered back into camp and dug a deep hole. The earth claimed Prince Brodermann just as it eventually claims all, making no distinction of class.

Smoke piled rocks on the grave, picked up his rifle and gathered up a saddled horse and the two remaining pack-horses. He rode slowly back to the rear entrance of the fort.

He told what happened while the others were going through the supplies.

"My God!" Blanche said. "Champagne and caviar."

"I'd let it settle down some before I popped that cork," Gilbert said. "The bouncing it's taken, that stuff would go off like a shot."

"What did you do with the other dead?" Thomas asked.

"Left them for the varmints," Smoke said shortly. "Any activity out front after the fireworks started?"

"Yep," Walt said. "They was men out there just like you suspected. But I don't think they ever got in place. They pulled out. Angel climbed up yonder," he pointed to a ledge off aways from the falls, "where the rocks wasn't so wet he couldn't get a handhold, and seen 'em leave. Then we used field glasses and seen 'em way over yonder ridin' hard." He pointed. "They musta picketed their horses and walked in the last mile or so."

"Pack it up," Smoke said. "Now. And do it fast. We're pulling out of here."

"But . . ." Carol said.

"No buts, lady. We're moving. Now."

"Yes," Gilbert said. "I see the logic in that. Our horses are well-rested. We have regained our spirits and strength. So while the opposition is running chaotically, in total disarray, we make our final dash to freedom."

Smoke smiled. "Took the words right out of my mouth, Gilbert."

22

The final ride to park headquarters was uneventful. The acting park superintendent had already sent a messenger to the Army, advising them of the missing patrol, and a full mounted platoon was only a day away and riding hard.

The ladies immediately went off for a hot bath and a change of clothing. The small garrison of Army engineers went on full alert. All six of them.

"They won't come here," Smoke calmed the acting superintendent down. "Once they see we made it, they'd be riding into a death trap, knowing we got word out. But let the Army stay on alert. It'll be good for them."

"Well, the law will now take care of this von Hausen and those hooligans with him."

"No, sir, they won't."

"I beg your pardon, Mister Jensen?"

"I will," Smoke said flatly.

The man took one look into Smoke's hard eyes and backed up a step. "Yes, sir. I do believe you will."

Smoke had told no one about Hans Brodermann's money.

That evening, after supper, he took Angel and Walt aside and told them. He gave them the money.

"My God, Smoke," Walt said, after looking into the sacks and the wallet and finding his voice. "There must be four or five thousand dollars in here."

"Probably more than that," Smoke said. "There's two thousand dollars in greenbacks and several thousand more in signed checks on Wells Fargo. That's not counting the gold. Why don't you two buy you a little spread somewhere and settle down?"

"That's a good idea," Angel said, looking at Walt. "How about it . . . partner?"

The three men shook hands.

"Keep in touch," Smoke told them. "I'll be pulling out at first light."

"You want some company?" Walt asked.

"No. This is something I have to do myself. You both understand that."

They did.

When the others awakened the next morning, Smoke had already left. When questioned, not even the Army guard on the last duty watch had heard him leave.

"He's going to track them all down, isn't he?" Gilbert asked.

"Yep," Walt said. "To the last person. They could have pulled out. Smoke gave them that option. But they turned their backs to it. And they messed up real bad when they done it. They made Smoke mad."

"That is quite a man," Carol said.

Walt glanced at her. "All man, lady. Some say he's the last mountain man."

"The lard's done hit the hot skillet now," Montana said, lingering over the last of the morning coffee. "And she's a-bubblin' and a-spittin'."

"He is just one man," Valdes said.

"I used to think you had good sense," Montana replied. "Now I'm beginnin' to think you fell off your hoss and landed on your head one too many times. He's a-comin' after us, Valdes. And he's mad clear through. And when he's mad, and knows he's in the right, Smoke Jensen don't give a damn about the law. They's been a dozen times over the years when more men than us tried to stop him. When the gunsmoke cleared, Jensen was still standin'."

"I think I am in the company of old women," Valdes said scornfully.

John T. Matthey smoothed out the saddle blanket, slung his saddle on and cinched it up. He said nothing. But he felt that Valdes' pride was setting the Mexican gunfighter up for a killing. His own.

It had been four days since the fight at the fort on the ridge, and the men had swung wide and then cut east. Dodge City, Kansas, where their money was being held, was a long way off. And those of them with any sense knew that Smoke Jensen was coming hard after them.

"Where are we?" von Hausen asked, walking up to the men.

"Wyoming," Roy Drum told him. "Just a few miles south of the Montana line. 'Bout twenty miles south of us, on the Shoshone River, they's a little settlement. It ain't got a name. 'Least it didn't have last time I was through there."

"Is there a railroad there?" Gunter asked. "We have to get east as quickly as possible."

"Don't know. But I'd fight shy of railroads, was I you," Roy told him. "I got me a good strong hunch that the word's done gone out on us. The law'll be lookin' hard at folks buyin' train tickets."

"That doesn't leave us many options, then, does it?" von Hausen asked.

"We done run out of options," Gil Webb said. "Slap dab out of them. All but one."

"And that one is? . . ." Andrea asked, a haughty note in her voice.

"We run, lady," John T. said. He was tying his bedroll in place behind his saddle. "We ride hard for Dodge, you folks pay us off, and then we all scatter like leaves in the wind. Jensen's comin', lady. Comin' hard. And he's mad. Killin' mad. He's snarlin' like a big lobo wolf, sniffin' the ground and stayin' on our scent. We run."

"You ever seen a buffalo wolf, lady?" Roy Drum asked. "No. 'Course you hadn't. They 'bout all gone now. Folks killed them out. Big one would weigh a hundred an' fifty to hundred an' seventy five pounds. One—just *one*—could bring down a buffler. Jump on its back and kill it. That's what Smoke Jensen is, lady. Are we afraid of him? No. But only a fool don't respect him. Now if you folks don't mind, get them hosses of yourn saddled and let's go. Like right now!"

"We have to have supplies," von Hausen said. "We'll travel to that settlement you talked about."

Roy opened his mouth to argue. John T. cut him off. "We're out of coffee, Roy. We lost several packhorses back yonder in that meadow. We ain't got no bacon, no flour, no beans. We'll head for the settlement."

"All right!" Drum said savagely. "Then damnit, let's ride."

They managed to get Ray Harvey on his horse. His broken leg was swollen badly, and it was all he could do to keep from screaming out in pain.

"We got to leave you when we get to the settlement, Ray," John T. said. "You got to get some doctorin' on that leg 'fore gangrene sets in and you die. We'll make sure you get your money. And that's a promise."

That was a lie and both men knew it. Ray's leg was stinking from infection. Gangrene had already set in and his blood was poisoned by it.

The party provisioned at the trading post and pulled out that same day, leaving Ray Harvey in the barn on some hay. Jerry Watkins took all the man's money. So much for honor among thieves. The settlement had no doctor. Smoke rode in the next day, early, and found Harvey nearly gone.

"Shoot me, Jensen!" the hired gun begged. "Put me out of my misery. I can't stand the pain no more."

Smoke shook his head. "I won't do that, but I will buy you a case of whiskey. You can die drunk if you like."

"I'd appreciate it. That'll help a lot. They've gone for Dodge, Jensen. You ain't but about a day behind them. They stole my money and left me here to die. I don't figure I owe none of them a damn thing."

Smoke bought a case of whiskey and arranged with the livery owner to let Harvey stay there until he died. Which was not going to be long. His leg had turned black and vivid streaks of infection were shooting out from the poisoned leg.

Smoke rested his horses, feeding them all the grain they wanted. He had a bath and a haircut and a shave and had his clothing washed and ironed. He left his packhorse, taking only a few things he could carry in his saddlebags and rolled up behind his saddle.

At dawn, he swung up into the saddle. "Let's go, boy," he told his big Appaloosa. The horse stepped out eagerly, knowing the hunt was on.

The livery owner watched Smoke ride out in the darkness. He told a buddy, "I'd not want that man after me. They'll be hell to pay when he catches up with them folks that wronged him."

"I hope he gut-shoots Watkins," Harvey said, his words slurring from the whiskey.

Roy Drum had cut south from the small settlement, and Smoke knew then the route he was taking. They would angle southeast and cross the North Platte at that little town just east of Emigrant Gap. From there, they would touch the corner of Colorado then turn due south toward Dodge.

"Looks like I don't buy any bulls this summer," Smoke told his horse.

* * *

Once von Hausen and party crossed the Greybull, they had about fifty or sixty miles of nothing until they hit the north/south stagecoach road. Smoke remembered a trading post—that by now might be a settlement of sorts—on the old Bridger Trail, at the confluence of Fifteen Mile Creek and the Big Horn River. They would have to stop there—the ladies would want that—and resupply. Sixteen or seventeen people went through a lot of groceries on the trail. Then, too, there was another point to consider: from the trading post to the next settlement, that being on the North Platte, there was about a hundred miles of nothing.

Smoke frowned as he rode. If they stayed on the route that he, himself would take, it would put John T. Matthey about twenty miles south of the Hole-In-The-Wall. John T. just might know some pretty salty ol' boys who would like to pick up a few bucks—namely by killing one Smoke Jensen.

It was something to keep in his mind.

Von Hausen and party, with Roy Drum at the point, crossed the Greybull and pressed on. Some of the swelling in Jerry Watkins' face had gone down, but he still looked like someone had taken an icepick to his face. Many of the birdshot had been picked out; the rest he would carry for the rest of his life. Which, with Smoke Jensen hard on them, might turn out to be very short.

Tom Ritter's left arm had to be carried in a sling, due to a .44 slug that had passed right through his shoulder. Pat Gilman had been wounded in the hip. He could ride, but his face was pale and his lips were tight against the pain. Paul Melham's left arm was out of commission; like Tom, he toted that arm in a sling.

It was a sad-looking bunch that rode toward the Big Horn.

"You know any boys at the Hole, John T.?" Pat asked, riding alongside the man. They were walking their horses to save them.

"Could be. I been thinkin' on it. That's a good hundred miles down the trail. But I don't know how many of them would want to tangle with Smoke Jensen."

"If we could just slow him up some . . ."

"Yeah. I know. Jensen gave us more breaks during this . . . craziness than I figured he would. That's over now. He sees us, anywhere, anytime, he's probably gonna drag iron. For a fact, he ain't gonna give us no more breaks."

"I give up on tryin' to ambush that feller. Seems like he can smell a setup."

"He was raised up by mountain men. Preacher, in particular. He ain't got no better honker on him than we do; but he senses danger. Preacher schooled him good."

"We're just gonna have to make up our minds to stand and face him, John T."

"I been thinkin' on that, too."

"And? . . ."

"You best keep in mind that if we do that, we're gonna take some lead. Jensen ain't gonna just step out in the street and face fifteen of us. He's the farthest thing from a fool. He faced them old boys at that silver camp—eighteen or so of them—and he rode off after the dust settled. And he wasn't nothin' but a kid hisself. He's a ring-tailed-tooter, Pat."

"Sounds like you sort of like the man, John T."

"Oh, I do, in a way. I ain't really got nothin' agin him, I'm just gonna kill him, that's all. How's your hip?"

"Hurts bad. I'm gonna pull out at the settlement or the river. Maybe I'll get lucky with Jensen."

A couple of days later, when they swung down from the dusty saddles at the settlement on the Big Horn, Valdes pulled his rifle from the boot and said, "No more of this for me. I am staying here and settling this affair once and for all. I am weary of running like a frightened child."

"Count me in on that, too," Jerry Watkins mumbled through still-swollen lips. "I got a real personal score to settle with him."

"I can't ride no more," Gilman said. "I was plannin' on pullin' the pin here anyways."

The others just looked at the men and shook their heads. John T. said, "I wish you boys would think on that some. I'm goin' to head for the Hole later on and round up some more boys."

Valdes shook his head. "No. This is as far as I run." He handed von Hausen a slip of paper. "That is my mother's name and address in Mexico. You will see that she gets my share of the money, por favor?"

Von Hausen nodded his head. "Yes, I will, Valdes. I give you my word on that."

"This is adios, then." He solemnly shook hands with everybody and led his horse to the stable.

"See you, boys," Pat said, meeting the eyes of the men and the women. The women seemed indifferent about the whole matter. Then limped off, following the Mexican gunslick.

"I reckon that about sums it up," Jerry mumbled, and followed Pat and Valdes.

"We'll resupply and immediately move on," von Hausen said. "We can't afford the luxury of bathing and grooming. Let's buy what we need and get out!"

Valdes, Jerry, and Pat watched the party ride out of town from a table by the window in a saloon. Pat had not sought the advice of the local doctor about the festering wound in his hip, because he didn't figure he had much longer to live anyway.

He took out a pen and started laboriously printing on a piece of paper he bummed from the bartender, who was nervous about the men being in his place of business. He had

heard about von Hausen—news traveled swiftly in the west—
and wanted no part of Smoke Jensen.

"What are you doin'?" Jerry asked.

"Makin' out my last will and testament," the gun-for-hire
said. "Then I'm gonna give it to that lawyer across the
street."

"I didn't know you had anybody to leave nothin' to."

"I don't. I'm leavin' it to my horse."

"Your *horse?*"

"Yep. He's a good'un. I ain't worth a damn, but that
shouldn't be no reflection on my horse. I'm gonna see to it
that he lives out the rest of his days eatin' and gettin' fat and
bein' lazy."

"That ain't a bad idea," Jerry said. "Do it for my hoss,
too. How about you, Valdes?"

"I don't give a damn what happens to my horse," he said
sullenly. "And how do you know we're not gonna ride out of
this dismal place?"

" 'Cause the telegraph down the road says Smoke Jensen
is about a half a day behind you boys," a rancher spoke from
a couple of tables over. "That's why. I'll see to it that you
boys' horses are put out to pasture and live a good life, if you
want me to. I admire a man who takes care of his horse."

"Thanks," Pat said.

The rancher looked at Valdes. "You can go to hell."

Valdes started to get up from the table. He stopped
halfway out at the sound of several hammers being eared
back. Four of the rancher's hands stood at the bar, six-guns
in their hands.

"Sit down," one told him. "Way I figure it, you got maybe
six or eight hours to live—at the most. You might as well
enjoy that time. 'Sides, I don't want to miss this fight."

Valdes sat, being very careful to keep both his hands on
the table.

"I'll take care of your horse, too, Mex," the rancher told
him. " 'Cause I like horses."

"You serve up food in this place?" Jerry said.

"Got a stew that's good," the barkeep told him.

"That'll suit me just fine," Pat said. "Then I'm gonna take me a snooze under that tree yonder." He pointed. "I reckon I'd better get in the habit of bein' stretched out," he added drily.

23

The day wore on with its usual never-deviating pace. But to the three hired guns in the saloon, time seemed to drag. The saloon filled as word spread around the area. Buckboards and wagons rattled into town, carrying entire families; many had packed box suppers. This was the biggest thing to happen in the community since the outhouse behind the church collapsed and dumped the minister into the pit. Took twelve men half the day to haul him out. Folks never dreamed that a man of the cloth would know all those bad words.

A cowboy galloped into town and jumped from the saddle in front of the saloon. He slapped the dust from him and ran inside. "Rider comin'! Big man on a big Appaloosa."

"That's Jensen," Jerry Watkins said.

Valdes stood up and slipped the thongs from the hammers of his guns. Jerry rose and slipped his guns in and out of leather a couple of times. Pat Gilman shifted his chair around. His hip was hurting him so bad he was afraid if he stood up, he'd fall down.

Smoke rode slowly up the short street. Jerry started to

208 *William W. Johnstone*

pull iron and shoot him through the window. He froze as the rancher who had stayed at the table through the long afternoon eared back the hammer on his Colt.

"I'll shoot you myself, boy," he said. "Lord God, you got him three to one as it is. What kind of lowdown snakes are you people?" He shifted his gaze to Gilman. "Git up and take it like a man."

Pat got to his boots and stood with an effort. "I'm surrenderin'," he said. "I want a trial."

"We ain't got no badge-toter here," a cowboy said. "Law's a hundred miles away, near 'bouts. 'Sides, we heard all about you boys ambushin' that Army patrol and tryin' to murder them women in the park. You're gonna get a trial, all right. And the judge is comin' through the door right about now."

Spurs jingled on the rough boardwalk and the batwings were slowly pushed open. Smoke stepped inside, and there was no doubt in anyone's mind that this was Smoke Jensen. He seemed to fill the whole doorway and his cold eyes put a sudden chill in the room. Smoke sized up the situation and deliberately turned his back to the hired guns, walking to the bar.

"Beer," he told the nervous barkeep.

Every inch of space along the front of the saloon was filled with people. The minister who had first-hand knowledge of excrement and knew it when he saw it, began praying for the lost souls of the hired guns.

Smoke drank his mug of beer, wiped his mouth with the back of his hand, and turned to face the trio. "Mighty good beer. Tasted good."

"I'll buy you another," the rancher said.

"I'll take you up on that in just a few minutes," Smoke said. He stared at Valdes. "Valdes," he said softly. "The backshooter. Angel told me about you."

Valdes spat on the floor and cussed his former friend until he was near breathless.

"Pat Gilman," Smoke shifted his gaze. "Raped and then

killed your stepsister. Broke jail and killed a deputy in the process."

"You writin' a book, Jensen?" Gilman asked. His face was shiny with pain and fear.

Smoke smiled and looked at Jerry, with his birdshot-peppered face. "One of the women you big brave boys were trying to kill did that to you. I don't know your name."

"Watkins. Jerry Watkins. If I'd a got my hands on that woman, she'da been fun for a couple of days."

"Yeah," Smoke spoke softly. "That's just about what I figured. Scum, all of you."

"I don't take that kind of talk from any man," Valdes said. His voice was high-pitched, and he was sweating. He was in a half crouch, tensed, his hands over his guns.

"Then I guess it's time, Valdes," Smoke uttered the quiet, deadly words. That was his only warning that their time was up. He drew his right-hand .44 and let it bang.

The reports of the .44 were enormous in the room. Smoke fired six times, the shots seeming to be as one long, thundering roar. Valdes took two slugs in his chest and fell back against a wall, his hands empty. Smoke's draw had been so swift that the Mexican gunfighter had not even seen the initial move.

Pat Gilman took a round in his chest and another slug in the hollow of his throat as he was stumbling backward. He went crashing through the window to fall on the feet of those gathered on the boardwalk.

Jerry Watkins did not have to worry about his birdshot-peppered face any longer. He had a bigger hole right in the center of his forehead and another hole in his cheek.

The barroom was very quiet after the thunder of the deadly gunfight. Smoke ejected the empties and they fell tinkling to the floor. He reloaded calmly. No one spoke. No one even moved. Outside, the minister was shouting to the heavens.

"Sweet Jesus," a cowboy breathed. "I never even seen his pull."

The rancher, western-born and western-reared, shook his head in disbelief. Up to this point, he thought he'd seen it all.

The barkeep stood rooted to the floor, his mouth hanging open, his hands on the bar.

Smoke holstered his .44. "They have plenty of money on them," he said to no one in particular. "Von Hausen was paying them well to kill me. You can either give them a fancy funeral, or roll them up in a blanket and dump them into a hole. I don't give a damn." He looked at the rancher. "I'll take my horse over to the stable and see to his needs. Then I'll be back for that beer."

The rancher nodded his head. "My pleasure. Jim, take his horse and see to it, will you?"

"Right now, boss," a cowboy said, and stepped gingerly around Smoke.

"Grain, hay, and have him rubbed down good."

"Yes, sir, Mister Jensen," the cowboy said. "I'll see to it personal."

"Get that crap outta my saloon!" the barkeep finally found his voice. It was high and shrill with excitement. "Drag 'em over behind the barber shop."

Some of the good ladies of the town started singing church songs, still standing on the bloody boardwalk.

"When we heard about this von Hosensnoot feller," the rancher said, "I sent a hand down to the nearest wire office and telegraphed the sheriff's office. Told him I'd be glad to round up some boys and tend to this matter personal. He wired back and told me that couldn't nobody arrest this feller. Is that right?"

"I'm afraid so," Smoke said, sitting down just as the bodies of Valdes and Watkins were being dragged past his table. "I don't really understand it all. Something about being immune from prosecution."

"Well, that don't make a damn bit of sense to me!"

"It doesn't me either. But I guess it's the law." The barkeep sat his mug of beer down on the table, gave Smoke a nod, and quickly backed off.

The church ladies were singing the Lord's praises loudly, as they all trooped across the street, following the men dragging the bodies. The minister, when he'd heard Smoke telling about the dead outlaws having lots of money, was really pouring on the shouting and preaching and planning an elaborate funeral. He followed the singing ladies. A giggling gaggle of young boys and girls followed the minister. A pack of the town's dogs followed the kids, barking and playing and rolling in the dirt. All in all it was quite a parade.

"The sheriff said that you'd probably be in trouble if you killed this von Hossenhoof," the rancher said.

"Well, I'll just have to get in trouble then. 'Cause I'm damn sure going to kill him."

"What about them women?"

Smoke shook his head. "I don't know. I'd sure hate to hurt a woman. If I can help it, I won't." Then he told the rancher about Andrea killing her husband, and how she shot him and left him to die.

"You don't mean it!"

"Sure do. I talked with the fellow for a few minutes before he died. He was a real prince."

"I seen 'em when they come in this mornin'. Them was some hard ol' boys ridin' with the nobility. I recognized John T. and Cat Brown. Funny thing, Smoke, that von Hossenheifer and them folks with him all dressed up like nothin' I ever seen . . . they didn't none of them look crazy." He thought about that; took off his hat and scratched his head. "Well, them hats looked sort of stupid."

"Pith."

"Oh. Sure." He pointed. "It's out back."

"No," Smoke said. "That's what they call those hats."

"You got to be jokin'!"

"No. Pith helmets. P-I-T-H. I think that's the way it's spelled."

"Well, that makes it some better," the rancher said.

"I've got to rest my horse," Smoke said, after draining his mug. "Then get something to eat and rest."

"They may try to recruit more men at the Hole."

"Yeah. They probably will. These people seem to have money to burn. I'll just have to deal with that problem—if it arises—when I come to it." He pushed back his chair and stood up.

The rancher sized him up. 'Bout six, three, and probably two hundred and twenty or thirty pounds. One hell of a big fellow.

Smoke smiled at the man. "Thanks for the beer."

"Luck to you, Smoke."

"What exactly is the Hole?" Gunter asked.

They had camped for the night, eaten supper, and were drinking coffee before turning in.

John T. said, "It's about fifty miles south of a brand new town called Buffalo, and due east of the Powder River. Used to be run by a man called Poker-Face Carey. I don't know whether he's still there or not. It's a shanty town of shacks and a couple of saloons. I'll angle over that way in a couple of days and see if anyone's interested in hookin' up with us."

"How many days to Dodge City?" Marlene asked.

"Long, hard ride, missy," Utah Red said. "I'd hate to even guess. We're days away from Dodge."

"Get ten men," she told John T. "Ten good men who are fast with a gun and who aren't afraid of Smoke Jensen. We'll pay each one a hundred dollars a day and a thousand dollar bonus apiece if they'll get us to Dodge City."

John T. smiled. "I don't except I'll have much trouble gettin' ten pretty good ol' boys."

"One-Eye's there," Gil Webb said. "I know him. And I'm pretty sure Dick Dorman's still there."

"You know Dick?"

"Sure."

"Soon as we hit the Bighorn's, you angle off and beat it for the Hole. We'll meet up on the south fork of the Powder. You know the crossin'?"

Gil nodded.

"I had me a partner once. Name of Slick-Finger Bob. He'll do to ride the river with. He was usin' the Hole 'fore it became so known. Get him if he's there."

"See if an ol' boy named of Barton is there," Paul Melham said. "Henry Barton's his name. Tell him to come on; mention my name."

"Ask around for Sandy Beecher," Utah Red said. "He's a good one, too."

Later, Marlene lay beside von Hausen. They talked in whispers. "Getting to Dodge City is only part of the trip, *mein liebling*," she said. "What happens to us after the men are paid off and gone?"

"Gunter will go in alone. You've noticed the beard he's growing? He'll be dressed like a cowhand. He'll contact that attorney and get the money. We'll pay the men off and one by one go in and catch the train. Jensen will be looking for us east. We won't go east. We'll head back west, to San Francisco, and take the long way home. By the time we get back, all this will have been forgotten."

"I wish we did not have to go to Dodge City. We are placing ourselves in a great deal of danger by doing so."

"So do I. But we couldn't risk taking that much money with us. These desperadoes would have killed us the first night on the trail. I had to set it up this way for our safety. I think with the men from this Hole place, we'll make it. If nothing else they'll buy us some time."

"Do you suppose Valdes and the others might have killed Jensen?"

"I doubt it. But it's a nice thought to go to sleep on, isn't it?"

She laughed. But it was an ugly laugh.

When Smoke crossed the Bighorn River he cut slightly south, skirting the Bighorn Mountains and angling down to catch the stagecoach road that led to the settlement slowly being built around Fort Caspar on the North Platte.

He had a plan, and he thought it would work. Alone, with the big strong Appaloosa under him, he was making about ten miles a day more than those in the large von Hausen party. He'd get to Fort Caspar at least two days ahead of their planned arrival. At Fort Caspar, he would resupply and then head back west and see what damage he could do, plus he wanted to turn the party more north.

Von Hausen would not dare show his face at the Fort, so the only flaw in Smoke's plan was if the party decided to change directions on him. But he didn't think they would do that. They had to have supplies. Von Hausen and party would camp well away from the Fort and send some of their hired guns in for supplies.

Fort Caspar was named for Lt. Caspar Collins, who was killed by Indians while trying to rescue a wagon train. Casper came about due to the misspelling of the railroad clerk who filed the plat for the town.

Gil Webb rode to the Hole and came away with ten salty ol' boys who thought they could handle Smoke Jensen. What they were were thugs and petty thieves and riff-raff and horse-stealing bums. They were good with a gun, give the devil his due, and any of them would kill for the pennies off a dead man's eyes.

Smoke had found a tinker on the stagecoach road who was more than willing to sell him coffee and bacon and flour for inflated prices. Since he did not have to go to Fort Caspar, he headed straight north about the time Gil was leaving the Hole with his band of thugs.

The rendezvous on the Powder was going to be very interesting. And quite lively.

24

"This here's One-Eye Slim," John T. introduced the man to von Hausen.

Von Hausen looked at the man. Both his eyes seemed fine.

"He likes to gouge out the eye of anyone he fights," John T. explained.

"It's my trademark," One-Eye said proudly.

"Wonderful," von Hausen replied. "We all have our little quirks."

He was introduced to Dick Dorman. "He can do a border roll faster than you can blink," John T. said.

Von Hausen and company did not have the foggiest idea what a border roll was and none of them were particularly interested in finding out.

"Slick-Finger Bob," John T. pointed to another man.

Von Hausen waited for some explanation for the nickname.

John T. shrugged his shoulders. "I don't know why they call him that."

Von Hausen sighed.

He was introduced to Henry Barton, Sandy Beecher, Frank Clover, John Flagg, Joe Elliot, Terry Smith, and Ed Clay.

They were the most disreputable-looking human beings Von Hausen had ever seen in all his life. He was loathe to turn his back on them. "We pull out in the morning," he said.

Smoke stopped to chat with a drifting cowboy on the trail.

"They's some bad ol' boys camped up yonder by the crossin'," the cowboy said. "That many bad ones all in a bunch spells trouble for somebody."

"How far ahead?"

"No more'un five miles. You'll see their smoke. Altogether there must be twenty or twenty-five of them. I got the hell outta there."

Smoke thanked him and rode on. When he spotted the smoke from their campfires, he found a good place to picket his horse. Smoke took off his boots and slipped into his worn moccasins. He took the .44-.40 from the second saddle boot and moved out while he still had about an hour of light. He stopped about five hundred yards from the big camp and looked it over.

Then he threw back his head and howled like a great gray timber wolf.

"What the hell!" John Flagg said, as the wild howling came again.

"That ain't no wolf," Utah Red said. "It's real close to it, but not quite."

"Jensen," John T. said. "He's found us."

The howling stopped for a few minutes. Everyone in the camp had armed themselves and taken cover where they could find it.

The howling came again. This time it was coming from a different direction. The men and women in the camp looked at each other nervously.

"He's playin' games," Cat Brown said. "The dirty son is playin' games with us."

"Then he's a damn fool," Dick Dorman said. "One man against all of us. Who the hell does he think he is?" A .44-.40 slug from Smoke's rifle screamed off a rock about two inches from Dick's head. Rock fragments bloodied Dick's face and sent the outlaw hugging the ground. A second slug tore into his exposed boot and shattered his ankle. Dick screamed in pain and doubled up, both hands to his bullet-broken ankle.

Another slug punched a hole in the coffeepot and coffee spewed out into the fire. Another round from the .44-.40 whined wickedly off the big cook pot and started it rocking.

Paul Melham jumped up and jerked his rifle to his shoulder. That move got him a slug right between the eyes that blew out the back of his head. He fell backward without a sound.

"Damnit!" von Hausen yelled from his position behind a tree. "Rush him. Drive him back. If you don't he'll pick us off one at a time. It's our only chance. Come on, let's go!" von Hausen leaped from his position and zigzagged a few yards forward.

The hired guns could not hang back while the man who was paying them risked his life. They charged, running and ducking and twisting.

Smoke faded back and slipped away into the waning light of early evening.

Roy Drum found his tracks. Cautiously, the men followed the tracker. "He's runnin' hard," Drum pointed out. "See how his moccasins is diggin' in? He's way ahead of us."

The men pressed on, cautious, but eager for the kill.

Smoke jumped into the saddle and headed straight back for the camp while the main body of men were a good three quarters of a mile away and getting further. Smoke hit the camp screaming like a wild man.

Marlene shrieked and grabbed for a rifle just as the shoulder of Smoke's horse hit her and knocked her sprawling. She fell hard to the ground, knocking the wind from her.

Smoke rode right over a big tent, the Appaloosa's hooves shredding the canvas and destroying equipment.

Andrea ran screaming from the onslaught. Smoke leaned over in the saddle, grabbed her by the belt and lifted her off the ground. She was wailing in fright. He dumped her unceremoniously on her butt into the river and left her splashing and sputtering and screaming. He turned and headed back for the camp. Maria was lifting a rifle to her shoulder when Smoke started putting rounds from his six-gun into the ground around her feet. She shrieked and made a run for it. She didn't get far.

With the reins in his teeth, Smoke grabbed her by the seat of her pants and turned her flipping and rolling, her aristocratic posterior catching up with her boots. She landed on her belly and went sliding in the dirt.

He stampeded the horses, sending them racing in all directions, then made a final pass through the camp, tearing down the second big tent and dragging it into the fire. The barons and princes and princesses would have to sleep under the stars from now on.

Marlene was just getting to her feet, screaming her rage and calling Smoke some really terrible names, when Smoke turned and raced toward her. She reversed herself and took off. He grabbed her by the shirt collar and dragged her toward the river just as Andrea was reaching shore. He tossed Marlene into Andrea and the two women got dunked.

Smoke headed out, driving the frightened horses ahead of him and screaming like a Comanche.

When the men got back into camp—or what was left of it—they were out of breath from running. Von Hausen jerked his pith helmet off his head and threw it on the ground. "He's taken the women!" he shouted.

"He's damn welcome to 'em," John T. muttered.

"There's two of 'em," Utah Red yelled, pointing to the river.

Marlene and Andrea were climbing out of the river, slopping and sloshing to the bank.

"I'll kill him slow!" Marlene screamed. "I swear it'll take him days to die."

Maria groaned and got to her feet. Her face was skinned from her abrupt hard slide on the ground. Gunter ran to her side. She shoved him aside and screamed, "He put his goddamned hands on me!" she squalled. "Treated me like dirt! *Me!*" She whirled at the men. "Five thousand dollars for the man who kills Smoke Jensen."

"I'll add five thousand more!" screamed Marlene.

"And I'll add five thousand to that!" shrieked Andrea.

"I'd fight a grizzly bear and make love to an Eskimo woman for that," Slick-Finger Bob said. "Or vicey-versey," he added.

"Now, ladies," von Hausen tried to calm them. "Our mission is to get to Dodge City. We simply can't . . ."

"You go right straight to *hell!*" Marlene screamed. "I want Smoke Jensen's . . ."

She named a couple of things she wanted cut from Smoke.

"Whoa!" Montana Jess whispered. "That there's a real mad woman."

Smoke rounded up as many horses as he could and cut the cinch straps off the saddles. Then he slapped them on the rump and sent them running off, free and happy. He emptied out the men's saddlebags and took what food they had and threw the rest of the contents in the river. Then he swung back into the saddle, recrossed the Powder, and found him a good campsite, high up on a mesa and tucked behind some huge boulders.

His supper that night was sandwiches of biscuits and salt

meat he'd taken from someone's saddlebags. He went to sleep smiling at how furious he'd made those fancy women.

There was no placating the women, so von Hausen soon gave up trying. They had been manhandled and humiliated by Jensen, and none of them were forgiving creatures. But, von Hausen thought, sitting and drinking coffee that night, perhaps they were right. The women maintained that they would never reach Dodge City; that Smoke Jensen would track them down and kill them all. That it was just a matter of time.

John Flagg recollected that Smoke had traveled clear across country to New Hampshire one time to settle a score, so why not just deal with him now?

Von Hausen had started to argue that surely Jensen would not come to Europe to settle a score. But he'd shut his mouth before the words could form. Jensen probably would do that.

And von Hausen was going to do something else. He'd set up a code word with the lawyer in Dodge City; a code word that would release the money to the men. A little item he had kept from everyone. As soon as they got to a town with a telegraph office, he'd free up the money and take his party into Canada. They would travel east and sail out of a port there . . . even though he would have to be friendly with those damnable French for a time. He felt better now that that was settled in his mind.

Now all they had to deal with was Smoke Jensen, von Hausen thought ruefully. And for the first time on this long hunt, he admitted—to himself—that he had made a mistake in chasing Smoke Jensen.

Frank Clover felt his guts churn and sweat pop out on his face when the cold voice spoke from behind him.

"Get off your damn horse."

Frank froze in the saddle. He didn't want it in the back. He'd shot men in the back, but he didn't want to go out that way. "I'm gettin' off. Jensen?"

"Yeah. Turn your horse so I can see your moves."

"Whatever you say, Jensen. Slow and easy. You gonna give me a chance?"

"Oh, yeah."

Frank dismounted and turned to face Jensen. Lord, lord, but the man was dangerous looking.

"Slap your horse on the rump," Smoke told him. "Get him out of the way."

Frank slapped his horse and the animal moved off a few yards. He grinned at Smoke. "I don't want to hit him too hard. I'm gonna need him to ride out of here."

"You're not riding anywhere, hombre. This is your last day to do anything. You should have stayed at the Hole."

Frank looked puzzled. How in the hell had Jensen known about that?

"My name's Frank Clover."

"Heard of you. Two-bit thief and back-shooter. Like to slap women around. You're a real brave boy. Drag iron, punk."

Frank tried. He got as far as closing his fingers around the butt of his .45. Two shots rang out, twin lightning and thunder bolts that slammed into his chest and knocked him down. The last thing Frank Clover remembered was that the sky was so blue. So blue . . .

Smoke unsaddled the horse and turned him loose. He left Frank Clover stretched out on the trail. Both his guns were still in leather. He should have listened to his mother and stayed on the farm in Minnesota.

John Flagg found the body and looked nervously around him. He was growing increasingly nervous until Joe Elliot and Terry Smith rode up. That made him feel better.

The howling of a wolf sent chills scampering up and down their spines. The wolf howl came again, and their horses got jittery at the sound.

A rock about the size of a grapefruit came hurling down from a mesa and slammed into Joe Elliot's shoulder, knocking the man to the ground.

"Jesus Christ!" he bellered. "My shoulder's broke. Oh, damn, it hurts."

Another rock about the size of a big fist came flying down and hit Terry Smith in the head, knocking him flat on the ground and unconscious.

John Flagg hit the saddle and got the hell gone from that crazy place.

Joe Elliot looked up and saw Smoke Jensen standing on the rock above him.

"Strip," Smoke told him. "Right down to the skin. Then get your canteen and pour some water on your buddy on the ground."

Elliot peeled down to the pale buff. He was in very bad need of a bath.

"Throw your guns in the bushes," Smoke told them. "Then start hiking."

"This ain't decent!" Elliot hollered.

Smoke jacked back the hammer on his .44. The naked pair started hiking back to camp.

"And take a damn bath when you get to the river," Smoke shouted at them. "You stink!"

Dick Dorman saw them coming. His wound had been cleaned out and his ankle set and he was in camp with the women. "You ladies best turn your heads," he called. "We got some company comin' and they're nekkid as a new born."

"Tell them to take a bath in the river before they come in," Andrea said. She picked up a bar of soap and hurled it at the limping men. "Bathe, goddamnit!" she yelled at them.

Dorman, using a sturdy branch for a crutch, hobbled over to the men's bedrolls and found clothing for them.

"And tell them not to put on those stinking pile of rags until they wash them, too," Andrea screamed.

"Yes'um," Dorman said.

"And it wouldn't hurt you to take a bath, either," Marlene squalled at him.

"Yes'um," Dorman said, thinking for the umpteenth time that day that if he could find his horse he'd leave this crazy bunch 'fore Jensen kilt them all. Never again would he be so stupid as to tie up with anybody who wanted to hunt down Smoke Jensen.

Von Hausen and Gunter rode in and looked at the men, bathing in the river.

"Jensen kilt Frank Clover and took our clothes," Elliot said. "We had to walk back."

Von Hausen had a dozen questions to ask about that. But he only shook his head and walked his weary horse over to the picket line. Marlene met him.

"Any luck?" she asked.

"We couldn't even find his trail," von Hausen admitted. "The man's hid his horse somewhere and is on foot. And he's not leaving any tracks."

All the women were bruised and somewhat the worse for wear after their brief encounter with Smoke, and they were in no mood for excuses.

Marlene said, "We have hunted man-killers all over the world. We have always been successful. Tomorrow, we," she waved at Andrea and Maria, "shall take to the field and show you big, brave men how to hunt."

"Marlene," von Hausen said, his temper barely under control, "as of this moment, I do not give a damn what you ladies do."

Marlene tossed her head and stalked off, Maria and Andrea with her.

Von Hausen had to clench his fists in order not to give the backs of the ladies a very vulgar gesture.

25

Smoke shook his head when he spotted the women the next morning. They were riding without men. Smoke concluded they were either the dumbest females he had ever run into, or just so arrogant they did not realize the danger they were in. He decided on the latter. He flattened out and let them come on. His clothing blended with the earth and Smoke had the patience of an Apache. Ol' Preacher had drilled into his head that many times movement gives away position more than noise.

Smoke did not want to hurt the women. A dunk in the river and a good shaking up was about the limit he was prepared to go with them, even though they were as vicious as any man he had ever encountered. What would he do if they started shooting at him? He didn't know.

As they drew closer, Smoke thought again that this was not his favorite terrain for fighting. He liked the high mountains and deep timber. Where he was now was rocky and sparse. There were peaks here: Roughlock Peak was to his north, Deadman Butte lay to the west, but nothing to compare to the High Lonesome.

Andrea made up his mind.

The women reined up about ten feet from him, and Andrea said, "This is a good spot. I'll stay here. Marlene, you ride on about two hundred and fifty yards. Maria, you ride on an equal distance past Marlene. We've got rocks behind us and a good field of view in front of us. As long as we stay within shouting distance of each other, we'll be fine."

Maria and Marlene rode on. Andrea dismounted. The last thing she would remember for about an hour was something crashing into her jaw and the ground coming up to meet her.

"What the hell do you mean, she's gone?" von Hausen roared.

"I mean she's vanished," Marlene screamed at him. "One minute she was there, the next minute she was gone. The tracks lead straight north."

"Break camp," von Hausen ordered. "Jensen's got her."

The men had found most of their horses and repaired the cinch straps. They quickly saddled up and broke camp. Dick Dorman could sit a saddle. But he had to have help dismounting. He gritted his teeth against the pain and rode. Joe Elliot's left arm was in a sling, and he was hurting something awful. But he followed along, riding Frank's horse. Searchers had found Terry's horse and brought it to him.

Henry Barton was riding a packhorse that had the worst gait of any animal he had ever tried to ride. Sandy Beecher rode a mule that tried to bite him every time he mounted and tried to kick him every time he dismounted.

"You are the most despicable man I have ever met in all my life," Andrea told Smoke. "This is outrageous. I have never been treated like this in my life. This is kidnapping. I will have you arrested."

"Shut up," Smoke told her.

He had tied her hands to the saddle horn and was seriously considering wrapping a sack around her mouth.

"I suppose you intend to violate me," Andrea said.

Smoke looked back at her. "You have to be kidding! I'd sooner bed down with a skunk."

She spat at him. She wasn't a very good spitter. With spit on her chin, she said, "You are certainly no gentleman. You are a brute and a boorish oaf."

"Lady, shut up."

She screamed so loud it hurt Smoke's ears.

"Go right ahead and squall, lady. No one's going to hear you. In case you're interested in geography, that's Roughlock Hill right over there."

"I hate you, I despise you, I loathe you!"

"This is really going to be a fun trip. I can sense that right off."

"Where are you taking me, you pig?"

"To the mountains, lady. I'm glad you had sense enough to bring a coat with you. You're going to need it."

"Why did you kidnap me?"

"So the others will follow."

"I shall have you whipped to death, you barbarian."

"Right, lady."

"If you attempt to violate me I shall give you no satisfaction."

"You're as safe with me as you would be in a nunnery."

"Don't you find me beautiful?"

"In the same way a rattlesnake is pretty."

"These bonds are too tight. My hands hurt."

"My ears hurt."

She cussed him.

"You have a very dirty mouth, lady."

"I'm hungry."

"We'll eat this evening."

"I have to go to the bathroom."

"Later."

She cussed him.

"I'm not so sure this was such a good idea," Smoke muttered.

On the third night out, Andrea finally got it through her head that Smoke was not going to violate her precious wonderful flawless perfect body. And that made her madder than the kidnapping.

The man was infuriating. He seemed to sleep with one eye open. She could not escape because Smoke tied a rope around her waist and the other end to his arm before they went to bed. Three times she'd tried to slip away. Three times Smoke had jerked her back to the ground so hard her eyes crossed, her teeth rattled, and her butt hurt from the impact.

While the fire burned down to coals, Andrea asked, "Why don't you sleep with me tonight?"

"I'm married, lady."

"She isn't here."

"Yes, she is. In my mind."

"Is she beautiful?"

"Yes."

"She probably weighs three hundred pounds and has a head like a hog."

Smoke laughed at her.

"You find me amusing?" she flared at him.

"I find you dangerous, Andrea. Vicious and unfeeling and very dangerous."

"It was only a game, Mister Jensen," she said softly.

"Lady, you people were going to *kill* me."

"When this started, we thought of it as the ultimate hunt. You are depicted as a notorious gunfighter. A killer. We assumed there would be arrest warrants on you. That no one would care if you got killed. We . . ."

"Stop it, Andrea. You're lying. Stop lying. You found out

about me before the hunt started. You could have stopped it before you left Dodge. And you killed that Army patrol. A cold-blooded ambush. So stop lying and making excuses for yourself and your lousy damn friends. And Andrea, I buried your husband. We talked at length before he died. You shot him with that little hide-out gun I took from you. And he didn't die easy."

She refused to meet his eyes. "If you turn me over to the police, I won't be prosecuted."

"I know that. I don't know what I'm going to do with you. But believe this, Andrea if you believe nothing else: if you try to kill me, I'll hurt you."

"Big brave man, aren't you?" she sneered the words at him.

"No. Just a man who is trying to survive. Now shut your mouth and go to sleep."

"And if I don't?"

"I'll stuff a gag in your big mouth."

She lay down and closed her eyes.

"He's leadin' us back into the mountains," Roy Drum said. "Just as sure as hell that's what he's doin'."

"And then? . . ." Gunter asked wearily.

"He'll start killin' us," John T. said, his voice flat. "That's why he grabbed Andrea. So's we'd follow him."

"Heading back to the mountains," von Hausen said, scratching his unshaven chin. "And he'll make his final stand there, won't he?"

"You better believe it," Utah said. "Howlin' and snarlin' and spittin' and scratchin' and shootin'." He looked back at the group. "If any of you boys feel you're comin' down with a case of the yeller belly, git gone now. 'Cause once we git up in the High Lonesome, there ain't gonna be no runnin'."

No one left. They sat their saddles and stared at the man, defiance in their eyes.

"Don't say you wasn't warned," John T. told them. "Let's ride."

Smoke rode through Powder River Pass and took a deep breath of the cool clear air. He smiled, smelling the fragrance of the high country; he was home. Halfway between there and Cloud Peak, he set up his first ambush point, after securing Andrea's mouth so she could not scream and warn her blood-thirsty friends.

She tried to bite him and kick him, but he was expecting that and got her secured with only a small bruise on his shin.

"Now you be a sweet girl," he told her, after stepping out of kicking range.

She bugged her eyes and fought her bonds and tried to kick him again.

"Relax, Andrea. You're making your bonds tighter."

She soon realized he was right and ceased her frantic struggling. She fell back on the ground and glared hate at him.

"Hans was probably glad to die after being married to you," Smoke muttered. He picked up his rifle and moved to a spot several miles away.

Smoke watched the long, single-file column come up the old trail, Roy Drum watching the ground, tracking Smoke like the expert he was. Roy passed within ten feet of Smoke.

Ed Clay was the last man in the column. When the rider in front of him had rounded the sharp bend in the trail—a place Smoke had deliberately chosen—Smoke leaped from the ledge and knocked Ed out of the saddle, clubbing him with a big fist on the way to the ground. He threw Ed across his shoulder, grabbed his rope from his saddle horn, and slapped the horse on the rump, sending it back down the trail. Smoke slipped into the brush and climbed back up to the ledge.

There, he hog-tied Ed and gagged him with the hired

gun's own filthy bandana and picked up his rifle, slipping back into the brush, paralleling the trail.

"I sure will be glad to get shut of this damn mule, Ed," Sandy said. "You wouldn't like to trade off for a spell, would you?"

He got no reply as they rode further into the dimness of thick timber and brush.

"Did you hear me, Ed?" Sandy asked, twisting in the saddle.

Ed wasn't there.

"We got trouble!" Sandy called. He looked up in time to see a stick of dynamite come sputtering out of the ridge above him. "Oh, hell!" he yelled.

The charge blew, the mule walled its eyes and bowed up, and Sandy's butt left the saddle and he went flying through the air. He landed on the west side of the trail and went rolling down the slope, hollering and cussing all the way down. He landed in a creek and banged his head on a rock, knocking him silly.

Marlene's horse reared up at the huge explosion and threw her off. She landed hard and immediately started bellering.

One-Eye's horse fell against the slope and Smoke took aim and conked One Eye on the noggin with a fist-sized rock. One Eye slid off the saddle, out cold.

Smoke added more confusion to the riders on the narrow trail by jerking out his left-hand six-gun and emptying it in the air. Then he threw back his head and howled like a wolf and screamed like a panther. The horses went crazy.

Smoke found some good-sized throwing rocks and started pelting those below him. One cracked von Hausen's pith helmet and knocked the Baron slap out of the saddle. He landed belly down on the edge of the trail and about fifteen seconds later, he joined Sandy in the creek, sitting in the cold water, addled goofy by the blow to his head.

Smoke had had his fun, but he wasn't going to play

games with skilled gunhandlers like John T. and those of the original bunch. He pulled his rifle to his shoulder and blew Tom Ritter out of the saddle. The outlaw was cooling meat when he hit the ground and went slowly tumbling down the slope to the creek.

"Damn you, Jensen!" John Flagg screamed, struggled to get his horse under control and finally managing to jerk his .45 out of leather.

Smoke shot him between the eyes.

John Flagg's horse bolted and ran right over Maria, knocking the woman over the side of the slope. She rolled and tumbled down the bank and hit the creek just as von Hausen was getting to his feet. She hit him squarely across the knees and both of them went under, flailing and waving their arms and slipping and sliding on the slick rocks in the creek.

Smoke lit another stick of dynamite and dropped it to the trail below him. Then he cut out at a fast run through the timber.

The charge blew and knocked Utah Red off his horse. The hired gun went rolling down the slope and slammed into von Hausen and Maria just as they were crawling out of the creek. They returned to the creek.

Slick-Finger Bob was tossed out of the saddle and landed on his belly on the trail. He had just enough wind left in him to roll frantically off the trail to avoid having his head smashed by the hooves of the panicked horses. He felt himself going over the edge and grabbed at an ankle. Marlene's ankle. The two of them went over the side of the steep embankment and began the fast tumble down.

Von Hausen had just enough wind left him to crawl up the bank of the creek. He almost made it. Slick-Finger Bob and Marlene banged into him and knocked him clear to the other side of the fast-rushing mountain stream. Von Hausen's head hit a rock and he was out.

The mountain trail grew quiet. John T. peeped around a

tree trunk and took in the sight before him. Two men were down and dead as a hammer. Tom Ritter lay on his belly and John Flagg was on his back, a hole right between his eyes. One-Eye looked dead; then John T. saw his fingers began to twitch. A whole bunch of people appeared to be in the crick below, squallin' and bellerin' and cussin' and hollerin' for help. John T. couldn't see Ed Clay nowheres. Dick Dorman had been tossed from his horse and landed on his bad ankle. He had passed out from the pain.

John T. motioned toward Cat Brown to take the south end of the trail while he climbed the bank on the north end. It only took a couple of minutes for them to see that Jensen was gone.

Marlene had crawled up the slope, her eyes wild with hate and fury, her mouth working overtime, spewing out every cuss word she knew in several languages. She was mud from head to boots.

John T. looked around and finally found his horse and tied a rope to the saddle horn, dangling the other end down to the creek. "Tie it around his majesty's shoulders," John T. called. "We'll pull him up."

"What about me!" Maria shrieked.

"Drag your own ass up here," John T. muttered, "We'll git to you," he hollered. "Just take it easy."

Von Hausen was hauled up the slope. He lost his boots and his pants during the salvage effort.

Slick-Finger Bob was crawling up the slope, pushing Maria ahead of him.

"Get your hands off my backside!" she screamed at him.

"Well, goddamnit, lady, what else am I gonna push against?"

"Don't touch me!"

"All right," Slick-Finger said, and removed his hands and got out of the way.

Maria hollered all the way back down.

26

Smoke put the muzzle of a .44 against Ed Clay's head. "I'll give you a choice, partner," Smoke told him. "Leave or die. What's it going to be?"

"You give me a chance, Mister Jensen, and I'm gone. I won't join up with the others. You don't have to give me a horse, a gun, or nothin'. Just let me leave and you'll never see me again."

"Head straight east," Smoke told him. "There's a settlement on the Clear. If I see you in these mountains, I'll kill you."

"The only people that's gonna see me from now on is my momma and daddy, back in Nebraska."

"Get gone."

Ed Clay got gone. Smoke doubted he'd return to Nebraska, but he also felt he'd never see the man again.

Smoke tossed Andrea into the saddle, tied her hands, and swung aboard his Appaloosa. He headed north, deeper into the Bighorns.

* * *

"Found Ed's horse," Henry Barton said. "But there ain't a sign of Ed."

The camp looked like a field hospital. Dick Dorman and von Hausen were stretched out side by side. Maria was off to one side, badly shaken and bruised up from her trips to the creek. Utah Red had hurt his leg on the way down the slope and was bitching and moaning. Slick-Finger Bob had a cut on his face and a knot on one knee. Sandy was still addled and acting goofy from his head impacting against a rock. One-Eye had a egg-sized lump on his noggin from Smoke's thrown rock.

Marlene finally got von Hausen awake and was pouring hot soup down his throat. Roy Drum had retrieved von Hausen's boots and pants, falling into the creek himself. The pith helmet was ruined, cracked wide open.

Gunter knelt down beside von Hausen. "Two dead," he told him. "Ed Clay's missing. Several of the men are injured, but not seriously."

Von Hausen coughed up creek water. "The spirit of the men?" he questioned.

"As long as we keep paying them, they'll continue."

"We'll continue," von Hausen said. "As long as he has Andrea, we really have no choice, now, do we?"

Cat Brown rode back in and swung down. "I found Jensen's tracks. He's headin' straight north. The woman's still with him."

"And leaving tracks a fool could follow," von Hausen said, not putting it as a question.

"That's right, boss."

"We'll rest here and push on at first light."

Marlene glanced at him. There was a grimness in his voice that she had never heard before. She wondered what it meant.

* * *

"When are you going to turn me loose?" Andrea asked.

Supper was over. She had the rope around her waist; the knots so tight she had broken off her nails trying to loosen them—to no avail.

"When the hunt is over," Smoke told her.

"You mean, after you've killed them all."

"I didn't kill that fellow this morning, now, did I?"

"I could talk to Frederick. I'm sure he would cease immediately once he sees I am safe and unhurt."

"Frederick is mine," Smoke told her. "I'm going to kick his face in."

"You!" she said mockingly. "Frederick will destroy you. He is a skilled pugilist."

"We'll see."

"I've seen him fight two men at once and whip them both."

"Good for him. In a ring?"

"Certainly. One of Frederick's opponents would tire and the other would come in."

"Rules to it, hey?"

"But of course."

"I'll have to say a little prayer before bed tonight that when we do lock horns, Frederick doesn't beat me up too bad."

"Now you're being sarcastic."

"Go to sleep, your ladyship. Tomorrow is going to be very exciting."

Sandy Beecher heard a rustling behind him. He left the saddle and stared hard at the thick brush. The mid-morning was cloudy and cool, with the skies looking like rain. The bushes did not move again.

For the first time he noticed the thin vine that stretched across the trail. From ground level, he could see that it was attached to the bush that had moved. Sandy got to thinking on that. Now if the vine was attached to the bush, that meant that whoever jerked on it was . . .

"Oh, hell," he muttered. "Behind me."

"That's right," Smoke whispered. "You're a mighty young man to die."

"Do I have a choice?"

"You might. That's up to you."

"The others are fanned out all over this mountain, lookin' for you. You let me get back on my horse, and I'm gone. That's a promise."

"Why should I believe you?"

" 'Cause I'm tellin' you the truth. Where's Ed Clay?"

"If he's not dead on the trail, he told me he was heading back to Nebraska."

"That's him. Me and him was pards. You let me go and you'll never see me no more, Mister Jensen. Never."

"Tell me about the others."

"They're bad ones. They got big money in their eyes. I got me a couple hundred dollars from that Baron or whatever he is, and that's enough to get me back to Missouri."

"That your home state?"

"Sure is! About thirty miles east of Springfield."

"I was born not far from there."

"You don't say? You know the Blanchard's?"

"Doc Blanchard tended to my ma when she was sick."

"Well, I'll just be damned. He's my momma's brother."

"He still alive?"

"Was when I left, about five year ago."

"Tell him Emmett Jensen's youngest boy said howdy."

"I'll sure do it. Smoke?"

"Yes. Them others'll kill you if you get careless. I've stole from time to time, but I ain't never killed nobody."

"I hope you never do. Take off."

"You want my guns?"

"No."

Smoke watched him leave, and true to his word, Sandy headed south without so much as looking back.

Smoke stood up and began stalking those who hunted

him. Henry Barton sat his gray and studied the stillness of the timber. He wished Jensen would step out and challenge him. He'd like to be the man who killed Smoke Jensen. He could write his own ticket after he done that. "Looking for me," the voice came from off to his left.

Henry knew he'd been suckered. He was right-handed, and Smoke had studied him, waiting for just the right moment. If he drew now, he'd be shooting across his body. "Jensen?"

"That's me."

"Do I get to turn my horse?"

Smoke chuckled. "Why sure you do."

Henry said to hell with it and jerked iron. Smoke's .44-.40 roared and Henry was knocked from the saddle, the slug taking him just under his rib cage and blowing out the other side.

Terry Smith came galloping up the mountains trail, hollering for his buddy. He reined up when he saw the gray, standing riderless in the timber.

"Here I am," Smoke called.

Terry cussed, wheeled his horse and lifted his six-shooter. Smoke blasted him out of the saddle, the big slug taking him in the center of his chest.

Smoke faded back into the brush on the mountain and jogged to a small knoll set in the middle of the timber. He punched two more rounds into his rifle and eared the hammer back, waiting.

A yell came to him, faint but understandable. "This here's Dick Dorman, Jensen. Joe Elliot's with me. We're gone. You hear me, Jensen. I got a broke ankle and Joe's shoulder is busted and tore up. We're out of it and gone."

"This ain't no trick, Jensen," Joe hollered. "We're headin' back to the Hole. Just let us pass and you won't hear no more from us."

Two rifles crashed. Smoke heard the sounds of bodies falling to the earth.

"Good shooting, darling," von Hausen said.

"And the same to you, sweet," Marlene said.

Smoke shook his head. Fine people to work for, he thought. Very caring about the hired help.

Montana Jess, Gil Webb, John T., Cat Brown, Utah Red, and Roy Drum were by now old hands at chasing Smoke. None of them were about to expose themselves and enter those dark woods. But the two left of the men from the Hole just weren't that smart. Slick-Finger Bob thought he was slicker than he was. He slipped into the timber unseen, so he thought. It was his last thought.

Smoke drilled him at two hundred yards, the slug punching right through Slick-Finger Bob's head.

"I'm a-gonna tear both your eyes out, Jensen!" One-Eye called. "Then I'm gonna let you stagger around blind a couple hours 'fore I shoot you."

What a nice fellow, Smoke thought. I wonder what he does for an encore?

"Jensen!" he hollered. "You're surrounded. You can't get away. Step on out here and fight me."

Smoke picked up a rock and tossed it to his right. It thudded to the ground and One-Eye fired. Smoke put three fast rounds in the area of the gunsmoke. One-Eye staggered out, both hands holding his belly. He grunted in pain and slumped to the earth. He was still on his knees when Smoke backed out and disappeared into the lushness of the timber.

John T. sighed. "Anybody seen Sandy?"

"Not since breakfast," Montana told him.

"Well, that means he's either dead or pulled out."

"Do we go in there after him?" Utah asked.

"Not me," John T. said. He slipped back and into the timber on the other side of the game trail Smoke had been using. One by one, the others joined him.

They grouped together, very conscious of the bodies of Dorman and Elliot, lying not thirty feet away, back-shot by their employers.

"Comes a time, boys, when a man's got to use some common sense," John T. said. "Personal, I think we should have used it about a month ago."

"What are you sayin', John?" Gil asked.

"That it's time for us to go. We got some money out of this. More'un we'd have made in five years ordinarily. Boys, we've left bodies all over the place durin' this so-called hunt. It's time to pull out."

"That's what Dorman and Elliot tried to do," Cat pointed out.

"That ain't gonna happen to us, now that we know what to expect."

"How about our money down in Dodge?" Gil asked.

"Hell with it. We can take that check that Miss Hoity-Toity wrote us back yonder in the park. How about it?"

"You boys go on," Roy Drum said. "I want Jensen and the real big money."

"It ain't worth dyin' for, Roy."

"I'm with Roy," Cat Brown said. "But we'll see to it that you don't get back-shot."

"I'm stayin'," Utah Red said.

"I'm goin'," Montana Jess said.

"I'm with Montana and John T.," Gil Webb said.

The six men walked over to von Hausen. "I'll take that big money check you offered back in the park," John T. said. "We're pullin' out."

"Who is 'we'?" Gunter asked.

"Me, Montana, and Gil. Hand over the check."

Von Hausen noticed that the gunfighter's hand was close to the butt of his six-gun. He reached into his jacket and took out a waterproof pouch and opened it. He handed John T. the check.

John T. looked at it, then folded it and put it in his pocket. "Thank you kindly, von Hausen. Roy and Utah and Cat will see to it that you good folks don't back-shoot us on the way out. Adios, ladies and gents."

Several long moments ticked by before anyone spoke. The sounds of the hired-guns' horses faded into silence as the men left on the trail south. Finally, Gunter said, "Does anybody have a plan?"

"Hire more men?" Marlene asked.

"Forget it," Utah told her. "No time for that."

"I think I'll make a pot of coffee and fry up some bacon," Roy Drum said. "What about them bodies?"

"Push 'em over the side of that ravine yonder," Cat said. "I don't feel like diggin' no damn holes."

"We don't have a shovel anyways," Utah pointed out. "It got lost yesterday when Jensen ambushed us."

Roy built a fire while Utah and Cat hauled the bodies away and shoved them over the side, into the ravine. Roy had the bacon frying when the men returned.

"It might work," von Hausen said, looking at the trio of gunslickers. "Those are the hardest of the hardcases. We're a very small force now, and we'll be able to move faster and much more quietly."

He looked up, then stood up. He thought he'd heard a very faint yell.

"What's the matter?" Maria asked.

"I thought I heard something. A yell. Yes. I'm sure I did." The faint yelling reached them all.

"That's Andrea," Gunter said. "She escaped!"

"I doubt it," Utah said, not getting up from his position by the fire. "Jensen probably got tired of listenin' to her complain and cut her loose."

"You men go get her," von Hausen ordered.

"You hired us to kill Jensen," Roy said. "Not find lost females. Just give a shout or two. She'll wander over here."

"Heartless brutes," Marlene said.

"Right, lady," Utah replied.

Von Hausen and party began shouting and waving their arms and jumping up and down. After a few minutes, Andrea staggered in, collapsing by the fire, telling all sorts of wild stories about being beaten and raped by Smoke Jensen.

"You're a goddamn liar," Roy Drum said flatly. "He wouldn't touch the likes of you with a coup stick. I hate Smoke Jensen, but he never raped no woman in his life. I'd be willin' to bet everything I own he ain't never even been unfaithful to his wife. So why don't you just shut your lyin' damn mouth."

Andrea glared hate at the man, but she said no more about being assaulted. She slurped at a cup of coffee and said, "He said he was going to whip you in a fight, Frederick. Said he was going to kick your face in."

"Nonsense!" von Hausen said. "The man has better sense than to think he could best me in a ring. I've fought the best of fighters and never lost. He was just blowing off steam, that's all."

"Don't tangle with Jensen in a fistfight," Utah said. "'Cause you'll lose."

"Ridiculous!" von Hausen snorted.

Utah shrugged his shoulders. "Don't say you wasn't warned."

"What else did he say, Andrea?" Gunter asked, getting a blanket and draping it around her shoulders. The day was growing increasingly cool and damp.

"That tomorrow you all die."

27

It was a sensation, an emotion, that all skilled gun-handlers experience at one time or the other; that feeling of knowing that today is the day.

Utah and Cat and Roy knew it. They did not speak of it, but each knew the other was sharing the emotion.

Cat almost dropped his coffee cup when the wild howling of a wolf cut the early morning air. It was from the throat of someone very close to the camp.

"Let's do it!" Roy Drum said. "Let's by God get this over with once and for all."

He picked up his rifle and walked to the edge of the timber that surrounded the camp. A single shot rang out. Roy slumped to his knees and leaned up against a tree. His rifle fell from his lifeless fingers.

Cat looked at Utah. Both men shook their heads. They rose as one and saddled their horses.

"What are you men doing?" Marlene screamed at them.

"Pullin' out, lady," Utah told her.

"What about your money?" von Hausen asked. There was

a tremor in his voice that no one among them had ever heard before.

"I 'spect that John T. knows a way to shake it out of that Dodge City lawyer feller. If he don't, I do," Cat said. He rolled his blankets and groundsheet and tied it back of his saddle.

"Smoke!" Utah called. "Me and Cat are the only ones left. We're pullin' out. I'd be obliged if you'd keep these foreigners from back-shootin' us."

"I'll do that," the call came from the damp woods. "I let a couple of others go. I'll do the same for you boys."

" 'Preciate it. See you around, Smoke."

"I hope not," Smoke called. " 'Cause when you do, you better drag iron."

"It was just a job of work," Utah called.

"Get out of here before I change my mind," Smoke called.

They got.

"Either strap on guns or toss them all in a pile," Smoke called.

"Kill him, Gunter!" Maria yelled, grabbing at his arm. "Kill the arrogant bastard."

But Gunter had lost the taste for the hunt. He unbuckled his belt and let his sidearm fall to the ground.

"You coward!" Maria screamed at him. She jerked up a pistol and emptied it into the dark timber.

"You missed, lady," Smoke told her, his voice coming from behind her.

Marlene grabbed up a rifle and fired at his voice, working the lever until the weapon was empty.

"Over here," Smoke called, from a new location.

Andrea put her face into her hands and began sobbing.

Marlene threw the rifle to the ground and stood trembling with rage.

"The Army's coming," Smoke called. "I saw the patrol about an hour ago from a ridge. They had some rough country to get through, so I figure they'll be here in about an hour or so. Then I'll do what somebody should have done a long time ago."

"And what is that?" von Hausen called.

"Stomp your damned guts out."

Von Hausen laughed at him. "I accept your challenge, gunfighter. But why wait until the Army gets here? I don't understand that."

"Because I don't trust any of you back-shooting bastards and bitches."

Von Hausen removed his gunbelt and tossed it to one side. "All of you, put your weapons in a pile. Every weapon. All the military can do is escort us to the ship. We might as well have some fun waiting for them to get here."

Every weapon, including hunting knives was piled onto a blanket. Von Hausen pointed to a long flat rock about three feet high. "All of you sit over there," he told his friends. "And do not, under any circumstances, try to assist me in any way during this brief boxing match." He raised his voice. "Is that satisfactory, Mister Jensen?"

"Suits me," the voice came from behind von Hausen and it startled him. Smoke hung his gunbelt on a limb and pulled on a pair of leather work gloves.

"We'll now set the rules," von Hausen said.

"No guns or knives," Smoke said. "Those are the rules. No time limit, no neutral corner, no knockdown rules. So anytime you're ready, you pompous, overbearing, arrogant jackass, come on and fight."

Von Hausen assumed the boxer's stance: his left fist held out from his body, elbow bent, his right fist up, protecting his jaw. "You may approach and make the initial move, Jensen."

"OK," Smoke said, then jumped at the man and hit him in the face with both fists.

Von Hausen backed up, not really hurt, just startled at such a move. He flicked an exploring punch at Smoke.

Smoke ducked it and busted von Hausen in the belly. That got Smoke a hard fist to the side of his head. Smoke spun around and kicked von Hausen on the knee. The German yelped and backed up.

"Oh, foul, foul!" Gunter yelled.

Smoke ignored them and pressed von Hausen, hitting him with a combination that bloodied the man's mouth. Smoke followed that with a hard left to the man's belly. The German tried to clench. Smoke threw him down to the dirt and backed up.

Von Hausen jumped to his boots and charged Smoke. Smoke tripped him and clubbed the man's neck on his way down. The German got up, spitting dirt. Now he was mad, which is exactly what Smoke wanted.

"You peasant!" von Hausen hissed at him.

Smoke put one of his peasant's fists through the nobleman's guard and busted von Hausen's regal nose, sending blood flying. Smoke ducked a punch and waded in, smashing both fists against the man's belly and landing a vicious uppercut that snapped von Hausen's teeth together. The German was having to breathe through his mouth; his honker was busted.

Smoke caught a fist to the side of his head, another got through: a glancing blow on his jaw. Smoke back-heeled von Hausen and sent the man crashing to the rocky ground. Von Hausen came up snorting and bellowing. He came at Smoke, both big fists flailing the air. Smoke caught von Hausen's forearm, turned slightly, and flipped the heavier man, sending him hard to the ground.

With a roar, von Hausen was up and trying to get set. Smoke never let him. Smoke stepped in and smashed the man's face with hard left's and right's. The blows staggered von Hausen and tore his face. Smoke timed one perfectly and sent von Hausen to the ground, on his hands and knees.

"Time, time!" Gunter yelled.

"Shut your damned mouth," Smoke told him.

Gunter shut up.

"Get up, Baron," Smoke said. Then all the rage he had kept under control for weeks boiled to the surface. He cussed the man, calling him every filthy name he could think of. And being raised among mountain men, he knew more than the average fellow.

The Baron was a little slow getting up. Smoke kicked him in the belly, the blow lifting the man off his hands and knees about six inches. Von Hausen rolled and slowly got to his feet. He raised his hands and Smoke started a punch about a foot behind his shoulder and gave it to von Hausen. The German's teeth flew from his mouth under the right fist and Smoke tore one ear off with a thundering left that whistled through the air. It sounded like a pistol shot when it landed.

When the man was sinking down to his knees, Smoke came under his jaw with an uppercut. All present could hear the jaw pop when Smoke hit him. Frederick von Hausen hit the cool damp earth and did not move. Marlene screamed and ran to his side.

Smoke walked over to Gunter and before the startled man could move, Smoke knocked him slap off the rock. Gunter tumbled over the flat rock and lay unconscious on the ground.

Smoke pointed a finger at Maria and Andrea. "If you two even so much as twitch, I'll shoot you." He walked over to von Hausen, jerked off the man's wide leather belt and grabbed Marlene by her long blonde hair. He dragged her over to the rock, sat down with her across his knees, and proceeded to give her fanny a long overdue beating with the belt.

When Smoke finally released the woman, her screaming had been reduced to low whimpering moans of pain. He knew he had blistered her butt; he also knew it would be a long, painful ride for Miss Marlene, sitting a saddle out of the mountains.

"You brute!" Maria hissed at him.

Smoke smiled and jerked her across his knee. He gave

her fanny the same workout he had given Marlene's derriere, reducing the woman's squallings to tiny whimperings for mercy. When he finished, he dumped her on the ground and dangled the belt for Andrea to see.

"You have anything to say to me?"

She shook her head and kept her mouth shut.

Gunter was moaning and crawled around on his hands and knees, his mouth a bloody mess. He got to his feet, leaning against the rock for support. He didn't need it.

"Oh, no," Gunter said as Smoke approached him.

"Oh, yeah," Smoke said, and popped him again. Gunter kissed the ground.

The Army patrol, which had arrived at the scene just seconds after Smoke and Frederick squared off, and whose members had thoroughly enjoyed every moment of the thrashing and spankings, rode into the clearing.

"Captain Williams, sir," the officer said, saluting Smoke. "We've come to escort these people to the nearest train depot and to see that they leave this country."

"You can sure have them," Smoke said. "No way they can be held accountable?"

"I don't think so, Mister Jensen. Their families have a lot of political influence in this country. Statesmen and diplomats and that sort of thing."

Smoke told the Captain about Hans and where he was buried. "I'll write Prince Hans Brodermann's parents personally. He really wasn't a bad sort of fellow."

"Why did he get mixed up with this bunch?"

Smoke looked over at the now not quite so haughty Marlene. "Well, I reckon, Captain, that the man had a good eye for horses and mighty poor judgment when it came to picking friends."

EPILOGUE

Smoke rode into Sheridan and sent a wire to Sally, assuring her that he was all right. He told her he was going to ride back to the Sugarloaf, sit on their front porch, play with his dogs, and wait for her to join him. He closed with: *I'll stay here in town and wait for your reply.*

The next morning, over breakfast, a boy brought him the reply from Sally. It read: *Taking next train. Will be there long before you. I'll play with the dogs. You can play with me. Love, Sally.*

THE FIRST
MOUNTAIN MAN:
BLOOD ON THE
DIVIDE

PROLOGUE

He was called Preacher. No one knew his real name. Sometimes even he had difficulty remembering it. He had left his home in the settled East as a boy and had never been back. He'd been to St. Louie several times, but that was as far east as he'd chosen to go. His preferred home was the mountain wilderness, the High Lonesome, the Big Empty.

He was called Preacher because he had, years back, been taken captive by a warring tribe, and when he saw they were about to torture him to death, he started preaching. He preached all day and all that night. The Indians finally concluded he was crazy and let him go. He'd been Preacher ever since and he was known from the far north of Canada down to the deserts of the Southwest, from the Mississippi to the Pacific. He was also known as one hell of a bad man to tangle with.

Preacher was not a big man, more of average height for his time. But he possessed great upper-body strength. He was lean-tripped and whang-leather tough. He was handsome in a rugged sort of way. He was of the breed called mountain man.

Those men roamed the western wilderness for a few decades, then vanished into history. When the fur trade played out, most drifted on into obscurity. A few did not. Preacher was one who did not. Preacher saw the writing on the wall about furring and gave it up long before many did.

He wasn't worried about making a living. If he never saw another gold coin again, he would survive. He could do everything there was to do in the wilderness, and had done most of it. He could pan for gold (Preacher always kept a small sack of gold for hard times), scout for the Army, or lead a wagon train through. He could catch wild horses and break them (he preferred to gentle-break them), and he even knew how to farm. But that was at the bottom of his list of things to do.

He thought he was about thirty-five years old. Give or take a year or two.

And he knew or had known most of the famous and infamous mountain men of his time. Jedediah Strong Smith. Joe Walker. Bridger. Beckwourth. The Cherokee-Negro Ed Rose, who became a Crow chief with a harem of four wives. Old Bill Williams, that sour and secretive man who was more than once accused of cannibalism. Kit Carson, who could write only his own name and read nothing at all but yet became a brigadier general in the U.S. Army. Hugh Glass, who was badly mauled by a grizzly but took so long to expire, his friends got tired of waiting around for him to croak and left him to die alone. But Hugh fooled them. He managed to crawl to a Sioux village and the Indians nursed him back to health. Mountain men were notoriously hard to kill. Preacher knew them all and they respected him.

While Preacher was by no means the very first mountain man, he certainly was there during the heyday, and lasted long after that chapter was closed and all but forgotten. Preacher was the first white man to see many areas of the West. He rode trails that before him had been ridden only by

Indians. Preacher named creeks and rivers and the names stand today.

Indians still sing songs about Preacher. And some say Preacher still rides the ghost trails of the High Lonesome.

BOOK ONE

Put your faith in God, my boys, and keep your powder dry.
Valentine Blacker

1

Preacher had been smelling smoke for a couple of days, and when the plumes finally came into view, he had steeled his mind and stomach to the horrible sight of dead and mutilated and tortured bodies of men and women and children.

Too damn many people in their wagon trains trying to move west and getting themselves ambushed by hostiles. "This land ain't ready for settlers," Preacher muttered, as he rode up toward the crest of a ridge. "Why in the hell don't people see that?"

He topped the ridge and stared in utter disbelief. No burning wagons here. No tortured and savaged bodies. He couldn't believe his eyes. It was a damn settlement. A diddly-damned settlement right in the middle of nowhere. He counted the houses. Five houses and a big, long log building that was probably some sort of community meetin' house that also served as church and schoolhouse.

Disgustin'.

Preacher had seen some white folks just last week, and now he'd run up on some more. The wilderness was fillin' up faster than a city. Why in the hell didn't people stay to home?

Preacher stayed just inside the stand of timber on the ridge and thought that if this kept up, in two, three more years they'd be a damn road all the way from New York State to the blue of the Pacific. Women a-flappin' their dress tails and shakin' their bustles and a-battin' their eyes and doin' all them other strange things that women is prone to do when a man is around, and they'd have hoards of squallin' kids a-runnin' around and farmers cuttin' up the land and growin' things. And the Injuns would get all riled up and go on the warpath and they'd be graveyards fillin' up faster than who'd a thunk it.

Pitiful. Made Preacher sick to his stomach just thinking about it.

"Horse," he said to Hammer, "do we want to go down yonder and listen to a whole passel of nonsense out of the mouths of them pilgrims?"

Hammer swung his head around and gave Preacher a very dirty look. Hammer didn't like people no more than Preacher did. Although neither man nor beast disliked humans as much as he let on.

Preacher swung down from the saddle and stretched, then squatted down on the ground, eyeballing the settlement from his position on the ridge. He had to admit, though, that somebody among the movers had them an eye for land and had picked them a right nice spot to light. There was a pretty little creek runnin' soft and sweet nearby, with stands of cottonwood and willow and oak and elm dotted all about. Preacher guessed that Fort William was about forty miles away. He'd been figurin' on meetin' up with some ol' boys there and gettin' drunk and tellin' lies and dancin' and shootin' and lots of other good stuff.

But this totally unexpected sight had shaken him right down to his moccasins. He couldn't figure just what the hell these folks was doin' out here. The summers were hotter than the fringes of hell and the winters were brutal. This wasn't crop land. Preacher figured those folks down yonder could raise kids, but that was about it.

"Just ride on around these crazy folks," Preacher muttered. "Leave them be. 'Cause if you ride down yonder, they gonna be askin' your opinion on matters and wantin' you to stay and help out and they'll be some white woman, sure as hell, without no man, and she'll be sashayin' around a-winkin' and a-gigglin' and a-wigglin' this and that and knowin' you, boy, you'll be trapped down there for the winter." Which was a long way off, since it was early spring.

The mountain man called Preacher shook himself like a big dog and stared down at the settlement. It was either '38 or '39—he wasn't sure. So that made him about thirty-five or thirty-six—he wasn't sure about that either. Close enough.

There was a grimness on his tanned face as he stared at the homes below him. He could just about predict with deadly accuracy what was going to happen to them folks down yonder. And that was something he didn't like to think about because of the kids. Preacher rubbed his smoothly shaven face. He'd shaved his beard off, leaving only a moustache. This time of year fleas tended to gather in a woolly beard.

Preacher had gotten shut of people last fall, leaving them over to Fort Vancouver. Missionary types, come to spread the good word to the savages. He'd spent a quiet and peaceful winter holed up in a favorite cabin of his and he was in no mood to put up with another bunch of silly pilgrims who should have stayed back in Pennsylvania or New York or wherever the hell they came from.

Movement caught Preacher's eyes and he shifted his gaze without moving his head. Hammer's head came up and his ears were pricked. "Steady, ol' hoss," Preacher said. "They ain't Injuns, but I 'spect they ain't up to no good. Not the way they're movin' so quiet like."

The half dozen riders were approaching the settlement from the northeast, keeping the line of trees along the creek between the buildings and themselves. And taking great pains to do that, too, Preacher noted. The buckskin-clad mountain man remained where he was, watching the valley below him. Pretty little valley it was, too. The settlers had them plowed-up gardens about to sprout, and milk cows and goats and chickens and the like. Sure looked to Preacher like they'd come to stay. During the time he'd squatted on the knoll, he had counted five growed-up men, eight filled-out females, four good-sized teenagers, and what looked to be a whole tribe of kids. Two of the women were ample ladies. Didn't appear to Preacher that none of them folks down yonder had ever missed a meal; but them two ladies in particular would near about take a whole bolt of cloth to make just one of them a dress. Well . . . not quite, but close. Howsomever, ample ladies could keep a man warm in the winter and cool in the summer. They give off lots of shade.

Preacher leaned against his Hawken rifle and watched as the half dozen riders reined up, still hiding behind the line of trees, and dismounted, just like if anyone was watchin', it would appear that they was gonna have them a drink and a rest by the creek. But Preacher didn't believe that for a second.

"They ain't up to no good, Hammer," he said. Then with a sigh, he stood up and stepped into the saddle, taking up the lead of his packhorse. Staying in the timber, Preacher angled around and headed toward the creek. When he reached the banks, he cut north and headed into the cottonwoods and stopped. He was curious as to what the suspicious-acting riders were up to. But he thought he had him a pretty good hunch. Preacher was close enough to the settlement to hear the sounds of children playing and the laughter of a woman. He could also smell bread that was fresh baked. Got his mouth to watering, for he was mighty low on supplies. He could just about taste hot bread all smeared with butter and a tall glass of milk from the coolness of the well ledge.

"Well, hell, Hammer," he said as he moved his horse out of the trees and toward the cabins. "Might as well go on up and be sociable. I ain't forgot all my upbringin'."

The riders had moved out of the trees. "If they was decent folks, Hammer, they'd have already made their presence known, so I got to figure they ain't nothin' but a pack of highwaymen who run out of highways back East and come out here to rob and kill. I reckon we'll see about that in a short enough time."

Preacher sat his saddle and waited. He had him a hunch the riders would pretty soon ride on into the settlement, all smiles and howdy-do's, and then when the settlers was unexpected of it, they'd jump them.

Then it came to him. Six riders. The Pardee brothers. Sure. That pack of no-counts from Ohio. Least that's where they claimed to have been whelped. Preacher wasn't sure about that. The Pardee brothers was so sorry, he doubted any woman would have the nerve to lay claim to them.

He heard their ponies splash across the creek, and leaving his packhorse in the trees, Preacher rode Hammer straight up into the clearing on the knoll, arriving a couple of minutes before the Pardees could make it. Men and women and kids all rushed up to meet him. Once they saw he wasn't an Indian. Preacher noticed with some degree of satisfaction that the men were all armed. That meant they wasn't all totally ignorant.

"You got a bunch of scalawags ridin' up here, folks. Don't trust 'em and don't present your backs to 'em. I think it's the Pardee brothers. And them's the sorriest pack of white trash that ever sat a saddle on a stole horse."

The children all stared wide-eyed at Preacher. They had probably never seen a mountain man before, for if that breed of man did not wish to be seen, he wasn't. Preacher's old black hat was battered and had a musket-ball hole in it. He was dressed all in buckskins and wore high-top leggin's. Behind the sash around his lean waist were two .50 caliber pistols. On holsters attached to the saddle were two more pistols of like kind. He carried one of the biggest knives any of the children—or the adults—had ever seen. It had been hand made for him by a top knife maker in New Orleans. The scabbard for the razor-sharp blade was beaded and very elaborate.

"Riders coming, Pa," a boy who looked to be about fifteen said.

"Yep," Preacher said, twisting in the saddle and eyeballing the riders. "It's them damn worthless Pardees all right. Do anyone here know what year it might be?"

"It's 1838, friend," a man said.

"I was close," Preacher muttered.

"Hallo the settlement!" came the call from down on the flats. "We're friendly and white."

"Just like I figured," Preacher said. "They comin' in all smiles and grins, and when they get you to trust them, they'll cut your throats and have their way with the women." He looked at several girls, ten or eleven years old. "And with them, too. Don't doubt it none."

"Why should we believe you?" a haughty-sounding lady asked. One of the ample ones.

"Ain't no reason to," Preacher told her. " 'Ceptin' I'm known from Missouri to Oregon as a man of my word." He swung down from the saddle, Hawken in hand, and flipped the reins to a youngster. "Stable him safe 'fore the shootin' starts. If it starts. And be careful. He bites and kicks." He faced the line of approaching riders. "Malachi Pardee!" he shouted. "Hold it right there, you snakehead."

The riders abruptly stopped. "Who you be, friend?" the call came from the line.

"I damn shore ain't your friend, Malachi," Preacher called. "You or none of them damn worthless brothers of yours. Now you hear me, Malachi, you'll not snolly-goster these good folks like you done them poor movers up on the Paintrock."

"I don't know what you mean, friend!" Malachi called, standing up in the stirrups, trying to see who was hurling the insults at him.

Movement down by the creek caught Preacher's attention. "All your people gathered here?"

"Yes, sir," a woman said. "Why?"

"More of 'em down by the crick. I heard that Malachi had him a regular gang now. All the petticoats and kids in the buildings. You men see to your families. Move. I think we're only minutes, maybe seconds from bein' attacked. If they're stupid, that is. And they is."

"They all appear to be nothing more than harmless vagabonds to me," the haughty, ample lady said.

Preacher looked at her. Or as much of her as he could in one gettin'. "Lady, you best get movin'. As much as you got to tote around, you're gonna be the last one in the house anyways"

She huffed up. "Well! I never!"

Preacher let that alone . . . with an effort on his part. "Move, people."

"It's that damn meddlin' Preacher!" one of the Pardees hollered. "Where in the hell did he come from? I thought he'd be down at the rendezvous."

The line of men and women and kids stopped suddenly and slowly turned around. Everybody from St. Louis to Vancouver knew that name. "The mountain man . . . Preacher?" a man questioned.

"I been called that. Get in the buildin's, damnit!

"Pa," a boy said. "He's famous."

"And vulgar," the ample lady said. "Besides being an uncouth ignoramus."

One of the Pardee brothers let loose a ball that whined wickedly close to the lady. She let out a squall, jerked her dress up past her knees, and went up the grade like a buffalo headin' toward a wallow. Whoopin' and hollerin' and huffin' all the way up. She was the first one inside the big building.

Preacher ducked down and took shelter behind one of the wells the men had dug. "Stay in the stable, lad, he called to the boy tending to Hammer. "If you can shoot, they's a brace of pistols on the saddle."

"At a man?" the teenager questioned.

"Forget it," Preacher said. He eared back the hammer on his Hawken. "Pilgrims," he muttered. "They gonna be the death of me yet."

But the one shot appeared to be all the Pardees wanted to give this time around. They had lost the element of surprise and they hadn't counted on Preacher being anywhere within five hundred miles of the settlement. Preacher listened to the splash across the creek, then he ran up the slope to the flats where the buildings were located and climbed up on the sod roof of a cabin. He stood and watched the Pardees link up with half a dozen more men and ride off.

"Scum and trash," he muttered darkly, hopping down to the ground.

A settler came out of the community building and stood by Preacher. "They'll be back, won't they?"

"More than likely. You got food, clothin', possessions, and fair females. Yeah, they'll be back. You men stand ready. You had any problems with the Injuns?"

"A bit. But once they saw we would fight, they left us alone.

Preacher grunted as the others gathered around. "That didn't have nothin' to do with it, pilgrim. Injuns is notional folks. They might have taken a likin' to you. They do that sometimes. Maybe on that day they felt their medicine was bad. But out here in the Big Empty, you always stay ready for a fight with the Injuns. More and more people comin' out here is really gonna stir 'em up. This is Cheyenne and Arapaho country mostly. But at one time or another, you'll have bands from a dozen tribes wanderin' through. Any of them can and will lift your hair. Exceptin' maybe the Crow. They'll just steal your horses, usually. How long you folks been here?"

"We arrived last summer and just managed to get our homes built before the winter came. I'm Robbie MacGreagor and this is my wife, Coretine."

"Pleased, I'm shore. I'm Preacher. Y'all got anything to eat?"

The children sat on the floor and watched in awe as Preacher ate. They had never seen anybody his size eat so much. When he was through, he belched loudly and wiped the grease from his hands onto his buckskins. "Helps keep 'em soft and waterproofs 'em, too. You ever get invited to eat in an Injun camp, you be sure and belch like I done when you're finished grubbin'. If you don't, the Injuns'll think you don't like what they served you and be offended."

"Where is your home, Mr. Preacher?" a lady who had been introduced as Rosanna asked. She was married to a Millard somebody or other.

"Just Preacher, missy. My home? Anywhere I want it to be, I reckon. I left my folks' home back East when I was just a tadpole. Twelve, I think I was. I been out in the wilderness near 'bout all my life. Why'd you folks come out here?"

"To settle the new land," a man called Efrem said. His wife was the lady who bore a striking resemblance to a buffalo. Maddie did not like Preacher and made no attempt to hide her feelings. They had four kids—two boys, two girls. Fortunately, they took after their father.

"It's too soon, folks," Preacher tried to caution them. "Besides, this ain't farming country."

"Oh, but I beg to differ," Efrem said. "I think it is. We shall certainly see, won't we?"

"You might, I won't."

A man who was named Gerald Twiggs opened his mouth to speak. A young girl of no more than three or four who was standing in the open doorway said, "Daddy? There are a whole bunch of wild red Indians in the front yard."

2

"Easy!" Preacher said sharply as everyone reached for weapons. "If they'd wanted us dead, we would be. Just stand quiet and ready." He walked to the open door and stood there looking at the dozen or so Cheyenne who had silently walked their ponies up the slope and onto the flat of the settlement. Preacher breathed easier. He knew the subchief leading this band. "Lone Man moves as silently as ever." Preacher spoke the words in Cheyenne as he made the sign of peace. "It is good to see that he is too great a warrior to make war against women, children, and peace-seeking men."

A smile flitted across the Cheyenne's face. He grunted and spoke in rapid-fire Cheyenne. What he said, loosely translated, was that while Preacher was still as full of buffalo turds as ever, it was good to see him.

Preacher was quick to notice the many hands painted on the Cheyenne horses. Each hand represented an enemy killed in hand-to-hand combat. The paintings were fresh and so were the scalps hanging from lances and tied into the manes of the horses. All were Indian scalps.

Lone Man had followed Preacher's eyes and said, "Crow.

They have been warned many times to stay out of our land. Now these will—forever. I have not seen Preacher in two seasons. Have you now decided to scratch into the earth?"

Preacher laughed at that and a twinkle appeared in the Cheyenne's eyes. He knew Preacher better than that. "I visit friends of mine here. These are good people who wish only to work the land and get along with all things of this earth. They cause no trouble."

"We shall see," Lone Man said. He turned his horse and rode out, the others following him.

"My God!" A man introduced as Charles Nelson had finally found his voice. "Did you see all the scalps?"

"Crow hair," Preacher told them. "They made one-too-many raids into Lone Man's territory. It's usually the Dakota—Sioux to you—that don't much get on with the Crow. But you get the Cheyenne all stirred up and you got yourselves a world of hurt comin' at you."

"What did they want here?" a woman asked.

"Curious. Injuns is mighty curious folks. They were just checkin' you out. Now, I told Lone Man that you all was friends of mine. He may or may not believe that, and it may or may not have some bearin' with him. But I've wintered with the Cheyenne and get along right good with them. They may leave you be. But they's renegades in every tribe. The Crow gets along fair to middlin' with the white man; but you always keep a gun handy. You be on the lookout at all times."

Buffalo Butt puffed up and haughtily announced, "We shall tell them all that we are God-fearing people and mean them no harm. We shall be perfectly safe here. It's people like you stir up all the trouble."

"Yeah," Preacher said dryly. "Well, I'll be long gone by the time you folks roll out of the bed come the mornin'. I'll be back this way from time to time to check on you and partake of your cookin'. Good night."

The next morning, as the sky was beginning to silver before dawning, when Robbie made his bleary-eyed way to the outhouse, Preacher was gone.

"Damn fool people," Preacher said, as he rode toward the trading post located near the Laramie and North Platte rivers. "Bringin' all them kids out here to the wilderness. Bunch of igits is what they is."

He was following the trail of Malachi Pardee and his gang, for as long as they rode toward the post, and while making good time, he was riding with caution. Malachi despised Preacher. They'd locked horns in the past a couple of times and Preacher had always come out on top. Preacher was no saint—far from it. But like most of his time, he operated under a strict code of conduct. And Malachi Pardee and his followers violated all the codes Preacher lived by. They were brigands and worse. As he rode, Preacher pondered what all he knew about Malachi, and none of it was good.

Pardee sometimes hooked up with a worthless bunch of Injuns who roamed about up in the Medicine Bow country. These particular Injuns were from all tribes, and they'd banded together after their tribes had kicked them out for one reason or another. But this time Preacher hadn't seen any Injuns in Pardee's pack. Just no-good whites.

The last time Preacher locked up with Malachi, Preacher should have killed him. He knew it then and knew it even better now. But Malachi had yielded and Preacher had stepped back and let him live. Big mistake.

Preacher nooned by a hidden spring—known only to about ten thousand Injuns and several hundred mountain men—and built no fire. He ate a thick sandwich he'd made that morning in the kitchen of the MacGreagor house. Hadn't woke a soul up as he did it. If they slept that sound, Preacher didn't give the pilgrims much chance of living very long out here. But most of them had seemed like real nice people. Except for Buffalo Butt.

Before eating, Preacher had let his horses roll and then picketed them and let them graze. Then he had him a long drink of cold water and ate his sandwich. He stretched out on the ground and rested. He'd been doing a lot of ruminating of late, and decided this was a dandy time to do some more head thinkin'.

The future just didn't look real bright for men like Preacher. He'd predicted the trapping and the fur trade would play out, and it sure was doing just that. He hadn't done much of it the past couple of years anyway. But he knew he had to think about doing something. He was too proud not to work at something. Many of his friends had packed it in and gone back East. But most of them were coming back faster than they went out, all of them saying they just couldn't live back yonder no more. There wasn't no place for men like Preacher in the civilized East. *Po*-lite society, some was callin' it.

A mountain man by the name of Hogjaw had come back to the wilderness with a tale of horror. Seems like he was having him a drink in a tavern and a local called him a son of a bitch. Hogjaw whipped out his good knife and cut that citizen from brisket to breakfast. Damned if the constable didn't put Hogjaw under arrest and tote him off to the hoosegow. Charged him with murder. Hogjaw busted out of jail and lit a shuck for the Big Empty just as fast as he could flee.

After hearing that story, Preacher knew damn well he could never live back East. There was such a thing as being just too civilized.

Laying on the ground, Preacher heard the sounds of horses' hooves and got to his feet, moving to his horses. He calmed them and whispered to them so's they wouldn't whinny when they got the scent of other horses.

The Injuns passed close, and they was painted for war. Preacher made out several Crow, some Blackfeet, Mandan, and some he didn't recognize. A good-sized band of renegades, and they were riding the trail left by Pardee and his kin and trash. Preacher's tracks had blended in with the others and he'd been careful when he left the trail for the spring.

They were all gathering for some reason, and Preacher could guess what that reason might be: more settlers coming in. More damn fools heading this way, bound for the glory land in the Northwest.

Preacher said a very ugly word as he saddled up and pulled out. If there were more wagons coming, they'd more than likely stop at the post for supplies and for talk about the trail ahead of them.

Preacher had had his gutful of pilgrims and decided he'd head the other way and get himself back into the mountains. Then he stopped and, with a sigh, turned Hammer's head toward the post. The folks had a right to know what dangers lay ahead of them, he reckoned.

"Here we go again, Hammer," he said. "But this time, only part of the way."

When Preacher arrived at the post, he was startled by the size of the wagon train and relieved to see an old friend of his was going to be the man to guide the wagons westward. Jack Larrabee was a man to ride the river with. He was about fifteen years older than Preacher and had been out in the wilderness for nigh on to forty years.

The two men hoo-hawed each other and whacked each other on the back a time or two and then went to the cutler's for a round of drinks.

Preacher nearly swallowed his cup when Jack said, "The movers ain't goin' on to Fort Vancouver, Preacher. They're going to settle just west of the Rockies."

"Wagh!" Preacher spat the word. He knocked back his whiskey and, when his vision cleared from the hooch, said, "Then they're fools, Jack."

"Maybe not. Long Hair's done told me personal that he wouldn't bother them."

"That's Long Hair. He's a Crow. Crows will steal their horses and possessions, but Crows don't kill whites except in self-defense. Usually." Long Hair got his name because, when measured, his hair—and it was all his own—was almost twelve feet in length. Crows were known to take horse hair and attach it to their own to make it appear longer.

"For a fact," Jack agreed.

"How about the Cheyenne and the Arapaho and the Shoshoni and the Dakotas? To mention just a few who might lift some hair along the way?"

Jack shrugged his shoulders. "I warned the movers, Preacher. What else can I do?"

Preacher knew the fix the man was in; he'd been there personal. Jack was just trying to make a living and Preacher couldn't fault him for that. "And how about the Pardee boys and that gang of no-counts with them?"

Jack's eyes narrowed. "You seen them, Preacher?"

"I seen them." He told Jack what had happened at the little settlement and what he had seen while resting at the spring.

"Oh, they know about the wagons," Jack admitted. "But we're too many for them. This is the largest train to ever try to cross the Rockies."

Preacher looked out the open window at the fifteen-foot-high adobe wall that surrounded the trading post. Beyond it, a wilderness that seemed to stretch endlessly for hundreds and hundreds of miles. Preacher shook his head at the thought. And he had a right to be a doubter: he'd taken a train all the way to the Pacific the year past.

"They'll make it, Preacher."

"Oh, the hell they will!" Preacher said, pouring another cup from the jug. "They might make it 'crost the Rockies, but they ain't gonna survive alone where you're takin' them, and you know it, Jack. Who the hell do you think you're talkin' to? I know about them folks same as you. Maybe more. They's fleein' the bankrupt eastern part of the country, that's who they is. Hell, I can read. I found me a paper last year. They done sold ever'thing they couldn't pile on them wagons and they can't go back. They got nothin' to go back to. And they got only misery ahead of them. Goddamnit, Jack, they're merchants and clerks and coin counters and the like."

"You're just upset 'cause the fur's gone and you can't abide crowds noway."

"That's part of it, yeah. But it's too soon for these folks, Jack. They got no protection from the government. A bunch of that territory's in dispute 'tween England and America. I snooped around, Jack. Them pilgrims just barely got enough shot and powder for their personal needs. What are you gonna do if you're attacked?"

"You know the odds of Injuns attackin' a wagon train of this size is slim, Preacher," Jack said stubbornly.

"Mayhaps you be right, Jack. Mayhaps you can get them movers 'crost the Rockies. But like I said: what happens after you get there and leave them? You know damn well good as me that's when the Injuns will hit them."

But the scout's jaw was set in determination.

"You know what would be smart on the mover's part, Jack? Huh? If you was to take these pilgrims about twenty-five miles from this post and settle them. Then the next bunch go twenty-five more miles past that, and so forth. Then you'd have, sooner or later, a supply line that ran all the way to the blue waters. But this way, Jack, is dumb!"

Jack stood up and looked down at his old friend. "We'll be leavin' at first light, Preacher. Feel free to tag along. The grub is better than passable."

Preacher shook his head. "No, thanks, Jack. But I'll wish you luck." 'Cause you're damn sure gonna need all you can get, he silently added.

The next morning, Preacher stood with several other trappers and watched the long line of wagons stretch out. No one spoke for a long time. Finally, a long, lanky drink of water all dressed in buckskins said, "I got me a bad feelin' about those folks yonder, boys."

Preacher looked at the man. "So do I, Caleb. So do I."

The men turned as one and headed for the store. Preacher wanted to get him a jug and get rip-roarin' drunk and try not to think about those pilgrims heading into the raw and dangerous wilderness.

On a bright and clear spring morning, Preacher rolled out of his blankets and stretched the kinks from his joints and muscles. He was about two days' ride from the post and the whiskey he'd consumed was clear of his system. He had stayed in an alcoholic fog for near'bouts a week. He and Caleb and the other mountain men who gathered at the post had swapped lies, jugs, thrown axes and knives at targets, and in general had them a high ol' time. Then, without anyone putting it into words, the men had drifted away, each hearing the silent call of the wilderness beckoning them back to the High Lonesome.

After carefully looking all around him and listening intently for several minutes to the birds singing and the squirrels chattering, Preacher decided there were no Injuns about and shucked out of his clothes and jumped into a pool created by a cold, clear creek. He washed quickly, before he turned blue, and jumped out, running around the camp naked as a jaybird until he was dry. Then he put on fresh longhandles he'd bought at the post and slipped into buckskins a Mandan squaw had made for him. He fixed coffee over a smokeless fire and set about figuring just what he was going to do with himself and where he wanted to go.

Problem was, he'd been damn near everywhere there was to go in the wilderness. Preacher had been born restless, and, in his more than two decades in the Big Empty, he had gained a reputation as not only a fierce and respected warrior, but also as scout and explorer, helping to guide many a government team through the seemingly impassable reaches of the mountains and the rivers.

Preacher saddled up and gave Hammer his head and let him go. Hammer soon began following wagon tracks and Preacher, with a sigh, let him have his way. He found no fresh signs of graves along the way for the next two days, so the pilgrims were staying lucky. So far. Two days later, he saw the buzzards circling. He checked his weapons and pushed on, steeling himself for the awful sight that would soon present itself to him.

He came up cautiously on what was left of the wagon train he'd seen back at the post. It was anything but a pretty sight. The men and women and kids had been hit whilst they were abed. Nearly all of them was dressed in bed clothes, which was something Preacher never could understand about pilgrims. They dress up to go to bed, then take off their dress-up-to-bed clothes to dress up again when they got out of bed.

Rifle in hand, Preacher walked among the silent and stiffened dead. The women and the girls had all been raped and the men tortured pretty bad. Preacher had seen sights similar, but not on this large a scale. A man might say it didn't bother him—as Preacher had often said—and a man might say that a man gets used to it—as Preacher had often said—but a man really don't get used to it. A man just steels himself for the task, that's all.

The buzzards were everywhere, many of them too bloated from human flesh and entrails to fly. They just waddled around and looked disgusting. Preacher found an intact shovel amid the wreckage and rubble and knocked half a dozen of the big, lumbering carrion eaters in the head until the rest of them got the message and waddled off a few yards away from the bodies, to stand out of harm's way and stare malevolently at the man who spoiled their dining.

Preacher began the laborious task of dragging what was left of the bodies off the trail and over to a ravine. There, he dumped them over the side. It wasn't very sedate, and certainly no one would call it Christian, but it was the best the mountain man could do. Damned if he was going to dig a lot of holes in the rocky ground. It would take him a week. By that time the bodies would be stinking so bad not even the buzzards could stand it. He really had no idea how many men and women and kids had been massacred, for they'd been dead several days and the buzzards and the varmints had been hard at work, dragging bodies and parts of bodies off into the woods to eat or stash for later.

Preacher changed out of his buckskins and into homespuns and worked all that day. It was late afternoon when he had nearly filled the small ravine with bodies and caved in the top to crudely cover the remains. He made a cross out of rocks, like a T on the ground, carefully working the rocks into the ground so's they'd stay put . . . at least for a time. He'd gotten used to the smell, but knew the vile odor had permeated his clothing and they'd have to be thrown away. Which was the reason he'd changed into homespuns. He found some soap amid the rubble and stowed the bars in his pack. He camped a mile from the ambush site and the next morning, after a bath, began casting around for a sign. What he found disturbed him more than a little.

While he was gathering up a few stray horses that had wandered back to the ambush site and building a crude corral for them, he ruminated on the sign he'd found.

It appeared that maybe half a dozen or so people had escaped the slaughter and headed into the woods. And from the size of their footprints, they either was women or kids or both. There wasn't a man-sized print to be found.

"Lord have mercy," Preacher said. "Little children adrift in the wilderness. If they was borned out here, they might have a chance. But these is town kids, and I bet most of them don't know left from right."

He went off the trail and into the timber, staying with the tracks of the survivors. It wasn't that hard to do. A piece of thread, a tore-off bit of dress that had snagged on a branch, a strand of blond hair hooked on a twig . . . all these things were easy to follow if a body knowed how, and Preacher knew how.

He finally concluded that there was six kids and one growed-up woman. Three boys, three girls, and one woman. Alone in the Big Empty, probably without even a weapon of any kind, and no flint to start a fire, for he hadn't found any sign of old ashes.

The renegades who attacked the train—and they were renegades, for he'd found several bodies—were long gone. Preacher had made sure of that before he started totin' off the dead. Red Hand's bunch, he was sure.

"Damn that renegade bastard!" Preacher said. "I just keep runnin' into that bad Injun."

Preacher found where the small party of survivors had stripped off berries and gobbled them up right then and there. He had to smile. He'd be catchin' up with them 'fore long. These berries would give a body the rear-end squirts real quick, and a belly-hurt, too. But Preacher knew how to fix that, once he caught up with them. Rhubarb was good, and so was honey. Dandelion was pretty good and chamomile was good for the bellyache.

But first he had to find them that got away. And then that very thought sobered him as he muttered, "What the hell am I gonna do with them?"

3

Preacher spotted the group and hunkered down in the brush, taking a slow and careful look around to be certain that no renegades were using them as bait.

Then he stood up and the small group spotted him. Before he could open his mouth, the girls started screaming and shrieking to high heaven and the boys started chunking stones at him. They must have had quite a pile of them. The air was filled with stones of various sizes. Preacher hit the ground.

"Wait a minute!" he hollered. "Damnit, I'm here to help you. Stop throwin' them rocks at me."

The stone barrage ceased and Preacher carefully got to his feet and cautiously moved forward, not wanting to get conked on the bean by an apple-sized stone, for these people were still some bad scared.

"I found what was left of the wagon train," he called, approaching the group. "I done my best to bury the dead."

"I saw you back at the fort," a boy said. "You're the mountain man called Preacher. Mr. Larrabee said you were famous."

"I wouldn't know about that," Preacher replied. He looked at the group. Boys and girls about the same age. Ten to twelve, he figured. The woman was a looker. Maybe twenty-one or -two years old. Fine figure of a female, mussed up hair, dirty face, and all. Poked out in all the right places. Defiant type, too, for she met his appraising eyes with no blinking. "Come on. I found horses back yonder and corralled 'em. I found food that wasn't touched by the Injuns—"

"It wasn't just red Indians," the woman said. "There were whites among them."

"That don't surprise me none, missy. The Pardee brothers probably hooked up with Red Hand like Bum and his boys done last year. I killed Bum and his bunch; should have tracked Red Hand down and kilt him too. Sorry I didn't now. I will this time, you can bet on that. You kids line up and stay behind me. Sister, you bring up the rear and don't let none of these babies stray off. Come on."

It was not far back to the ruins of the wagon train, only a few miles, and Preacher set an easy pace because he could see the group was very tired. "What's your name, sister?" Preacher called over his shoulder.

"Betina. Betina Drum."

"You lose family in the attack?"

"No. I was traveling with a family, but they were no relation to me."

"You ain't got no man?"

"I'm spoken for. He's back East. He is to join me later."

Preacher muttered darkly and profanely, not quite under his breath, about the caliber of men who sent their women alone into the wilderness. The girl behind him giggled at his words.

Preacher stopped the group in the timber and brush a few hundred yards from the still-stinking wreckage of the wagon train and told them to stay put. From the edge of the timber, he checked out the ruins and then waved the group forward.

"Betina, you take the girls and see what you can salvage

from this mess. Clothing and food and money that might be hid in secret compartments in the wagons. Movers do that. Red Hand and Pardee might have missed some of it. Most Injuns ain't got no use for money. Don't know what it is. These children got to have something to get them back East. I'll take the boys and do the same. Now, there might be some bodies I missed under some tangle, so be careful."

He stood for a moment, watching her walk away, and admired the sight for a few seconds. Then he remembered the boys and got them busy digging and pawing through the rubble.

They found food aplenty and articles of clothing and underthings and the like. Several knew where their parents had hidden money and they brought it to Preacher. He shook his head.

"We'll put it in the saddlebags and let Miss Drum see to it. That's a lot of money and I don't want no part of it. Come on, let's get saddled up and get gone from this place."

"We want to conduct a memorial service first, Mr. Preacher," Betina said. "Over the mass grave. It's the Christian thing to do."

"All right. You have at it, lady. I'll just see to the horses."

The horses were all riding stock, and that had surprised Preacher, but obviously the outlaws and renegade Injuns had been too busy raping and torturing and looting to gather up all the livestock. They had driven off the cattle to eat later. Preacher had found saddles among the rubble, and had repaired those that had been slightly damaged. The attackers had made only a half-hearted attempt to torch the wreckage.

Preacher waited with the horses while the little band of survivors had them a prayer service over the grave site. But he did take off his battered hat. Preacher did some thinking while the others was prayin' and singin'. Sounded right nice, too. The girls had good voices.

Preacher figured he was closer to that little settlement he'd come up on than he was to the post. So he'd head there and see if those good folks would take in the kids for a time until they could see their way to get back to the post. Betina had told him she was a trained schoolmarm, so maybe she could stay there with them until her man come out from the East.

Preacher was amazed at how well the kids were holding up in the face of all this. But then, he knew that kids really had no grasp of death. When you're young, you think you're gonna live forever. One girl had cried when she found the body of her little dog. She had carefully and lovingly buried the arrow-shot pup. Those had been the only tears shed so far. That Preacher had seen. Maybe nothing had really set in yet, he figured.

That got Preacher to thinking about when he was a little boy and the dog he had. Got him to feelin' plumb emotional there for a few minutes.

"Come on, people," Preacher muttered, looking at the little group. "We're losin' daylight."

The group was silent as they rode away, the females riding astride just like the boys. Preacher figured the settlement was about two days' ride away from the ambush site. They'd have to spend at least one night on the trail. And he had no way of knowing how near or far away the renegade Injuns and Pardee's bunch might be. But he had been watching and had spotted no signs of smoke.

"I sure can get myself into some pickles," he muttered.

Once, on the crest of a long hill, while the coffee was boiling and the meat cooking, Preacher rested his charges and pointed out to the seemingly empty vastness. "That's the way I remember it," he said to Betina, a note of wistfulness in his voice. "Not a white man as far as the eyes could see. It'll never be the same no more."

"Civilization is moving westward. It's called progress, Preacher."

"Pain in the butt is what I call it."

"It's so . . . big," one of the girls said.

"It's that, all right, button," Preacher told her. "You get lost out yonder and we'd never find you. Remember that." He watched as the heads of the horses came up and their ears pricked. "Get out of sight," he told Betina and the kids. "Stay low and quiet no matter what happens. Take the horses and move into the timber. If anything happens to me, you know where to go, Bet. So move. Right now."

A moment later, the little party and their mounts had vanished into the timber and brush. Preacher kicked some dirt over a mess of little shoe prints and waited by the fire, his Hawken at hand. It wasn't a long wait. Four men rode slowly toward him, coming from the west. Preacher knew only one of them, a no-good who called himself Son. But if the other three had tossed their lot in with Son, they were just as sorry as he was.

"Hi-ho, the fire," Son called. "That shore smells like coffee to me."

"What the hell else would I be boilin'?" Preacher said sourly. "Hot water to bile my socks in? I ain't got no socks so it must be coffee water."

"Preacher," Son said, walking his horse up to the edge of the tiny clearing. "I thought it was you. You just as ill-tempered as I recall."

"I ain't ill-tempered neither, Son. I just don't like you. So don't bother dismountin'. There ain't nothin' here for you or them with you."

"You wouldn't let no poor tarred travelers git down and stretch the kinks out whilst partakin' of coffee and that there fine-smellin' meat, Preacher?" Son asked.

"No."

"Then by God we'll just take it!" one of the men with Son hollered. "And if you don't like it, Slim, you can just go to hell!"

Preacher slowly turned his head. The mouthy man had no way of knowing it, but he was only heartbeats away from sudden and violent death. He should have expected it; that was the way he had lived. "You think you'll do that, huh?" Preacher asked.

"Yeah," the man said with an evil grin. His teeth were blackened stubs. "But first I think I'll kick your ass around this camp just for the fun of it."

Preacher shot him with the .54 Hawken. The big ball slammed into the man's chest and knocked him out of the saddle, his arms flung wide. He hit the ground and lay still, his heart shattered. His horse trotted off a few yards and stopped. Son and the other two were in momentary shock.

Preacher was on his feet, a cocked pistol in each hand. "They's both double-shotted, boys. Who wants it?"

Son and the two others stared at the dead man for a moment, their faces pale under the whiskers and dirt. Outlaws and scum, they were accustomed to always having the upper hand. They were not accustomed to this. They tore their eyes from the dead and stared at Preacher.

"I just flat out ain't got no use for you people," Preacher told the trio. "Now flop your friend across his saddle and get the hell gone from here."

"You're a mean man, Preacher." Son had found his voice and croaked out the words. He cleared his throat. "That was an un-Christian and turrible low thing you just done. That poor wretch was only funnin' with you."

"I didn't see no joke to it. Man pushes me, I just ain't got no sense of humor. You got any idee what's in the Hereafter, Son?" Preacher asked him.

"No."

"You want to find out this day?"

Son shook his head. "I reckon not."

"Then get off your horse and get that dead man and yourselves gone from here. I ain't got no time to waste with the likes of you people. And keep them hands away from your guns. I might mistook sudden movement as a hostile thing and lose my patience with you boys. I don't think you'd like that."

"You're a cruel and vile person, Preacher," Son told him, slowly and carefully dismounting, all the while being very careful to keep his hands clear of the pistols stuck behind his wide belt. "I say this to you as a man who fears the Almighty's wrath. The Lord will not smile kindly upon you come the day of the trumpets' sound."

"You best worry about your own salvation, Son. I'm re-callin' all them widder women you robbed back East, before you run from a noose back yonder and slithered like a snake to the wilderness, and all them trappers out here you kilt for their pelts. You want to deny any of what I said?"

Son glowered hate and fury at Preacher, but made no attempt at rebuttal.

The two with Son stepped down and gingerly hoisted the bloody body of the dear departed across his saddle and tied him down. They mounted up and looked at Preacher.

"Ride!" Preacher told the three of them. "I don't never want to see your ugly faces again. And I mean it, boys. Son, you come ridin' in here with evil thoughts and bad intentions. I could smell the nastiness in you 'fore I smelled the stink of you personal. I ought to do the world a favor and kill you here and now. But you can ride. Now go 'fore I change my mind."

When they had ridden off, Preacher put away his pistols and charged his Hawken. "Stay hid," he called softly. "They might work up some courage and decide to come back. They know I wasn't here alone. They ain't stupid. They's enough meat cookin' for a damn army."

"You're a violent man, Mr. Preacher," Betina called from the brush. "You could have shot to only wound that poor man."

"Yeah, I could have. But I didn't, did I? Now sit still and hush up."

Preacher ran up a hill and climbed a tree, watching Son and his party fade from view. He had him a hunch he'd see them someday, but for this day they'd had enough. Preacher also figured they wouldn't take the time to bury the body—they'd just dump it along the way.

"Let's hurry up and eat and get gone, people," Preacher told Betina and the kids.

Preacher ate with one eye on the trail Son had taken. He hadn't told Betina or the kids, but there hadn't been enough bodies back at the ambush site to match up with all the wagons he'd seen leave the post. And Jack Larrabee had not been among the dead. Preacher had made sure of that. He took into account that some women and girl kids might have been taken for hoppin' on later, but he was pretty sure that some others had taken to the woods and the brush and had made it clear. If possible, he would leave the woman and the kids at the settlement, and then head for the Lonesome and try to find some of those who had escaped the slaughter. He had him a notion that Jack was on the trail of the ambushers, and outnumbered or not, as he surely was, Jack was riding to take his vengeance.

As for any of the others who escaped the massacre, Preacher could only wish them the best. Grown-up men could look after themselves and try to stay alive. But the thought of little kids wanderin' around hurt, scared, and hungry didn't set well with him.

Preacher halted the parade an hour before dark, built a small fire, and fixed bacon and bread and coffee. Then he moved several more miles before bedding the kids down for the night in a cold camp. He made sure they were safe and had cover aplenty, then sat with his back to a tree, his Hawken across his knees.

"Those men back there in the clearing," Betina asked, sitting close to Preacher in the darkness, "Why—?"

" 'Cause they're no good," Preacher cut her off, knowing what she was going to say. Or he figured he knew. "Anyone who hooks up with Son just ain't no good. Son's a murderer, a thief, and a rapist. If he was to ever go back east of the Mississippi, the law would hang him."

She paused a moment and then said softly, "I see."

"No, you don't neither, missy. It's different out here than back where you come from. You told me you was from Albany. That's in New York State. Town's real old; maybe two hundred year old. Used to be called Beverwyck, I think. Missy, I ain't entirely stupid. Whenever I can get my hands on a newspaper or a book, I read it. But them things is kinda scarce out here. Back where you come from, you got uniformed constables, right? You can walk the streets and be safe at night, right? You can sit on your front porches, enjoyin' the cool of the evenin' drinkin' tea and eatin' cake and a-passin' a gentle time talkin' to friends and neighbors. You should have stayed back yonder, missy. But you didn't. So here you are with your man more'n two thousand hard miles away. And for the second time in less than a year, I find myself explainin' to pilgrims that this is wild country. There ain't no law out here 'ceptin' the gun and knife and arrow and war axe, and there ain't likely to be none for many a year to come. Probably not much law will ever be out here in our lifetime. So what are you goin' to do, missy?"

"Stop callin' me missy. My name is Betina. Friends call me Bet. Do? Why . . . teach school."

Preacher was silent for a moment, listening to the sounds around him. "You mean you don't have no noble thoughts about educatin' the savages?"

"Heavens, no."

"Well, that's a relief. 'Cause the so-called savages got they own way of life and don't want nobody tryin' to change them. You might make it out here after all."

A wolf flung his howling message into the night sky and then another called and then the pack all began singing. Betina scooted a little closer to Preacher and he chuckled softly. "Afeard of wolves, are you?"

"Shouldn't I be? Everyone else is."

"Stupid people are. There ain't no reason to be afeard of wolves. They won't bother you if you don't mess with them.

I like wolves. They're good company as long as you know their ways."

"Wolves are good company?"

"Sure. I've took up with several over the years. And I've had several take up with me. They're social critters. Strong family bonds. Devoted to their mates. Some folks say that a wolf won't never mate up again if'n they lose a mate. I don't know about that. I like to think it's true. Wolf ain't like a human person. It won't kill 'ceptin' for food, family, territory, or self-protection. They better than humans in that way. Wolf eats what it kills and keeps its family fed and protected. They a persecuted animal and there ain't no need for it. I been out here in the wilderness all my life, near 'bouts, and I ain't never heard of no healthy, full-grown wolf ever attackin' a human bein' unless that human bein' messed with it first. Injuns will tell you the same thing." Preacher smiled in the night. "Ain't that the God's truth, ol' feller?"

Betina looked at his shadowy shape. "Just who are you calling an old fellow?"

"That big ol' lobo wolf right over yonder at the edge of the timber. See him? He's lookin' right at us."

Betina squealed and got so close to Preacher he could feel the heat. Right nice feeling, too. Then he chuckled.

"Oh . . . you!" She scooted away.

Preacher laughed softly. "Bet, for ever' time you seen a wolf, a wolf has seen you a hundred times. They real shy critters. Relax, you're safe enough here. We'll be at the settlement tomorrow afternoon."

Movement at the edge of the small clearing cut Preacher's eyes. He saw the cold and unblinking eyes of a big gray wolf watching them from the timber. Preacher and the wolf stared at each other for a moment, then the big gray vanished silently into the night.

"What if the settlement isn't there?" Betina asked, unaware of the wolf's presence.

"I done give that some headwork."

"And . . . ?"

"I don't know. Cross that bridge when, or if, we come to it. Ain't no point in worryin' 'bout something that might or might not have happened."

"Preacher, what about the people in the wagon train who got away from the ambush?"

Sharp little gal, Preacher thought. "What people. Bet?"

"Don't fun with me, Preacher. You are perfectly aware that men and women and children got away from the attackers. Just as I am aware of it."

"I seen signs of that, yeah."

"Mr. Larrabee was not at the train when it was attacked. He had gone on ahead to scout, or something. They struck us just after everyone had settled in for the night."

Preacher had not pushed her to talk about the attack. This was the first time she had offered to say anything about it. He let her talk softly while the children slept the deep sleep of the exhausted.

"We all wondered and thought the worst when Mr. Larrabee didn't return before dark."

That's it, then, Preacher thought. More'n likely, Jack's dead. They nailed him 'fore he could get back to the train. Arrow or lance, probably. A gunshot would have alerted the pilgrims. But if the renegades hit the settlement, they didn't come this way. And this is the easiest route.

"They dragged some of the younger women away," Betina continued after a moment. "The white outlaws were ripping the clothing from them as they rode off. It was awful. I had not taken off my dress to sleep. Just laid down on the blankets under a wagon. Melinda and Lorrie were sleeping next to me."

We're in bigger trouble than I first thought, Preacher mused. That smoke I seen this afternoon . . . or thought I seen. It was comin' from the direction of the settlement. Or what's left of it. Damn!

"The boys had gone into the bushes for personal reasons," Betina said. "I grabbed Jody as she was running past the wagon and the four of us made it to the woods and ran for our lives. But I saw others made it to the woods. What happened after that, I just don't know."

But I more'n likely do, Preacher thought. Them folks that made it away from the ambush is either dead or lost and scared out of their minds. And a scared person will get turned around faster than a whirlwind.

"I hope that settlement is there," Bet said, covering her mouth as she yawned.

So do I, Preacher thought. But I'll wager it ain't.

4

The large meeting building was the only structure that had not been burned.

Preacher had circled wide and come up with the creek and line of trees between the settlement and himself. He had smelled the unmistakable odor of charred wood long before he reached the creek. Leaving Betina and the kids hidden in the line of trees, Preacher rode on up to the settlement—or what was left of it. It was an ugly and savage sight.

"Lord God A'mighty!" Preacher had whispered.

The bodies of the dead lay naked, stiffening and bloated in the yard. The men and teenage boys had been tortured, scalped, and mutilated. What had been done to the women and girls was even worse—as bad as anything Preacher had ever seen. And Preacher had just about seen it all.

Preacher turned to see Betina riding up the slope. "Don't come up here!" he shouted. "Get back. Stay with the kids."

Naturally, she came riding up. And promptly fell off her horse and got sick all over the place. She got to her feet and staggered around blindly for a moment before she could take her hands from her face.

"Take a good look at it, Bet," Preacher told her in a hard voice. "And then don't ever lecture me again 'bout shootin' a man out of the saddle."

"Horrible!" she gasped, wiping her mouth on the sleeve of her dress. "Do you . . . can you recognize any of them?"

"Yeah. I think that's Efrem and Maddie something-or-the-other over there. She's got the heft to her."

"What did they do to the man?"

"Held his head in a fire. Brains cooked, built up steam, and the head busted open. I've seen it before a time or two. That's Gerald Twiggs and wife Pauline over yonder. I don't know the names of them little girls. I think them two boys there belong to Efrem and Maddie. The renegades took the rest of the girls and womenfolk. I'll start gatherin' up all the bodies. You see if you can find a shovel, Bet. We got some holes to dig."

"What type of human being would do this to another? Filthy, horrible, despicable . . ." She threw her bonnet to the ground and broke down and wept.

Preacher hunkered down and let her squall. He was not unfeeling or uncaring. It was just that he had seen it all before. He let her bawl for a time and then grabbed her and stood her up and shook her as he would a petulant child. "Now, listen to me, Bet. Damnit, *listen to me!* We ain't got the time for this. We got to get these people in the ground and get the hell gone from here. They ain't been dead more'n a day, so that means that whoever done it ain't far off. Now you go find us a couple of shovels and then you hump your back heppin' me dig. Then—"

"Mr. Preacher?" The small voice spun the mountain man around and filled his hands with pistols.

The MacGreagor kids, Andrew and Mary, stood by the corner of the meeting house, hand in hand, staring at him with wide eyes set in dirty faces.

"Lord God, kids!" Preacher said, shoving his pistols back behind his sash. "Did anyone else make it out alive?"

"Our mother's hid out in the tater cellar out back. Mr. Nelson is alive, but he's been hurt real bad. He took an arrow in the belly. It poked out his back."

"He's gone, then," Preacher told Betina. "They'll be poison spreadin' all through him. I've seen it. It ain't pretty. Go with the girl and see what you can do. Me and the boy will dig the holes. Come on, lad. Let's find us some shovels."

Betina took Mary's hand and walked around the only building left standing and Preacher and the boy started looking for shovels. As they dug, Preacher asked, "What about your pa, boy? You ain't said nothin'."

"He's over yonder in the cornfield. He was plowing when the savages and the white men struck. He never had a chance. I saw some white men shoot him down while they laughed and whooped and hollered like it was a game. But he had told us kids and Ma what to do should the savages come. You see, Pa dug a tunnel from the house to the cellar out back. It's small, but reenforced right good. Ma yelled for me and Mary and we slipped into the tunnel and hid. I guess we was lucky that we couldn't hear much of the screamin'."

"I'd say so," Preacher replied, as he rolled Maddie into the shallow grave and put her husband in on top of her. At least he thought it was her husband. His condition, it was kind of hard to tell. He looked across the flats from the ridge. "Yonder's a pony, boy. And two more to the north of that one."

"It's Heck!" Andy said. "He's mine."

"Well, go fetch him and the others and get them kids I told you about down at the crick. We got to look around for any food left here and then get the hell gone."

"My pa didn't hold with cussing, Mr. Preacher," the boy admonished.

Preacher looked at the boy. He started to tell him he wasn't his pa. He bit back the words and said, "When you get a few more years on you, boy, then maybe you'll be big enough in the poot to tell me what I can and can't do. For now, do like I tell you."

"Two to a grave, Preacher?" Betina asked, walking up behind him.

"Less work. They can comfort each other on their way to wherever it is they're goin'. Grab a shovel."

"The man died, Preacher."

"Figured he would. You and Coretine drag him out here whilst I go out in that stupid cornfield and get MacGreagor. I told them all to tie a rifle boot to the plow and to keep a brace of pistols handy. Can't tell a goddamn pilgrim nothin'. They think they know it all."

She studied his face. "And that makes you angry, doesn't it, Preacher?"

"Mighty right it does. 'Cause it's a waste of good human life. These was decent people we're plantin'. Even Maddie, and she didn't like me worth a whit. For some reason. But she weren't no bad person. And she shore deserved a better end than what she got. Betina, you can't put eastern ways of life to work out here. Maybe someday, but not now. It's wild and untamed and savage. You lookin' at what I mean. I tried to tell these folks that. It was like talkin' to a tree stump." He threw down his shovel and swung into the saddle. "I'll go fetch MacGreagor. We got to get gone from here. Red Hand's bunch done this, and that's one bad Injun."

"You know him?"

"I know him."

Preacher took a tattered and somewhat scorched blanket and went after MacGreagor. Hammer was not real thrilled about totin' any dead body and he let Preacher know this by trying to bite him. But Preacher was ready for it and jerked his arm away just in time.

"I don't like it either, Hammer. So just calm down and let's get this done."

MacGreagor had been scalped and mutilated, so Preacher made sure the blanket covered the man's head so Coretine and the kids couldn't see what all had been done to him.

Preacher didn't want the kids to have to carry that image of their pa all the rest of their days.

The bodies covered with the earth they had traveled a thousand miles to work and live on, Betina and the others prayed while Preacher kept a lookout. He'd caught a glimpse of smoke to the west, and wanted to get gone from what was left of the small settlement.

The women and the kids all started bawlin' and carryin' on something fierce and Preacher could do nothing except let them squall. He figured the full load of grief had finally overtook the kids from the wagon train. So while the survivors whooped and hollered, Preacher tightened cinches and made certain what supplies they had managed to salvage were secured down tight for the ride.

Finally, Preacher had to break it up. Each second they delayed was a dangerous one. "Get on them horses!" he said sharply. "We ain't got time for no more of this. Can't nobody here do nothin' for them that's in the ground. That's all up to God now. So let's ride."

About five miles from the ruins of the settlement, Preacher found the remains of Millard and Rosanna whatever-their-last-names-were. Both of them had been stripped naked and tortured long and hard.

"Filthy red savages!" Coretine said.

"This was white man's work. Injuns got more style than this," Preacher told her. "This is the work of Malachi Pardee and his no-count brothers and them other white trash with them. And all Injuns ain't the same, lady. They's just as many peaceful tribes as there is warrin' tribes. One of you boys fetch them shovels from the packhorses and let's get these folks all covered up."

"Smoke to the west, Mr. Preacher," Josh said.

"I seen it, boy. You're doin' real good. Keep your eyes sharp, now."

What Preacher didn't tell the others was that the smoke was not from campfires. It was talking smoke. It might mean that they had been spotted. It might not. No way of knowing. Yet.

The tortured bodies buried, Preacher took the lead and moved them out. He had him a place in mind that just might mean their salvation. If he could get to it. There would be graze for the animals and plenty of water. There was one way in and one way out of the little valley, and one man with two or three rifles and a brace of pistols could hold off an army, if he had people reloading for him.

"The children are tired, Preacher," Betina called from the rear of the line. "They need to rest."

"You can rest when you're dead," Preacher called over his shoulder. "Keep moving."

He pushed them hard the rest of that day. Some of the girls began to cry from exhaustion. Preacher remained stoic and did his best to ignore them. Their whimperings touched him, and he truly felt sorry for the kids. Maybe they'd never forgive him, but that was no matter if they were kept alive. Betina and Coretine were giving him dark looks, but he could live with that, too. He pressed on.

An hour before dusk began settling over the land, Preacher saw the upthrustings of rocks in the distance and turned in his saddle. "We're almost there," he called. "A few more minutes and we're safe."

He stopped at a line of trees and told the exhausted party to dismount and wait—he'd be right back. Preacher disappeared into the trees and was back in five minutes. "Lead your horses and follow me," he told them. "Quick now. We ain't got no whole lot of time."

"But we're safe!" Coretine protested. "You said we were safe here."

"Lady, move!" Preacher told her. "I got to clean up where we stopped here. They's horse droppin's and hoofprints and footprints all over the place."

There was just enough light left to show the weary party the lushness of the peaceful little valley, although it was more like a well-concealed box canyon. Preacher didn't waste a moment of precious time.

"Strip the saddles and pack frames from the horses and let them roll and drink and graze. Let them wander where they will. I'll fix the pass so's they can't get out. You people lay out your bedrolls and eat cold this evenin'. No fires. We're in a lot of trouble, folks, and I can't make that no plainer. We could easy be trapped in here if we're not all real careful. So stay quiet. I'll be back."

Preacher moved quickly to clean up the area where they had stopped outside the hidden valley. He worked fast, but thoroughly, using twigs and leaves and handfuls of fine dirt and sand. He'd come back at first light to do a better job of it, but for now, he felt he'd done all he could do.

Back inside the towering rock walls, Preacher longed for a cup of coffee, for he was a coffee-drinkin' man. Instead, he bellied down at the spring and contented himself with a long pull of icy cold water. He noticed that the younger kids had already rolled up in their blankets and were sleeping.

He squatted down beside the women and said, "Tomorrow, we'll gather up some dry wood and build a small fire back yonder under a cave overhang. We can have a hot meal and coffee. We got plenty of supplies—last us ten days or more with nobody on short rations. By that time, Pardee and Red Hand will have done their evil deeds in this part of the country and be gone. Then I'll get y'all to the post."

"I'm sorry I was so testy with you today," Coretine said. Her voice was numb with grief and exhaustion.

"It don't matter," Preacher told her. "Forget it. I was pushin' you folks pretty hard. And I was mad 'cause I had to bury some decent folks back yonder."

"Yes. I know. My husband was a decent man. Would it have made any difference if he had mounted a musket boot on his plow, Mr. Preacher?"

"Might have. Folks see a gun, they think twice about startin' trouble. Least he might have gotten one or two of the attackers and the shot would have alerted the others. Don't make no never mind now. What are you going to do, Mrs. MacGreagor?"

"I guess I will return to the East. I don't like this dreadful country."

Preacher smiled gently. "I can understand how you might feel that way, Mrs. MacGreagor. But tell me this: the feller who come back East talkin' up the new promised land, what all did he have to say about this country?"

"That the land was free and it was ours for the taking. That it was lush and lovely and so rich that crops seemed to just leap out of the ground with hardly any work at all. Of course, we didn't believe that last part, but we did pay him, signed on with the forming-up wagon train, and left a few months later."

"And nobody asked nothin' about how Injuns was gonna take to a whole bunch of people movin' in on them?"

"Well . . . yes. But Mr. Sutherlin said that the Indians were peaceful and liked the white man. They welcomed the whites coming and settling. He said the Indians were anxious to learn the white man's ways."

"Did he now?" Preacher shook his head. "Mrs. MacGreagor, your Mr. Sutherlin fed y'all a bunch of bull. You know that now, don't you?"

"Yes. Certainly. But he was such a grand figure of a man, in his homespuns and buckskins. He was so tanned and fit and looked to be the very essence of a frontiersman."

"Probably never been west of Illynoise," Preacher said sourly. "A damned huckster and snake-oil salesman. So he took your money. Did you ever see him again?"

"No. He was supposed to meet us in Missouri, but he sent word that he'd be delayed and for us to push on. He would try to catch up with us."

"Sutherlin." Preacher rolled the word around. "Seems to me like I've heard that name before."

"Oh, he is a very famous mountain man. He has written much on the West and its people."

"He ain't no famous mountain man out here, Mrs. Mac-Greagor. Least not under that name. I know them all. Lots of folks has read words written by men who come out here 'fore I did and in their minds twisted them words all around. Others has writ words about this place who ain't never set foot near here. I 'spect your Mr. Sutherlin is one of them . . . and maybe worsen. He'll get his comeuppance. Bet on that. Now you go wrap up in your blankets and get some rest. We're reasonable safe here."

Preacher was alone with his thoughts for a time, and then Betina come to where he sat, his back to a tree. She spread a blanket on the ground and sat down beside him. "Coretine is a very nice person, isn't she, Preacher?"

Something in the way she said it warned Preacher that he'd better be careful how he answered. Betina had taken to battin' her eyes at him of late, and a-wigglin' this and that, too. And he'd seen her givin' them both sharp and hard looks as they sat together, talkin' low. "I reckon," Preacher replied, choosing his words careful. "She says she's headin' back East just as soon as possible."

"Attractive, too, isn't she?"

"I ain't paid no attention to that, missy." Which was a lie he hoped he could pull off. Coretine was a mighty handsome woman. Not near 'bout as pert as Betina, but full-figured and handsome.

Betina decided to give it a rest. She sat quiet for a time and then said, "You think they're out there, don't you, Preacher?"

"Yeah. I do. Not far away, neither. I think Red Hand has people out lookin' for us. The next few days are goin' to be chancy ones, Bet. It'll be up to you and Coretine to keep the kids quiet at all times. No runnin' around and playin' and carryin' on. They's a cave about five hundred yards over yonder. It runs about two hundred feet into the rocks. First light,

I'll check it out for critters and you and Coretine take the kids in there. And don't come out until I tell you to."

"All right, Preacher. You get some rest. You've got to be as tired as the rest of us."

"I'll catch me a few winks."

Preacher slept close to the canyon entrance that night, and slept very lightly. He'd found a few pistols and rifles at the ambush site and had taken them and what powder and molds and lead he could find. Before he'd laid down for the night, he'd loaded a few of the weapons and stashed them for the ladies in case of trouble. He didn't know about Betina, but Coretine had shocked him slightly when she said she would gladly shoot any savage red Indians or trashy white bastards who bothered them.

Preacher believed her, too.

At first light, Preacher checked out the cave and moved the people into it. Then he slipped through the narrow passageway and stood for a time near the hidden mouth, all senses working hard. He could neither hear nor smell anything out of the ordinary.

Moving slowly, Preacher went over the area where they had stopped the afternoon before and cleaned it up. Satisfied it would pass any quick inspection, he slipped back into the passageway and into the canyon.

He gathered up dry wood and twigs and carried them to the cave. At the mouth, under the overhang, he built a small, nearly smokeless fire and told the ladies to fix coffee and something to eat, and then put out the fire.

"They're close, I'm thinkin'," he told them all as they gathered around the fire, waiting for the meat to cook. "They've lost our trail and know we're somewhere nearby. The next couple of days will tell the story."

Preacher looked at the group, eyeballing each of them for a moment as he waited for the coffee to make. "Y'all was complainin' yesterday 'bout bein' tired. Well, you gonna get lots of rest durin' the next few days. Except for one lookout here in the mouth of the cave, I want you all to stay back in the cave unless you got to come out to do your business. Stay quiet. Do what I tell you to do and we'll come out of this pickle barrel alive." *I hope,* he silently added.

Preacher ate his bacon and drank his coffee. He allowed himself a short smoke from his old pipe and then checked his weapons. He told Andy to take the first watch at the mouth of the cave and went to sit at the entrance to the canyon. One thing Preacher had learned early on was patience, and he had a deep well of that to draw on.

He wasn't at all sure about the others.

After several hours of sitting very still near the entrance, Preacher picked up the very faintest of sounds. He waved at the lookout and the boy disappeared instantly into the blackness of the cave. Preacher eased his way through the narrow passageway—just wide enough for a horse to make it through—and knelt down in the sand, listening. He could hear faint talking, but could only make out a few words.

Renegade Utes, Preacher finally concluded. Three of them. And they were very close. If he was going to take them out, it would have to be with knife and war axe. He couldn't risk a shot. Others were probably within hearing distance of the canyon.

He leaned his rifle against the wall of the passageway and slipped out into the brush and timber. Preacher, he thought, you sure can get yourself into some high-lacious predicaments. He heard movement behind him and spun around, coming face to face with a big, war-painted Ute.

5

The Ute was startled for a split second and did nothing. Preacher was startled and killed the brave, slashing out with his long-bladed knife and nearly cutting the man's head off. The Ute's scream died soundlessly in his ruined throat. Kneeling beside the cooling body, Preacher looked around. There was the Ute's pony, a short distance away, its mane thick with tied-on scalps. Some of them, Preacher noted, were very fresh. And two of them were hair from women.

"Brave son of a bitch," Preacher muttered, as he wiped his blade clean on the Ute's shirt and then sheathed it. "I'll call you Killer of Women."

He heard the sounds of a walking horse draw closer. He shoved the dead Ute under some brush and jumped up into the lower branches of a thick-trunked old tree.

Preacher pulled his tomahawk from behind his sash and waited amid the leaves. He had every intention of opening up this Ute's head with his war axe. Might have worked out right well if the limb hadn't broken off just as the Indian was walking his horse under the tree.

When the limb cracked it sounded like a gunshot, and the

horse bolted, leaving the startled brave sitting on his butt on the ground for about one second before Preacher and the limb landed on him and broke his neck. The third Ute charged his pony at the noise and Preacher just had time to roll away from the axe in the brave's hand.

Grinning savagely, the renegade Ute leaped off his pony's back and ran to face Preacher just as he was getting to his feet. Both Preacher and the Ute held war axes in their hands. They slowly circled each other, each one attempting to see just how good the other was.

The Ute called Preacher a very uncomplimentary word and Preacher responded by calling him a lowlife son of a bitch whose mother slept with prairie dogs.

The Ute cried out and pulled a knife. Preacher pulled his own knife out with his left hand and the Ute frowned at that. The blade looked just about as large as the long knives the horse soldiers carried. Almost.

The Ute leaped silently as Preacher and the steel heads of the axes clanged as they met. Preacher took a wicked swipe with his knife and drew first blood as the razor-sharp blade cut the Ute's belly, although not deep enough to be called much more than a serious scratch. The Ute jumped back as warm blood oozed out of the cut.

The men once more began warily circling each other. The Ute insulted Preacher again and Preacher replied in the buck's own language, calling the Injun something slightly less than a rotting piece of maggot-infested skunk meat. It lost something in the translation. The Ute hollered and jumped at Preacher. Preacher sidestepped, leaped, and kicked the buck in the balls, doubling the brave over in sudden sickness and pain. That was all that Preacher needed. He brought the tomahawk down and split the Ute's skull open. The brave died with his eyes staring in astonishment that this could happen to him.

Preacher caught his breath and then quickly gathered up all the bows and quivers of arrows from the dead. He kept the best of the bows—it was a dandy—and filled one quiver with the best arrows. Then he ran back into the canyon and up to the cave.

"I'll be gone for most of the day and maybe part of the night. Stay absolutely quiet and away from the mouth of the entrance. I'll be back, but I can't tell you rightly when. So don't worry about me. I got to leave a false trail for the renegades."

Out of the canyon, Preacher did some fast work in cleaning up the area and then tied the dead Utes across the backs of their horses. On foot, he led them several miles from the killing site, staying in a meandering creek most of the way, then across a rocky bank. The Indian ponies were unshod, so they would leave no slashes on the rocks.

Preacher scalped the Utes and mutilated the bodies before stringing them up with rope by their heels from a tree limb. He then jumped onto the back of a pony and, leading the other two, set out on a hard run across the grass. He walked and ran the horses for miles before jumping off and heading back to the valley on foot.

Preacher almost ran right into a Cheyenne war party, but this was not a band of renegades. And it was a war party returning from battle, not going into it. While he got along well with the Cheyenne, most of the time, he did not feel like pressing his luck this time. It would be sometime in the future before Preacher would learn that this Cheyenne war party had struck at a Kiowa camp and, during the battle, two chiefs had been killed, Gray Thunder and Gray Hair. That battle would start negotiations between four tribes: Cheyenne, Arapaho, Kiowa, and Comanche. They would later make a peace that has lasted to this day. A pact of nonaggression between their tribes.

But on this day, all Preacher wanted to do was save his white butt. He jumped into a muddy ravine and hugged the mud until the war party had passed. Slipping and sliding and cussing, Preacher made his way back out and on to the valley. It was full dark and he was tuckered when he reached the entrance.

He told Betina to stoke up the fire and fix him some coffee and food whilst he cleaned up at the spring. Then, with the mud washed off of him, and over bacon and bread and coffee, Preacher told the group what had happened.

"You *killed* three right outside the entrance?" Betina gasped.

"Yeah. One of them by accident." He told the kids about the limb breaking and his falling out of the tree and onto the Ute and that got them all giggling.

Even Preacher smiled at his own antics.

"How many miles did you run today, Mr. Preacher?" a girl asked.

"Oh, mayhaps twelve or fifteen, I reckon. Not far enough for me to get my second wind though. I like to run. Keeps a body in good shape. I usually win all the footraces at the rendezvous. Which I was goin' to this year," he added glumly. "On the Wind River."

A little girl snuggled up close to him. "Don't be sad, Mr. Preacher," she said. "We'll all see that you don't get lonesome."

Preacher was at first startled, then amused. He was not a man to whom emotions such as gentleness and compassion came easy. "I 'spect you will, button," he said with a gentle smile. "Yes sirree, I 'spect you will at that."

The group stayed in the valley for a week, with only Preacher venturing out daily to check for signs and smoke. If any renegades came close, he did not hear nor see them. The group was running low on supplies, and Preacher decided it was time to head for Fort William, which was a trading post, not a military fort.

"Are the bad people gone, Mr. Preacher?" a girl asked.

"Bad people will never be gone, honey," the mountain man told her. "They'll be bad people around you all your life. You just got to keep one eye out for them all the time. Let's pack up and get gone, folks."

With Preacher in the lead, Hawken across his saddle horn, the party started out across the Lonesome Land, as some called it. Short-grass and sagebrush country. The name Wyoming came from the Delaware Indian term *maughwau wama,* meaning "big plains." In the late 1830's, Fort William—named after William Sublette, William Anderson, and William Patton, later to be called Fort John, for John Sarpy; and then later to be designated a U. S. military fort and renamed Fort Laramie—was a busy, bustling place. In 1836, the rotting logs that made up the outer walls were replaced with a fifteen-foot-high adobe wall, with higher bastions. Friendly Indians traded there, and it was a safe haven for weary travelers, of which, Preacher had noted sourly, there was a-plenty of lately.

All work stopped when a lookout spotted Preacher and his party approaching the fort and gave out a shout. The men, and the few women at the fort, all turned out to stand and watch silently. They all could accurately guess at what had happened.

Preacher looked around for a face he might know and spotted the mountain man named Caleb. "Where's the soldier boys, Caleb?"

"Gone out chasin' Blackfeet, Preacher. This all that's left of the wagon train?"

"Yep." Preacher swung down and took the jug offered him by Caleb. He took a deep pull and sighed as the whiskey hit his stomach. "Mighty refreshin', Caleb. Good goin' down." He cut his eyes to the bedraggled party of boys and girls and two women. "Three of them yonder in that pack is all that's left of that settlement I told you about. Woman and her two kids. Red Hand and the Pardee brothers hit them. It was bad. I don't know what in the hell any of 'em is gonna do. I'm right glad to be shut of them, personal. I've 'bout had my fill of people for a month or so."

"I do know what you mean. I was fixin' to head out in a couple of days. Figurin' on headin' up towards Pierre's Hole. You shore welcome to travel along if you like."

"Since you ain't no hand when it comes to flappin' your gums, Caleb, I'll take you up on that invite. I best get these poor sad pilgrims settled in. I'll catch up with you later on."

"I'll be around. I got to supply."

Preacher walked over to Betina and Coretine. "Ladies, I plan on pullin' out in a couple of days. So I reckon I'll get my goodbyes said here and now."

"How can we ever thank you?" Coretine asked.

"Ain't no thanks needed from nobody. I done what most any man out here would have done. Y'all got your mind made up as to where you're goin' from here?"

"We're . . . talking about it," Betina said. Preacher picked up on the hesitation but thought nothing of it.

"Luck to you all," Preacher replied, and then he walked away after waving at the kids. He was no hand at prolonged goodbyes. He headed to the store to get him a jug and then settle down for a night of serious drinking.

Preacher and Caleb pulled out two days later, long before dawn touched the skies. Preacher had deliberately avoided all contact with Coretine and especially with Betina. He didn't know what the ladies had in mind, and wasn't all that interested in finding out. Preacher had years back decided that his was to be a solitary existence in the Big Lonely. While he enjoyed an occasional dalliance with the ladies, red or white, there was no room in his life for a permanent female companion. By noon of the second day on the trail, the mountain man had put Betina and Coretine out of his mind.

Preacher and Caleb started out for Pierre's Hole, but as mountain men are wont to do, they got sidetracked, piddlin' around, lookin' at this and that, and running into a friend or two they hadn't seen in months or even years.

"Another year," Caleb said, breaking the silence that had lasted for hours as they rode along, "furrin' will be all gone. Done. Two year at the most."

"Seen it comin' three, four year ago," Preacher replied. "That's why I quit. Mainest reason I quit when I did. You know we're bein' followed?"

"Yep. Blackfeet."

"I sold me a pelt at the rendezvous back in '33 for six dollars," Preacher said. "Two year ago same quality fur brought one dollar. Knew it was time to quit. How many you figure they is tryin' to sneak up on us?"

"Too damn many people comin' into this country ain't heppin' none," Caleb replied. "I swear this country's gettin' crowded. Oh, 'bout ten, I reckon. Three, four of 'em done broke off and circlin'. I figure they'll set up an ambush at the pointy rocks."

The two mountain men had headed west from Fort William, riding for the Sweetwater Crossing. Once past that, they had planned on heading through the Rattlesnake Range and then on up to the hot springs. Maybe. Who the hell knew for sure? Neither man had anyplace in particular to go and nobody waiting on them should they decide to head there.

"You primed and ready to blow?" Preacher asked.

"I'm ready to bang all the way around."

"I have done everything I know to do to be friends with the Blackfeet," Preacher mused aloud. "And I have made a few friends. But them and the Pawnee has woofed me around for years. I'm a-gettin' right tired of it. Did you gleam how they was armed?"

"Arrows, mostly. Some old muskets."

Until the repeating rifle came to be, most Indians preferred to stay with bows and arrows or lances, for eight to ten arrows could be aimed and let loose in the time it took to reload a musket. And the Indian never had enough powder or shot.

"I'd rather not have no trouble," Preacher said. "If they'll just go on and leave us be, I'll not be the first to fire a ball." He chuckled. "Ol' John Colter finally had his belly full of the Blackfeet. Way I heared it, after they grabbed him and stripped him nekked as a newborn, they made him run. Chased him for hours. Wasn't long after that John give it up and said he'd never come back out here again."

"He didn't, neither," Caleb said. "Died back in '13, I think it was. St. Louie."

Preacher nodded his head and cut his eyes. "Them Injuns done vanished on us, Caleb. We best be ready."

"Yeah, you be right there, ol' hoss. They gonna be 'spectin' us to take the easy way. So how you want to play this?"

"We'll take the south end when I holler. By the time them hid in the rocks get over to the south side, we'll be around the rocks and sittin' there cocked and ready to reduce their number considerable."

"We there."

"You ready?"

"Give a shout."

"Now!" Preacher yelled, and their mounts and packhorses leaped forward. From the rocks, shouts of disgust and anger rose from the throats of the Blackfeet as they realized they had been tricked.

Preacher and Caleb slid to a halt, leaped from their mounts amid a jumble of boulders, and waited. The Blackfeet, unable to tell where the mountain men had gone, were confused for a moment, shouting at one another. Two leaped nimbly to the highest point of the maze of rocks and carelessly sky-lined themselves for just a moment. Two Hawken rifles roared, their huge balls tearing great holes in the chests of the braves.

"Reload," Preacher said, pulling out his two pistols.

A brave came screaming around the south end of the rock pile and Preacher shot him off his pony. Another jumped down from the rocks and Caleb smashed his face in with the butt of his rifle. Preacher's second .50 caliber pistol belched fire and smoke and another buck's days of warfare ended.

Caleb rammed home ball and patch and cocked his rifle just as a Blackfoot flung himself inside the circle of rocks. The mountain man dropped the muzzle of the Hawken and pulled the trigger, the muzzle only inches away from the buck's face. The brave was unrecognizable as he hit the ground.

To any Indian, fighting what appears to be a losing battle is stupid. The attack broke off and the remaining Blackfeet vanished. Preacher and Caleb quickly reloaded and got the hell gone from that area. They left the dead where they had fallen, knowing their friends would be back for them. Neither Preacher nor Caleb felt any rancor for the Blackfeet. No hard feelings. It was just one way of life clashing with another. Other tribes, such as the Crow, were working with the white man and making peace. But the Blackfeet would remain hostile for years, as would the Cheyenne, the Comanche, the Dakota, the Apache, the Kiowa, and many other tribes.

The mountain men were the first to see the writing on the wall, so to speak, although had it been really visible in print, many would not have been able to read it. The white man was coming, and in many cases bringing his wife and kids with him; they were coming just as surely as one season follows another. And the Indian would have no more success in stopping that westward advance of the whites than he would in stopping the snow that fell or the sun that shone. They would kill a few, but for every one killed, fifty, a hundred, a thousand would take their place.

And to the mountain man, it was sad, in a way. For their way of life was being taken from them as well.

Preacher and Caleb moved on, once more assuming their

northwesterly course. Just wandering, hoping to see a valley they had not yet seen, or to belly down by a cold, rushing creek for a drink of water from a mountain runoff. They were of a breed whose time had just about run out. They had made their mark upon a land and the land would always bear that signing. Many mountain men would simply disappear into history and never be heard from again. No one would know what happened to them, or where they were buried, or if they were buried. For in the wilderness, death in a hundred different ways waited around every bend and twist in the trail. Some would go back East and write about their adventures for an eager public.

But not Preacher. Preacher would go on to become even a larger legend. He would be a larger-than-life guide, tracker, scout, warrior.

Miles from the site of the brief but deadly battle with the Blackfeet, Caleb whoaed and sniffed the air. "You smell that, Preacher?"

Preacher did. "Yeah." His words were softly spoken. "That smell don't never change. Death up ahead."

6

It was Jack Larrabee. His back was to a tree and his weapons were by his side. They had been carefully placed there. Two arrows protruded from his chest. Blackfeet arrows. Out of respect for his fighting ability, the Blackfeet had not scalped or mutilated the body of the mountain man. They had left his eyes in his head so he could see his way into the land that lay beyond earth life.

Casting about the battle site for a sign, Preacher found four blood trails and Caleb found two more.

"He put up one hell of a fight," Caleb remarked. "Two musket balls in him and two arrows 'fore they brung him down. They'll be singin' songs about Jack come this evenin' and for many more evenin's to come."

"For a fact."

The Blackfeet had also left his horse and his possessions, meager though they were.

The man had escaped the renegade attack on the wagon train only to be ambushed by the Blackfeet.

"He was trackin' the Pardees and another small group," Preacher called, studying the sign on the ground about fifty yards from where Jack lay.

Caleb looked up from his digging in the rocky ground with a small shovel and nodded his head. "We'll take it up," he said quietly. "What do you think about that, Preacher?"

"I reckon so, Caleb." Preacher walked to his own pack-horse and got a shovel. "Ain't no law books nor constables out here. Seems to me if any sort of decency is gonna prevail, those of us who are at least tryin' to do some right has got to act as the law."

"They's a word for that."

"*Vigilante*. Do it bother you?"

"Cain't say it do, mainly 'cause I don't know what it means or how to spell it. Somebody's comin'."

"I know. I been watchin' Hammer. But he ain't all that upset. Must be somebody whose scent he's familiar with."

But just in case, the men dropped shovels and picked up rifles.

"There ain't no need for nothin' like that." The voice came out of the rocks and brush.

"Hell, it's Windy," Caleb said, lowering his rifle. "Come on in, Windy. You can hep us plant Jack. You alone?"

"Rimrock's with me. You boys got any coffee?"

"Shore," Preacher said, easing the hammer down on his Hawken as the two mountain men came into view. "But we ain't gonna boil none here. Let's get Jack decent, or as decent as he'll ever be, and then move on a few miles."

Windy and Rimrock were just about as disreputable look-ing as two men could get, and just about as opposite. They were shaggy and woolly and had fleas, but their courage was limitless and they knew the country from Canada to Mexico. They dismounted and walked over to where Jack lay, look-ing at the body, the arrows still sticking out of the body.

"Goddamn Blackfeet," Rimrock rumbled.

"Get something to dig with," Caleb told the pair. "But don't stand too close to me and Preacher. We had us a bath last week and we're still fairly fresh and pure. Did you never heared of no soap, Windy?"

"I run out. But you take Rimrock here, I don't think his mamma ever introduced him to soap."

"Rimrock never had no mamma," Preacher said. "He was found as a child in the woods and bears raised him."

Caleb stopped his digging and looked at Rimrock. "Come to think of it, you and a griz do favor."

Rimrock just smiled. He was one of the easiest-going people in the mountains, until he lost his temper, which wasn't often. Then he was awesome. Rimrock stood about six and a half feet tall and weighed about two hundred and eighty pounds. His horse was huge, looking more like a dray animal than riding stock. Windy, on the other hand, would have to stand on tiptoes to hit five feet two inches, and probably weighed about a hundred pounds . . . but it was all muscle and gristle and bone. To get on his pony, Windy usually had to find a large rock to climb up on. If one was not handy, Rimrock would just pick him up and throw him into the saddle. The two men had been partners for years, only occasionally going off on their own.

"Two musket balls and two arrows, hey," Windy said, shaking his head. "He give them a run for it, I'll say that. And they respected him for it."

Preacher told the newcomers about the wagon train and the settlement.

"We been up north, along the Powder. We ain't heard nothin' or seen nothin'," Rimrock rumbled in a deep bass voice. " 'Ceptin' movers comin' in. Why, we seen five families 'tween here and the Powder. Place is gettin' all crowded up with folks. I never seen nothin' like it. Gettin' to be a regular city out here."

"Trappin' up there?" Caleb asked.

"New. That's about over. We're just ramblin' around," Windy told him. "I wonder how many made the rendezvous?"

"Probably a goodly number," Preacher said, breaking off the arrows and trying to fold Jack's arms across his chest. They were locked in place. He gave up. "But I'll wager that in two, three years, there won't be no more rendezvous, no-where. Anybody want to take me up on that bet?"

"You don't mean that!" Rimrock said, aghast at just the thought of it.

"It's over, Rim," Caleb told the man. "Furrin's done. We all got to find something else to do. Me and Preacher, we're travelin' light. No traps."

"We don't have none either," Windy said quietly. "It ain't worth the bother no more."

"Gimme Jack's blanket over yonder," Preacher said, pointing. "Rim, help me wrap him up. He's done stiffened up tight as a drumhead."

They placed the mountain man on his back in the hole and buried his weapons with him.

"Put his blade in there with him," Rimrock said. "He might meet up with a big-assed griz on his way. Windy, strip the saddle offen his horse and turn the poor animal a-loose. He was wild when Jack caught him, so he'll cut wild again."

The men buried Jack Larrabee deep and covered him up and then layered the mound with heavy rocks to prevent the animals from digging up the body. Then the mountain men stood in silence around the mound for several minutes.

"Jack was a good man." Windy finally broke the silence.

"He didn't have no back-up in him," Rimrock said.

"He went out a-clawin' and a-scratchin' and a-bitin'," Caleb added.

Preacher put his battered old hat back on his head and said, "See you, Jack." Then he turned and walked toward Hammer.

The others fell in line with him.

"Ain't gonna be no one left 'fore long," Rimrock muttered, after tossing Windy into the saddle.

The men had settled in for the night, some miles from where Jack Larrabee lay cold in his grave. A hat-sized fire kept their coffee hot while they lay in their robes and blankets and drank coffee and jawed of men they had known and places they had been and sights they had seen.

"I heared you saved some pilgrims and then took them folks and their wagons all the way to the blue waters last year, Preacher," Rimrock said.

"I did. Me and Nighthawk and Jim and Dupre and Beartooth. I can't say as I ever want to do nothin' like that again."

"I'd left 'em along the trail," Windy said. "Damn pilgrims."

Preacher smiled. Windy would have done no such of a thing and everybody around the fire knew it. He just liked for people to think him sour and jaded and coldhearted. Preacher said, "If you'd a seen them fine-lookin' females I took over the mountains and rivers to the blue waters, you'd a still been out there with 'em, Windy."

"Women!" Windy snorted. "I ain't got no use for women. Always wantin' to tie a man down."

"What about that little Crow gal up on the Yellowstone?" Caleb asked with a smile.

Windy glared at him from across the fire and everybody hoo-hawed at him. Windy had come back to the lodge after too long a stay runnin' his traps and she had throwed all his possessions out on the ground, moved the tipi, and took up with another man.

Windy had been sorta testy about women ever since.

A fallen branch snapped out in the darkness and the four mountain men were out of their robes and blankets in a heartbeat, grabbing up rifles and flattening out behind cover, well away from the small fire.

A moan reached their ears. The mountain men did not move. They waited, rifles cocked. Something stirred in the brush, then another moan.

"I'm hurt, boys." The words came weak and in no more than a whisper. "I'm Shields. Tom Shields."

"I know him," Windy whispered. "He's all right. Can you make it to the fire, Tom?"

"If it's the last thing I ever do, and it just might be. I'll make it. Them damn Pardees got lead in me."

"You stay put," Rimrock called, getting to his feet. He went out into the darkness and carried the badly hurt man into the camp and laid him down by the fire, his back against a rock. Preacher started to open Tom's bloody shirt and the injured man's hand stopped him.

"Don't waste your time, t'ain't no use in that. . . . Say, you be Preacher."

"Yeah. Now I 'member you. You was at the rendezvous up on Horse Crick back in '35, I think it was."

"Yeah. Just give me some of that coffee, boys," Tom said. "And talk to me whilst I pass. I got lead hard, high and low. One lung's gone and my innards is on fire. I thought for a time I was gonna pass with no one clost to hear my tale."

"The Pardees did it?" Caleb asked.

"Mighty right. Them and their kin and followers. They was drunk and mean and fixin' to burn my feet for fun when I broke and run. I been runnin' for might near two days. Walkin' and crawlin' and staggerin' is more like it." He took a big gulp of coffee and all could see that the hand holding the cup had no fingernails.

Preacher looked at the hand and felt a killing coldness creep over him. "The Pardees tear out your fingernails?"

"Yeah. They did. They got some poor women and girls with 'em, too. And them poor creatures is bein' abused so's it's a mortal sin, it is. It's the most pitifulest sight I ever did see. I 'spect they all dead by now. They'd shore be better off if they is." He took another slug of coffee and drew a long, shuddering breath. "Them men is worser than any Injun that ever lived." He coughed up blood.

"Where be they now, Tom?" Rimrock asked.

"Oh . . . I wouldn't have no idee. They said something 'bout attackin' some wagon train of pilgrims somewheres.

But I was in so much pain the words just didn't register in my head." He closed his eyes for a moment and then said, "It's funny, boys. The pain is plumb gone. My head is real clear now. I was just then thinkin' how it was when we all furst come out here. You could ride for months and not see a white man. Now they's cabins a-poppin' up all over ever' place. They must be two hundred people out here now."

Tom began to ramble and Windy took the cup from his hand before he could spill the hot coffee. He met the cold, dangerous eyes of Preacher staring across the dying man at him and sensed that their wandering was going to come to an end. He'd seen that look in Preacher's eyes before.

"Mighty peaceful, boys," Tom said. "Things is all misty and sparklin' lights and blue like. I guess the Good Lord has decided to let my clock wind down."

"We're goin' after the Pardees, Tom," Caleb said. "At least, I am."

"Count us all in," Rimrock said, his face hard with anger. "We'll avenge you, Tom. You can go out knowin' that much. You got my word on that."

"It's a good thing to have friends, I swear it is," Tom said. "Gimme another swaller of that coffee 'fore I pass, boys. Say, you reckon they got coffee over on the other side? I've often wondered about that. I'm a coffee-drinkin' man."

"Shore they do, Tom," Windy said, his voice very gentle. "I'd bet on it. As a matter of fact, I want you to keep a pot hot for us. Will you do that?"

"You know I will," Tom whispered. "It's all dark boys. I can't see nothin'."

Rimrock took one of the man's tortured hands into his own big paw. "It's all right, ol' hoss. We're here with you."

Tom Shields smiled and died.

The men stood around the rock covered mound in the new light of day. Preacher took off his hat. "Lord," he said.

"We done buried two good men in the past few hours. We ask You to receive them with kindness and charity. They wasn't perfect, but they were men to ride the river with. And I can't say no more good about a man than that. Amen." He plopped his hat back on his head. "Let's ride boys. We got some snakes to stomp on."

7

Preacher held the razor-sharp blade to the renegade's throat. The renegade was wearing the buckskin dress of a Ponca *berdache*. A homosexual. Many Indians believed that the moon appeared to boys during puberty and offered both a bow and a woman's pack strap. If the boy hesitated in reaching for the male symbol, the moon gave him the pack strap, and a female lifestyle. It was as good a theory as any.

"I ain't belittlin' your way of life, Pretty Little Fallin' Star," Preacher said sarcastically, speaking in the *berdache's* tongue. He had no way of knowing what the Ponca's name was, but he wanted him to know that he spoke it and knew all about him. "But if you want to continue your way of life, you better not tell me no lies."

The Ponca was no coward, for he was a veteran of many battles, but the look in Preacher's eyes spoke silent volumes. And the Ponca knew about the mountain man called Preacher. Many in his own tribe—before he got kicked out—called Preacher White Wolf. The Mandans called him Man Who Kills Silently. The Dakotas called him Bloody Knife. The Crow sang songs about his bravery and fierceness, as did most of the tribes, including the Blackfoot.

"I will not lie," the Ponca said.

"The Pardees and Red Hand. Where are they?"

"Red Hand has left Pardee for a time. Probably half a moon or more. They will meet again when the next wagons try to cross. I do not know where Pardee and his people have gone, nor do I care. I left them and Red Hand. Their viciousness sickened me. War is one thing, but they go too far. A puking vulture would make better company."

Preacher pulled the knife away from his throat and stood up, sheathing the huge blade. "Get out of here," he told the Ponca. "Go on back to matchmakin' in your tribe."

"I cannot," the Ponca said. "They have banished me forever. I am nothing. I am nobody. They even took my name. I would be better off dead."

"All right," Windy said, hauling out a pistol and cocking it, ready to give the Ponca his desires.

"Wait a minute," Preacher said. "He leveled with us. Let him go his way."

The Ponca stood up from the ground, straightened his dress, and then swung onto his pony, showing a lot of leg. It was not a thrill for any of the mountain men. He looked at Preacher. "They plan to steal children from the next train."

Rimrock's face grew hard. "To sell them to slavers?"

The Ponca shook his head. "To use them and then kill them." He rode away without looking back.

"We might not be able to wipe out Red Hand's bunch," Preacher said. "But we can damn sure put a dent in the Pardees' operation."

"Providin' we can find them," Caleb said, mounting up.

Preacher stepped into the saddle and picked up the reins. "We'll find them. 'Cause if we don't, a lot of kids is in for a rough time of it."

The Pardees and their followers left the abused and tortured body of the last woman captive dead on the ground. The carrion birds and the varmints would soon take care of the body. To the best of their knowledge, no one was now left alive to connect them with any atrocities. The gang of cutthroats and brigands saddled up and headed out.

The Pardee gang had long been a scourge in the wilderness. They were a totally ruthless, savage, and lawless pack of degenerates in a land that had never known any type of law except for tribal law . . . and no tribe would have anything to do with the Pardees. Only tribal outcasts, like Red Hand and those that followed the renegade.

Miles and days behind the Pardee gang, four men rode. They rode with rifles across the saddle horn. Small bands of Indians saw the four men and did not bother them. A band of warring Blackfeet saw the four men and let them pass without trouble. There was something in the way the men sat their saddles and held their rifles that caused the Blackfeet to hesitate. And they knew that one of the men in the group was the man the Blackfeet called Killing Ghost. The band of warriors who watched the four men ride on were not afraid of Killing Ghost, known to the white as Preacher, but they respected him. They knew that should they attack, there would be heavy losses and no gain for them. So to attack was foolish.

The Blackfoot raiding party sat their ponies and watched the four men ride out of sight.

"They ride after the white renegades," one brave said.

"Good," the subchief said. "I hope they catch them and kill them all." He turned his pony's head and the others followed.

"Wonder why them Blackfeet back yonder let us go?" Caleb asked, during a break for water.

"By now, that Ponca's spread the word that we're after the Pardees and no one else," Preacher said. "Most Injuns hate the Pardees as much as we do. But they're 'feard of them. I had a Pawnee tell me one time that the Pardees had good medicine workin' all the time. And there ain't never no less than ten or twelve of them."

"A Pawnee?" Windy questioned, knowing how Preacher felt about the Pawnees. "You actual had a conversation with a Pawnee?"

Preacher smiled. "I had my good knife to his throat. He had to talk to me."

The great monetary collapse of the late 1830s was sending people westward by the hundreds. Most were cautious enough to populate states and territories east of the Missouri River. But there were others who heard the westward-ho call and ventured on. Naturalist Henry David Thoreau wrote: "Eastward I go only by force; but westward I go free."

Most of those who went west knew very little about the country into which they were traveling. Much of what they did know was wrong. Actually, very little was known about the wilderness west of the Missouri River. There were those movers who turned back, telling tales of savage hordes of wild red Indians, and of terrible sicknesses and bad water that killed when tasted. Still others told of the awful loneliness of the great plains that drove some people mad.

But still they came. For whatever reasons, they came. Alone, in pairs, often entire families. The story is told about the pioneer who, when he glimpsed the Pacific Ocean, fell to his knees and wept because he could go no further west. No one knows if the story is true or not, but it is attributed to the British novelist Charles Dickens.

By the late 1830s, cabins were beginning to dot the wilderness. Many of them belonged to trappers, but many were also family dwellings of easterners who headed west and, for one reason or another, came to a spot and went no further. All too often in the early days, they were never heard from again.

*   *   *

"That's a damn cabin down yonder!" Rimrock said.

The four were resting their horses on a ridge.

"It wasn't there last year," Preacher commented. " 'Cause I come this way." He stared at the lonely cabin. "Anyways, it ain't much of a cabin."

"You be right about that," Caleb said. "But it's new. I don't think they's anybody to home. The day is cool and they ain't no smoke from the chimney."

"Why would anybody build a cabin here?" Windy questioned.

"Who knows why an easterner does anything?" Preacher posed the question as he gave Hammer his head and started down the ridge. The others followed.

The men stopped just out of good rifle range of the cabin and spread out, studying the lonely cabin set well back from the banks of a creek.

"I'm goin' in," Preacher said, and kneed Hammer forward. He stopped in the weeded-up front of the cabin and hallooed it several times. His shouts of greeting echoed back to him. Preacher swung down and walked up to the front door, noticing that it was hanging slightly open on its leather hinges. The hinges were cracked and dried nearly useless.

Standing to one side, so the logs of the wall would stop any ball, he pushed open the door with the muzzle of his rifle. Before he could step inside, Rimrock called, "I'm going around back."

"I'm goin' inside for a look around," Preacher said.

Dust covered everything. But not one thing was out of place. A musket hung over the fireplace, and a brace of pistols in holsters were hung on the back of a chair. The table had been set for a meal, with four plates and four cups and real silverware. Preacher picked up a dust-covered spoon and hefted it. Good quality stuff, too. He looked in the blackened kettle hanging over the long-dead ashes in the fireplace. Something had been cooking in the pot, but all that was now left was a hardened glob of whatever it had been.

Pack rats had been at work; their sign was evident. But by and large, everything was as it should be.

There were three rooms and a loft. Preacher climbed the loft ladder and looked around. Nothing out of order. Two floor pallets had been made up and they had not been disturbed by any human hand. He climbed back down and walked out into the back.

"We got some skeletons out here," Caleb said.

"This is spooky, boys," Preacher said. "Damn strange. Any arrows about?"

"Nothin'," Caleb said. "And we been castin' about for sign. Critters got at the bodies, o' course, but none of the skulls has been cracked open by war axes."

"Pox might have got them," Preacher opined. "The reason the house was untouched might be 'cause the Injuns consider this an unnatural place of death and won't go near it." But he really didn't believe that. If they had the pox, why would they all run out into the backyard? He had no idea what had happened to the pioneer family and realized that, like so many other mysteries, he probably would never know. And it really didn't matter.

"What about the bones?" Windy questioned.

"I reckon we can scoop them up and plant them," Rimrock said. "That skull over yonder probably belonged to the man, and that one there is the woman. Them two over yonder was the kids."

The men got their shovels and started digging. "Seems to me like we're shore buryin' a lot of folks this go-around," Caleb remarked.

"You should have been with me at the wagon train," Preacher said, ending that topic.

No one knew where the Pardees hid out when they weren't rampaging around the ever so slowly populating wilderness, stealing and killing and raping. Preacher and his friends looked for the gang, but they had dropped out of sight.

In the wilderness, if one wished not to be found, it was easy to disappear within the millions and millions of acres of plains and timber and mountains. But not so easy for a large gang. They had to cook, had to have coffee, and that meant more than one fire for a dozen or so men. Somebody would see the smoke.

"Have not seen them, Preacher," a Cheyenne called Big Belly told him. "But Red Hand went north and west, to the mountains. This much I know is true."

"Why so far away?"

Big Belly shrugged his shoulders. "I cannot say what I do not know."

Preacher and his friends pushed on, all sharing the feeling they were chasing a will-o'-the-wisp. They headed west, and when they came to a spot that seemed familiar to them, they made camp. The Indians knew they were there, of course, but the mountain men had long ago made friends with most of the tribes . . . except for the Blackfeet. Most of the Indians looked upon the mountain men as being one of them, wanderers and hunters and lovers of the earth. But the men kept a sharp eye out nevertheless. You just never could tell.

"No point in us wearin' ourselves out looking for the Pardees," Preacher said. "They got them a hidey-hole and they's dug in tight. If there is any wagon trains headin' west, and I pray they ain't, they'll be loathe to leave the safety of the fort with all the killin' goin' on."

"You hope," Caleb said, as he dug a shallow pit for the fire and lined the rim with rocks. "Movers bein' what they is, some of them would walk through the hellfires to get west. I never seen the like."

Windy brought back a battered and blackened coffee pot filled with water and set it to boil. "Reckon what month this is?" he asked.

"May, I think," Rimrock said. "Since I give up furrin', I

don't pay much attention no more. Preacher, we best be mindful of what that driftin' Mandan told us about them Contraires."

Preacher nodded his head in agreement. The Cheyenne warrior society called Contraires were extremely unpredictable. If they meant no, they said yes. They washed in dust and dried off in water. Nearly everything they did was backwards, except in battle. They was nothing backward about them in battle. The Cheyenne believed they possessed magical powers, but Preacher knew from personal experience that they bled and died just like anyone else. But they were fine warriors and to be feared.

"You got somethin' gnawin' at you, Preacher," Caleb said. "You want to spit it out?"

"Yeah, I do," Preacher admitted. "Any of you boys ever heard of a man named Sutherlin?"

Caleb, Rimrock, and Windy exchanged glances. "How come you ask that?" Windy inquired.

" 'Cause I think he's crooked as a snake. I think the bastard's workin' with the Pardees."

The men chewed on that for a moment. "I heard of him," Windy said. "He lives back East. Ain't he some kind of organizer of wagon trains west?"

"That's him. Betina told me he was the one who spoke to her and them others back East. He was supposed to meet them for the trip west, but backed out. Now I got me an idea that he's done this before."

"Sounds reasonable to me," Rimrock said. "But you ain't got no proof of that."

"Not a bit. Just a gut hunch is all."

"Who would know that we could ask out here?" Caleb questioned.

"One of them damn Pardees, that's who," Preacher said.

"They ain't likely to be givin' that up easy like," Windy pointed out.

"I 'spect not. But you let me get my hands on one of them,

and I'll make you a bet I get the news out of him. Count on that. Dump in the coffee. Water's boilin'."

"That would be a low thing for a man to do, if this Sutherlin's doin' it," Rimrock said. "A terrible mighty low thing."

The men sat silent with their thoughts for a time. Then, strong black coffee poured, they leaned back against their saddles and relaxed. "I knowed it," Rimrock said, breaking the silence. "I knowed I been here 'fore. Right here in this same spot. It just now come to me." He looked around. "Yep. Right over there is where I buried Jake Maguire. Right over yonder on that rise in that stand of cottonwoods."

"I 'member him," Caleb said. "Injuns get him?"

"Nope. He started complainin' 'bout his stomach hurtin' and it just got worser as the days wore on. We stopped right here on this very spot and he passed the next mornin'. His belly was all swoll up. Something went wrong with his innards, I 'pose."

The men followed Rimrock as he walked over to the stand of trees and up the rise. "Right there," he said, pointing. "I scratched them words in that big rock."

JAKE M. DYED 1821
OF INNARD SIKNES.

"I didn't know how to spell his last name," Rimrock confessed. "But I got them other words right!"

8

The eyes of the mountain men popped open and everyone lay still in their robes and blankets, alert and listening as the very faint and unnatural sound came out of the night and to the now-wide-awake camp. The fire had burned down to only a few embers and the night sky was cloud-filled, limiting vision to no more than a few yards. With their hands on their weapons, the mountain men waited. They could smell the wood smoke and grease from the bodies and clothing of the Indians and knew from long experience in the wilderness that when the attack came, it would come either in a silent deadly run or in a wild screaming rush of killing frenzy. They also knew the Indians were very close. No one had to ask if the others were awake. These were men who had lived all their adult lives on the cutting edge of danger.

Preacher cut his eyes to the bulk of Rimrock, who was lying only a couple of yards away. He could see the whites of his eyes and practically feel the tenseness in the big man's body.

Across the dying embers, Windy had his hands outside

his blankets, and both hands were filled with pistols. Caleb lay on his side, one hand on his rifle.

Any second now, Preacher thought. They're as close as they dare come before they leap. If we make every ball count, we can break the attack at the first rush . . . maybe. If they get inside the circle, we've got a fight on our hands.

Preacher knew that every man there was thinking the same thing. He also felt that these were Red Hand's renegades rather than the Cheyenne Contraires the Mandan had warned them about; but he wasn't quite certain why he thought that. Then he knew why. The smells were many, signifying men from different tribes. Not all tribes ate the same thing, hence their body odors were different. Some Plains Injuns, such as the Blackfoot, Crow, and Comanche, would not eat fish, considering it taboo. Apaches would eat a horse, but Plains Injuns worshipped the horse, oftentimes staging elaborate burial ceremonies for a favorite. A few tribes would eat dog, but most would not; some even worshipped the dog as a minor god. Some Injun tribes considered the coyote as sent from the beyond, so they revered it.

Just some of the dozens of little things a man must learn quickly in the wilderness . . . if he plans on keeping his hair for any length of time.

Then there was no more time for thinking as the renegades came screaming out of the darkness, charging the camp with rifles and war axes and knives.

Preacher threw back his blankets and rose to his knees, cocking and leveling one pistol. He fired, the ball taking the brave in the chest and stopping him cold. Before the dying attacker hit the ground, Preacher turned and leveled his second pistol. The night blossomed with muzzle flashes and Preacher's second shot hit a brave in the face. The Injun's face exploded and he was flung backward, dead before he stretched out on the ground. Preacher grabbed for his Hawken.

A buck jumped on his back and rode Preacher to the cold

ground. Preacher flipped him off and jumped into the middle of the man's chest with both feet. He heard bones break under his feet. The renegade screamed in pain as Preacher rolled away, grabbing up his rifle and cocking it as he came to his knees.

The rifle was torn from his grasp and Preacher ducked a savage blow from a war axe. On his back in the dirt, Preacher got his feet all tangled up in the Injun's feet and ankles and brought him down. Kicking out, Preacher's foot smashed the buck's nose and the other foot caught him in the throat. The Indian started gagging and gasping for breath through his ruptured throat.

Rolling to his feet, his rifle lost in the dust, Preacher hauled out his big blade and went to cuttin'. He nearly severed the head off of one buck. The man went down, blood squirting with every beat of his heart. Turning, Preacher drove the blade into the throat of another warrior, abruptly stilling the wild cries. He jerked the blade free and jumped to one side, avoiding the screaming charge of a brave with the hair knot that some Cheyenne favor. Preacher stuck out a foot and tripped the buck, sending him rolling and sprawling. Preacher jumped on the man's back and drove his blade into the buck's neck.

Rimrock had dropped his empty pistols and snapped the back of an attacker, and he was now wrestling with a huge brave. He clamped one big hand around the buck's throat and squeezed with all his might. Blood erupted from the buck's mouth and Rimrock let him drop to strangle on the ground.

Windy had fired his last charged weapon and was now fighting with a lance he'd taken from a dead Sioux. He impaled a buck, and when he jerked to free the lance, the tip broke off. Windy started using it like a club.

Caleb was swinging his empty rifle and doing some fearful damage with the heavy weapon. Dead and dazed Indians lay all around his feet.

Preacher grabbed up a war axe and planted it in a Cheyenne's head.

Suddenly, as it nearly always is, the attack was over. Indians ran back into the timber and rode out. The mountain men found their weapons and quickly charged them, working fast but smoothly from years of practice. One Indian rose up and tried to stab Windy in the back. Preacher shot him in the chest.

Windy built a small fire and soon had the coffee hot. The men began dragging the dead Indians out of their camp area. Then they sat back down and caught their breath. When they had swallowed some coffee, each took a firebrand and inspected their grisly work.

"All renegades," Preacher said, as they walked around the area where they'd dumped the bodies. They were not worried about the Indians returning this night. This bunch had taken a terrible beating at the hands of the mountain men, and wanted no more of them. And since they were renegades, they would not be back for the bodies. But the men weren't careless, either. They quickly broke camp and moved about a mile. Since it was nearly dawn, they did not attempt to sleep.

"I killed a Ute," Caleb said. "And I seen Preacher drop him a Cheyenne. Rimrock killed a Dakota. Something big is in the works, I'm thinkin'."

An Indian with blood all over his face and chest staggered into the camp and fell down before he could do any damage with his axe, and before any of the men could shoot him.

Preacher squatted down beside the dying brave and tossed his axe into the graying early morning. "You a damn Kiowa," he said. The dying Indian glowered up at him. "You sort of out of your territory, ain't you?"

The Kiowa cursed and spat at him, showing Preacher that he was not afraid. But also giving away that he spoke some English. He had taken a ball in the chest and his head was busted wide open, the skull bone showing.

"You better talk to me," Preacher told him. " 'Cause if you don't, when you die, I'll cut out your eyes and take your hands and feet. You'll never find your way to the beyond and you won't be able to see it if you do stumble into it."

The Kiowa's eyes narrowed at that. Finally, he said, "What is it you wish to know?"

"You're part of Red Hand's bunch?"

"Yes,"

"Where is he?"

"That I do not know. We broke from him for the time he spends away from the wagon trail. In this I speak the truth." He coughed up blood, pink and frothy, and that was a sure sign that he was lung-shot.

When he had finished coughing, Preacher asked, "Where is the Pardee hideout?"

"No one knows that. Not even Red Hand. I know only that it is in the mountains."

Preacher believed him. He didn't know why, but he did. "How do you want to be treated at death?"

"You would do that for me?"

"Why not? I ain't got nothin' agin you."

The brave sighed, the expulsion of air sounding more like a death rattle. "I want to be left to rot. That is all I deserve." His head lolled to one side.

The men drank coffee and waited for the Indian to die. He died about an hour after dawn. "I wonder what he done to get banished from the tribe?" Windy asked.

"Don't have no idea," Preacher said. "Must have been something awful." He rolled the Indian up in a tattered blanket he was going to throw away and secured it. "We'll wedge him up yonder in that thick fork" he said, pointing to a huge old tree. " 'Bout the best I know to do."

The men packed up and pulled out. A mile from where they'd left the dead Kiowa, they found the body of another Indian. They did not dismount, just looked at the body and rode on. That made fourteen renegades the mountain men had killed in one brief battle. When the news reached Red Hand, it would make the renegade leader much more wary of the four, pointing out to him that their medicine was very strong.

The men pushed on, heading for the high mountains in the faint hope they could find the hideout of the Pardee gang. Chances of them doing that were slight, something they all knew, but all four felt it was something they had to do. They cursed the ever-growing numbers of movers that were heading across the Great Plains to the Pacific, and cursed those who were stopping to settle in the wilderness. In all the days they'd been in the saddle, they'd seen two new cabins. Place was really getting crowded. But the curses were mainly without rancor. The men realized it was progress, and like the Indians, they could do nothing to prevent it. But unlike the Indians, they could live with it and try to adjust to it.

"This here's where the pilgrims cross," Preacher said, dismounting and stretching.

They were west of Three Crossings, standing on the east side of the Sweetwater River.

"If somebody was ambitious," Preacher continued, looking around him, they'd build them a post right here and make a fortune sellin' to the movers."

"Tend store?" Windy said. "Wagh!"

The mountain men all shuddered at the thought. Just the idea of being trapped inside four walls was disgusting. And having to deal with people was even more disgusting. Especially pilgrims. Pilgrims didn't appear to have a whole lot of sense. If they did, they'd stay to home and hearth.

"But that ain't for the likes of us," Preacher said, summing up all their feelings. He looked around him at the silent loneliness. "The Pardees got to be just west of here. Somewheres between the Wind River and South Pass. Or at least they got lookouts close by."

"Mayhaps you be right, Preacher," Caleb said. "Let's split up. We're all gettin' a tad sick of each other's company, and that way we can cover a lot more territory and be shut of one another for a time."

The mountain men parted company that day, agreeing to meet back at the crossing in a week or so. They rode the land, going into areas where few white men had ever been. They searched for sign and inspected the horizon for smoke. They could find nothing. They all came back more than a little disgusted. None of them had found hide nor hair of the Pardee gang.

"They ain't within no twenty-five or thirty miles of this place, Preacher," Caleb said. "Or if they is," he amended, "they ain't cookin' 'ceptin' after dark and under a tent or in a cave."

That last part triggered something in Preacher's brain. But he couldn't pin it down. He let it lie dormant for the time being. It would come to him.

"Hello, the camp!" The call came out of the late-afternoon air. "I'm uncurried and mangy and got fleas, but I'm told I'm right friendly."

"Carl Lippett," Caleb said. "I'd know that voice anywheres. Come on in, Carl."

Carl sure wasn't lyin'. He definitely was uncurried and mangy. He looked and smelled like he hadn't had a bath in weeks. And as for the fleas, Preacher started scratching five minutes after Carl joined them around the fire. But he did have news, so the men could scratch in exchange.

"Big doin's at the post, boys," Carl said, after taking a swallow of coffee. Since he came from the east, the post would be Fort William. "Got some pilgrims who pulled in and some of them wanted to sell their wagons and possessions and head back to home. Had some pilgrims there who jumped right in and bought the wagons. But here's the funny part: these pilgrims ain't goin' over the mountains west of here. No sirree. They're sayin' they're gonna settle just north of here. Permanently. Up where the Wind River bends."

Preacher leaned back against his saddle and drank his coffee. He dismissed what Carl had just said. He didn't believe a word of it. Carl must have had his head in a jug of whiskey and got things all twisted around. Nobody in their right mind would settle anywhere near this location.

". . . And kids," Carl continued. "Lord, I have never seen the like in all my borned days. Looked like a herd of midgets. And they was two women travelin' without no men; they had about ten kids 'tween 'em."

Preacher sat up and looked at Carl. "*What* two women travelin' alone, Carl?"

"Well, I disremember their names right off. But they was both comely ladies, I can tell you that. One a few years younger than the other. The younger one was the real looker. And they must have had a right smart poke to buy them wagons and outfits."

Preacher stared at him, a sick feeling in the pit of his stomach. It just couldn't be. "What . . . ages . . . were . . . the . . . kids?" he asked in a low and slow tone. Caleb, Windy, and Rimrock all gave him strange looks.

"Why . . . I'd have to say they run 'tween nine and thirteen," Carl said. "And that puzzles me. How do you reckon them ladies done that? I can't figure it out. There wasn't no twins amongst 'em. It's a mystery to me."

"Done what?" Rimrock questioned.

"To be so young and to have all them younguns so close together? Don't none of them kids favor a-tall."

"Well, hell, igit!" Windy said. "They probably adopted 'em. Any fool could figger that out."

Rimrock and Caleb shook their heads. Preacher's face was a real study.

"Oh," Carl said. "Mayhaps you be right. I never thought of that."

"What else in the way of important events has you got to tell us?" Caleb asked.

"They left the post about a week 'fore I did. They ought to be along in about ten days. Oh, Preacher. I do recall one of them females' names. Drum, it was. Betina Drum."

9

It took the men about fifteen minutes to calm Preacher down. They were all pretty good cussers, but after listening to Preacher unload, they all had to admit that he could probably outcuss anyone they had ever been around. Preacher stomped around the camp, kicking this and that and hollering and running off any animal within a five-mile radius who wasn't picketed. He did make an exception for a small band of friendly Shoshoni who had silently walked their ponies up on a ridge above the camp and sat listening to their old friend Preacher rant and rave.

"I ought to throw you in the damn river!" Preacher told a startled Carl Lippett.

"Me? What'd I do, Preacher? Now you just calm down. Me and water don't get along."

That was the wrong thing to say but spoken at just the right time. Preacher scratched at a flea bite and glanced at Rimrock, who smiled and looked at Windy, who grinned and winked at Caleb, who had a wicked look in his eyes.

Preacher said, "You got any soap in your possibles bag, Rimrock?"

"Brand new bar I bought up north. Strong soap hand-made by some movers."

"I seen him buy it," Windy said. "It's strong all right. Man can get clean just by standin' near it." Windy scratched at a bite. "Carl, you got en-tarry too many varmints on you. I'll fetch the soap."

Carl began looking wildly around him for a way out. There was none. The men had him blocked. Carl spotted the Shoshoni warriors on the ridge and yelled for them to help him. They laughed and pointed at him.

"Weasel Tail!" Preacher shouted. "Keep an eye out for us, will you?"

"You have your fun, Preacher," Weasel Tail shouted. "We watch good."

"Now, rookie here, boys," Carl protested. "I had me a right good wash back some months ago. That'll do me for the rest of the summer."

"Now!" Preacher yelled, and the men grabbed him, one to each arm and leg. They carried him squalling to the river. They all piled into the water.

The Shoshoni were laughing and pointing. They would have stories to tell when they returned to their village.

"Goddamnit!" Carl roared. "Unhand me, you heathens! Too much water ain't good for a body. Rots the skin."

Carl was dunked into the water several times and Rimrock lathered his long hair with the strong lye soap. Fleas were leaping and hopping for their lives by the hundreds. If they could shriek, they would have been doing that, too. But since those bathing Carl had just about as much soap on them as did Carl, the fleas were exiting the other mountain men as fast as they landed on them. Articles of clothing were tossed on the bank and soon the men were all as naked as the day they came into this world. Tell the truth, they all needed a good scrubbing, and they got it, in addition to some black eyes, busted lips, and various other contusions and abrasions from Carl's fists.

"Halp!" Carl hollered.

Windy jammed a fistful of suds into his mouth and that closed that.

For the mountain men, it would have been a terribly inopportune time for a band of outlaws or renegade Indians to come along. But Weasel Tail was a mighty war chief of the Shoshoni, and it would take a large band to attack him.

But they were lucky, for the Shoshoni were enjoying the show and more than happy to guard over the rambunctious and frolicking men of the mountains.

The men finally decided that Carl was clean enough—probably the cleanest he'd been in years—and allowed him to exit the water, which he did with great haste, running around the camp drying himself off and cussing the other men.

"I'll probably die of pnew-moanee!" he hollered at them, frantically looking around for his clothing. Where's my damn clothes?" He had not noticed when Preacher tossed all their clothing into the river. Windy grabbed them and commenced washing.

"I got 'em!" Windy hollered. "I'll get the varmints out of them, too." He waved at the Shoshoni and they waved back. "Look at Weasel Tail, Preacher. He's gettin' a real laugh out of all this."

Preacher waved at the five Shoshoni and motioned for them to come on down, pointing at the coffeepot and making the sign for eat. They did not need a second invitation. While the mountain men were drying off and dressing in spare clothing—except for Carl; he didn't have any spares and Caleb loaned him some britches and a shirt—the Shoshoni dismounted and sat around the fire, waiting patiently for their hosts to join them. To eat and drink first would not be at all polite. They ignored the rantings and ravings of Carl.

Over coffee and venison steaks, the men ate in silence—no talking until the food was gone. Finally, Weasel Tail belched and spoke. "You all look very hard for something, Preacher. What is it you seek?"

"Band of no-good white men. The Pardees."

"They live in caves in the mountains. Just across the Wind River." He pointed and that little worrisome thing that had popped into Preacher's mind was now clear. He knew now the general area of the Pardee gang. "But the way is guarded. Two men with rifles could hold back an army."

"How many ways in and out?" Rimrock asked.

"I do not know. It is a bad place and Indians do not go there."

No one asked why. That would not be polite. Probably something terrible had happened there, perhaps centuries back, and the story was passed down through the generations by the keepers of those things.

"I have to tell you that more whites are coming," Preacher said.

"From out of the fort to the east. Yes. We know. They won't be bothered by my tribe. I cannot speak for the Sioux or the Cheyenne." He spat on the ground. "Who would want to?" The Shoshoni were bitter enemies of the Sioux and the Cheyenne, and didn't have a whole lot of love for the Crow, either, since neither the Sioux or the Crow would admit that any other Indian tribe had the right to exist anywhere.

"Red Hand?" Preacher asked.

"Red Hand will die if he attempts to fight us. So he does not. I do not know where he is."

Preacher figured Weasel Tail was lying about that. But he didn't push the issue. Preacher waited, sensing something else was on the subchief's mind and that he would get to it in his own good time. Preacher took out tobacco and they all smoked.

"There will be no stopping the whites, will there, Preacher?" Weasel Tail asked.

"No. If all the tribes in the West came together, you would only stop them for a little while." Preacher wasn't sure about that, either, but he figured he'd better plant some doubt in the brave's mind. And his remark would be repeated, he knew that.

"What is it like where you came from, Preacher?"

"I couldn't tell you now," Preacher admitted. "I been out here since I was just a boy. I ain't never been back. I had a person tell me last year that they got great iron steam engines that run on steel tracks. They're all over the place. Call them trains. Some folks say that they'll be out here 'fore long."

"Trains," Weasel Tail repeated. "What do these trains do?"

"Carry goods and people, I reckon. Be a right interestin' sight to see, I 'pose. Some folks back East even got toilets in their houses."

"Inside the lodge?" Weasel Tail was appalled.

"Yep. 'Fraid so."

Weasel Tail shook his head at the thought. "That would not be a good thing. I cannot imagine why people would want such a thing."

"Me, neither."

"What are you going to do now, Preacher? You did not trap this season."

"I don't know," he admitted.

"You could come live with us," Weasel Tail suggested, his face brightening. "Preacher is always welcome in our lodges. Why not? You are a great hunter and provider and my village has some fine-looking young women and you could choose one and she would make you a good partner. Your way of life is almost gone, Preacher, and . . ." His voice trailed off and he sighed his frustration. "I mask my own fears, Preacher. I am afraid I will live to see the end of my own way of life. The whites just keep pushing westward and bringing sicknesses that we have never known before and do not have the power to combat. Many tribes have been nearly wiped out. Tamsuky of the Cayuse is already making talk against the Bible-shouter Whitman west of us. The Cheyenne and Ute and Arapaho and Sioux and Blackfoot say we must fight to keep the whites out. I do not want to fight the whites."

"We would rather be friends," a young warrior said. "But it is hard to be friends with whites who come now. They are not like you men. They are fearful people and they leave great mounds of stinking garbage behind them when the wagons leave."

Preacher knew that to be fact. He'd personally seen it. He nodded his head in agreement. "The Nes Percé?"

Weasel Tail met his eyes. "They are as we. They do not wish to fight the whites. But a fight is coming, Preacher. If the advancing whites do not respect our land, and our way of life, and you know they will not, there will be war."

Preacher was a simple man; he did not have the words to be profound, even though he was considered fairly well educated among his peers, being able to read and write and do sums. He could but shake his head in agreement, for he knew the words of Weasel Tail to be true. Already, many of the tribes along the West Coast had been wiped out, had succumbed to sickness, or, for the most part, had been tamed. But Preacher, despite his gripings about the steadily growing numbers of people moving west, knew that many of the folks back East who moaned about the plight of the Noble Red Man did not know all the truth. The truth was that the whites were not stealing the land from the Indians, for the Indians didn't own it. Most did not believe that anyone could really *own* part of the earth. They could not comprehend that. And the Indians were not poor, simple savages. They certainly could be savage—to the white man's way of thinking—but on the plus side, many Indian tribes had very complex societies and laws and rules.

"I don't know what to say to you, Weasel Tail," Preacher replied. "I ain't no educated man, but I know that what you say is true. You and us here, we think alike on most things. That's why we can get along. We respect your way of life and don't try to change it. But these new folks comin' out . . ."

He sighed, wishing he could tell the Indian about how the movers felt. But to tell the truth, he didn't understand them. either. "Yeah, you gonna have to change, Weasel Tail. They gonna make you change—or kill you."

Preacher had heard the stories about the Fox and the Sauk, and how back in '32 a warrior named Black Hawk had tried to lead about a thousand of his people back to their homelands, part of which included western Illinois. His original intent had been peaceful, not warlike. Black Hawk and his followers just wanted to go home. What they got was slaughtered as they fled, trying to swim across the Mississippi River back into Iowa.

"Now Preacher is sad," Weasel Tail said.

"Yeah, I reckon I is. Farms and factories now are where the Ojibwa, Menominee, Iowa, Winnebago, Ottawa, and Potawatomi once lived. And that ain't altogether right."

"What is a factory, Preacher?" a brave asked.

"Well, it's a place where people work to make things. Sort of like when your women all gather to sew together skins for a tipi."

"Ahh! And then when what they make is made, they go back to . . . what?"

"Well, they ship them goods out and then they start all over makin' more goods."

"Why?"

"So's the people . . . ah, so's other people don't have to make the goods that are made in the factory."

Weasel Tail sighed and shook his head. "These other people, what do they do that makes them so important that other people must do their work for them?"

Preacher smiled. "Well, it ain't that they's so important. It's just that the people in the factory makes things for the people in the other factory . . . sort of."

"Ayee!" Weasel Tail cried. "My head is reeling from confusion. Let me see if I understand all this. When both factories have finished making whatever it is they make, they all get together and trade, correct?"

"Not exactly," Preacher said—his own head was beginning to reel from confusion. "You see, white people use money. You've all seen the metal coins. Well, they have value to white people. So they give the coins for the goods that are made in the factories."

"There is more than one or two factories?"

"Oh, yeah. Hundreds of 'em."

The Indians looked at one another. Weasel Tail said, "There are not that many things that have to be made."

"There is in the white man's world."

"What makes these *co*-ins worth something?" another brave asked.

"Well, I ain't real sure about that," Preacher admitted. "But it boils down to gold and silver is valuable."

"To who?"

"The white man."

"Why?"

"I . . . don't know. It just is."

Weasel Tail picked up a rock. "Could this be as valuable as gold or silver?"

"If enough people thought so, yeah."

"So if enough people thought this rock was the worth of twelve horses, and I had twelve horses, they would give me this rock for the horses?"

"Yeah . . . that's about it, I reckon."

"What would I do with the rock?"

"You could use it to buy more horses from another person."

"There is no one in my tribe that stupid."

"Yeah . . . well, you do have a point. I think."

"Will we have to use these *co*-ins you speak of?" a Shoshoni asked.

"Probably. Someday. Yeah, you will."

"And how will we get them?"

"You work for them."

"Where?"

"In the factories and on the farms and things like that."

Weasel Tail stood up. "My head is aching from all this confusing talk about *co*-ins and factories and rocks that are worth twelve ponies. Why don't whites just give a sack of potatoes for a shirt, or a horse for a wooden box that whites live in, or a gun for a shoe and be done with it?"

"Well, because not all whites have a gun or a horse or a sack of potatoes."

"But they have *co*-ins?"

"Well, yeah, some of them. Most of them."

Weasel Tail looked down at Preacher and shook his head. "Your people are very strange. Your people want to possess so many things that are useless that you complicate your society so you must carry around pieces of metal to purchase more things that you really do not need. I think I will never understand the mind of white people. They make my head hurt. White people live in houses that cannot be moved. What do the white people do when they get tired of looking at the same thing all the time?"

Preacher chuckled. "Well, they sell their houses, I reckon."

"Then the people put the *co*-ins in their pockets and go chop down more trees to build another wooden box they cannot move."

"That's . . . just about it, Weasel Tail."

"Well. That is very foolish. What happens when all the trees are gone?"

"Weasel Tail, the trees ain't never gonna be *gone!*"

"What will prevent that from happening? I have been told that there are so many whites they cannot be counted. If that is true, if they all cut down trees to build their useless wooden houses, soon there will be no more trees, am I not right?"

"Now he's got me worryin'," Rimrock said.

"Me, too," Windy said. "He's got a point, Preacher."

"I don't even know what in the hell any of you is talkin' about," Caleb said.

"These clothes smell funny," Carl said. "I'm gonna smell like a laundry for a week."

"Oh, hell!" Preacher said. "They's trees all over the damn place. They grow up out of the ground natural. Stop worryin' about trees."

"Somebody better worry about them," Weasel Tail said somberly. "Trees are life. Indians know this. Whites do not. I am afraid that someday white people will cause the earth to die. Then see if you can buy another earth with your *co*-ins." He waved his hand, and without another word, he and his party left the encampment.

Rimrock took the empty coffeepot down to the river for more water. Windy placed another stick on the fire. Caleb leaned back against his saddle and looked reflective. Carl was fanning himself, trying to dispel the soap smell.

Preacher shook his head. "Maybe Weasel Tail is right and we're wrong. Hell, I don't know. I just wish everybody would get along. Might as well wish for the moon." He lay down and pulled a blanket over him. "Wake me up when it's time to eat."

10

All they could do was wait, and that was something they could do well. Carl pulled out a few days after Weasel Tail's gloom-and-doom talk, saying he'd see the men around . . . when they got shut of that damn bar of soap.

"I still smell like a laundry," he muttered as he rode away. "At least the fleas was company."

"What's your plan, Preacher?" Windy asked, as the men lay around the fire, drinking coffee.

"I really ain't got one. I know the wagons got to pass right by here. So mayhaps I'll see to it that they get clear of the Pardees. I don't know exactly what I'll do. I'll damn shore try to talk them out of cuttin' north and settin' up yonder. That's plumb foolish."

"Well, I don't mind waitin'," Caleb said.

"You boys want to pitch in with me and see to the needs of a bunch of hammerheaded easterners, hey?"

"It ain't as if we had a whole lot of pressin' engagements, Preacher," Windy said.

"We ain't got nothin' else to do, Preacher," Rimrock said. "Throw another stick on that fire, Windy. It's our lazy day."

The men did nothing but eat, sleep, hunt for game, fish, and tell totally outrageous lies to each other and about each other. The days drifted by and blended in. Time was unimportant. They could almost make themselves believe it was very nearly like when they first arrived in the Big Lonesome. But they all knew it was not. Already, wagon ruts were being carved in what some were calling the Oregon Trail.

Then one morning the men heard the very faint sounds of bullwhips and the shouting of human voices.

"Yonder come the pilgrims headin' to the promised land," Caleb said.

"Yeah," Rimrock said. "They in for a jolt, I'm thinkin'. 'Cause they ain't no milk out here and the only honey usually has a bear close by it."

"One thing about it, though," Preacher said, recalling last year when he led a party of pilgrims to the West Coast, "by now they'll have gotten rid of much of the stuff they thought they just couldn't live without. And they'll be plenty trail wise, too."

"What I can't figure out is just exactly where they think they'll settle up north of here," Rimrock mused. "And what they're gonna do oncest they get there."

"That's a mystery to me, too," Preacher said. "But I reckon we'll know directly."

"I wonder why the scout didn't come up on us hours ago?" Windy said.

"The fools probably don't have one," Preacher replied. "And don't nobody go lookin' at me."

The men and women and children stared at the four mountain men. And stared. Finally a man mounted on a fine bay horse stepped out of the saddle and pointed a finger at Preacher.

"You there!" he shouted. "Come here."

The mountain men looked at each other and all smiled. Preacher raised his voice and told the man, "You got something you want to say to me, get over here and say it. The distance is the same for you as it is for me."

The man flushed a deep red. "I am not accustomed to such impudence, sir," he called. "My name is Samuel Weller."

"I'm proud you know your name," Preacher told him. "If a man don't know nothin' else, he shore ought to know his name. I fought a bear oncest in the woods and lost, so he took my name. Folks started callin' me Preacher. So if you run into a bear with a Christian name, leave him be. It's me."

Weller stared at Preacher for a moment. Then he walked toward the men, stopped, and shook his head. "That is utter balderdash, sir. Are you mad?"

"I ain't even upset. Are you?"

Several of the men and women in and alongside the wagons at the front of the train started laughing, and Weller's face again turned crimson. Preacher figured right off that he hadn't made any points with Weller. Not that he gave a damn.

"You there!" Weller pointed his whip handle at Rimrock. "We are in need of an experienced guide to lead us to our final destination. Are you interested?"

"I ain't even curious." Rimrock told him.

Weller opened his mouth, then abruptly closed it as the name Preacher began sinking in. *Preacher!* The man who had rescued the missionaries and then led the wagon train to the Pacific. My word! The man was a living legend.

Weller walked over to where Preacher and the other mountain men stood, rifles in hand, pistols and knives hung all about them. Good Lord, he thought, facing the men, but they certainly were a disreputable-looking bunch. But they all seemed . . . quite capable. He looked at Windy. For a man of his small size, he certainly had a bold and reckless demeanor about him.

Weller looked at the bulk of Rimrock. The man was very nearly a giant. Certainly capable of breaking a man in two. Rimrock grinned at the man.

Caleb was a long and lean and lanky man, but Weller knew those types of men could possess extraordinary endurance and strength. Preacher was, well, Preacher. Wide shoulders and hard-packed muscle in his arms. Huge wrists. The man had only a stubble of beard, so obviously he shaved quite often. But there was one more thing about Preacher that Weller had missed at first glance, but not now. The man was dangerous. Not dangerous in the unpredictable sense, but dangerous in that he would be a bad man to have as an enemy.

Weller cleared his throat and was about to speak when a woman's voice cut him off.

"Oh, Preacher!"

Miss Drum came rushing up, quite unladylike, Weller thought, and threw her arms about Preacher's neck and boldly kissed the man right on the *lips!* Weller was taken aback by the utter brazenness of it.

"Preacher! I just knew I'd see you again," she exclaimed, and kissed him again.

Preacher's eyes were wide with shock. Embarrassed, he disentangled himself from the woman and held the well-endowed young lady at full arm's length. "Betina. You're lookin' well."

"To say the least," Rimrock muttered.

"Amen, brother," Windy whispered.

Caleb stared at the woman.

"I just knew we'd meet again, Preacher," Betina gushed. "Were you waiting for us to come along?"

"Well . . . tell you the truth, yes. I was wantin' to talk you folks out of this crazy notion of headin' north, and point you either west to the Oregon Territory or back home."

She shook her curls. "Preacher, we are going to build a town just north of here. Along the banks of the Wind River. We shall have shops and stores and a church and a school. Isn't that right, Mr. Weller?"

"That is correct, Miss Drum," the man said—a bit stiffly, Preacher thought.

Preacher took off his hat and rubbed his forehead with a hard and callused hand. "Betina, listen to me, girl. There ain't nothing up there where you're talkin' about 'ceptin' Injuns. It's too soon for all this, girl. You've had you a taste of how wild and savage this land can be. But you ain't seen nothin' until you winter out here. That is, providin' you and the rest of these good folks *survive* 'til the winter. Betina, there ain't nothin' up yonder. No trails, no roads, no civilized folks, no nothin'. There ain't nothin' 'tween Fort William and Fort Hall 'ceptin' wilderness, Injuns, and renegades. It's a fool's errand you're on, girl."

She stared at him for a long moment and Preacher knew he had not dissuaded her. "I am determined, Preacher. We shall have our town to the north."

Then Weller had to stick his mouth into it. "We shall trust in the Lord, Preacher," Weller said. "He has guided us this far, and we shall continue to bask in the light of His providence."

"Mayhaps you be right, Weller," Preacher said.

Weller beamed his delight at that.

" 'Cause I reckon that old sayin' holds true," Preacher added.

"And what might that be, sir?"

"That the Good Lord looks after drunks, children, and fools!"

"This ain't right what you're doin', Preacher," Rimrock bluntly told him.

Preacher stopped in his rolling of blankets into canvas groundsheet and looked up at the man. "You don't mean to tell me that you're stayin'?"

"I got to, Preacher. These people ain't got a prayer out yonder on their own."

Preacher stood up. "Rim, there ain't even no good *trail* that leads up yonder to where these fools want to go. You know that as well as me. We've all been there. There ain't nothin' there. So why there, Rim? Answer me that."

"I don't know the answer to that, Preacher. But that there little gal thinks the world and all of you, and if you turn your backside to her at this time of need, then you a mighty sorry excuse for a man."

Preacher's eyes narrowed and he cocked his head to one side and stared at the man. "I've killed men for sayin' a hell of a lot less than that to me, Rimrock."

Rimrock met the stare without blinking. "I don't think you ever kilt no man just 'cause he spoke the truth," the big man said calmly.

That stung Preacher. He frowned and shook his head in disgust. He'd been friends with these men for too many years to have something like this drive a rift 'tween them. He sighed heavily. "All right, Rim. All right. Hell, I'd a probably been back come the mornin' noways. I'll help you take these people into the wilderness. Has any of 'em told you exactly where it is they want to go?"

Preacher listened and his eyes grew wider. When Rimrock finished, Preacher said, "Now I know they're all plumb crazy. That ain't farmin' country. That country ain't good for nothin'. Are you sure about this?"

"He had the location all writ now and he read it off to me."

"Something is bad wrong with this, Rim. That's a good thirty-five or forty miles north of this trail. The only visitors they'll have will be them lookin' for scalps."

"I done pointed that out to them. Weller said the Lord would see to their safety."

"Is he a gospel shouter?"

"If he ain't, he shore ought to be. Are you goin' to talk to him about this folly?"

Preacher shook his head. "No need. We ain't gonna

change their minds. But I thought Betina was bound and determined to reach the Oregon Territory and that Coretine person was headin' back East with the kids?"

"I reckon they changed their minds."

"I reckon they did at that. When do they want to make the turn north?"

"Right here, come the mornin'."

"Lord help us all." Preacher nodded his head and secured his bedroll behind the cantle of his saddle. "You know the way, Rim. I'll leave sign along from time to time. I'll see you in a couple of days. I want to travel light, so see to my pack animal and possessions, will you?"

"I'll do it, Preacher. See you."

Preacher swung into the saddle and rode out, past Betina's wagon. She was tending a small fire and had coffee on. She smiled up at him. "Coffee, Preacher?"

"Thank you kindly, but no. I got to push on. I'll see you in a couple of days. Then we'll talk."

Her face brightened. "I'm looking forward to that."

"Yeah," Preacher said dryly, then rode away.

He made a lonely camp that evening not too far from a slow-moving little creek. If it had a name, Preacher didn't know it. "Fools," he muttered to his tiny fire hidden in rocks. "Someday this might be a settled land. But it's too damn soon now for people to even try."

He emptied his coffeepot and put out the fire as the shadows began creeping in. Drinking his coffee and munching on a biscuit he'd swiped from a mover's wife that morning, Preacher tried to make some sense out of this move. He'd asked Weller, but the man turned mum on him. No sense in that either. He could understand people wanting to go to California or the Oregon Territory—sort of—but this move . . .

Then it came to him.

"Shore, there it was, right there in front of me all the time," Preacher muttered to the shadows. "So damn plain I couldn't even see it."

He could see Sutherlin's fine hand in this. Had to be. And the reason the Pardees couldn't be found was 'cause they wasn't back at their mountain hideout . . . they was waitin' up on the Wind River. Or at least was headin' that way. Had to be it. Sutherlin would have the wagons leave the more-or-less-established trail west and head north to settle in a country that only mountain men, a few Army scouts, and Indians had ever seen. Then when the movers was busy with building cabins and such, they'd hit them, Pardee's gang and Red Hand. They wipe them out, burn the wagons and structures, sell the women and girls for slaves and whores, and then vanish. The movers wouldn't be missed for months, at least until spring, and by that time, their bones would be bleached white and scattered by varmints. And the odds were, no one would ever know what happened to them.

"Quite a plan, if I got it figured out right," Preacher muttered. "But how did Sutherlin get tied in with the Pardee bunch? And what did he get out of this?"

Preacher knew the answer to that immediately. The fee for organizing the train, of course. But how many times could he get away with something like this?

"Plenty, if he's smart," Preacher said aloud. "Let two or three trains through, and hit the third or fourth one." And Preacher knew then why the Pardee bunch was sometimes not heard of in the Big Lonesome for months at a time: they staggered the territories where they operated. They'd ride hundreds of miles to strike, and then beat it back to the Lonesome with their booty and hide out for a time. Then they'd move to another location to strike again.

"Quite an operation," Preacher muttered. "This Sutherlin must have a lot of men workin' for him. He organizes a train back East, then sends riders west with the news." And, he thought, no tellin' how long this has been goin' on. Preacher shook his head at the vastness of it.

Preacher had known some cold-blooded ol' boys in his time, but Sutherlin and Pardee and Son and men of that ilk took the prize for bein' pure evil. To date, those workin' with Sutherlin must have been responsible for the deaths of no tellin' how many men and women and kids along the trail. No tellin' how many young girls and boys had been sold into slavery, or indentured to someone, which to Preacher's mind was the same thing as slavery.

And so, he thought, summing it up in his mind, here I am stuck a hundred miles from nowhere, knowin' what's goin' on, and now what am I goin' to do about it?

He pondered that for a time, then nodded his head as he came up with a plan. "Might work," he said. "At least I can give 'er a try."

Satisfied with it, he rolled up in his blankets, Hawken close to hand, and went to sleep.

The next day, he rode into Weasel Tail's camp and met with the Shoshoni war chief.

"A terrible thing," Weasel Tail said, after listening to Preacher. "I will help. Your plan is good one, I think. And you are right about the Pardees disappearing for long periods of time. Now we will eat and smoke and rest." He smiled sadly at Preacher. "Treachery knows no color or way of life, does it, my friend?"

"I'm afraid not," Preacher agreed. "We all got good and bad amongst us. When the time comes, Weasel Tail, you be careful what you agree to with the whites." He was silent for a moment, then added, "Some amongst us are prone to lie."

11

Weasel Tail started sending out riders that day. They were to range as far out as they dared, talking to friendly tribes and gathering news of any wagon-train ambushes or of any recently built cabins and settlements being wiped out. Weasel Tail said his riders would be back when they would be back. Time was not that big a deal for an Indian.

Preacher expected the wagon train to make no more than five or six miles a day at best. Ten days, he figured, to that miserable spot somebody had conned them into taking.

Then Preacher leveled with Weasel Tail about the final destination of the wagon train. The war chief was neither angry nor surprised. Instead, he smiled.

"We have known that for weeks, Preacher," Weasel Tail said. "Some of my people slipped close to the wagons one night and listened to the men and women talk."

"They took a chance," Preacher told him.

"Not without someone of your caliber there," the war chief replied, with a twinkle in his eyes.

"You know where I'll be," Preacher told his friend. "As soon as you get some news, let me know."

As Preacher rode the land, he was once more reminded that this part of the country was not his favorite by a long shot. He never could figure out exactly what this country was good for. And he hoped that when the members of Weller's party got themselves a good taste of it, they'd see the folly in staying and either push on west or turn around and go back home.

But it was a faint hope and he was fully aware of that. He was beginning to understand the mentality of movers.

Preacher reined up and studied the land for a moment, looking all around him. Then he smelled dust. He and Hammer went immediately into a ravine. Ground-reining the horse, Preacher slipped from the saddle and climbed up the bank and sought a little cover behind a bush that was growing tenaciously in the rocky soil. That was the only thing that prevented his head from being exposed.

It was a small war party of Utes, and they had them a couple of prisoners. Preacher knew from experience that the Utes could be real inventive when it came to torturing prisoners. But from where he squatted, he couldn't see any way in hell he could help them poor men lashed to their saddles. Then he watched as the Utes stopped and swung down off their ponies.

"Hell," Preacher muttered. "They're gonna do the deed right in front of me."

There were six Utes, all young braves, a couple of them just into manhood, it looked like. None of them had rifles or pistols. Two carried long lances, the rest bows and arrows. All had war axes.

Preacher stared hard at the prisoners. He didn't know either of them. They looked and dressed like pilgrims. With a sigh, Preacher knew he just couldn't squat back behind a skinny bush and watch two white men get tortured to death. The screamin' and hollerin' tended to get on a person's nerves. So that left only two options: leave or fight.

He slipped back to Hammer and fetched his other two

charged pistols, checking them carefully and hoping they wouldn't misfire when he most desperately needed them. He rubbed Hammer's nose and whispered to the animal, calming the big horse and taking comfort from him.

"I'm a-fixin' to stick my nose into the fire ag'in, Hammer. Way I see it, I ain't got no choice in the matter. Goddamn pilgrims is gonna be the death of me yet. So you just rest for a time and be here when I get back."

Preacher slipped up the ravine until it narrowed down to nothing. He crawled on his belly for a few yards until coming up behind another skimpy bush. There would have been nothing to this in the lushness of the real wilderness, with thick stands of timber and growth aplenty.

He peeked around the scrub bush and saw smoke beginning to rise. These young Utes were fixin' to have themselves a high ol' time with the prisoners. Probably going to start out by burnin' the feet of the men. That way even if the men did get loose, they couldn't run away. The backs of the Utes was toward him, so Preacher closed the distance by a few more yards, then a few more as a wild shriek of pain tore from the throat of one of the captives.

"Hell with this," Preacher muttered, coming up on one knee and leveling the Hawken. He let a ball fly. The big ball caught one buck in the center of his back and the brave pitched forward, landing with his face in the fire. His hair caught on fire and sent up a fearful odor.

Preacher dropped his rifle and jerked out two pistols, running toward the momentarily confused scene. One older Ute, reacting faster than the others, quickly notched an arrow and let it fly. It missed Preacher by a good foot and he never stopped his running charge. He let a pistol bang. The ball struck the buck in the hip and turned him around, knocking him to the ground. He pulled the trigger of the second pistol and it misfired. Preacher added some pretty fancy cussing to the wild hollering of the Utes and jerked out the last brace of pistols, knowing that he was in real trouble now. There were four pissed-off Utes standing facing him, and he had two charged pistols.

One of the men all trussed up kicked out with his bare feet and caught a Ute behind his knees, knocking the buck to the ground. A brave with a lance in his hands and a scream on his lips charged Preacher. Preacher gave him a ball of lead at nearly point-blank range and the Ute's chest was suddenly smeared with blood. An arrow missed Preacher's head by inches and Preacher gave that brave his last ball. The shot knocked the Ute down, but didn't kill him right off. He lurched to his feet and staggered toward Preacher, a knife in his hand.

Preacher grabbed up the lance and met the brave, just as the Ute the man had knocked down jumped to his feet. The buck with the knife tried to fake Preacher out, but the mountain man was an old hand at this. Preacher gave him the point of the lance in the belly, driving it through. The Ute screamed, dropped the knife, and wrapped his fingers around the shaft of the lance as he sank to his knees.

Preacher broke the lance off in him and met the two Utes charging him, screaming their rage and hatred at this interloper. Preacher swung the lance like a club and took one out with a wicked blow to the head. He jammed the broken end of the lance into the belly of the last Ute and the Ute fell back, jerking the lance from Preacher's hands. The last Ute standing faced Preacher with a knife. The trussed-up captives were methodically kicking the hip-shot Ute in the head with their bare feet.

Preacher could see out of the corner of his eye that the buck was unconscious and would probably not survive the vicious kicks to the head. But the prisoners were plenty mad and scared and taking that out on the Ute's head. Preacher knew their feelings very well.

The Ute facing Preacher told him in no uncertain terms what he thought of Preacher. Preacher replied in the warrior's own tongue that he pretty well felt the same about the

Ute, then grinned and added that he felt the Ute looked like a stinking pile of buzzard puke.

The young Ute lunged and Preacher drew the first blood with his good knife. The wound was not serious, but it did give the brave something to think about.

The Ute cursed Preacher.

"You better sing your death song," Preacher told the war-painted brave.

The Ute leaped and Preacher's knife ripped into the brave's belly as Preacher's left hand clamped down on the Indian's wrist and held the knife hand firmly away from him. Preacher twisted the knife, ripping upward with the cutting edge. The Ute's face grimaced as the pain tore through his guts and the blade finally ripped into the heart. The pain turned to death. Preacher jerked out his knife and let the Ute fall to the bloody and churned-up ground.

He ran to the trussed-up men and sliced their bonds with the bloody knife. "Grab up a pony and let's get gone from here. Them gunshots was probably heard by other Utes. How come them Injuns didn't take your weapons when they overpowered you?"

"The first bunch did," the one with the slightly charred foot said. "Then they took off after our partners and left us with this bunch."

"How far back?"

"A good eight to ten miles," the second man said. "If our friends can find any kind of shelter, they'll hold off the savages. I'm sure of that."

Some of the tenseness went out of Preacher. The sounds of the shooting would not reach eight miles. Preacher gave the men a longer second look. Pilgrims. Their clothing was store-bought and their hats new. Burned Foot even had him a gold watch on a fancy fob.

"All right, you boys take it easy. Look around and strip you some moccasins off a dead buck and get you a knife from them. I'll get my guns and horse."

"One of these red savages is still alive."

"That's his problem. Either kill him or let him be. Don't make no difference to me." Preacher quickly reloaded and trotted back to Hammer, who was waiting patiently for him in the ravine. "Place is fillin' up with amateurs, Hammer." Preacher swung into the saddle. "Seems like all we been doin' is pullin' pilgrims out of trouble. It's gettin' to be a right wearisome thing."

"I cannot find footwear that fits me properly," Burned Foot complained as Preacher rode up.

"Well, my goodness!" Preacher told him. "I guess that means we'll just have to ride right out and find where them Utes tossed your boots, won't we?"

"There is no need for sarcasm," he admonished Preacher. "We are strangers in this savage land."

"I never would have guessed. And the land ain't savage. It just ain't worth a damn for nothin' around here. Mount up. Let's go find the bodies of your partners."

"The *bodies?*"

"Yeah. The bodies. If they're still alive, I'll eat a raw skunk. Let's go."

Preacher turned Hammer's head and rode off, not waiting to see if the men were following. The trail left by the Utes was plain as the nose on a man's face, and he figured even a pilgrim could follow it.

The men caught up with him and Burned Foot said, "There are dead people back there."

"Do tell? What about them?"

"Well, it's the Christian thing to bury them, wouldn't you say? I mean, they did inflict some horrible pain upon my person, but they are human beings."

"I don't know whether I'm a Christian, or not. But if you want to bury 'em, you can just ride on back there and start diggin'."

The two men thought about that for a moment and said no

more about it. "What were you doing out this way, sir," the second man asked. "Exploring?"

Preacher sighed mightily. He shook his head. "No, pilgrim, I was lookin' for the man in the moon. Do you two have names?"

"But of course," Burned Foot said. "I am Miles Cason and this is my best chum, George Martin."

Preacher looked at him. *Chum?* "Pleased, I'm sure."

The two men waited. And waited. Finally, George said, "To whom do we owe our lives, sir?"

"Your mamma and daddy, I reckon."

"My foot hurts like the devil!" Miles said.

"What is your name, sir?" George asked.

"Preacher."

"Preacher?"

"Yep. Just Preacher. See the smoke over yonder, boys?" He pointed. "Did y'all have wagons?"

"Yes. Two of them. To carry our supplies. We're out here hunting gold."

Preacher looked at the man. "Gold? Here? You're huntin' gold . . . *here?* Who told you there was gold around here?"

"A geologist."

"A *what* ologist?"

"What is that smoke over there?" George asked. "Is that a settlement?"

Preacher chuckled. "The next settlement west, pilgrim, is several hundred miles from here. That smoke you see yonder is the burnin' bodies of your partners and anything else the Utes didn't take. See the buzzards already circlin'? Now follow me down into this draw and don't ask questions."

"Why are we going into this ravine?" Miles promptly asked. "I simply must have a doctor see to my foot."

"We're goin' into this draw 'cause the Injuns is still over here havin' fun with your friends. Although I don't much imagine your friends is seein' no humor in it."

"How do you know the savages are still over there?"

" 'Cause of the damn dust!" Preacher said irritably. "They must be draggin' one of them."

"Are you going to their rescue?" George asked.

"Hell no! Even if I was a mind to—which I ain't, by the way—by now there ain't enough left to save. We will give them a proper burial, though. Tomorrow."

"Tomorrow?" Miles asked, horror in his voice.

"That's right, pilgrim. Tomorrow. If we're still alive, that is. You can bet your boots, if either of you had any, them Injuns over there is seasoned braves. Not like them young bucks that had you two. We can't risk movin' out of this draw 'cause we'll kick up dust in this goddamn, godforsaken place. We'll just sit this out here and hope them over yonder don't take the same way back that we come. So just sit down, shut up, and don't ask me no more questions. I'm tired of it."

"I'm hungry," George said.

Preacher reached into his parfleche and tossed them some jerky and pemmican. "Stuff that in your mouths and chew on it. If it don't do nothin' else, it'll keep you quiet."

"You really are a very rude man," Miles said.

Preacher just looked at the man and said nothing. Although there were a great many words he thought about saying.

The men opened their eyes in the grayness just before dawn. Preacher was sitting on the ground, his back to the wall of the earth bank.

"The Utes pulled out hours ago," Preacher informed them. "Get the kinks out of your legs and saddle up."

"My foot hurts," Miles said.

"It'll either get better or it'll rot off," Preacher told him. "Good Lord, man. I've hurt myself worser than that cookin' breakfast. Quit your bitchin'."

"Are you sure the savages have gone?" George asked.

"Yeah, I'm sure."

"It's going to be a dreadful sight, isn't it?"

"Yeah, it is," Preacher replied, tightening the cinch on Hammer. "But if you're plannin' on stayin' out in this country, it's a sight you better get used to."

"I could never become that callous," Miles said, his lip still stuck out over Preacher's mild castigating.

"Then you best run on back to wherever the hell it is you come from, pilgrim. 'Cause out here, you either toughen up or you die. And that's the way it is. Now saddle up and mount up. We got some buryin' to do."

George and Miles got the heaves as soon as they rode up to the site. Both of them staggered off a ways and fell down on the ground, coughing and gagging. Preacher prowled the still-smoking ruins.

Preacher had seen this many times. He kept his face impassive to the horrible sights around him as he looked at what was left of the men who had come west in search of gold. Preacher breathed shallow and through his mouth. The stench was terrible.

"That's poor Willie over there," Miles said, his face pale and drawn. "He came out here for the adventure of it. We went to college together. He graduated with honors."

"Didn't do him much good out here," Preacher remarked. Under a torn over bundle, he found a pistol and tossed it to Miles. "Start lookin' around for things that you might could use, you two. I seen some boots over yonder. And there's a shovel. I'll start diggin' the hole."

"You mean holes, don't you?" George asked.

"No. I mean a hole. One. Pile 'em in there together. We can't waste of whole lot of time tarryin' around here. Them damn Utes might decide to come back. You can bet they've found the ones I kilt yesterday and they'll be hoppin' mad."

"What you're suggesting is very indecent and most un-Christian," Miles told him.

"But very practical," Preacher responded. He'd dealt with enough pilgrims to know that most of them didn't use a lot of common sense once they got west of the Missouri. Not for a while, anyways. Then they either smartened up or got killed. "But you boys can take the time to speak some words over the grave," he told them.

"How very kind of you," George said.

"Think nothin' of it." Preacher let the sarcasm roll right off of him. "I do have my good points. Start rumblin' around and stop all this jawin'."

Preacher grabbed a shovel and started digging. "When you two get done grubbin' about in the rubble, start bringin' some rocks over here. Dump them yonder. We got to pile them on the mound so's the varmints won't dig up what's left of the bodies and eat on them."

"That's disgusting!" Miles said.

"Not to a varmint."

"Do you have a Bible, Preacher?" George asked.

"No. Had one. Give to me last year by a gospel shouter. I lost it somewheres."

"I hate this savage land," Miles said.

"Good. Glad to hear that," Preacher said, digging in the ground. "Maybe you'll go home now."

"We came out here for gold, and we won't leave until we have found it," Miles said firmly.

"That means you both gonna be here forever," Preacher muttered.

12

Preacher waited patiently while the two men conducted services over the large mound of earth. Sounded to him like both of them were part-time gospel shouters. They sure did praise the Lord and such. Didn't sound too bad, though; man needs a little gospel hollerin' every now and then. When the two had wound down and he got them back in the saddle, he headed them toward the wagon train. Preacher damn sure didn't want to be stuck with them out here all by his lonesome. Although he had to admit, they showed some spunk all trussed up and kickin' that buck down. It helped, for a fact, it did.

Windy was scouting far ahead of the train and whoaed up when he saw Preacher and the pilgrims. He eyeballed the two men, questions in his eyes.

"Gold hunters," Preacher told him.

"In *this* part of the country? There ain't no gold around here."

"A what-ologist told them they was. They had them a streak of bad luck by runnin' into a Ute war party not too many miles up ahead."

"Do you have a physician with your party?" Miles questioned.

Windy blinked.

"He means a doctor," Preacher said.

"I ain't scoutin' for no hospital," Windy told Miles. "You sick?"

"I have a horribly burned foot. I was tortured savagely by those filthy wild red Indians."

"Do tell? Lookin' at you, I'd have to say that you stood up to it right well."

"The Utes stuck his foot in the fire one time," Preacher said. "Stick a poultice on it when you get these lost sheep to the train, Windy. I'm gone." Preacher wheeled his horse and rode out without looking back.

"We certainly owe that person our very lives," George said. "But I have to say that he is the most irritable-behaving man I have ever encountered."

Windy smiled. He knew some mountain men that would make Preacher look like a cross between Solomon and Moses. "Come on, children," he said, lifting the reins. "Let's get you back to your own kind."

"And what kind is that, sir?" Miles inquired.

"Igits," Windy told him, and rode off.

Preacher snared him a big fat rabbit for supper, and after eating every scrap of meat and sucking the marrow from the bones, he carefully buried the remains, put out his fire, and moved on another couple of miles before he found a good spot to bed down for the night. He checked his guns carefully. That Ute war party would have long since found the six dead young braves and they would be angry and looking for revenge. And Preacher didn't think the ones who attacked Miles and George and the others was the main party—more like a splinter band. Right about now, they would be all linked up and there would be a whole passel of them whoopin' and hollerin' and singin' their songs and workin' themselves up into a killing frenzy.

Whether they would attack the wagon train was something he could only guess at. But if the main bunch was fifty or more, they'd try it.

But a man alone would be easy pickin's for them, so he'd ride careful come the morning. Not that he didn't always . . . but a little extra caution never hurt.

It sure paid off. Preacher had not ridden two miles from where he'd camped when he smelled dust. A lot of dust. Then from a draw, he spotted the Utes. And this was no small party. Preacher figured at least seventy-five strong. He pulled back and walked Hammer slowly to an upthrusting of rocks and got behind the huge natural barricade.

"Now, Hammer," he told the big horse. "This ain't no time for conversin' with some long-lost cousin of yours. Since you with me, them Utes just might decide to eat you!"

Hammer looked at him mournfully.

"That's a fact, horse. So you just be quiet now. Be real quiet."

The Utes were riding with a purpose in mind and did not have many outriders flanking them or none ahead of them that Preacher could spot. He thought that strange, but then the Utes probably figured they were in safe enough territory. As soon as they had passed by, Preacher headed back for the wagon train, since that was the direction the Utes were taking. He stayed several miles to the east of the war party. This bunch was going to hit the wagons, Preacher would bet his hat on that. And they just might do it at night. It was a myth that all Indians never attacked at night. It all depended on whether or not they felt their medicine was strong enough. Preacher had once opined, over a jug of whiskey, that a man ought to be always careful at night, 'cause supposin' you run up on a whole bunch of atheist Indians who didn't believe in no kind of afterlife. Man would be in a real pickle then.

Preacher rode hard, pushing Hammer, until he was sure

he was ahead of the Utes; then he cut toward the train. They had just circled for the evening's camp when Preacher rode in and tossed the reins to Caleb.

"War party of Utes not more'n two, three hours away," he told Weller and the mountain men. 'Comin' down from the north and they ridin' with a purpose. I think it's the main bunch of that smaller party that hit Cason and Martin's friends."

"I was told that the savages never attacked at night," Weller said, then noticed all the mountain men smiling at his words. "Obviously, I was misinformed."

"Yeah, you was," Preacher said. "Best double the guard tonight. And have ever' man charge ever' weapon they got and keep them close by. Check powder and shot, too. Have the women break out the molds and get some lead heated up for balls."

When Weller had gone, Rimrock asked, "How many did you see, Preacher?"

"At least seventy-five, maybe a few more or less than that. Only a few of 'em armed with rifles, I'd say."

"Well, they'll hit us for sure," Caleb said. "There ain't nothin' out here 'ceptin' us."

"Did you ever make the spot where these pilgrim want to light?" Windy asked.

"I come close enough to it to know that it don look like no farmin' country I ever seen and there sure as hell ain't gonna be no town there no time soon." He told him what he suspicioned about the Pardees and Sutherlin and also what he had Weasel Tail's braves doing.

"Sounds right to me," Rimrock said. "You musta really put your head to workin', Preacher. This Sutherlin feller, he's shapin' up to be a real blackheart."

"He'll stop bein' when I put a ball through it," Preacher replied.

* * *

Preacher grabbed him a short snooze—'cause he didn't figure on dozin' none that night—and then ate a plate of stew that Betina brought to him. She sat on the ground beside him all goggle-eyed and watched him eat every bite. Made Preacher nervous. Female had marriage on the brain. He knew from experience. He had a squaw follow him around one time, actin' just like Betina was doin'. Preacher finally pulled out of that Cheyenne village in the damn dead of winter just to get shut her.

"I can hardly contain myself," Betina said. "I am so anxious to get our new town established. We'll have us a fine schoolhouse, too. I'll see to that."

"Betina—"

"Do you remember your school days, Preacher? Oh, my, but I certainly do."

"Ma mostly taught me writin' and readin' and figurin'. Betina, about this here town—"

"Schools are so dismal," she prattled on. "But ours won't be. I attended a great barn of a school. Sometimes, when the winters were very harsh, we would be dismissed because of the lack of proper heating. But that won't be the case with my school. We must educate our children and see to their comforts while doing so. Don't you agree?"

"Yeah. Sure." She had stressed *our* and that sent shivers up and down Preacher's spine. "Betina," he tried again, "you gotta understand something about this town—"

"And I want to give each student some personal attention. I think that is very important, don't you, Preacher?"

"Oh, yeah," Preacher said wearily. " 'Specially with a good strong board when they act up."

"Oh, I don't believe in corporal punishment, Preacher. I believe that is the wrong approach."

"Wished I'd been in your school," he muttered. The brief times he had attended a regular school he got a lickin' damn near every day. And another one from his pa when he got home. He smiled. He had deserved every one of them and more.

"What are you smiling about, Preacher?"

"The hidin's and the knucklin's I got when I did go to a regular school."

"Was it horrible for you?"

"Hell no. I deserved twice that many for the stunts I pulled and didn't get caught doin'."

"They're out there, Preacher," Windy called softly. "And workin' their way in."

"I'm scared, Preacher," Betina admitted. "I've been prattling on like a magpie because I am scared to death. I don't want to go through this again."

"It'll be all right," he assured her. "You get into the center barricade with the others and try to keep the kids calm. Go on, now."

The livestock had been pulled inside the huge circle and several wagons placed there for the children and for those women who would take care of them. Brush and logs had been hurriedly pulled in to fill in the large gaps between wagons. Betina ran for protection and Preacher took up a position by the rear wheel of a wagon. He had four pistols and two rifles, all freshly charged. He had shoved his war axe behind his sash.

The women had good reason to be afraid, for it was Ute custom to repeatedly rape all women they took captive. They might let them go afterward, but the women would have a rough time of it while in Ute hands.

Preacher also felt that the party he'd seen earlier was only part of a larger bunch. The Utes were a little north of the usual territory, so that meant they had declared war against another tribe. The wagon train was just an added pleasure for them, and a chance to take more scalps and women prisoners.

Preacher also felt that many of the bunch he'd seen were

made up of the highly skilled warrior society of the Ute tribe. They were fierce fighters and did not give up easily.

Weller came up to Preacher's side, moving quietly in the early night. He carried a rifle and had two pistols behind his belt. "We came this far without experiencing a speck of trouble with the savages. Now we may well be fighting for our lives at the next blink of an eye."

"We sure will be doing that," Preacher agreed. "In about two, three more minutes. And these Utes are tough. Believe it. Now let me tell you the real bad news. You've led these people into what might be a death trap."

Weller opened his mouth to speak and Preacher cut him off and shut him up.

"Shut up and listen to me, Weller. It's about time you listened to somebody. You and your damn town in the promised land. That's crap, Weller. Puredee crap. We're in trouble, man. We're cut off. Alone. There will be no help comin' our way. None. Do you understand all that? Injuns are the most patient people on the face of the earth. Especially Utes. I know. A band of Utes kept me and four other men pinned down tight for days when we was furrin' south of here. We had ample powder and shot and just wore 'em down. But we was in the mountains, Weller. In good cover. Not stuck out here on the flats like we are now. We're gonna lose some men, Weller. Women and some kids, too, probably."

Weller stood silent for a moment, his gaze shifting from Preacher to the unknown that lay waiting in the darkness outside the ringed wagons. When he spoke, his voice was filled with resignation. "I was told that the trail west would soon move to the north—to the area we hoped to settle. I was assured of that move."

"Why should the trail move north?" Preacher softly questioned. "It's been used for years right where it's at. Further on, it's the only logical way through the Rockies."

"Mr. Sutherlin—"

"I knew it!" Preacher said hotly. "I knowed it had to be

him. I was right. I'll tell you later. If we live through this night, that is." Weller again opened his mouth and Preacher shushed him. "Go on back to your post, Weller. They're about to rush us. Move, man."

Weller was learning, for he asked no questions. He vanished into the canvas-ringed circle of night, moving swiftly back to his post. Preacher turned all his attentions to the vast expanse of dark that lay before him.

The Utes would be very close now. They'd had several hours of darkness to creep close, sometimes moving no more than an inch or two at a time. Preacher was just glad they were not Apaches. They were the best at making the most out of every scrap of cover. Or no cover at all.

Preacher had briefly spoken with most of the men in the wagon train. None of them had much experience when it came to fighting, for most of them came from the cities and towns back East. There were a few who came from rural areas, and knew something about fighting. A couple had actual combat experience, having fought with Jackson in the War of 1812. But fightin' Injuns was a tad different from fightin' the British, who for the most part just stood all in a line and let you cut 'em down. And the U.S. Army wasn't much better. Dumbest damn way of fightin' Preacher had ever seen. Injuns was a whole lot smarter when it came to fighting. And Preacher and the other mountain men had quickly adapted to their ways of stealth and ambush.

Then Preacher saw a bush that hadn't been in that spot a couple of minutes back. He lifted his rifle to his shoulder and sighted in. The bush moved a few inches and Preacher put a ball right through it, about six inches off the ground. A scream ripped the night and the bush flew up into the air as a mortally wounded brave reared up on one knee, a hideous wound pouring blood from his neck. He fell forward and was still just as other Utes charged the wagons.

Preacher picked up his other rifle and let a ball fly. A brave doubled over like he'd been hit with a thrown anvil. He bounced on the ground and jerked in pain. Preacher jerked out a brace of pistols, both of them double-shotted, and let them bang. When the smoke cleared briefly, he'd put two more Utes on the cool, rocky ground.

All around him, the night was exploding in gunfire. There was no breeze at all, and the gun smoke was thick and smarting to the eyes. Preacher's immediate area was momentarily clear of all living things, and he took that time to recharge his weapons, looking up and around him every two or three seconds.

The men of the wagon train had broken the first charge and the Utes seemed to just drop off the face of the earth. But Preacher knew better. He knew they were out there, and very close. One Ute tried to drag off a wounded brave and Preacher cut his spine with a ball.

"Sing out!" Preacher shouted.

"One mover over here took an arrow in the chest," Rimrock called. "He's dead."

"Got one wounded over here," Caleb called out. "He'll be all right."

"Everybody's all right over here," Windy called.

Preacher looked left and right of his position. "Anybody hurt along here?"

"No," a mover said. "Just scared."

"Stay that way," Preacher told him. "It'll help to keep you alive."

"What's next?" another one asked.

"Probably fire-arrows if they stay true to form. Charge up all your weapons. Everybody got a hatchet or axe close by like I told you? Good. We might be hand to hand 'fore this is all over. And brothers, them Utes is good at that. Don't play around with them. Just whack off anything in reach. Arm, hand, head, anything at all."

"I don't know that I can do that," a mover said.

"You want to have your hair jerked off and live long

enough to see your wife and daughters raped?" Preacher tossed that at the man.

"No."

"Then you'll do it."

"Yonder comes the fire-arrows," Rimrock called. "Grab the buckets and stand ready."

Preacher squatted down by the rear wheel and waited. He knew from experience that a rush would follow the fire-arrows. The Utes—among other tribes—had quickly learned that movers would drop their guns and grab up buckets of water in an attempt to save their possessions.

"Let the women handle the water buckets," Preacher called. "Every man stay with his gun."

Fire-arrows zipped through the air, shot from well-concealed positions. The canvas on one wagon burst into flames and the women began tossing buckets of water on the fire. They had it out in half a minute. The other fire-arrows fell to the ground and burned out harmlessly.

Then the Utes came silently out of the night, some of them mounted, others running on foot, waving war axes and holding decorated lances.

"Fire, goddamnit!" Preacher shouted. "Don't let them get inside the circle."

Preacher felt if they could contain this charge, the Utes would feel their medicine was bad and break it off to talk it over. But it was a big if.

A war-painted Ute reared up in front of him and Preacher shot the brave in the center of the forehead, the big ball almost taking the top of the Indian's head off. He smashed the butt of the rifle into the face of another and then jerked out his pistols and fired into a mass of brown bodies just outside the circle of wagons.

And still the Utes came.

A warrior jumped his horse inside the circle, leaped off, and landed right on top of Preacher, taking both of them hard to the ground. The brave lost his war axe and scrambled for it. Preacher and the Ute rolled around on the ground for a few seconds until Preacher smashed the buck's head in with the butt of an empty pistol and then leaped to his feet, grabbing for his last two charged pistols.

More canvas had been set ablaze and the wind had picked up, fanning the leaping flames that highlighted a frantic life-and-death struggle amid the circle of wagons on the plains. A woman was smashing a brave's bloody head in with what remained of a wooden bucket. Several movers were locked in hand-to-hand combat with Ute warriors. One woman lay on the ground, an arrow in her chest and a crying child on the ground beside her. Preacher observed all this in a split second as he worked to charge his pistols. A wild scream turned him around. A brave was running toward Weller, his axe raised to crush Weller's head. Preacher shot him and the brave stopped in his tracks and stumbled forward, landing on his face. Weller looked at Preacher and nodded his thanks.

Windy had grabbed up the lance of a fallen Ute and had driven it through another brave, pinning the writhing buck to the earth.

Then, like it began, it was over, silence falling around them as the Utes vanished into the night.

"Reload," Preacher called. "Right now, before you do anything else." He left his post and walked toward the area where the kids and a few women were located in the center of the circle. He smiled at Betina. Her face was sooted up some and her hair all mussed, but she managed a wan smile.

"Will they be back?" she asked.

Preacher nodded. "If they feel their medicine is right, they'll hit us just at dawn."

"If their medicine is bad?"

"They'll leave."

"I'll say a little prayer."

"Shore wouldn't hurt none. While you're askin', tell Him to send some help, will you?"

13

Preacher took charge of the defense of the train and began posting guards, telling those not on guard duty to get some rest. He told the women to have coffee and hot food available at all times, and to work in shifts, some cooking while the others rested.

"Them Utes know we're total cut off from any kind of relief," Caleb said in a low tone as the men squatted down in the darkness, cups of coffee in their hands. "So it's my thinkin' they might try to wait us out."

"They might," Preacher agreed. "But we got food and a ready supply of water behind the train. They's maybe two days' graze for the stock if we limit them, and then another two days of grain for them on short rations. You all and me, we know this battle ain't gone unnoticed. Other Injuns has seen the fire and smelled the smoke and all the dust. Some might come to investigate. And that could be good or bad, depending on the tribe."

"If it's Crow they'd hep us," Windy said. "And so would Weasel Tail's bunch. But if the Snake and the Crow both show up, they'll start fightin' each other."

"I don't know," Rimrock said. "They been right friendly to each other the past couple of years. I think they might have made peace."

"Did you talk to Weller about this here Sutherlin person?" Caleb asked.

"Just done it. Shocked him down to his socks, it did. To be a religious sort of feller, he done some right smart cussin'. Sutherlin is the one who told these pilgrims to cut north from the trail. I told Weller to take pen to hand and to write down the whole story and seal 'er good and give it to me. Later on, I'll take me a trip east. Maybe even go as far as the Missouri. Find me a regular Army fort, like Leavenworth, and talk to the generals and colonels about Sutherlin."*

"Maybe we'll all go," Rimrock said, as Caleb and Windy nodded their heads in agreement. "I ain't been back in so many years I forgot what civilization looks like."

"Take a look at these pilgrims." Preacher said dryly. "That's what it looks like."

"Maybe I won't go," Rimrock said.

"Gone," Windy said, after slipping back into the circle of wagons. It was not yet dawn and the little man with more guts than most had been gone for over an hour. "They pulled out durin' the night. Headed south."

"We hurt 'em bad, all right," Caleb said. "I reckon we killed a good thirty of 'em. Probably wounded another fifteen or so real bad. Injuns ain't gonna stand for that. They're headin' for home."

Preacher went to Weller and was as uncommonly blunt

*Fort Leavenworth was established in 1827 as protection for the Santa Fe Trail. It was originally called Cantonment Leavenworth. It is the oldest U.S. fort west of the Mississippi still operating.

with him as he had been the night before. "You understand that you were on a fool's mission headin' north, don't you?"

"Yes," the man admitted "I do. But Preacher, we've come too far to turn back now. I . . . ah . . . would you lead us up to the Oregon Territory?"

"No. No, I won't do that. But we'll see you back to the trail and you can either wait there for another train to come along or I'll take you back to the post and you can wait there. Talk to your people and see what they want to do."

"They will not turn back to the post, Preacher. I can assure you of that. We would lose too much time. We have to get across the mountains before the snows come."

"You sure got that right."

"A rider coming from the west," a lookout shouted. "And he's alone."

Rimrock squinted and smiled. "That's Carl Lippett. I recognize the horse. If he sees us he'll run thinkin' we're gonna give him another bath."

"Does this man know the trails?" Weller asked.

"As good as any man."

"Perhaps then he might be persuaded to lead us on westward," Weller said with a hopeful note in his voice.

"He might," Windy said. "He's just about crazy enough to take the job."

Preacher faced Weller. "Weller, take these people on back a ways. Take them to Missouri or Iowa Territory. Wait a few years and then come on out. It's too soon, Weller. It's just too soon for this."

But the man would not budge from his decision. "We shall press on westward."

Shaking his head and muttering, Preacher walked back to the wagons of Betina, Coretine, and the kids. Betina took one look at his face and said, "No, Preacher. We shall not go back." It was spoken softly but firmly.

"Nor shall I," Coretine said, standing by her side. "This

savage land shall not defeat me. My husband had a dream, and I shall see it come to be."

"No point in my sayin' nothin', then." Preacher walked away without another word.

Carl Lippett agreed to guide the party on to the Pacific and the wagons were made ready for the trail. The train turned around and headed back toward what some had begun calling the Oregon Trail. Preacher and the other mountain men tagged along.

"Way I look at it," Carl said, as Preacher rode along with him at the head of the stretched out train, "either I take them on west or they go it alone. Least with me along they'll have a chance. They won't get lost. Preacher, you took a train across last year. I'd 'preciate anything you could tell me about it."

For the next two days, Preacher told the man everything he could remember about the way west to Oregon Territory—the way a train could get through. When he had exhausted his memory, Carl shook his head.

"Looks like I just might have a mighty big job on my hands," Lippett said.

There was nothing Preacher could add to that statement.

A few miles before they reached the trail, Preacher and his friends left the pioneers and rode away without saying a word to anybody. Farewells had been said and there was nothing more that anyone could add.

"I said it back at the post some weeks ago," Caleb said, breaking the silence after a few miles, "and I'll say it again. I got me a bad feelin' about that train."

"We done all we could do to talk them out of goin'," Windy replied. "I ain't gonna feel bad about it."

But he did. They all did. Grown up men like Miles Cason and George Martin going into the wilderness was one thing (George and Miles had been persuaded to join the train and press westward toward the Pacific)—they were men and could make choices, whether they be right or wrong. A woman usually followed her man. But little kids had no say about it at all.

Of late, the mountain men had buried entirely too many people who sought a new land and new life. And it did weigh heavily on their minds.

When they made camp that evening, the men were not in their usual joking and kidding mood. They all sat silent and reflective around a slowly dying fire, chewing on rabbit meat and drinking coffee.

"Feels like I'm at a funeral," Rimrock finally said.

"The only funeral I'm lookin' forward to attendin' is the plantin' of the Pardees and Red Hand," Preacher said.

Caleb tossed a stick on the fire. "It ain't that we're so damn busy doin' other more important things."

"What are you talkin' about?" Preacher glanced up.

"I know," Windy said. "And that ain't the point, Caleb. Point is, they was *told* that goin' on was crazy." He tossed the dredges of his coffee into the brush behind him. "Aw, hell! Them movers don't have to know that we're even about."

"I ain't gonna be about," Preacher said, catching on.

"I ain't neither," Rimrock said. He poured another cup of the coffee. Black as sin and twice as hot.

"Speak for yourself," Windy told his friend.

"What say you, Preacher?" Rimrock asked. "You changed your mind about the movers?"

"No," Preacher told him. "If a big enough band hit the train, either stretched out or circled, four more guns won't make no difference."

That the four mountain men were able to stay together this long was nothing short of a miracle, for the mountain man was by nature a solitary creature and few of them made lasting bonds with others of their kind. Only a few, like Rimrock and Windy, ever rode together on a full-time basis, and even they split up from time to time.

But as their way of life came closer to an end, and it

would end almost abruptly, some mountain men looked up others of their kind and in twos and threes they wandered the High Lonesome until their deaths, finally wandering onto the pages of history and into oblivion.

"I think come the mornin', I'll just ride back to that train and tag along," Caleb said. "Food's good."

"I'm with you," Windy said firmly, surprising his long-time partner, Rimrock.

Rimrock stared at his small friend for a moment and then smiled. "You never did have no sense, Windy. But I wish you well anyways. Me, I'm for ridin' up toward Canada." He stretched out on his robe. "I ain't been up there in a while. It's nice up there this time of year."

"How 'bout you, Preacher?" Caleb asked.

"I ain't made up my mind yet," he replied glumly. Which was a lie, but what he had in mind he wanted to do alone. "I reckon whichever way the wind is puffin' in the mornin', that's the way I'll go."

Since it was dead flat calm when the dawning broke, Preacher lingered long by the fire, drinking coffee and watching his friends ride off. There was little conversation. Caleb and Windy rode toward the wagon train, Rimrock headed north. Windy and Rimrock would probably hook up again, but out here, you just never did know. They'd gone their separate ways before, but never for very long at a time.

As Preacher sat alone by the quiet fire, in the silent camp in the wilderness, the thought entered his mind that with furrin' all but gone, he didn't have the faintest idea what he was going to do for a living. He didn't know anything but the Big Empty. Couldn't imagine living anywhere else. He sat by the fire until it had burned down to coals. He watched an eagle soar high above him and listened to the birds sing and the squirrels play and chatter. Then he smiled.

He knew how the Indians felt. He could understand it. All this magnificence was his and all this was theirs. Nobody liked to see a way of life come to an end. Preacher had read

somewhere that all things change . . . or something like that.
And that to fight against change was useless.

Maybe so, he thought with a sigh.

Right now, shut of his friends, Preacher could more easily
take the fight to the Pardees. For this was the way he liked
it—alone.

The wagon train prodded on westward and Preacher
hunted for the Pardee gang in the high country. They'd had
time to run back there after the Wind River ambush fell
through. So they lived in caves. That was well and good, but
they had to come out of those caves, and whenever they did,
they would leave tracks. More than that, they had to have a
trail to follow in and out. Or they made one when they decided to make the caves their hideout. If there was a trail,
Preacher would find it. He hadn't yet seen a river he couldn't
cross, a range he couldn't find a way through, or a horse he
couldn't ride. Preacher would find the Pardees.

"Preacher just don't give up," Radborne Pardee told his
older brother. "We been hearin' stories 'bout Preacher ever
since we come into these damn mountains. I hate him. He
shore messed up a good thing back yonder on the Wind."

Malachi Pardee shook his head and tried to dismiss the
talk of Preacher with a wave of his hand. A very dirty hand.
"Preacher's just a man, like us. All them stories is a bunch of
bull. Just bull. He's like all these mountain men, a wanderer.
Preacher is long gone and nowheres near here. So just forget
him, boys."

Renegade scouts of Red Hand's bunch had reported the
wagon train had moved on west after the Ute attack. The
Pardees were restless and apprehensive. They had not seen
civilization for a long time. And Malachi didn't know if Red
Hand was going to join them for the attack against the wagon

train. Red Hand was getting a little spooky about Preacher's medicine.

Preacher's medicine.

Radborne was not to be put off. "Brother, we have stretched our luck far . . . maybe too far. We've got gold aplenty from the raids and no place to spend it."

"Radborne's right," brother Henry said. "Somebody's got to be addin' all this up and gettin' close to figurin' out what's goin' on. It's just a matter of time 'fore Sutherlin gets caught up to. And when he do, he'll tell all he knows 'bout us to save his neck. And then where'll we be?"

Malachi gave each of his brothers a long, hard look. "How about you, Ansel? Where do you stand? Do you want to ride back 'crost the Missouri?"

Ansel shook his head. "No, I don't. But I do want to go somewheres where they's real white women and whiskey and people to talk to and civilization. I'm gettin' tarred of humpin' squaws."

Valiant Pardee stuck his penny's worth in. "We got gold enough from the wagons to head to Californy and open us up a tavern. We can get some whores a-workin' for us and fleece the travelers like we done back in Ohio."

"Keep talkin'," Malachi said. "I want everybody to get it all said."

Kenrick Pardee said, "Whilst I am tarred of livin' in caves like moles, I think we ought to play this string out. Three or four more raids and we'll have enough gold so's we won't ever have to work agin. Not never no more. Not that we ever worked much," he added.

"Boys," Malachi Pardee said, standing up and pacing the cave floor. The cave smelled like a skunk's den, for the Pardee boys were not big on personal hygiene. "Let me see if I can't get something through your heads. Now I want you all to hear me good. We can't ever go back 'crost the Missouri. Not now, not tomorrow, not never. The onliest thing that's waitin' for us back there is a hangman's noose. We're known from Ohio clear through to the Pacific. I ain't sayin' that someday we can't quit this business and settle down. But what I am sayin' is that this ain't no time to do it. And when we do pack it in, we can't be nowheres near no settled place for a long time. That won't work a-tall. And if I have to explain the why of what all I just said, then I got to figure I got a bunch of igits for brothers."

The Pardee boys all looked at the floor of the cave and said nothing in rebuttal. Malachi walked out into the sunlight and let his younger brothers stew for a time. Tell the truth, Preacher did worry him just a bit.

Tell the truth, although Malachi would never admit it to anybody, especially his brothers, Preacher worried him a whole hell of a lot.

Malachi kicked at a rotten branch, sending bits and pieces of it flying. "Preacher," he muttered under his breath. "What a goddamn stupid name. He's about as much a preacher as I is."

What Preacher was, and Malachi was well aware of it, was a tough, mean, and dangerous fighter and a bad man to have on your trail. Twice he and Preacher had locked horns, and both times Preacher had stomped the snot out of him. Malachi had swore on his poor old mother's memory (even though she had been a mean old bitch and Malachi had hated her guts) that he would someday kill Preacher.

"Be a fine day when that happens," Malachi muttered darkly. He squatted down and proceeded to think things out. And of all the brothers, he had to be the one to do that. That weighed heavy on his mind at times.

Malachi was no mental giant, but compared to most of his brothers, he was a genius. Malachi could read and write and figure some, as could Kenrick. The rest of the Pardee clan were all dumb as dirt. If Malachi wasn't around to look after them, he just couldn't imagine what would happen to the ninnies. Especially Ansel. Ansel was just plain stupid.

But his brothers had their good points. They would kill

without hesitation on his orders . . . matter of fact, they liked to kill mayhaps a tad too much. And brutalize women! Lord, but them boys loved to put the hurt on a woman. They wasn't much left of a woman when his brothers got done with her. And they could torture a man in ways the Injuns hadn't even thought of. Malachi loved to watch them at work. But Malachi didn't fret too much about his brothers.

Basically, they were real good boys.

14

"Gotcha!" Preacher whispered, his eyes hardening and his smile becoming more like a wolf's snarl.

He had found a track. Just one. But that was enough. He pressed on, on foot, leading Hammer. He found where a branch had been broken. Another spot where a horse had dumped a load and the rider had been unaware of it. Preacher stopped and looked up. He had been on the trail for days before picking up the first hopeful sign.

The mountains loomed up majestic before him. The air was fresh and cool and scented. He was home. The mountains comforted him, and always pulled him back. And he knew them intimately. The Pardees had made a bad mistake if they were up there, and Preacher believed they were.

"Now, you child-killin', baby-rapin', torturin' no-count bastards. Now I'm gonna give you all some mountain justice and rid the world of you."

He searched carefully until he found a tiny valley nestled behind an almost impenetrable wall of brush. He was delighted to find the valley was lush with grass, belly-high to Hammer, with a deep pool of spring-fed water. Preacher stripped the saddle from Hammer and the rig from his pack-horse and let the animals roll while he inspected the mountain meadow. There was another way out, and he blocked that carefully with transplanted bushes, watering them so they would live. He worked slowly and carefully, for he had time. He now knew the trail the Pardees and their ilk used from their caves high up, when they went on their murderous raids. As long as the lush grass and the water was plentiful, and it was, his horses would not attempt to leave the peaceful little valley. So Preacher had plenty of time to hunt the Pardees.

When he was satisfied his horses would be safe when he left, Preacher chanced a small fire under an overhang and boiled coffee and chewed on jerky. He had not seen one sign of Indians, and neither had he found any signs that this particular valley had ever been entered by humans, red or white. In his prowlings, he had not found a single trace of the ashes of old fires. Preacher had him a feeling that he was the first white man—maybe the first human—to ever enter this tiny bit of pristine wilderness. And that left him with a good feeling.

And that feeling stirred emotions within him that he had not experienced in years. The feelings he had had years back, when he stood on a ridge overlooking a wild and roaring river, or a lovely undisturbed valley, or a stretch of grass that looked so large and so long it seemed to be one with the sky.

"A little piece of what it used to be like," Preacher muttered, a little bit of sadness in his voice. He dumped the coffee into the boiling water, and then he took the pot off the fire and tossed in some cold water to help the grounds settle.

Actually, it was still pretty much the way it was when Preacher and the other mountain men had arrived, years back. But they were feeling the first tentative push of pioneers westward. Only a ripple for now, but soon it would turn into a huge, roaring wave of humanity sweeping over the land. Preacher and the others hadn't seen a thing yet.

His fire out, Preacher slept soundly and dreamlessly that night, his horses picketed nearby. Anything alien or out of place with nature moved in the valley during the night, they would wake him in an instant. Hammer was as good as any trained dog.

Up before the skies turned silver, Preacher carefully packed a few things in his blanket and groundsheet and rolled it, securing it with rawhide strings and slinging it across his back. He checked his pistols. The bright sash was gone, replaced by a wide sturdy strip of deerskin that tied securely. The pistols went behind that. His horn was filled with powder and he had plenty of shot. His bow was good and his quiver filled with arrows. His big knife was honed to a fine edge. He was ready to go hunting.

He was going to do his best to put the Pardee brothers out of business.

"Don't you get too fat now, Hammer," Preacher told his horse. "I'll see you in about a week, or less, the Good Lord willin'." He picked up his rifle and headed out of the lovely little valley in the mountains.

He had enough pemmican and jerky in his parfleche to last him a good long time, and he planned to once and for all rid the wilderness of the Pardee trash and anyone stupid enough to ride with their wicked way. Also any renegade Injuns he might chance upon.

Which was what he spotted not an hour after leaving the valley. Preacher recognized him as a Comanche, and this Comanche was a long way from home. He had evidently broken some hard-and-fast tribal rule and gotten himself booted out. And here he was, big as life. Which was going to end, very quickly.

The Comanche must have thought himself safe in these mountains, for he was not exercising much caution as he rode the country. Had him a fine lookin' horse, too. Preacher immediately coveted that animal.

"Might as well take him," Preacher muttered low, and

climbed a tree to the lower limb that dangled over the nearly invisible trail.

When the renegade drew near, Preacher dropped and kicked the buck in the head on the way down. Addled, the renegade staggered to his moccasins just in time to receive Preacher's big blade in his belly, the cutting edge up. Preacher finished the Comanche and let him fall.

Looking around, he noted with disgust the scalps tied to the horse's mane. One of them was from a woman's head. Blond hair. He calmed the spooky horse and untied the scalps, throwing them into the brush. Then he stuffed the body of the Indian up into a hollow log. He'd let a bear work for his supper.

Preacher led the big horse off the trail and back to his little valley. Hammer snorted a few times and let the new addition know who was boss real quick. When they got all that settled, all three of them went to grazing.

The horse the Comanche rode to his death was an Appaloosa, and a big one for that breed. The renegade had either made or stolen, probably the latter, a buckskin pad saddle, stuffed with buffalo hair and grass. Preacher had read some accounts of the wilderness—written by eastern writers—which stated that Indians never used saddles. That was pure bunk. It all depended on the Indian. Many Injun women used a high-backed Spanish-style saddle made of wood, and they rode astride like a man. Lots of Injun men used saddles of all types and styles and descriptions for long journeys and for ceremonies.

Preacher again took his Hawken in hand and moved out of the valley, exiting this time using a different route. He walked for several miles, and just as he reached a point a few hundred yards below the timberline, he smelled smoke.

He squatted down and inhaled deeply. Somebody was broilin' venison steaks and boilin' coffee. Made Preacher's mouth start salivatin', and it made him mad. Here he was trying to do the right thing and just get along with them that would let him, and these murderin', thievin' bums was eatin' high off the hog. Or the deer, as it were. Well, by God, he'd put a stop to that, and do it right now.

Preacher followed the scent trail with his nose and almost stumbled right into the camp. It was very well concealed. If he had taken two more steps, he would have gone over the edge of a ravine, and before he'd stopped rolling, he'd have been shot to pieces by them below.

"Hurry up with that there meat," a bearded, burly lout of a man said, irritation in his voice. "I got myself a bad case of the hongries."

"Peacify yourself, Reed," the man at the fire said. "I can't git this far no hotter and I shore can't cook the meat no faster than I is."

Reed stood for a moment with a frown on his face. He licked his thick lips. "I just don't like you a-tall, Franklin," he said. "I never have. You're a smart-aleck son of a bitch. If you couldn't cook, I'd have shot you a long time ago."

Franklin cut his eyes. "You want this here steak rolled in dirt, Reed? 'Cause you say one more word to me and that's how you gonna get it."

Reed said something that Preacher couldn't catch and Franklin stood up from the fire.

"That's enough!" the third man said sharply. "We got enough troubles without fightin' amongst ourselves. Reed, you said something about takin' a crap. Go do it and then go tell Asa to come in and eat. You relieve him at guard. Now move!"

Preacher noted the direction that Reed was taking and In-juned his way over. He had already spotted Asa the guard.

Just as Reed was dropping his trousers and preparing to hang his butt over a log, Preacher sliced his throat wide open and held him by the hair, lowering him silently to the ground. He stuffed the man's pistols behind his belt and then quickly scalped the man, cutting around the hair and jerking it loose. Preacher left the man and moved around to the guard. He notched an arrow and put one straight into Asa's spine. The man dropped as soundlessly as a child's rag doll and Preacher very quickly dragged him into the bushes and scalped him. He was getting loaded down with pistols, but no Indian would leave such fine weapons, so he took them.

"Goddamnit, Reed!" the shouted words came to him. "Will you hurry up with your crappin'? What's the matter with you?"

No reply. Naturally. If there had of been one, Preacher just might have decided it was time to take flight and get shut of these mountains.

"Asa!" the man called to the guard. There was a note of worry in his voice. "Where is you, boy?"

Preacher waited, another arrow notched and ready to fly.

"Something's wrong," the man said.

"Naw," Franklin said, not looking up from his broiling meat. "Reed's just a troublemaker and Asa's probably asleep, that's all. Nothin' to worry about, Simpson."

But Simpson wasn't buying that and Preacher could both see it and sense it. Simpson had a deep streak of suspicion in him. The man stood for a moment, listening, then picked up his rifle and stepped away from the fire.

"I'm goin' out to take a look for myself," Simpson said. "You 'member that Malachi said Preacher would probably be comin' after us."

"Oh, hell, Simpson!" Franklin said. "Preacher ain't nowheres nearer than five hundred miles. Y'all gettin' mighty spooky over nothin', say I."

"Just cook the damn meat," Simpson said. He began walking toward Preacher's location.

I'm gonna have to be quick and true if I pull this off, Preacher thought. It was far too early in the game to risk a shot, and he wanted this camp's attack to be blamed on the Indians. He hauled back the bow string and let the arrow fly. He was notching another arrow before the man called Simpson took the first arrow in the center of his chest. He grunted and dropped to his knees just as Preacher stepped out of the thin brush and let another arrow fly toward Franklin.

It was a clean miss.

"What the hell!" Franklin yelled, jumping to his feet and leaping for his rifle, which was leaning up against a boulder across the clearing.

Preacher won the wild race by a second, leaping on the man's back just as his hand closed around his rifle.

Preacher rode the man down to the ground, pounding at his face with big hard fists. Franklin twisted and threw Preacher off his back. Preacher rolled and came up, his knife in his hand.

"Bastard!" Franklin panted, blood from a busted nose streaming down his chin. He reached for his own blade.

Preacher jumped at the man and kicked out, his foot catching the man on the knee and putting him down with a yelp of pain into a dusty heap. Franklin rolled and came to his boots, slashing out with his knife. Preacher sidestepped and cut the man's arm to the bone. Franklin screamed in pain and dropped the knife. He turned to run for the sparse timber and Preacher reversed the knife and let it fly, the big blade sinking into the man's back. The blade had centered Franklin's back, severing the spinal cord. Franklin went to the ground in an uncoordinated heap, falling almost soundlessly.

Preacher pulled out his knife and knelt down, quickly scalping the outlaw. He went back to where Simpson lay, the ground all around him wet with blood, and took his hair. It was not something Preacher enjoyed doing, but to pull this off, laying the blame on the Injuns, it had to be.

It didn't damper his appetite, however.

After he had finished his gruesome work, Preacher carefully hid the spare weapons and then returned to the fire, leaving the bodies where they lay. He washed out a cup and drank the coffee, then slowly ate the meat, savoring each bite and ignoring the dead men.

After he had eaten his fill and polished off the pot of strong coffee, Preacher turned the men's horses loose and then set about disguising his tracks to make it look like several Indians had attacked the camp. What he was doing would not fool anyone who had enough sense to sit down, think it out, and then carefully examine the signs. But Preacher was hoping no one among the Pardee gang would do that.

He left a piece of venison broiling over the fire so it would be burned to a crisp, only adding to the scene he hoped would convince the others of the suddenness of the attack. He knew he should mutilate the bodies and he tried to steel himself to do that, but he just couldn't bring himself to do it. It had been bad enough scalping the men.

When he was satisfied he had done all he could, Preacher stood for a moment, inspecting the surroundings. He had played hell here for a fact. Finally, he nodded his head and slipped away from the camp of the dead. It would not take the carrion birds long to find the bodies and it would not be long before the Pardee brothers or some of their followers took notice of the slowly circling flesh eaters and come to investigate.

He stopped at the edge of the camp and looked back. "Oh, to hell with it," he said. "That ain't gonna fool no one." He returned to the camp, found a piece of paper and the stub of a pencil, and wrote out a short note, smiling as he did so. It took him awhile 'cause it had been a long time since he had written any words.

He left the note stuck on the end of a branch and then melted back into the Lonesome. He figured it was gonna get right interestin' when the Pardees discovered the camp and the note. He was hoping they'd follow him. That was why he was leaving a trail even a pilgrim could follow. A mile from the camp of the dead, Preacher paused long enough to carefully construct a booby trap. He smiled grimly as he worked. Somebody was going to be in a world of hurt when they hit this one.

He backed off and waited. All in all, he thought, it was starting out to be a right nice day.

15

"They never had a chance," Radborne Pardee said, after he and his brothers ran off the gloated carrion birds. The birds didn't go far from their snack. They waited and watched patiently. "Injuns snuck up on 'em and finished 'em."

No one had yet discovered the note. Very observant bunch of outlaws.

Malachi wasn't at all sure it had been Indians. He stood in the middle of the carnage and looked slowly all about him. "Something is wrong with this," he finally said. "I don't think this was done by Injuns."

"How come you to say that, Malachi?" his brother Henry asked, a stupid look on his stupid face. "What else could it have been? Them's arrows, ain't they?"

"I know they're arrows, Henry," Malachi said. "I can see that. But something's mighty wrong here. Mighty wrong. It's just . . . I can't put my finger on it."

"I'll say this," Kenrick Pardee said, looking at the trail. "Them Injuns, if it was Injuns, was either drunk or it's a setup. A blind man could follow this trail."

Malachi nodded his head in agreement, thinking that he

was very grateful to have at least one brother with sense enough to come in out of the rain.

"What is all this scribblin' on this here paper?" Radborne said.

Malachi took the note from the branch and slowly read the words. He and Kenrick were the only ones in the clan who could read. His mouth dropped open and his face darkened with rage. He started cussing and balled up the note and threw it to the ground, then jumped up and down on it. It had been unsigned, but he knew who wrote it.

"Nobody calls me a stupid son of a bitch!" he yelled. "Goddamn that Preacher."

"Preacher!" Kenrick said.

"Yeah. Preacher. He writ that note. I know it was him."

"Then let's don't take no chances, Malachi," Kenrick said. "Let's call in the whole bunch and take off after him. We try to go this alone and he'll pick us off one by one."

Malachi nodded his head. "All right. Put out the call, brother. Sound it long. We've got to get him. Before he gets us," he added grimly.

Preacher heard the mournful sounds of the hunting horn as it sounded around the high country. Malachi was calling his bunch together to come after him. He settled down for a wait.

"Come on, Malachi," he said. "I made the trail easy for you. But you'll have to look close to see this surprise I got rigged up down yonder."

Preacher had left the wider animal trail and worked his way into a stand of timber. Those following him would have to leave their horses and continue their tracking on foot, for Preacher didn't want to hurt anyone's good horse unless it just come hard to that. A horse couldn't help it if the man who rode it was a sorry son of a bitch. Preacher did know that most highwaymen took better care of their horses than they did themselves, for the outlaw's life often depended upon the speed and the stamina of the horse he rode.

Preacher waited behind the jumble of rocks and thin brush. From his vantage point, he had a wide view of the area just below him, a fairly thick stand of timber, and there was only one way the Pardee gang could come at him—straight ahead.

Down the trail, Malachi Pardee had halted the gang and they had gathered. They moved out slowly, in single file, for the trail was narrow and rocky, with bad footing. Now they had halted. Ned Blum had volunteered to take the point, as Malachi had suspected he would. Ned hated Preacher, and his hatred spanned a dozen years. Ned had braced Preacher once and Preacher had tossed down the glove and then proceeded to stomp the bejesus out of the outlaw from Delaware, publicly humiliating him in front of a dozen men. Ned had sworn to kill Preacher.

"I don't need no help to take Preacher," Ned boasted to Malachi and the others. "Y'all just stay back here and let me handle this."

"You go right ahead, Ned," Malachi said, thinking: Maybe you'll really get lucky and get a ball in him.

Rifle in hand, Ned moved out, working his way carefully into the stand of timber, moving ever closer to the spike trap Preacher had laid out for anyone stupid enough to follow his trail. Ned was cautious, and he had good reason to be, for everyone in the wilderness knew that if Preacher was anything, he was a very dangerous man. But Ned figured he could take him now that Preacher didn't have his buddies around him. Not that his buddies had anything to do with Preacher whipping him that time, but Ned had convinced himself through self-lies that they had.

Ned dried his sweaty palms on his britches and once more gripped his rifle. He paused for a moment, looking around him. He could see nothing out of the ordinary. Damn that Preacher, he thought. He's a-layin' up yonder somewhere's like a stinkin' Injun. He's been out here in the Lonesome so long he ain't even a white man no more. He thinks like a damn Injun.

Ned moved on and up. After a few steps, he sensed something was wrong and paused, looking all around him. Something was wrong, but he didn't know what. He let his eyes linger on the trees, the brush, the rocks, the faint trail that Preacher had left. He looked behind him. The boys was clean out of sight. He took one more step, then another. He began to feel better. Maybe he'd been wrong. Maybe all them feelin's of gloom and doom was wrong. After all, Preacher was just a man, not no superbein'.

He took another step and felt the earth give beneath his foot. He tried to jerk back but it was too late. Ned screamed as the sharpened stakes tore through his foot and ripped into the flesh of his ankle and calf. He dropped his rifle as the pain became so intense he almost lost consciousness. He began screaming, over and over, the hoarse howlings echoing around the high country.

"I reckon Ned wasn't as good as he thought he was," Malachi remarked matter-of-factly, listening to the screaming.

"What you reckon Preacher done to him?" a thug called Van asked. He looked furtively all around him. That screaming was really unnerving.

"Why don't you go find out?" Malachi said, looking at the scared outlaw.

"Me?"

"I ain't talkin' to no damn tree, Van. Yeah, you. So move on out."

All the others looked at him as Van licked suddenly dry lips and hesitated for a few seconds. The wild screaming was now more animallike in nature. All of them were thinking that there was no damn telling what Preacher had done to Ned.

"Back him up, Dexter," Malachi ordered.

That made Van feel some better. Dexter was a good man and pure hell with a pistol, and in that stand of timber up yonder, a pistol was what a man was going to have to use. Van moved out, Dexter staying about twenty-five feet behind him.

As they slowly and cautiously closed the distance, both of them expecting a ball through the chest at any second, Dexter asked, "Van, what you reckon we've gone and done that's made Preacher so mad at us?"

"I don't know. I ain't never done him a hurt, that's for sure. Let's get Ned out of this mess first and then we'll tackle Preacher." They stepped into the timber. "Jesus, it's close in here. Watch yourself."

"Oh, may God help me!" Ned wailed. "My foot and leg is all tore up bad."

"Hang on, Ned!" Dexter called. "We're comin' in to hep you. Just hang on."

"Yeah," Preacher muttered, Dexter's words just audible to him. "Come on, boys. I got some surprises waitin' for the two of you, too."

Van was the first to reach the injured man and he almost got sick when he saw what Ned had gotten into. Preacher had dug a pit and rigged up sharpened stakes, with about half of the stake points up, the other half of the points down. Those pointed up had torn into Ned's foot, calf, and ankle. When Ned had tried to jerk his foot free, those stakes pointing down had ripped into flesh and trapped him.

"Good Lord," Dexter said. "Keep watch, Van. I got to somehow pull these stakes out. Damn a man who would do something like this. Christ, they's blood all over the place. I can't get no good purchase on nothin'."

Preacher had worked several hours in the building of his traps, and when Preacher wanted to be low-down mean, he could be one mean son, for a fact.

Dex stepped back a foot or so and his boot hit a vine stretched tight. He had time to look up and open his mouth to holler before the heavy log fell on him. The log crushed his skull and broke his back and neck. But Dexter didn't mind. He was dead before he hit the ground. He would rape and rob and torture and murder no more.

Van had jumped back at Dexter's shout; now he looked at the mess, horror in his eyes. Ned had passed out, and that was a good thing for Ned, for one end of the heavy log had landed on his shoulder and bounced off. In addition to his other woes, Ned now had a broken shoulder and broken arm.

Van gingerly stepped back from the dead and badly injured and his boot slipped under and triggered another stretched-tight vine. A green and thick and limber limb lashed out and slammed into Van's face, breaking his nose and knocking out a couple of teeth and loosening a few more. Van screamed in pain and fright, struggled to his feet, and went staggering back down the trail, almost blind from the involuntary tears that were streaming from his eyes as a result of the busted beak.

"What the billy-hell . . . ?" Malachi said, hearing all the commotion and then seeing Van come lurching and staggering out of the timber.

A rifle slammed and Van went down bonelessly and limp, a hole about the size of a teacup in his back. Malachi and the others hit the ground and went scrambling on all fours for cover.

"Anybody see the smoke?" Kenrick called from his cover behind a skinny tree.

"No," a ne'er-do-well called Hall said. "But it's got to be comin' from up yonder in them rocks above the trees. Hell, that's a good three, four hundred yards."

"Preacher can shoot," Malachi said grudgingly. "This ain't no good, boys. We got to pull back from here."

"What about Dex and Ned?"

"You ain't heard no more sounds from up yonder, have you?"

"Well . . . no."

"They're dead. Come on. Let's pull back and get gone. We got to plan some."

They left Van where he lay and slipped back, far back, well out of rifle range. They went so far back they were out of cannon range.

Preacher watched them leave and left his rocks and drifted down to where Ned lay trapped in the stake pit. He ignored the battered and broken body of Dexter and squatted down beside the unconscious Ned. While Ned was out, Preacher freed his legs and hauled him out of the hole, stretching him out on the ground. He could plainly see that the man's arm and shoulder were busted. He poured a little water from his canteen on the man's face and Ned moaned and opened his eyes. They were bright with the pain that rippled through his body.

"Your pals pulled out and left you," Preacher told him. "Mayhaps you should start thinkin' about associatin' with a better class of people."

"I'm dyin', ain't I?"

"You ain't in the best shape I ever seen a man to be," Preacher acknowledged. "But I reckon if I was a mind to, I could fix up some poultices and such for your legs and set that shoulder and arm."

"For the love of God, man—"

"Don't you be talkin' 'bout God to me, you trashy bastard. Anybody that would ride with the Pardees don't need to be mentionin' God."

"You a mighty cold man, Preacher."

"No, I ain't. I just don't like the Pardees nor anyone who consorts with them." He picked up his rifle. "I best be movin' on."

"Wait! Are you just going to leave me here?"

"I could shoot you, I reckon. I'd do that for a horse," Preacher said straight-faced.

"My God, man, but you a devil!"

"Well . . . you could make it easier for yourself by talkin' to me," Preacher suggested.

"About what?"

"Malachi Pardee and his plans."

"I don't know nothin' about no plans," Ned said, a sly look creeping into his eyes.

Preacher started to walk away.

"Wait!" Ned called weakly. "Don't leave me like this. I don't know much but I'll tell you what I do know."

Preacher squatted down beside the man. Ned wasn't going to die—providing gangrene didn't set in—but he would never be one hundred percent again. His shoulder was crushed and his arm broken in several places. If his legs weren't treated fast, both of them would rot off. Preacher told him that.

"You're gonna hep me, aren't you?" Ned begged.

"Depends on what you tell me."

Ned laid his head on the ground. "All right," he whispered. "All right. I ain't never in my life seen a man as hard as you, Preacher. Never."

Preacher fixed poultices for the man's badly injured legs—but the plants really needed weren't growing this high up. Then he set Ned's arm and shoulder as best he could. Ned passed out from the pain and Preacher left him like that. There was nothing else he could do for him. Ned hadn't known much, but what he did know was a help.

Only a few of Red Hand's renegades had stayed with the Pardee gang. The renegade leader had taken most of his followers and left out. Ned seemed to think they had gone east, believing that would provide them with easier pickings. Ned had the impression that Malachi Pardee was even too gamy for Red Hand.

Preacher doubted that. Red Hand was as cruel a man as Preacher had ever seen. He probably just wanted to get shut of the crazy Pardee brothers. Preacher knew them all, and with the exception of Malachi and Kenrick, the rest of them were as nutty as a pecan tree. Ansel was by far the blood-thirstiest. He was killing crazy.

As for Ned, he would die if his friends in the gang didn't take care of him real soon. And Preacher doubted any of them would take the time or expel the effort to do so. More than likely, Malachi or one of his goofy brothers would give Ned a ball right between the eyes. As badly hurt as Ned was, that might be a blessing. Or they might just leave him to die. This was no country to be badly hurt in. There was a doctor back at the post, but that was days away, and riding would be agony for the hurt outlaw. Preacher didn't have any sympathy for the highwayman. Ned had voluntarily chosen his vocation. No one had held a gun to his head and forced him to become an outlaw. There were some—mostly back in the settled East—who were starting to say that outlaws and the like should be pitied. Preacher thought that was some of the biggest crap he'd ever heard of. He couldn't imagine why anyone would think that. But he knew there were people in the world who always placed the blame elsewhere, never looking square at the problem, always looking for an excuse for bad behavior. Preacher didn't have any use for people like that.

Preacher moved on, staying just below the timberline and leaving a clear trail for those behind him to follow. As long as they wanted to play Preacher's game, he'd lay down the rules. And they'd be mighty damn savage ones. At least this way he was keeping Malachi and his crummy bunch away from what few settlers there were and the wagon trains that were beginning to prod slowly westward.

Preacher would have scoffed at any suggestion that what he was doing was noble. He would have had a good laugh at that. That thought had never entered his mind. He did know that what he was doing would be considered no more than murder by some folks back East. But folks who stay settled and safe in populated areas like cities tend to lose sight of matters. Preacher knew that for a fact. He didn't understand it, but knew it to be true.

The truth was, Preacher just didn't like Malachi Pardee nor anyone else who thought and behaved as Malachi and his followers did. No man had the right to take from another. It was just as simple as that. A man had a right to take gun in hand to protect what was his. Whether it be wife and family, hearth and home, or a man's horse or dog. A body had a right to use force to keep what was his. Preacher had heard that a lot of folks back East, them particular in the cities, had stopped totin' pistols and was leaving all the duties to the police and the constables. As far as Preacher was concerned, that was plumb stupid. If something like that kept on, soon they'd be laws forbiddin' a man to tote a pistol and protect himself.

Preacher shook his head and dismissed that thought. That was too ridiculous to even consider. That would never happen in America.

16

Malachi Pardee sat before the fire, a cup of coffee in his dirty hands. His thoughts were just as dirty as his body, and that was filthy. Malachi was between a rock and a hard place, and he knew it only too well.

That wagon train with the good lookin' women and the prime young girls in it was getting further and further away, and there was no telling when another one would form up and pass through. It was getting late in the summer and few would chance the crossing this close to snowfall. But Malachi knew he could not take his gang and leave the mountains after the train. Not with Preacher up here. Preacher would just swing in behind them and pick them off one at a time. No, Preacher had to be dealt with here and now and left dead in the Big Empty. That was all there was to it. The goddamn worthless, shiftless mountain man had been a thorn in Malachi's side for too many years. Just the thought made him angry. Who in the hell did Preacher think he was, anyways?

Brother Henry looked at his big brother from across the fire where supper was cooking. "Is we gonna have Preacher a-doggin' us forever, Malachi?"

"Yes, if we don't come up with a good plan to get shut of him," Malachi replied sourly. "Cut me off a hunk of that there meat, Henry. It's got me salivatin' something fierce."

Henry whacked off a hunk of hot, half-raw meat, and Malachi fell to gnawing. Thank the Lord they all was blessed with good strong teeth, he was fond of saying.

With blood and juices running down his chin, Malachi said, "I just can't figure why Preacher hates us all so. Lord have mercy knows we ain't never done a harm to him. We's just tryin' to make a livin', that's all. If folks that have would just share with us, we wouldn't have to do what we's doin'. T'ain't right, for a fact. The government ought to provide for poor folks like us."

Preacher knew that he'd made Malachi and his greasy bunch very nervous and very cautious, so they would be watching the ground for trip ropes from here on in. So he changed his tactics. Knowing that lazy, shiftless people rarely looked up, Preacher concentrated his efforts on up instead of down.

Preacher occasionally chuckled as he worked swiftly but carefully removing and relocating rocks of various sizes, placing them on the lip of a gently sloping ledge. The ledge was above a long and deep grade of very loose rocks, a slide area, some of the rocks huge boulders. Just above the newly piled rocks were several boulders that Preacher had tested and found he could dislodge by bracing himself and shoving with his feet. When they hit the newly placed rocks, a monumental slide was going to occur. And anyone caught on the trail below was going to be in real serious trouble.

Preacher climbed down carefully and moved some rocks and logs, partly blocking the trail he had used to get up above the timberline. He disguised his work and then made his way back up. The Pardee gang would be forced to leave their horses and follow his false trail on foot.

His work done, Preacher then deliberately built a fire and cooked some deer meat and boiled some water for coffee. He figured the Pardees would come rompin' and stompin' in the morning, hell bent on killing him. Well, they could damn well try it.

"Look, Malachi!" Valiant hollered, pointing to the thin line of smoke in the distance. "That's got to be Preacher."

"Goadin' us," Malachi said, after doing some pretty fancy cussing. "That damn Preacher. He's a-funnin' with us and a-woolin' us. Laughin' at us whilst he makes fun of us. Makin' fools out of us. Well, I ain't a-gonna stand still for no more of this. I've had all this I can take, boys. Tomorrow we're gonna do the bastard in for good."

Ansel Pardee did a little dance and slobbered down his chin. Ansel wasn't good for much, but he was a real good slobberer. "We gonna peel the hide offen him, ain't we, Malachi? So's we can listen to him holler. Cook his bare feet in a far and gouge out his eyes, ain't we?" Ansel was really a swell fellow. Lots of fun to be around.

"Wipe your mouth and chin, boy," his big brother told him. "Yeah. We can do that, I reckon. If we take him alive. That might be fun."

The Pardees could be quite inventive when it came to torture and the general abuse of prisoners. Ansel was so happy he did a little jig right there in the camp. Ansel was at his best hurting people. Especially women and kids. But someone like Preacher would be just as much fun . . . almost, he reckoned. Ansel danced around the camp, flapping his arms and humming.

"Mamma was too long in the tooth when she whelped Ansel and Radborne," Kenrick remarked to Malachi, both of them watching their baby brother prance around.

"Well, hell," Malachi replied. "Henry ain't but two year behind me and his bread ain't baked right neither."

"For a fact. But I always suspicioned that Uncle Dunbar slipped over the woodpile one night when Pa was gone and lifted up mamma's gown."

"There was that talk as I recollect. You know, Kenrick, to turn out as well and fine as we did, we shore did come from mighty poor stock."

"I will agree with both them things, brother."

"Shhhiiittt!" Valiant said, looking at the narrow and rocky trail that lay beyond the boulders blocking their way. "Don't tell me we got to *walk* again?"

Malachi did look up, suspecting a trap, but nothing seemed out of the ordinary. The birds and squirrels had grown accustomed to Preacher and were going about their business as usual. Still, he didn't like it.

High above them, Preacher was in place and braced. When the rocks started going, half of that grade of loose rocks would break free under the rolling and bouncing impact. Some of those below would have time to get clear, maybe. And some wouldn't. And every one that went down was one less Preacher had to worry about. Not that he was very worried about any of that damn trash down below him.

Malachi looked back at his men. "George," he called. "Go check it out. Go all the way across and see if his trail is over yonder on the other side and see how far it goes for a ways."

George didn't want to make himself a target, but he went, expecting to feel the rip of a bullet in his guts or in his back with every step he took. But he went. When he reached the other side, he paused to wipe the sweat from his face and from the inside of his hat, even though this high up it was cool. He found Preacher's false trail easily enough and shouted that news across the several hundred yards' distance that separated him from the bunch.

"He's headin' this way for a fact, Malachi. I can see where

he rested agin this here boulder for a time, catchin' his breath, I reckon."

Malachi had him a bad feeling about the passage that stretched out in front of him. A real bad feeling. But if they didn't make this crossing here, they would have to ride a dozen miles around the mountains and then be faced with a hard climb back up. As it stood now, he was going to have to send men the long way around with the horses.

Hell, Malachi, he told his mind. Give it up and leave. Look to another part of the country. Head for the Oregon Territory and be a road agent there. Preacher will never leave these mountains and you wouldn't have him to put up with.

But Malachi knew he wouldn't do that. Now it was down to a matter of pride.

But pride can get you killed, he reminded himself.

Got to be this way, another part of him said. Can't have the talk a-goin' around that Malachi Pardee backed down from the likes of Preacher.

"Start crossin'." Malachi gave the orders. "You, Coyote Man, take the lead. Harold, you and Slim follow after him. Cotter, you and Shockly go after them. Move out."

"I will go after that," Little Wolf said. "Kills the Enemy will follow me."

"I will go after that," Big Eagle announced. "I am not afraid of a rocky trail."

"All right," Malachi said.

Miles back, Ned lay unconscious and dying in the deserted camp of the Pardee gang. They had left him to go it alone with no more thought than they would have given a dying snake. Probably less, for one of them would have surely killed the snake.

From where he lay, braced and ready, hidden from the eyes of those below, Preacher could not make out individuals as they began their crossing. But he could count seven or eight of them all bunched up on the safe side. No one, it seemed, wanted to be the one to take that first step.

Not that Preacher blamed any of them for hesitating. But he knew *he* wouldn't have been dumb enough to fall for such an obvious trap.

Pride's got Malachi now, Preacher thought. Old Man Pride has done took control of his senses. He don't want to lose face by turnin' back. And that's liable to be the thing that gets you killed, Malachi.

"I do not like this," Crooked Arm whispered to a friend as they stood at the end of the line of outlaws. "Bloody Knife is playing games with us. Deadly games."

His friend, called Running Dog, nodded his head solemnly. "If we are smart at all, we will disappear from this band of fools."

"And go where?" Crooked Arm questioned. "To forever wander the land without family or company?"

"We will be alive," Running Dog said.

Crooked Arm thought about that for a moment. "That is surely something to be considered. Now?"

"Now."

The two renegades started walking backward and soon vanished around a bend in the narrow trail. They were the smart ones. They would be alive to tell others how the man called Bloody Knife tricked Malachi Pardee. The tales would spread and grow and so would the reputation of the mountain man called Preacher.

Eight men, nearly a third of the Pardee gang, committed themselves to the rocky trail. Preacher tensed his legs against the boulder. Just a few more seconds, a few more steps, and the outlaws would be caught with no place to run.

In the center of the narrow trail, Coyote Man stopped and carefully looked all around him. Something in his guts was telling him, silently screaming at him, that death was near. But he could see nothing.

"What is wrong with you?" Big Eagle called from the rear of the line. "We are standing out here as plain as a wart on the end of a nose. If you are afraid, then get out of the way and let me lead."

"Shut up, you fat cow," Coyote Man called. "You could not lead a horse to water." He started forward and the others crowded in close behind him.

Preacher shoved with all his might and the boulder went rolling.

All on the trail and at both ends of it felt the ground begin to tremble. Little Wolf looked all around him, not understanding what was happening. Kills the Enemy looked in but one direction—up. He opened his mouth and screamed in terror as tons of rock were gathering up more tons of rock and all the mass was hurtling downward.

There was no place for the men trapped on the rocky trail to run. They stood as if frozen in place and waited for death.

"Goddamn you!" Malachi screamed, his words unheard over the thundering roar of the avalanche. "I'll kill you, Preacher. I swear I'll kill you."

Then a cloud of dust the size of a mountain enveloped the area, shrouding everything, tearing the eyes of those left alive, and causing a fit of coughing. When the dust had settled and the area was deadly silent, what was left of the gang looked toward where the trail used to be. It was gone, swept clean and covered. There was no way across and there was not a trace left of the eight men. On the other side, George looked back in horror and terror. He was trapped and alone.

"Stay where you is, George!" Malachi hollered, not knowing that George was so scared he couldn't have moved even if the Lord had commanded it. Besides that, he had crapped his drawers. "Start workin' your way down and we'll meet you by the river with the horses. We'll wait for you."

Malachi and the others waited for some sort of taunting jeer from Preacher. But all that greeted them was silence and the low moaning wind.

"We ought to say something." A Pardee follower called

Curtis finally broke the silence. "I mean, I ain't no church-goin' man, but they's all buried under them rocks."

Ansel giggled and slobbered and picked his nose.

"Preacher!" Malachi hollered, the word echoing back to him. "You dirty son, can you hear me? Answer me, damn your eyes."

Silence.

"I know you're up there, you ambushin' no-count. Come down here and fight me like a man, you bastard!" Malachi was so mad he had forgotten that Preacher had already twice stomped the crap out of him.

But Preacher was a long way off and running hard. He had left under the cover of the enormous dust cloud. He reached the outlaw's horses and quickly went to work. He jerked the picket pins and sent them stampeding. He cut up the cinch straps, slashed the fenders and stirrups, and then set about destroying and scattering the supplies. He dented their coffee pots with rocks and threw everything he could lay hands on, including their saddles and bedrolls, over the side and into a deep ravine. They could reach them, but they'd have to work doing it. He quickly added one final touch and then Preacher slipped back about five hundred yards, found himself a safe and comfortable spot, and waited for the outlaws to return.

It was not a long wait. Malachi Pardee and his gang, minus seven or eight dead and two that had slipped away and one that was stranded on the other side of the avalanche, straggled back into camp and stood for a moment, dumbfounded. With Ansel, it was no act.

Malachi didn't even cuss at the sight. He sat down on a log and sighed. He was tired, his feet were sore, he was disgusted, and just about played out. "Some of you fellers see if you can locate the horses," he finally said, weariness in his voice. "Rest of you start gatherin' up what supplies we got left and somebody build a fire. Them ashes is dead. Get one of them beat-up coffee pots and get some water. If it don't leak," he added, then added, "Goddamn that Preacher." Makin' a joke outta this, he thought. That's what it is to him, just one big damn joke. He thinks this is funny. Funny! Well, if I get a chance, I'll make this joke on him. If.

But Preacher had left a surprise in the cold ashes—in the form of a black-powder bomb he'd made with spare powder he'd found in the supplies of the outlaws. Preacher lay in the rocks and watched, hardly able to contain anticipatory laughter over what was going to happen in a few minutes.

One outlaw began gathering up twigs and sticks and a few larger branches of dead wood. He got the twigs blazing, then laid on a few sticks. Malachi stood up and walked over to warm his hands, as did several others, for the day had turned off cold in the high country.

The men stood in silence, their expressions glum.

They'll soon be a lot glummer, Preacher thought. He had to stick his fist over his mouth to stifle his laughter.

"Far shore feels good," Kenrick said, rubbing his hands briskly.

"Shore do," an outlaw named Clifford said. "And some coffee would be right tasty too. I think Dillman done found a mite of it."

Dillman walked up just as the bomb blew. The fire pit contained most of the killing effects of the blast, but dirt and rocks and ashes were flung all over the place, and the force of the explosion knocked down those who were standing around the fire. The charge created a huge dust and ash cloud that completely engulfed the camp for a few seconds. Dillman's sack of coffee went one way and he went the other, tumbling ass over elbows. Malachi took a stone right between his eyes and it knocked him to the ground and out like a snuffed candle. Several horses had wandered back into camp and the explosion sent the already skittish animals off and racing away, galloping at full tilt. Ansel had dropped his trousers and hung his butt over a log just as the powder blew. He landed in what he had just deposited as a fist-sized rock impacted with the top of his head. If it was possible to be goofier than he already was, Ansel Pardee had reached the zenith. Kenrick had been completely lifted off his boots and thrown backward, slowly twisting in the air. He landed on his belly and the wind was knocked from him. Clifford had turned his back to the fire to warm his butt and the blast not only set his trousers on fire, but lifted him into the air and tossed him about fifteen feet from the fire pit. Clifford was now scooting around on the ground, bellowing and cussing, trying to put out the fire that was scorching his butt.

Animals were snorting and rearing and running around in a wild-eyed panic. Men were hollering and cussing and in a state of utter confusion. Finally, the shattered camp began to calm down as the dust began to settle.

Preacher knew it was foolish to stay around any longer— he'd taken a terrible chance by staying around this long—so while a bit of confusion still held sway over the outlaw camp, he took off. The last thing he heard was Ansel's voice. The fool was shuffling around the camp, his pants down around his ankles, singing an old church song. However, it seemed that he could only remember one line.

"Hark, the glad sounds, the Savior comes . . ."

Preacher shook his head and hit the trail. As soon as he was far enough away, he'd sure sit down and have himself a real good laugh about this day.

"Hark, the glad sounds, the Savior comes . . ."

"Aw, shut up, Ansel!" one of his brothers said. "And pull your britches up, you fool."

Malachi sat up on the cold ground, one hand to his throbbing and aching head. He listened to the song. "I've done died and gone to Heaven," he mumbled. Then he opened his eyes and saw Ansel, standing bare-assed and bellowing out a song. "Or Hell," Malachi added.

BOOK TWO

There is no arguing with Johnson for if his pistol misses fire, he knocks you down with the butt of it.

Oliver Goldsmith

1

"Preacher ain't fightin fair," Valiant Pardee said.

Malachi looked at his brother and shook his still-aching head. He used to think there might be some hope left for Valiant. But no more. "How much did you boys salvage?"

"Not near 'bout enough," Henry Pardee grumbled. He wore a bloody bandage around his head where a panicked horse had run over him.

"We lost eight or ten horses," Kenrick told his brother. "But then, we lost eight or ten men, too, so that all evens out. We got enough supplies to go on . . . if you want to go on."

"Damn right I want to go on!" Malachi snapped. "Way I see it, we ain't got no choice in the matter. None a-tall. We can't let this story get out. We wouldn't have no respect from nobody if it do."

"Running Man picked up Preacher's trail," Clifford said, wearing a pair of pants he had taken from the supplies of the dead men. They were too short and made him look about as stupid as Ansel was. "He said Preacher was a-layin' over yonder in them rocks just a-watchin' us all the time." He pointed.

"That sounds about right," Malachi said sourly. "Preacher

had him a good laugh, too, I reckon. On us. Well, from now on we don't fall for no more of Preacher's tricks. We got to sit down and work us out a plan."

"I been thinkin' some on that, Malachi," Ansel said, wiping the slobber from his lips and chin.

"Lord help us all," Kenrick muttered.

"I can't hardly wait to hear this," Malachi replied in a whisper. "All right, Ansel, let's hear it."

"Let's make Preacher come to us 'stead of us al'ays a-goin' to him."

The gang members all exchanged glances. Malachi was silent for a moment, then said, "You be right, Ansel. That there is a good scheme. You done come up with a right good plan." He was forgetting that Preacher came to them in the first place, with disastrous results for the gang.

"How does we do that?" Clifford asked Ansel.

"Don't strain his brain too hard," Malachi said quickly. He glanced at Ansel. "You done good, Ansel. Real good. Now go somewheres and rest for a time."

"How *does* we do it?" Kenrick asked his big brother after Ansel had danced away. His performance posed absolutely no threat to any ballet dancer in the world.

"I don't know," Malachi admitted. "I got to ruminate on that for a spell. Go on and leave me be for a time." Truth was, Malachi desperately wanted to just give it up and get the hell gone from this part of the world. More and more he was getting the feeling he had just about played out his string and what little was left on the spool was being controlled by that damn Preacher.

He looked around the ruined camp and at what was left of his gang. He shook his head. At one time, Malachi Pardee ran the most powerful and feared gang of road agents and outlaws west of the Mississippi. And not that many months ago, either. Sure as hell didn't look like much now.

Malachi had the sinking feeling that the game was just about over for him. He tried to push that emotion from his mind, but could not. It was just too incredible for him to accept that one man could destroy an entire gang of some of the meanest cutthroats in all the West.

But he had only to look around him to see the truth in the matter.

"Damn!" Malachi whispered.

Miles away, Preacher rested and waited. For the time being, he didn't have a clue as to what he might do next to harass the Pardees, but then this came to him: if he were in their shoes, he'd do nothing and try to draw the enemy to him.

Preacher chewed on some jerky and thought about that. The more he thought about it, the more he became convinced that was what the Pardees might try.

If so, what was next for him?

Preacher didn't try to kid himself a bit. He'd been lucky so far. Real lucky. He wasn't dealing with amateurs, even though the Pardee gang had behaved as such since this personal little war began. Preacher realized that had to end and he'd better stop treating the conflict as a joke and tighten up. No more stunts like the one he'd pulled this day, hiding in the rocks and stifling laughter at the antics of the Pardee gang. That had been dangerous and plumb foolish on his part.

True, his actions had taken a fearful toll on the Pardee gang. But he'd been brash in the doing of it. He'd have to cut back on some of that.

He wondered how the wagon train was faring. He'd been so busy of late he hadn't had much time to ponder on those folks. Well, at least he was keeping the Pardees busy and away from the train. And the train was of a size that it would take a goodly bunch of Indians to attack it. By now the train should be clear out of this part of the country.

* * *

In all the weeks that Preacher had been trailing and doing battle with the Pardees, the train had made good time. But sickness had overtaken the movers and brought the train to a halt. The sickness, a strange fever that weakened muscles and caused the joints to ache and brought on chills one minute and burning-up hotness the next, had even struck the mountain men, putting Carl and Caleb and Windy flat on their backs along with most of the others . . . except for the kids. Not a one of them had been touched by the odd sickness. Now it was the kids taking care of the adults and the seeing-to of the livestock and such.

As the days drifted by, the mountain men worried that none of them would have the strength to push on in time to beat the snows. And if they weren't over the mountains come snowfall, they would be stuck right where they was till spring.

What finally saved their bacon was the return of Rimrock. The huge mountain man had a change of heart and turned around, riding back and picking up the ruts of the train and following it. Rimrock took one look at the adults a-layin' flat of their backs, weak as sick cats, and the exhausted and drawn faces of the kids, who'd been doing all the work, and he pitched right in.

"I seen this 'fore," Rimrock told Weller. "I don't know the name of the sickness, but I seen it 'fore. You ain't gonna die from it, but it makes a body so sick and weak some folks might wish they was dead to get some relief."

"I certainly agree with that," Weller whispered. "Any news of Preacher?"

"Injuns say they's a big war goin' on in the high country. East of here. Two renegades that broke from the Pardee gang claim that Preacher brought a whole mountain down on some of the gang. Wiped 'em out without no trace left. I doubt if it was an en-tar mountain, but Preacher probably caught some in a slide. Preacher is something to behold when he gets his dander up."

"You'll stay and help us, Rimrock?"

"Shore. Wouldn't be fittin' for me to do nothin' else. You just lay back and take 'er easy. I'll see to the rest of it."

Squatting down beside Windy, Caleb, and Carl, he said, "I can't leave y'all for no time 'fore you get in trouble. I reckon I'm gonna have to nanny the three of you for the rest of your days."

"We've got to get these folks well fast, Rim" Caleb said. "We ain't got much time left 'fore the snows come. They'll die out here."

"Forget it," the big man said. "It's gonna take weeks 'fore ever'body gets their strength back. Like I told Weller, I seen this sickness 'fore. That winter you went to St. Louie, Windy. I told you about it."

"Then we're in bad trouble," Carl said.

"Maybe not. The Whitman Mission ain't far from here. 'Bout a hundred miles. Worst comes to worser, we'll winter there. They'll welcome us."

"They might," Windy said, his voice weak. "But them Cayuses might not."

"I know Chief Tamsuky," Rimrock said. "I've met with him and slep' in his lodge. He's all right. It's all them gospel shouters up yonder that he don't take to worth a damn. They gonna keep on stirrin' up them Cayuses and one day it's gonna backfire on them all. You boys rest now. Ol' Rim's here. So don't worry."

The first movers up were Miles Cason and George Martin, and tenderfeet they might be—in Miles case that was still more than true—but Rimrock welcomed their help. The big man had shouldered a terrible burden taking care of everything.

"I have never experienced anything like that debilitating malaise we just recovered from," Miles told Rimrock. "It rendered me quite impuissant."

Rimrock stared at him for a few seconds. "What the hell did you just say?"

"The sickness."

"Oh. Yeah. Ain't got no name yet, that I know of. But it's tough. I ain't never had it and hope I never get it."

Betina and Coretine and a few of the other pioneer women were soon up and moving around, able to cook and wash a bit. But they couldn't do much for any length of time, having to rest every few minutes. But what little they could do was a godsend to those few who were handling the whole load.

"First decent meal I've et since I happened along here," Rimrock said, spooning another plateful of stew that Coretine had prepared. "I never was no hand at cookin' fancy things like this here. And anything Miles and George dishes up tastes like a boiled moccasin."

Windy staggered up, using his rifle for a crutch, and sank down to the ground with a sigh. "I reckon I'll live," the little mountain man declared. "But for a time there, I shore had some serious doubts."

"I's a hopin' when you recovered your looks might have improved," Rimrock said, eyeballing his friend. "But you just as ugly as ever."

"I'd talk was I you," Windy retorted. "Thank God it's nigh on to fall and your beard is bushy-out. Any of these kids see your face, they'd run off into the woods and hide." He thanked Coretine for a plate of food and said, "Rimrock's the onliest man I ever knowed who could frighten a grizzly bear just by lookin' at the poor beast. He shaved off his beard one spring and come face to face with a she-bear out eatin' berries. You never heard the like of bellowin' and snortin' and carryin' on. That bear was so scared she took off runnin' and didn't stop 'til she reached the Canadian line. Never did come back."

"I think, Mr. Windy," Coretine said, "I know how you got your nickname."

Windy grinned up at her and winked. "Mayhaps you do, missy. Mayhaps you do."

* * *

Preacher went back down his trail and erased all the sign he had deliberately left for the Pardees. Then he found him a nice snug spot and waited. The Pardees and those with the gang, he felt, would not be good at the waiting game. Preacher could, and had in the past, gone without food for days. He did not believe any member of the Pardee gang had such patience. He had access to water and plenty of jerky and pemmican. He would do all right. He had strong doubts about the Pardee gang sitting still for very long.

The spot Preacher had chosen was in timber, about a hundred yards from a spring, and protected by rocks. He had a clear view of all that might go on in front of him. To his rear was the face of a mountain, loose rocks on both sides would warn him if anyone tried that approach. Now all he had to do was wait. And Preacher was real good at that.

Miles away, the Pardees made ready for the anticipated visit from Preacher. They fortified their camp and turned it into a minifortress. Then they all smiled at one another and waited. And waited.

On the afternoon of the fourth day, Malachi said, "It ain't workin'. Preacher ain't gonna fall for this."

They were nearly out of everything. They had no coffee, no salt, no beans, and were living mostly on what they could slip out and hunt. And a body can only live so long on rabbit. Man needs fat. Fat's scarce on a rabbit.

"We got to do something almighty quick," a gang member said. "We can't go on like this."

All the gang sure agreed with that and all were very vocal about it.

"I'll think on it some," Malachi told them.

"Malachi," Kenrick said when they were alone. "Let's call it quits and get shut of here."

Malachi looked down at his filthy hands and ragged clothing. Everyone of them, including Malachi, stunk worse than buzzard puke. None of them were prone to taking many baths, but he couldn't remember being this dirty and ragged.

He sighed and nodded his head. "All right, brother," he said softly. "But we got to ride far and fast to outrun the stories. We'll head for Californy. Get a fresh start out there. Change our names and Pardee will be no more. Pickin's ought to be good out there."

"I'll tell the boys, Kenrick said.

It did not take the outlaws long to pack up their meager possessions and saddle up. Malachi looked all around him at what he could see of the Big Empty. "You won this time, Preacher," he muttered. "But there will be another time. Bet on that." He grabbed hold of the saddle horn and stuck his boot into the stirrup. The patched cinch strap broke and dumped Malachi on his butt on the hard and rocky ground.

Flat on his back, Malachi said, "I hate you, Preacher. As God is my witness, I hate you!"

2

"Gone," Preacher said, standing in the middle of the deserted outlaw camp. He had tired of waiting and had sensed something important was happening in the high country. He had left his hiding place after five days and cautiously made his way to where he had last seen the outlaws.

"I never thought he'd do it," Preacher said to the winds and the emptiness. And to the cold. It had really turned cold. Preacher squatted down by the long dead ashes of the old campfire and tried to figure out what month it was. September, he thought it was. Where had the summer gone? Seemed like only yesterday he'd come up on that little settlement of people, and that had been back in the late spring or early summer. He remembered exactly.

He began the long trek back to the little valley where he'd left his horses.

Hammer was glad to see him and told him so by the way he acted. Horses get used to human company and miss that when they're left alone. Even the Appaloosa he'd taken from that dead Indian seemed glad to see him. The 'paloosa was a big animal, weighing, Preacher figured, about a thousand pounds, near'bouts as big as Hammer. He talked to them and petted them and got them calmed down and then saddled up. He wanted to get on the trail of the Pardees and see just where they were heading. Initially, they had headed west, the route they'd taken putting them well north of the new wagon-train trail. But with the Pardees, you just never knew.

It startled Preacher when the first snowflakes began falling. It was just too damn soon for that—unless he'd missed his calendar date by a month or six weeks, and he didn't think he had. No matter, he thought. By now Carl was probably nearing the last leg of the train's journey and weary pilgrims would be getting their first glimpse of the Promised Land. And judging from the gray and leaden skies, none too soon, neither. Preacher figured this was going to be a bad winter in the high country.

Several days later, Preacher reined up in some timber and watched as half a dozen riders cut in front of him, heading across a little meadow. He knew one of the men: that no-count Son. Now he'd picked him up three, four men and was headin' out to do some mischief. Preacher waited until they were long gone and then fell in behind them. Whatever Son and his friends were up to, it was no good. Preacher had never known Son to do anything for the general good of anything or anybody.

Several days later, Preacher ran into a hunting party from Weasel Tail's village and the men fixed venison and sat around the fire and talked.

"Much sickness among the wagon train," a brave named Bear Killer finally told him. "They have spent weeks without moving. Even those like you were sick."

"You have seen this with your own eyes?" Preacher asked.

Bear Killer shook his head. "Talked to some who have. They speak the truth. Too many saw it for it to be wrong. The wagons are moving now, but the snows have come to the high places. They will not be able to cross the mountains until spring."

Long after the Indians had left, Preacher sat before the

fire and thought about what he'd been told. According to Bear Killer, the train had not even made fifty miles before the sickness struck them and stopped everybody cold.

Preacher did a little figuring. As soon as they were able to travel, Carl would head them straight for the mission on the divide and hope to winter there. That would be the only logical thing to do, for the winter was coming early this year, and from all indications, it was going to be a hard one. The movers would be low on food, some of them probably out of food by now.

All in all, everybody was going to be in for a damn rough time of it 'fore spring poked her head up again. Preacher saddled up and pulled out.

Twice on his way toward the mission, he cut the trail of Son and his no-counts. Then, on the northwest side of the Little Popo Agie, he stopped and swung down at a deserted camp for a look-see. After carefully reading the sign, he concluded that Son and his bunch had linked up with the Pardees. And that damn sure meant trouble for someone—or a whole bunch of someones, for the tracks leading away from the camp were heading straight for the mission.

Preacher built a small fire in the old fire pit and broiled him a venison steak. He longed for a cup of coffee, but he was slap out of that. While he ate, he made up his mind. There was no way the movers would survive the winter without more supplies. So somebody was going to have to take mules over the mountains to a Hudson's Bay Company outpost and bring back supplies. Any of the mountain men with the train knew the horse trail and had been over it many times. It wasn't that far away from the mission. Getting there would be no problem without the wagons, if one discounted hostile Injuns, blizzards, outlaws, and such, but with winter looming so close, getting *back* might be somewhat difficult. But it had to be done if those in the train stood a chance of surviving. Dawn found Preacher on the trail and a day later he rode into the mission and there was the train.

The missionaries there had not hesitated in taking in the members of the wagon train, but existing supplies were not nearly ample enough to carry everybody through the winter.

Over a cup of coffee and a bowl of stew, Preacher laid his plan out for his friends.

"You're right about not enough supplies, Preacher," Windy said. "I'm game for the mules. How about you, Rim?"

The big man nodded his head. "Suits me. But them at the post sure ain't gonna give them supplies to us. What are we gonna use for money, our good looks?"

"Wagh!" Caleb said. "We're all dead from starvation if that's the case."

Rimrock looked at the rail-thin mountain man. "I shore better not tarry with them supplies. Strong breeze would carry you off now."

"I'll go talk to Betina and Coretine," Preacher said. "They'll know how these movers are fixed for money."

Preacher laid it out for the two women, not downplaying their plight one bit. "I can see the signs, ladies, and the winter is gonna be a bad one."

"The people have some money, Preacher," Betina said. "Enough, I believe, to purchase supplies."

Preacher nodded his head. "Place of the Rye Grass," he said.

"I beg your pardon?" Coretine asked.

"Actual the Cayuse call it The People of the Place of the Rye Grass. Waiilaptu. Why the hell Whitman ever chose this spot is beyond understandin' far as I'm concerned."*

---

*Marcus Whitman and his wife, Narcissa, built their mission in 1836 and maintained it until both were killed by rampaging Cayuse Indians in 1847. In addition, eleven other men, one woman, and three children were killed that night. The Cayuses took some forty-odd others captive and held them until Hudson's Bay Company officials ransomed them free.

More than two years later, after being pursued by a pioneer militia, five Cayuse warriors turned themselves in and were tried and hanged for the murders.

"To Christianize the savages, of course," Coretine said.

"Well, they ain't takin' hold of it much, girl. Injuns got their ways and we got ours. Bes' leave other folks' beliefs alone, I say."

"But they have to be baptized," a mover woman who was nearby said. "Or they'll not enter the Kingdom of Heaven."

Preacher smiled gently. "How 'bout them folks over to the Dark Continent of Afreeca? Or them heathens in India or all them yeller people? They don't believe like you do. Are you sayin' all them untold millions is a-goin' to burn in the hellfires?"

"Yes." The woman's reply was firm. "That is why we must carry the Word to all the savages of the world."

"Amen," Marcus Whitman said, strolling by.

Preacher shook his head. Marcus was a good man, and a fine doctor, but he didn't always get along with the mountain men. Marcus didn't like the language used by the mountain men or their penchant for strong drink. And some of the Cayuses didn't like him either.

Preacher looked up as snow began to fall. It was early for that. Too early. It was going to be one hell of a winter for sure. Within hours, the land was blanketed with white.

"She's gonna be a bad one, Preacher," Caleb said.

"Yeah," Preacher agreed. "I got to get these pilgrims settled . . . some way. Ain't no time for buildin' cabins and not enough know-how. Goddamnest place I ever seen for folks to settle. They're gonna have to winter in their wagons and we're gonna lose some to sickness brought on by the elements." Preacher shook his head and sighed. "And to make things worser, Son and his scummy bunch has linked up with the Pardees, and I don't know where they are."

"You think they'll attack us here?"

"No. Too many Injuns close by. But they may try to take the supplies. I think we'll all cross over. Be safer that way."

The mountain men began their journey across the Cascades the next morning. The men at the Hudson's Bay post were startled to see the five men and even more incredulous when Preacher told them why they had crossed the mountains.

"They'll never last the winter without proper shelter," one man bluntly stated. "This winter is shapin' up to the worst anyone can remember."

"Way I see it," Preacher said, handing the clerk the list of supplies, "they ain't got no hell of a lot of choice in the matter. You wanna try gettin' all them wagons 'crost the mountains axle-deep in snow? Them people is best right where they's at until spring comes. Then them that survive can cross the mountains to the valley of the Promised Land," he added grimly.

The man stared at Preacher for a moment, then shook his head and walked off muttering, "Fools. All of them. Wagons across the mountains. Can't be done."

Preacher just smiled at the man's remark. He knew it could be done. He'd done it.

Preacher's friends caught the smile and winked. Caleb said, "Let's be findin' us a jug, boys. That ride made me thirsty. And we'll get a couple of jugs to take back."

"Don't let them gospel-shouters back yonder discover no strong drink," Windy cautioned. "They do and they'll pour it all out on the ground."

"Now I love the Lord," Rimrock said. "But that would be pushin' my faith just a tad."

Back at the mission, Preacher knew damn well he wasn't going to stick around there the whole winter. First thing you know, Betina would be snuggled up with him in his buffalo robe and Preacher would have a permanent ring in his nose.

Caleb and Carl, Rimrock and Windy watched him pack up his gear and load up his animals. "You take care of this spotted pony of mine, now, Caleb," Preacher said. "I'll be back for him 'fore you know it, and I want to find him in good shape."

"Will do, Preacher."

"I'll be checkin' back in time to time. I want to find them damn Pardees and Son and his bunch. Makes me uneasy knowin' they're out there close and plannin' no tellin' what kind of mischief."

"You just want a good fight, Preacher," Rimrock said. "I know you too well."

"Mayhaps you be right, Rim. This thing between me and Malachi is personal; been growin' toward a showdown for years. It's bad enough when one of our own kind turns outlaw, but to have trash like the Pardees a-ridin' the high country don't set well with me worth a damn."

"You know where they are, don't you, Preacher?" Carl asked.

"I got me a good idea. 'Sides, I got to get back to Weasel Tail's winter camp and see what his braves come up with. I'm long overdue. Then I'll come back here. During my absence, you get Weller and the others to take pen to hand and write out all they know about Sutherlin." He mounted up and Hammer pranced a bit, wanting to hit the trail. He was a horse who liked to see the country about as much as his rider. "See you, boys." Preacher headed east at a lope.

Betina and Coretine stood by their wagons with a group of people and watched him ride out. One of the missionary women looked at the expression on Betina's face and said, "Never set your eyes for a mountain man. They're like the wind. You might never see him again."

"Even the wind rests every now and then," Betina replied, her eyes on the now dark dot in the distance.

"Not for long," the woman said, and turned away, walking toward her quarters.

"He'll be back, Betina," Coretine said gently, the words only for the other woman's ears.

Arm in arm, they walked around the mission complex.

The first snow of the season was gone, and they stepped carefully to avoid the mud.

"I know she's right," Betina said. "But I can't help the way I feel."

"Do you love him?"

"No. But I could. And that's just as bad."

Coretine looked at her friend. "Maybe worse."

3

Preacher was aware of a trading post on the Columbia that catered to both legitimate trappers and to outlaws and renegade Indians. It was run by an Englishman who, so the stories go, had been forced to leave England just ahead of the hangman's noose. Because he dealt guns and whiskey to the Indians, they left him alone. He would also buy stolen pelts from outlaw trappers . . . of which there was more than people liked to believe. As he rode, Preacher struggled for a time to think of the man's name. Finally it came to him. Dirk. That was what he was called. Dirk. Preacher had never been to Dirk's place, but he knew where it was. Odds were, that's where he'd find the Pardees and Son and his bunch. Or close by there.

Then something else came to him. He'd have to be doubly careful. Dirk, so the stories went, was a poisoner. Had disposed of several men and women in England 'fore he was caught. He was supposed to be some kind of expert with potions and such. Preacher made up his mind that he'd not drink nor eat at Dirk's place.

Then he smiled a hard curving of the lips. He just might

put Dirk out of business, too, while he was up this way. Might as well do the good people of the world several favors while he was in a favorin' mood.

Hammer's ears pricked and Preacher felt the big horse tense under him. Stopping in a glade, Preacher waited. He could now hear the prod of horses' hooves. He eased the hammer back on his Hawken, then slowly let the hammer back down as the rider came into view. The rider was a trapper named Quinn.

"Ho, Quinn," Preacher called out. "It's Preacher here."

"Wagh, Preacher!" Quinn yelled. "You 'bout skirred me out of my moccasins, boy. Blackfeet done monikered you right when they named you Killin' Ghost. You quiet, boy. Spooky so."

"Thank my good horse for that, Quinn. Hammer picked up on you long 'fore I did." Preacher kneed Hammer out of the glade and up to Quinn.

"You lookin' prosperous," Quinn remarked. "You been eatin' home cookin', maybe?"

"Movers been feedin' me from time to time. Whole passel of 'em down to that gospel shouter's mission."

"I'll fight shy of that place then. I know it ain't a polite question to ask, but I got reasons aplenty and I'll tell you. Where you bound?"

"Up to Dirk's place on the river."

Quinn shook his shaggy head. "You be in mortal danger up yonder, Preacher. The country is fairly aboundin' with scoundrels. I seen that damnable Son up there, and I also gleamed a couple of them crazy Pardee brothers. Talk is, they runnin' from you and has decided to flee no more. And you know well as me if you see one Pardee, the others ain't far away."

"For a fact, ol' hoss. For a fact. But they'll be a lot less Pardees when I'm done with them."

Quinn smiled. "I reckon they done tugged on your halter

'til they got you riled. Be a sight to see, I'm thinkin'. I'd go if
my woman wasn't waiting for me at the lodge. Winter gonna
be a hard one this season, Preacher, and my rummetism is a-
hurtin' me something fierce. I'm lookin' forward to hot fires
and warm robes this winter."

Rheumatism was the trappers' main complaint, for during
the trappers' two seasons, spring to midsummer, when the
beaver molts, and again from autumn to waters' freeze, they
stand in icy cold waters.

"I be headin' west come the spring," Quinn continued.
"Me and my woman done talked it over an' she's agree to go
west with me. We're bound for Californy where it's warm all
the time. They's a dozen or more mountain men done pulled
up stakes and headed there."

"What you gonna do when you get there?"

Quinn shrugged. "Beats me. But I'll find something to
do. It's over for the likes of us, Preacher."

Preacher nodded his head. He had been one of the first to
know that. "See you, Quinn. Good luck."

"The same to you, Preacher."

Quinn headed south, Preacher continued on to the north.
As of one mind, the two mountain men looked back. Both
lifted a hand in farewell and then they were gone. For one, a
way of life was ending; for the other, a new era was just
opening.

Preacher made his camp not far from the Crab, in the
Saddle Mountains. This area was the home and the range of
a half dozen Indian tribes, including the Walla Walla, the
Spokane, and the Yakima. But Preacher got along well with
those tribes, and while he rode cautiously, he was not particularly worried. The Indians knew Preacher and most accepted
him as one of their own. Preacher would fight if he was
pushed to it, but left alone, the mountain man could be a
good friend and the Indians knew it. Twice on his way north,
Preacher stopped in Indian villages to socialize and eat. Indians loved to talk and had a high sense of humor, although

most did not let that side show around whites they did not know.

As he drew nearer to the trading post of Dirk, Preacher began to ride with more caution, for the Indians he'd spoken with told him there were plenty bad men around the post and that they were up to no good. And that the trappers that were like Preacher did not come to that trading post any longer.

Preacher didn't tell them so, but if what he had in mind came true, there wouldn't nobody ever come to that trading post again—ever.

But he wasn't going to just ride in there big as brass. He'd have more holes in him than a tree full of woodpeckers if he done that. Preacher made his camp a few miles from the trading post and set about pondering just what he might do.

"Get it right," he told himself and the gathering shadows. "'Cause it could be that you ain't gonna get but one chance."

Come the morning, he picketed Hammer and the pack-horse on a few hidden acres of grass on the edge of the Cascades and pressed on on foot. Why that damn crazy Englishman ever wanted to build a trading post around here was a mystery to Preacher! Damn wind blew all the time, storms could whip up out of nowhere, and the place wouldn't grow diddly squat. But then, he figured, nobody ever comes here, and it damn shore was off any known and well-traveled trail, so maybe that Brit wasn't so stupid after all, considerin' the ugly business he was in.

He made his way to within sight of the trading post, and it was a run-down, ramshackle place, looking more like a roofed and walled hog pen rather than a place where human beings frequented. But, Preacher reckoned, considering the caliber of men who visited this place of late, it was fitting.

Preacher's cover was adequate, but not the best by a long shot. He watched as several riders approached the building and dismounted. He didn't recognize any of them. Whatever their business was, it didn't take long. Within minutes, the three men exited the building, mounted up, and rode off.

Preacher knew that out here, three visitors a day was considered a heady business. There might not be anymore customers the rest of the week, for that matter. Preacher made up his mind and carefully changed locations after taking a long, low look all around him. He worked his way around to the back of the building, taking the better part of an hour to complete his swing. Now came the hard part, for several acres around the building had been cleared and only stumps remained. He started to move forward, then checked the movement, every sense telling him that something was mighty wrong. He remained motionless behind a stump, his buckskins blending in with the early-winter terrain. Something was wrong, but what?

He scanned his surroundings, only his eyes moving. He could not check behind him without moving, and he wasn't about to do that. But he had inspected the flats behind him carefully before moving to his position and was secure in his belief that no one was back there. At the time, he amended.

Preacher watched the rear of the cabin, keeping his eyes on the windows. The "windows" of most buildings were no more than a small sliding door without glass. One window moved slightly, cracking open a few inches, and Preacher tensed. How could they know he was here? Or did they only suspect? Either way, he was in a pickle and knew it.

He could hear the murmur of voices from inside the cabin but could not make out any words. After several moments, one man said, "Oh, hell, Dirk! Preacher ain't nowheres near here. I'll show you." The back door opened and a burly man stepped out to the ground and stood there. "Hey, Preacher!" he shouted in a strong voice. "You no-good son of a bitch!" Then he proceeded to call Preacher every vile and foul name he could think of, which was a-plenty. He traced Preacher's ancestors back several thousand years, and just before running out of breath and names to call him, he compared the mountain man to a monkey in a cage, and worse.

Preacher lay behind the stump, on a slight backward sloping incline, and waited motionless. He would deal with this loudmouth in due time—and deal with him he would, Preacher silently promised.

"See?" the loudmouth said proudly, as what had to be Dirk stepped out of the door and stood looking around.

"I guess you're right, Hubert," the second man said. "From all that I've heard about Preacher, he certainly wouldn't tolerate all that name-calling. But that red savage certainly said he'd seen Preacher."

"He lied," Hubert said. "Tryin' to get in your favor for a drink of whiskey or a blanket."

"I suppose you're right. Let's get in out of this cold. It's going to be a bitter winter, Hubert."

Preacher wondered if there were any more men inside the small post and decided not. The instant the window slide was closed shut to keep out the cold breeze, Preacher made his move, leaping to his feet and dashing to the rear of the building and flattening out against the logs. Preacher moved around to the side of the building and pushed up against the base of the chimney to catch some warmth from the heated rocks. From about head-high on up, the rocks changed to a stick chimney, the sticks held together with a mixture of mud and clay. It was a common-enough affair.

On Preacher's side of the stones was the woodpile, stacked high, so Preacher moved around to the other side in case the wood box got low and Dirk or Hubert came out for more firewood. Preacher saw an old doghouse someone had made, and looked in it. Cobwebs had taken over, the dog long gone. With a smile, Preacher crawled in the doghouse. It was a large doghouse and Preacher hoped the long-gone dog would not return to claim its house anytime soon. A dog that needed a house this size would be big enough to give a grizzly some problems. Since the rear of the doghouse was built up against the side of the stone chimney—the outside of the fireplace— the hut was surprisingly warm. Preacher made himself comfortable and waited.

One side of the doghouse was the wall of the cabin, so with his knife, Preacher began digging out a hole between the logs, carefully working out the mud that was chinked between the logs and pulling it toward him until he had him a hole just big enough to see and hear through. The darkness of the interior of the doghouse would, he hoped, prevent those inside the post from noticing the tiny hole.

"Them others gonna get here?" he heard Hubert say.

"Today is all I know," Dirk replied. "Put us on some meat to cook, Hubert. This cold gives me an appetite."

Somebody is always cookin' when I'm in a position to do nothin' but smell it and salivate, Preacher thought. He stuck a piece of jerky in his mouth and chewed. Then he heard the sounds of horses.

"Son and his bunch," the voice of Hubert came to him. "I reckon the others will be along shortly. I hope they brought their own food."

Son and his bunch stomped in amid a lot of laughing and cussing and rough humor, on both sides, and after the jug was passed around, they got down to serious talking. Preacher had his ear pressed to the tiny hole.

"The way Malachi sees it," Son said, "is we hold off until spring and then hit the wagon train two, three days out of the mission. It'll be clear of the Hudson's Bay post by then and we can all take the wagons and possessions and sell them. I think it's a grand idea."

"And the people?" Dirk asked.

"All dead. And the dead can't hook us up with anything."

"I hear Preacher's tied in with them, as well as three, four other mountain men."

"Where'd you hear that?"

"From an Injun who passed through yesterday. He said he saw Preacher about twenty miles from here. He swore it was him."

"I don't believe it," Hubert said. "I just don't believe it."

"Neither do I," one of Son's bunch piped up. "He thinks

he's got the Pardees run clear out of the country and I believe he's 'way south with the train."

"It's a deal, then?" Son asked. "We take the train, and with your connections on the coast, we get rid of the stuff?"

"It's a deal," Dirk told him. "I've been wanting to leave this wretched country for some time."

"The both of you have to understand this," Son said. "Oncest we start, we can't have no soft hearts 'bout none on the train. They all got to die—men, women, and kids alike. We can hump the women and the girls, then they got to die."

"That's understood." Preacher recognized Dirk's voice. "I've done in all three in my time. I have no use for kids anyway."

And I understand it, too, Preacher thought. I understand that you all are the most black-hearted band of cutthroats I ever seen in all my borned days. And now that I heard with my own ears what you plan to do, I ain't got no sympathy for the lot of you.

In other words, Preacher added silently, you bastards are in for a world of woe—from me!

4

Preacher figured there wasn't no time like the present to get into action. The fact that he was outnumbered about ten to one didn't bother him at all. It never had.

He crawled out of the doghouse and turned all but one of the horses loose . . . quietly. Then he began working swiftly in the gathering up of dry grass and twigs and then larger sticks from the woodpile. He crawled around the trading-post cabin on all fours and placed the material on all sides. Then he set all the bundles burning. He led the best horse around back, took out both pistols, and waited, figuring it wouldn't take long for those ninnies inside to start smelling smoke. Both pistols in his hands and the two more in his sash were double-shotted, so Preacher was expecting to inflict some serious wounds.

So intent were the men inside the trading-post cabin in their planning of murder and rape and robbery that not once had anyone opened the sliding windows to look outside . . . and that was something Preacher had been counting on. The men had not disappointed him.

Preacher sat down on a stump and waited, his hands filled with pistols.

"Hey!" someone within the building hollered. "I smell smoke."

"Do tell?" Preacher muttered. "I was beginnin' to think your blowers was stopped up."

"The damn cabin's on fire!" another yelled. "Lemme out of here!"

He ran out the back door and Preacher shot him, one ball taking the man in the chest, the second ball striking him in the face, making a great big mess. Blood and bit of bone struck the man right behind the mortally wounded outlaw and he screamed in panic.

Preacher ended his screaming when he fired his second pistol, the double-shotted charge taking the man in the chest and knocking him backward. He fell against another man and both of them went to the floor.

The air around the post was now thick with smoke. Men were staggering out, nearly blind from the smoke, tears streaming down their cheeks and all coughing badly. Preacher had pulled out his other two pistols and stood up, waiting for a clear shot.

Hubert ran out, stumbling and staggering. Preacher ended his outlaw life with a ball directly in the heart.

"The damn horses is gone!" a man screamed from around the front, then broke out in a coughing fit.

Preacher put a ball into a fourth man, jammed the empty pistols behind his sash, and jumped on the horse he'd borrowed. Staying low in the saddle, he headed for the brush. Just inside good cover, Preacher leaped from the saddle and began quickly reloading. When his pistols were charged, he looped the reins around a skinny bush and grabbed up his rifle. He made his way back to the edge of the clearing.

The men were working frantically to contain the blaze, but from where Preacher stood, it looked hopeless. The dry logs had turned the building into a blazing ball of fire. Neither Son or Dirk could be seen. Dropping to one knee, Preacher sighted in a man and pulled the trigger. The man stood up on his toes, stiffened, then threw his hands into the air and fell to the ground, landing on his face. The boom of the Hawken was lost in the roaring of the flames and the cracking and popping of burning logs. Preacher reloaded and waited, trying to peer through the dense smoke for a target.

"Give it up!" a man shouted, just then noticing the newly dead man sprawled on the cold ground. "We're targets out here. Head for cover."

The men vanished into the thick swirling smoke and Preacher gave it up and ran back to the stolen horse, jumping into the saddle and taking off. He rode for about a mile, then circled around, coming up into the woods about half a mile in front of the source of the black smoke arching into the skies.

Sitting his saddle, he listened for a moment and picked up the sounds of many hooves pounding in his direction. Preacher took the prudent course and got the hell out of there. He hadn't killed any of the principals, but he'd blooded the gang some, and given them something to think about.

He left the horse and took off on foot, in a distance-eating trot, heading north and staying close to the river on the timber side. They'd come after him, he was sure of that. The outlaws had no choice in the matter. They had to kill him. Preacher smiled grimly. And that was going to take some doing.

"Lost everything," Dirk said sourly. He sat on a log, his face grimy with soot and his clothing coated with dirt and ash. "Everything I owned went up in smoke. Goddamn that Preacher. Damn his eyes, I say!"

"I do know how you feel," Malachi said. "Believe that."

"I can't believe that no man would have the balls to just walk up and set fire to a building and then wait outside and shoot folks down as they run from the flames," an outlaw called Gil said, as he looked around him for the tenth time in that many minutes. Preacher made him nervous being this close. Real nervous. The man was new to the West, having broken jail in Maryland the past year. The first thing he'd been told when he hit the wilderness was to leave mountain men alone. Especially one called Preacher. Everybody had told him that Preacher was bad news.

He had scoffed at that.

No more.

"Settle down, Gil," Malachi told him. "We'll never kill the bastard if we all get spooked."

"I still think we should have gone on west," Kenrick said. "This is a bad mistake we're makin', I'm thinkin'."

"I wish we'd had some fresh meat," Ansel said. "Them coals of the cabin is right for cookin' now."

Dirk looked at the hulking stupid oaf and resisted an impulse to flatten him with the butt of his borrowed rifle. He decided it just wasn't worth the effort.

"Let me go a-huntin', brother," Ansel said. "I be's hongry around the mouth."

"Shut up, Ansel," Malachi told him. "Sit down and be quiet. Keep a lookout for us."

"You think Preacher will be back?" Dirk asked.

"I don't know. Maybe. With him, you never can tell."

"Probably lookin' at us right now," Kenrick said. "Let's get out of here, brother. Like right now."

"No!" Dirk said sharply. "No, by God. We go after the man. I will not spend the rest of my life looking over my shoulder. And there is a very good reason for us doing that: Preacher probably was listening to us make plans. He knows what we're going to do. He's got to die."

Malachi reluctantly nodded his head. Lord knows he didn't want to pursue Preacher; Malachi had him a gutful of the mountain man. But there was wisdom in Dirk's words. He picked up his rifle. "Let's do it, people. Preacher's got to die if we's goin' to survive. There just ain't no other way."

* * *

Back in Missouri, in a small town on the Osage River, on the edge of the unorganized territory known at the Great Plains, Edward Sutherlin tossed out the dregs of his coffee cup and looked at the six men who had accompanied him from Ohio. They were all tough, very capable men—men who would do anything for money. And had.

Edward Sutherlin rose to his boots and began rolling his blankets and groundsheet. He knew it was a bad time to be heading west. But it was something that had to be done. He'd received word that his operation was in jeopardy and that some stupid, illiterate, unwashed mountain man with the improbable name of Preacher was to blame.

Well, he'd soon settle Preacher's hash. He had too good a deal going to let one man louse it all up. With Malachi and his boys, and the six tough men he was bringing, that should be plenty. They'd leave this Preacher person's body for the scavengers and then get on with their business.

He just couldn't imagine why Malachi was so afeard of one man. It just didn't make any sense. Ridiculous is what it was. "Let's ride," Edward said. "We've got a thousand miles in front of us."

One of Son's men showed his head and Preacher's rifle boomed. The slug took the man right between the eyes and removed the entire back of the outlaw's head, flinging him backward, dead before he hit the cold ground.

The two dozen or so trash that made up the gang flattened out and hugged the rocky ground on the edge of the Cascades.

They tried not to look at the careless outlaw who now lay with his brains leaking out.

Ansel got to his knees to shift positions and Preacher's rifle boomed again, its ball smashing into a rock and sending bits of rock into the outlaw's face. Ansel whooped and hollered and fell to the ground, wiping the blood from his face.

Dirk and his boys didn't move. Dirk knew all about the mountain man called Preacher and knew what he was capable of. A man took no chances when dealing with Preacher. None. Dirk cut his eyes, looking around him. He was safe from Preacher's bullets as long as he stayed put, but he was pinned down tight.

Malachi looked back at Ansel. His brother wasn't hurt, just bloodied up some and scared. Malachi's own position was like that of Dirk. He was safe, but he couldn't move. Preacher had picked a dandy spot for an ambush. Something that Malachi should have known.

Son lay on the ground, looked at his fallen companion, and cussed Preacher. Ted had been a good man. One moment of carelessness had cost him his life. Now there was one less to fight Preacher.

"Malachi," Son called in a hoarse whisper. "We's just in good rifle range. We can't go forward, but we can damn shore go backerds. 'Nother fifty yards and we'll be plumb out of range. I say we roll backerds."

"You roll backerds," Malachi said. "I ain't movin' 'til I'm shore it's safe."

Flat on his back several hundred yards away, behind rocks on the incline, Preacher pulled his bow into a U-shape and let the arrow fly, not dreaming for a moment he could hit anything. With their heads down, the outlaws did not see the arrow arch high into the air and start down. A man named Fabor suddenly let out a mighty roar as the arrow point drove deep into the right cheek of his butt. He leaped to his feet, dancing and howling in pain. Radborne tackled him and brought him down before Preacher could shoot him dead.

"My ass is on fire!" Fabor squalled.

"The next time Preacher fires, make a run for it," Malachi called. "We'll be out of range before he can reload."

"Oh, Lord, Lord, my ass hurts!" Fabor hollered. "Somebody do something."

"I'll be durned," Preacher said, peering through the rocks. "I hit someone."

Preacher studied the situation for a moment, then picked up his Hawken and shifted a few yards. He sighted in on what appeared to be a boot sticking out from behind a log and squeezed off a round. Wild screaming came his way as one of Son's men had several toes blown off. Son grabbed the man and dragged him downhill, the others quickly following as Preacher reloaded.

Preacher lowered his rifle. The crap and crud were well out of range. Fabor was hollering about his butt and Son's man was screaming in pain from his blowed-off toes. Preacher gathered his gear and slipped back into the timber and began slowly working his way down the grade.

"Get that son of a bitch!" he heard Dirk the Englishman scream. "You men, circle around and trap him up there. You three to the right and you three to the left. We'll have him in a box. Move!"

Preacher smiled and continued moving downward, working his way toward where they had picketed their horses. He pulled up short in the timber. Malachi was wising up. He had left a guard with the horses. Preacher notched an arrow and let it fly. The point drove through the guard's neck and he fell to his knees, coughing and gagging with blood pouring out of his mouth. Preacher ran to him and smashed his head with the butt of his Hawken. He gathered up all the reins, tied them together with rope from one of the outlaws' saddles, mounted the best-looking horse, and took off at a gallop, screaming out Cheyenne war cries as he raced off down the slope and into the valley below.

Malachi jerked off his hat and threw it to the ground. "God*damn* that man!" he yelled.

Preacher stopped and wheeled around. "I am Man Who Kills Silently," he shouted, his words clear in the cold air. "I am White Wolf. I am Bloody Knife. I am called Killing Ghost. I am Preacher. I've lived with wolves and fought grizzlies, I've tamed pumas and talked with eagles. I'm surlier than a badger, got more poison in me than a den full of rattlers, and I'm tougher than any man you ever seen. You hear my words well. You will all die. All of you."

Several of the brigands shuddered as the words sent chills racing up and down their spines. All the outlaws stood on the hillside and watched the mountain man as he sat the horse about a thousand yards from them. They were powerless to do anything except watch and listen.

"Leave now and never return, or you'll all die in these here mountains!" Preacher shouted. "From now on I show you no pity nor mercy. Get gone east and don't never come 'crost the Missouri again. You best hear me well and heed the warnin', for them's my last words on the subject."

Preacher put the horses into a trot and soon disappeared over a rise. When he knew he was safe from view, he cut west and then, after a mile, turned north and rode steady until he figured he was a good six or eight miles from the now afoot outlaws.

He found him a fast-running creek and let the horses blow and water. He stripped the saddles from them, including the one he'd chosen to keep for a time, and dumped out their saddlebags, carefully picking through the supplies.

He kept the coffee and a small pot and a side of bacon. Somebody had fixed up some pan bread and carefully wrapped it. Preacher washed out a small skillet and set about frying up some bacon and boiling water for coffee. While that was sizzling and boiling, he carefully loaded up all the spare pistols he'd found in the saddlebags and in holsters on the horns. He'd have to take an extra horse just to tote around all the guns he was now in possession of. But he figured they'd come in handy, for he knew damn well those highwaymen weren't going to heed his words to leave and that sooner or later they'd come a showdown.

He now had a right smart amount of powder, more than he'd use in a year's time, so he set about making some bombs, using pieces of britches and shirts he'd found. He wouldn't even think of touching the longhandles he'd found. Filthiest things he'd ever seen. Preacher had handled them with a long stick and then burned them.

This was fir, hemlock, and pine country. Come the spring it would be some of the most beautiful country in all the Northwest, with tall yellow spikes of false hellebore, clusters of bleeding heart, white and yellow daisies, the umbrella-shaped cow parsnips, white bunchberry dogwood, blue lupine, lavender fireweed, and scarlet paintbrush. It was a scene that, once witnessed, would stay with a body for a lifetime. Peaceful and serene. But for now, Preacher was making bombs to kill people.

The Pardees and Son and Dirk and their gangs had to come after him. He had their horses. And in this country, a man without a horse was a dead man.

Preacher piled up the saddles and bridles and burned them, knowing the gang members would see the smoke. Indians would, too, of course, but Preacher was on good terms with most of the Indians who roamed this part of the country. He had a hunch the gang members were not. But by now the Indians would be in their winter camps and not all that anxious to make war.

Preacher piled all the supplies and clothing he couldn't use on the burning leather and destroyed it. Now all the gang members had was what they had with them when they came after him back down the trail. And that would be precious little. Now they had no blankets, no food, no nothing.

Preacher knew he was sentencing some of the outlaws to a hard death. That fact didn't bother him a twit. He had given them warning the game was about to turn rough. Besides, there wasn't a man back yonder who hadn't tortured and raped and killed innocent people. Whatever they got in the way of misery, they richly deserved.

Preacher drank the last of the coffee, ate the bacon, and sopped out the skillet with a hunk of bread. He washed the pot, the cup, and the frying pan in the creek and carefully packed them away.

He saddled up and cinched the pack frame, carefully balancing the load. He started the horses north, toward the Entiat. He knew a spot where he would make his stand and win and put an end to this war. Then he'd get on back to the mission and help see to the needs of the pilgrims, for the winter was going to be a harsh one.

He looked back once and muttered, "Follow me and die, boys. I warned you."

5

"He's headin' for a spot of his choosin' for the show-down," Son opined. "And we ain't got no choice in the matter. We got to follow."

The others said nothing for the time being, just stood and stared at the hoofprints that headed north. They all knew that without horses, they stood a very good chance of dying in the Big Empty. They also knew that they stood a very good chance of dying if they went after their horses.

Dirk picked up his rifle and began walking the hoof trail. He did not look back to see if the others were following. One by one, the outlaws fell in behind him. They walked with a feeling of dread lying across their shoulders, but they simply had no choice in the matter.

They had no blankets or groundsheets, no robes or spare clothing, no supplies of any kind. They left the man with the blown off toes lying on the ground and walked away, ignoring his screams for help. He called after them until his voice was gone. No one looked back. The outlaw that Preacher had drilled through the noggin was left in the rocks where he had fallen. The varmits and carrion birds would feast on him.

The man with the ruined foot tried crawling after his gang. He crawled until his hands were bloody and nearly useless and he could go no further. He lay on the ground and cursed those whom he had called friends. When his panic had subsided, he gathered what wits he had left and fashioned a crutch of sorts and started back down the trail they'd blazed after Preacher. He hoped all those bastards who had so coldly left him to die would meet a horrible fate at the hands of Preacher. He could not know just how accurate his wishes were to be.

Preacher put the horses in a little valley that had good graze still and good water. He knew that as long as the food and water held out, they wouldn't wander far. He cachéd loaded pistols and shot and powder in spots, as well as packets of food and water and blankets. Preacher ranged about five miles in his hiding of weapons and supplies. Satisfied that he was ready, he found him a vantage spot and waited.

It was a sullen and silent group of outlaws that trudged on, following the clear trail that Preacher had left. The leaders had no illusions. They all knew that this was the final showdown. They would die, or Preacher would die. It was that cut and dried. They had to have horses. If they didn't find mounts, they would die. Already the nights were cold, and getting colder with each passing night. They had to get out of the high country.

"We're walkin' right into it, Malachi," Kenrick said. "Playin' right into Preacher's hands. This is his game all the way."

"I know it," Malachi panted the words. "You got any better plan?"

Kenrick was silent.

The outlaw who had taken the point suddenly threw up a hand, halting the column. "This is it, boys," he called. "Come take a look at this, will you?"

The outlaws crowded forward and everyone of them sucked in their gut at the sight. Huge peaks lay on both sides of the wide valley; no way over them. At the end of the long valley, four or five miles wide and about that deep, more mountains loomed, beginning with a gentle sloping and charging upward.

They all knew that at the end of the valley, hidden amid the rocks and brush and timber, was Preacher. Waiting. To a man they cussed.

"I suggest we break up into groups of two and three," Dirk said, squatting down and resting his tired legs. "I think we'd have a better chance that way."

"I agree," Son said.

"All right," Malachi said. "Kenrick, you take one group of our boys, I'll take one, and Radborne can take the other."

"Two groups of my boys," Son said.

"Three of mine," Dirk said, standing up. "No point in wasting time. We might as well do it."

The men got their positions and trails straight and began moving out. Alone, on the other side of the valley, Preacher looked through the spyglass he'd found in the saddlebags of the outlaws—it probably belonged to the Englishman, for it was said that Dirk had once been before the mast, probably as a pirate—and watched the men split up and come toward him.

Some were going to work both sides of the valley and try to get around him and box him, while others came straight in. "Ain't gonna work, people," Preacher said. "You'll be so busy lookin' for traps that ain't there, you ain't gonna be givin' your full attention to all the surroundin's. And that's when I'm gonna nail you."

Preacher chewed on jerky and waited. He was going to drop the first one that came into rifle range, just to give the others something to think about.

"Stop that damn gigglin', Ansel," Malachi told his goofiest brother. "This ain't no joke, you fool."

"Can I sing?"

"No. Just shut up and keep your eyes wide open for booby traps. You know that damn Preacher laid some out for us."

The man with the arrow point still embedded in one cheek of his ass hobbled along at the rear of one group. No one had wanted to dig the point out, so he just broke the shaft off and endured the pain . . . which was considerable. But it wouldn't be for long, as he was motioned up to take the point. His group was going straight up the valley.

"I really 'preciate you guys offerin' to dig out this damn arreyhead," he bitched, "Some friends you are."

"Aw, shut up and take the point, Fabor. No one wants to look at your smelly butt."

"When I get my horse back, I'm gone from this bunch. Jinked is what we is."

No one replied, but they all agreed with him.

Fabor limped along, his eyes trying to take in everything around him and, in doing that, missing much. The group made the center of the valley and stopped to rest by a creek. After a drink of water, they pressed on, each step taking them closer and closer to where Preacher lay in the rocks.

Preacher cocked his Hawken and waited.

The other groups of outlaws were moving out of the valley and onto the first gentle slopings of the mountain. No one had spotted Preacher's hideout.

"There ain't no traps," Malachi said. "That ain't like Preacher. Maybe he ain't here."

No one replied to that because all knew it was wishful thinking. Preacher was close. They all felt it.

Fabor stopped for a moment just at the edge of the slope. He stood still, his eyes inspecting the rocks and the brush and the timber ahead of him. He opened his mouth to speak just as Preacher fired. The big slug took him in the center of the chest and dropped him dead as a stone.

Preacher immediately shifted positions, reloading on the move.

"He's in them rocks up yonder!" a man called Curtis yelled from his belly-down position on the ground.

Preacher was in the rocks, but the rocks and boulders ran for hundreds of yards west to east, with twisting passageways weaving in and out. It was a death trap and the outlaws knew it.

Dirk motioned one of his men forward and the man reluctantly obeyed, moving very slowly and cautiously. He entered the rocks and the silence fell about him. The rocks blocked the cold winds, but the outlaw took no comfort from that. He'd much rather face the winds than Preacher. He paused for a moment, listening. But all he could hear was the low moaning of the winds.

He turned toward a narrow passageway and caught the butt of Preacher's Hawken square on his chin. The heavy rifle smashed his jaw and knocked out teeth. The outlaw was unconscious before he sprawled out on the ground.

Preacher picked up the man's rifle and checked it. He wasn't familiar with the rifle. It looked like a .69 caliber English rifle, which fired a very respectable ball. Preacher turned at a slight noise and fired. The ball struck the man in the belly, and the range was so close the wadding as well as the ball tore into the brigand's stomach. The force slammed the outlaw against a boulder and he sat down on his butt, screaming as waves of pain tore through him. He hollered and cussed Preacher as the blood leaked from his mouth, dripping onto his filthy shirt.

Preacher vanished into the maze of passageways he had thoroughly checked out that morning, marking the dead ends with small rock cairns.

"Roy!" someone called. "Peter! Answer me."

The wind moaning and sighing was the only reply, since Roy was gut-shot and dying and Peter's jaw was broken in so many places he was not capable of speaking . . . even if he was conscious. Which he was not.

Ansel suddenly left Malachi's side and went screaming into the maze of rocks. Preacher heard him coming and braced himself, not wanting to kill the fool. Preacher reversed the outlaw's rifle and waited. Ansel's screaming drew nearer. Behind him, Malachi was shouting for his brother to come back. Ansel rounded the curve of rocks, panting and cussing and hollering and slobbering. Preacher gave him the stock of the English rifle smack in the face. The stock broke off and Ansel went down in a sprawl of arms and legs, minus a dozen teeth and with his jaw smashed horribly. Preacher grabbed up the nitwit's rifle and took off, winding his way through the huge boulders.

"You hurt my baby brother and I'll tear your eyes out, Preacher!" Malachi screamed out his rage. "Ansel, you all right?"

It would be a long time before Ansel even woke up, much less managed to speak. Roy lay dead, his back to a boulder. Peter had not moved. Fabor's body lay cooling on the slope.

Preacher checked Ansel's rifle and waited patiently in the rock maze.

"Goddamnit!" Dirk shouted. "He's just one man. One man. Get him. Come on. Everybody into the rocks."

"Yeah!" Malachi shouted. "Surround him in there. We can starve him out if nothin' else."

Fools, Preacher thought. Nothin' but fools. I'm a-squattin' here in about ten acres of rocks and I know all the ways in and out. So come on, you sorry pack of worthless ne'er-do-wells. Let's settle this now.

"Baby brother!" Kenrick yelled. "Where are you, boy? Call out."

"Here's Peter," a man called. "His face is all tore up bad. His jaw's busted. Roy's dead."

Preacher picked up a fist-sized rock and chunked it over the boulders. It crashed against the side of a passageway and a dozen rifles roared. The sounds of ricochets screaming around the rocks was fearsome. Then a scream ripped the early afternoon's cold air as Preacher began working his way toward the unconscious Ansel.

"You bastards!" a man cried out. "You've shot me. Oh, God, help me."

"Hell with you," Radborne called. "Here's our baby brother, Malachi. Oh, Lordy, he's hurt bad."

Preacher stepped out onto the narrow path, leveled his Hawken, and dusted Radborne from side to side, the ball tearing through the man. Radborne screamed and fell across his brother, mortally wounded. He struggled to rise to his boots and failed. Preacher vanished back into the maze, reloading quickly.

"He's in the center of the rocks," Son called, frantically reloading his rifle. "Damnit, stay away from the center of these rocks."

"Radborne!" Kenrick yelled. "Where are your?"

That was a very good question, but money placed on Hell would probably be a sure bet.

Preacher mentally counted up the score in this deadly game. He figured six were out of it, dead, dying, or badly injured. Not a bad day's work, Preacher thought.

A cry of anguish went up out of the rocks as Henry Pardee found his brothers. "Radborne's dead, Malachi. And Ansel don't answer me. His face is all swoll up. *Preacher!*" he screamed. "I'm a-comin' after you, Preacher."

Come on, Preacher thought.

Son had linked up with Dirk. Each man wore an expression of hopelessness. The two men exchanged glances.

"Let's get out of here," Son whispered. "We'll find the horses and leave."

"I'm for that," the Englishman returned the whisper. "We'll not do nothing except die in here. Preacher is a devil."

The men began backing out of the rocks.

Henry began stalking the silent stone passageways, his

face grim and angry. He ignored the calls from Malachi and Kenrick to come back.

Preacher waited.

The remaining outlaws stayed put, afraid to move.

Valiant Pardee joined Malachi and Kenrick. His face was pale under the dirt and he was badly frightened. "Son and Dirk pulled out," he whispered. "I seen them leavin'. I'm afeard, Malachi. I truly am."

"Preacher!" Henry screamed. "Come out and fight "

Henry was very close as Preacher pulled out a pistol and placed one hand over the hammer to muffle the sound of the cocking. He could hear Henry's heavy breathing and the scrape of his clothing as he brushed up against the sides of the rock passageway. Henry stepped in front of the narrow, almost hidden passageway where Preacher stood, and paused for a second. Preacher fired, the ball striking the Pardee brother in the temple and blowing out the other side. Henry Pardee dropped soundlessly to the rocks; his life of crime and depravity was over.

"There's one less of your kin, Malachi," Preacher shouted above the echoing of the shot. "You want the body, come get it. I'd hate to see a buzzard get sick from eatin' on it."

Malachi cursed Preacher until he was breathless.

Son and Dirk had stripped the clothing from two dead men for extra warmth, leaving their naked bodies on the ground, and were now frantically searching for the hidden horses. They were not having much luck.

"They could be miles from here," Son said. "We got to chance walkin' out, Dirk. We stay here and Preacher will get us for sure and certain."

The Englishman thought about that for a moment. "All right. Let's go. We got ample powder and shot and we're sure to see Indians. We can shoot them and take their ponies."

"Grand idea. Let's get gone."

Preacher lit the makeshift fuse to one of the powder horns taken from the dead and chucked it in the direction of whispered voices. Sometimes black-powder bombs worked and sometimes they didn't. This time they didn't. It landed on an outlaw's head and knocked him to his knees and sent several outlaws screaming and racing away from the sputtering powder horn. Preacher stepped out and fired his double-shotted pistols. The four balls shrieked and howled off the rock walls of the passageways and took two of the outlaws down in a bloody sprawl, the flattened ricochets wounding them grievously. The wounded men lay on the rocky paths and screamed in pain.

"Don't be singin' no sad songs to me," Preacher muttered as he reloaded. "I didn't tell you to ride with this bunch."

"Bad," Malachi whispered to Kenrick. "We got to get Valiant and Ansel and get gone from here."

"What about the others?"

"Hell with them."

Valiant came crawling up, his eyes wild with fear. "Preacher just shot the legs from under Hosea and Campbell. It's a turrible sight to see."

"Go drag your brother back here, boy," Malachi told him. "We got to get shut of this place."

"Which brother?"

"The *live* one, you igit!"

"Oh. Right, Malachi. I'm gone."

"I been knowin' that for years," Kenrick muttered.

6

Preacher Injuned his way up on top of a huge boulder, bellied down, and had him a look-see. He smiled at the sight. Two were running across the valley. He couldn't tell who they were. Dead and dying men were sprawled all around the narrow passageways. Then he saw a Pardee slipping up to his brothers, one dead and the goofy one still out of it.

Preacher leveled his Hawken and squeezed off a ball. The ball knocked Valiant sprawling, one arm dangling useless. But he still managed to grab ahold of Ansel and pull him from under Radborne. Preacher slid off the boulder and worked his way to the north end of the death maze. That put him higher up on the slope and gave him a clear field of fire. He reloaded both rifles and started picking targets.

One of the men he'd seen back at Dirk's place got careless and it cost him his life. Preacher shot him right between the eyes and watched him slide down the slope and come to rest against a boulder.

"I surrender!" another shouted.

"The hell you do," an outlaw said, and shot the man dead.

"Shore is a nice bunch of people down yonder," Preacher muttered, reloading his Hawken. He watched as Malachi,

Kenrick, and Valiant dragged the still-unconscious Ansel out of rifle range. Out of the corner of his eye, he caught movement on the ridges about two miles or so away. Indians, and it was a big bunch of them. He couldn't tell what tribe, but he'd bet they were Shoshoni. Preacher slipped away, made the timber, and kept right on going to his little hidden valley.

All through the afternoon he heard the sounds of shots, and come the evening, faint screaming. The next morning, he turned the horses loose and mounted up. He rode down to just above the rocks, staying in the timber, and looked down at what the Indians had left. It was not a pretty sight. He saw where the Shoshoni had ridden off to the northeast, so Preacher headed south, leaving the bodies to the varmits and the carrion birds, which were already circling above. They were patient, knowing that death comes to all living things.

Preacher picked up sign almost immediately. Eight men, all scattered out and all on foot. And they would be runnin' scared as a rabbit with a coyote after him. Preacher chuckled without humor and fell in behind one group. Some would call what he had in mind evil. Preacher called it ridding the wilderness of undesirables.

Preacher could have struck at the outlaws within hours of picking up their tracks. But he wanted some distance between himself and that roaming band of scalp-hunting Shoshonis. Odds were they probably wouldn't bother Preacher, since he got along fairly well with most Indian tribes. But he decided to play it cautious this time.

He came up on the body of an outlaw and chased off the buzzards. They didn't go far. The body had been stripped of all clothing and was naked, stiffening in the cold air. Looked like to Preacher the man's own buddies had knocked him in the head and taken his clothing for added warmth. Two of them walked away from the scene, if he was reading the sign right. Preacher left him where he lay and moved on. Somewhere Preacher had heard about honor among thieves, or something like that. Sure wasn't none of that to be found in this bunch.

He was following a creek when he suddenly reined up. Hammer's ears had pricked up and Preacher took note.

About three hundred yards ahead of him he saw three men, staggering along. Their clothing was in rags and they were clearly exhausted. But all were still armed.

Preacher sat his horse and watched them until they were out of sight. He felt no pity for the outlaws. Preacher was a hard man in a harsh land. As far as distance went, the men were not that far away from a trading post. But the Cascades lay between some vestiges of civilization and them. The Whitman Mission lay a couple of hundred miles to the south—they would never make that.

Preacher lifted the reins and cut east of the trio, following the Columbia south toward the mission.

Son, Dirk, and the Pardees had fared much better than their men . . . in a manner of speaking. They had come up on a band of friendly Yakima Indians, men and women who were moving to winter campsites, and brutally murdered them all, taking their horses and robes. The outlaws had their way with the women and then strangled them. Preacher came upon the awful sight just as another band of Yakima warriors reached the site.

It got real chancy there for a few moments.

"I'm trailin' the men who done this," Preacher told the war chief. "But if you find them 'fore I do, you're welcome to them."

The Yakima looked at Preacher through steely eyes. Preacher was known to his people as a fair man who loved the land and coveted no Indian territory for his own. The war chief slowly nodded his head. "You have names?"

"The Pardee brothers, a man called Son, and an Englishman named Dirk. Dirk ran a trading post north of here."

"I know the men. They are evil."

A young brave said something and the war chief shook

his head. He looked at Preacher. "Leave now, Preacher. We must bury our own."

Preacher left without another word. The Yakimas were killing mad and some of the younger braves looked like they'd as soon kill him as anyone else. He resisted an urge to glance over his shoulder, knowing that would be considered a sign of weakness on his part. He began to breathe easier a couple of miles later.

He couldn't figure out where the gang was heading. It looked like they might be going into the Rattlesnake Range or the Horse Heaven Hills; but he had serious doubts about that. That was rough country, and as far as he knew, there wasn't a livin' soul down there. Then their trail cut due west and Preacher knew they were heading for Fort Vancouver, which some folks was already calling the New York of the Pacific. A regular little city it was, by western standards. Preacher figured they'd waylay some trappers or movers, steal their clothing to get duded up better, and then travel on to the fort.

Preacher swung down from the saddle and built a hat-sized fire for coffee while he ruminated some.

Snow had dusted the land again, thicker and heavier, and the nights were turning bitterly cold. His horses were rough looking in their winter coats and Preacher knew he was rough looking . . . and rough smelling, too. He hadn't shaved in several weeks and he'd been in his clothing for longer than that.

He drank his coffee and made up his mind. He'd head for the mission to see about the movers. He'd catch up with the Pardees and their ilk sooner or later. But for now, he'd be content with the knowledge that he'd pretty much pulled their stingers out. Come the spring, he'd start tracking again.

What was left of the gang had found several old abandoned Indian winter homes: semi-underground earth houses that many of the Northwest tribes used during the harsh winter season. Along the way, they had killed any trapper they found and seized the supplies, including precious powder and shot and coffee. Their existence this winter would be bleak, but they would make it. At least, they figured, they had succeeded in shaking Preacher off their trail.

Malachi had set Ansel's busted jaw and tied a rag around his head to immobilize it. But the jaw was healing crooked and the blow to the head had addled Ansel even more. Now he was just plain crazy as a bessy bug. He had trouble speaking and hardly anyone could understand a word he tried to say.

Dirk had fallen sullen and silent; he stayed alone and contented himself with cursing Preacher. He did not think he had ever despised a man as much as he did Preacher.

Son passed the long days and bitter nights by dreaming of torturing and killing Preacher in all sorts of ways.

Malachi would look at what remained of the family and would shake his head in sorrow.

Edward Sutherlin and his party had made the fort on the Laramie River and settled in to winter there. Along the way he had picked up four more toughs and come the spring he would make his move to settle Preacher's hash.

On a bitterly cold early winter's day, Preacher rode onto the grounds of the Whitman Mission.

"Ol' hoss," Caleb told him, "you look as mangy as a bear come out of hibernation."

"Feel like it, too," Preacher said, climbing wearily out of the saddle and handing the reins to a mover boy. "I got fleas and ticks and spiders and mites all over me. Is there a place to take a bath?"

"We built us a cabin," Windy said. "Come on. It's snug"

"Get me over there 'fore Betina sees me," Preacher replied, looking all around him.

"She's with Miss Narcissa," Rimrock said. "They's ed-ecatin' the Injun children."

"Good. Maybe she'll leave me be then. Stoke up the fire and heat the water. I got things *crawlin'* on me!"

Preacher took two baths before he felt clean. Carl Lippett came over to say hello, took one look at what was going on, and hit the air, saying he was going out for game. He'd be back when all that damn hot water and soap was gone.

Preacher trimmed his beard but left the face hair on as some protection against the cold. He'd shave come the spring. Then he walked over to the community building to see if he could bum something to eat. The movers had done themselves up right proud in the getting ready for winter. They'd built log floors under the beds of the wagons for more room and secured the sides with canvas and what lumber they could mill. When the Cayuses had learned the movers were not going to stay on permanently, they helped the movers get ready for winter. All in all, it was a fairly snug camp. But they would suffer come the long months of winter, Preacher had no illusions about that.

Betina was rather stiff and formal when she saw Preacher, which was fine with him. He didn't want to hurt her feelin's no more than he already had, but his life had no room in it for a female . . . especially an eastern female with settlin' down on the brain. Maybe she was finally gettin' that through her head. Preacher hoped so.

"Was your mission successful, Preacher?" Betina asked coolly, after introducing him to Narcissa Whitman.

"I reckon you'd call it that. I killed ten or twelve of them."

"Ten or twelve of what, Mr., ah, Preacher?" Narcissa asked.

"Men. You got anything to eat?"

"Men!" Narcissa cried, horrified.

"Sorry lot they was, too. World's better off without them. Is that stew over yonder?"

"I'll pray for you, sir," Narcissa said.

"Thanks. I probably need it." Preacher walked over to the

fireplace and ladled out a heaping plate of stew from the big blackened iron pot. He grabbed up a fresh loaf of bread and fell to eating.

"Did they receive a proper burial?" one of the mission's helpers asked.

"Buzzards seen to that," Preacher said.

"My word!" the missionary said.

"They was gonna hit the wagon train come this spring," Preacher explained. "Kill all the men, violate the women and girls, and sell the youngsters into slavery and bondage and whorin'. They wasn't very nice people."

"We must bring law and order to this land," the missionary said.

"In about fifty years, maybe," Preacher said, after swallowing a mouthful of stew. It needed salt but he wasn't going to complain.

Miles Cason and George Martin came in, and Miles went immediately to Betina's side. Preacher noticed that and hid a smile.

"Did you track down those miserable excuses for men, Preacher?" George asked.

"That I did. Two or three Pardees got clear of me, and I think Son and Dirk did too. But I left them terrible short of a gang. What I didn't get, a band of Shoshonis did." He looked over at Miles. "You two sparkin', I see."

"Sir!" Miles protested, as Betina flushed and fanned herself vigorously with a little hankie.

"Ain't nothin' to get all worked up about. You two make a mighty handsome couple. Hee, hee, hee!" he chuckled at their red-faced expressions.

"We must get back to work, Betina," Narcissa said, smoothly getting her off the hook.

"Yes, quite," Betina said, and the two women left the room.

Preacher finished his stew, sopped out the plate with a hunk of bread, then refilled his coffee cup. "Place looks pretty good," he remarked. "Y'all done a bang-up job in gettin' ready for the winter."

"Thank you," Miles said. "Might I have a word with you, Preacher?"

"Have two or three. They're free."

George and the missionary left the room and Miles sat down at the long table. "Betina and I have been taking a more than casual interest in one another, Preacher."

"Thought so. Good. Y'all get married and have babies. I give you my blessin'."

"You're not upset?"

"Hell no!"

"Her feelings toward the young man back East have faded considerably."

"He's there and she's here. 'Sides, she showed more nerve than him in comin' out here. Pioneer stock needs to breed together. Is George sparkin' Coretine?"

"Yes."

"Then it 'pears to me that everything is gonna work out all right, ain't it?"

Miles fiddled with his coffee cup for a moment. "I was on a fool's mission in my quest for gold. Those ideas are gone. Betina and I have agreed that we shall push on come the spring and settle in the new land and farm."

"Regular city over 'crost the Cascades now. Y'all will do well."

"And your plans, Preacher?"

Preacher smiled at the younger man. "You don't want me around here, do you, Miles?"

"I . . . I don't know, Preacher. Part of me does. We all owe you our lives. I can't—won't—forget all that you and the other mountain men have done for us, and are continuing to do for us. We all feel somewhat sorry for you men."

Preacher looked at the man, amazement in his expression. "You feel sorry for us? Lord God, man, why?"

"What will you do when this area is settled, Preacher? Any of you?"

"Boy, that's years down the trail. This land will be wild and woolly and full of fleas for another fifty years . . . maybe longer than that. Right now they's more outlaws and brigands and highwaymen in this country than pilgrims. Maybe ten to one. And the Injuns ain't even yet begun to fight you people for real. They can't understand that the white man is gonna pour into this country by the thousands. Right now, it's just a trickle. It'll soon turn into a ragin' river of people. That's when your troubles will really begin. Outlaws will pour in here, wantin' something for nothin' like outlaws always do, whole Injun tribes will go on the warpath, killin' and scalpin'. That's when people like you will start hollerin' for people like me to help pull your bacon out of the fire. So don't you be feelin' sorry for me. That makes me laugh."

"The Army will be in to protect us," Miles rebutted.

"Not for years, boy. This is disputed territory. You got British and French and Americans all squabblin' over this country. They'll get it settled someday. Until then, it's ever' man for himself 'cause there ain't no law west of the Missouri 'ceptin' the gun and the knife and the bow and the war axe. You best be mindful of that at all times"

"I am much more optimistic than you."

Preacher nodded his head and drained his coffee cup. He glanced out the window . . . a real window with glass and all. It was snowing again. Big, thick, wet flakes. He wondered briefly where the Pardees and Son and Dirk had holed up for the winter. He wondered, should he stay here or hunt him up a cabin for the cold season? Or mayhaps ride over the mountains and hole up with some trappers over to the Hudson's Bay post? One thing for sure, Miles and Betina didn't want him around, and he didn't blame either of them for that. Betina knew she had made a fool of herself earlier and that stuck in her craw.

"You folks set up huntin' parties, Miles?"

"Yes," he said shortly.

"I seen where you been draggin' in wood and stackin' it around. That's good." When Miles did not respond, Preacher stood up and said, "I reckon I'll ride." He walked out of the community building without another word.

7

"They don't want me here, Rim," Preacher said, saddling up. "It don't sadden me none 'cause I understand it. You boys stick around and see these pilgrims through the winter if you're a mind to. Grub's pretty good, if a body can put up with all the gospel-shoutin'. I'm gonna ride a ways and find me a good camp and then ponder for a time how come it is I keep gettin' myself in these situations."

Hammer was tired, but he was, as usual, ready for the trail. Preacher rode out within the hour and headed for the Blue Mountains. He knew he wouldn't near 'bouts make them, but he knew of a little place about ten miles from the mission that was out of the wind and near a creek. He made it before dark and picketed his horses in a protected area with some graze left and set about making his lonely camp. He rigged him a lean-to in front of a boulder so the stone would reflect the heat from the fire back into his open-front shelter. He gathered up wood to last several days and stacked it close. Then he fixed him something to eat and put water on for coffee.

People sure were funny, he thought. Hard to figure them out. When a body thinks he's doin' right, turns out he's doin' wrong. Strange. He give his blessin' to Betina and Miles, and still they got all swore up about him being in the mission proper.

Hell with them.

Preacher lay about the camp for two days and finally got restless and saddled up. Hammer was snortin' and pawin', ready for the trail. Preacher then began a lonely odyssey across the southern part of what would someday be called Wyoming. He camped very near the spot that would some-day become Fort Bridger. Only a few years in the future, Bridger and Vasquez would build a trading post on almost the exact spot where Preacher now sat before his small fire, pondering the fates that had led him to this desolate spot. But Preacher wasn't going to ponder long, for action seemed to find the man. In this case, in the form of two Arapaho In-dians who were wandering and saw the fire. Preacher knew they were there, but he made no move toward his Hawken. Just kept it very close.

"Shore is gettin' tiresome talkin' to myself," he said, rais-ing his voice to be heard. "I'd be pleased to talk to someone. Even two mangy Arapaho called Kicking Bear and Runs Fast."

Both the braves laughed and rode into the camp. "We thought it was you, Preacher. But we couldn't be sure. We have fresh buffalo hump if you have coffee."

"Gather 'round, pull up a rock, and sit. We'll eat and talk."

"It is good to see you, Preacher," Kicking Bear said, pour-ing a cup of coffee. "In more ways than one. But we bring trouble to you."

"My middle name. What's the matter?"

"A band of war-painted Pawnee trails us." There was a definite twinkle of high humor in his eyes. "But since we know how Preacher loves the Pawnee, perhaps we should ride on. Preacher might not want to bring harm to his favorite people."

Preacher looked at the man and smiled. "Oh, yeah. Them's

my favorite, all right. I been stuck with several arrows over the years, all of them Pawnee. How many and how far away?"

"Ten or twelve. Perhaps they will hit us at first light."

Preacher took note that both Arapaho were carrying new Hawken rifles in addition to bows and quivers of arrows. He did not ask where they got the guns, the powder horns, or the shot. "We'll eat and then move over yonder in them rocks. A trickle of water flows through there and they's some graze for the horses. Pawnees are a little out of their territory, ain't they?"

"They are mostly young men, hunting scalps to impress the girls," Runs Fast said, fitting hunks of meat on sticks. "They will be mostly dead when they find us, I am thinking," he added very dryly.

"They are also ugly," Kicking Bear added. "They paint themselves and make them even more ugly." He spat on the ground. "They look like something out of a nightmare. I hate the Pawnee."

The men ate their fill and more, belched loudly, then drank two pots of coffee. Preacher took out tobacco and they smoked and were content for a time. The fire was warm, the late afternoon still peaceful and safe, for the birds were singing and the little animals playing.

"White men from the East are wintering on the Laramie River," Kicking Bear said. "They have plans to come west in the spring." He smoked for a time and Preacher waited. "The leader of the group is the man who has an alliance with the renegade, Red Hand."

"Sutherlin," Preacher said.

"That is the name, I believe. But since the names of white men are so strange and one must twist his mouth all out of shape and almost swallow his tongue to speak them, I cannot be sure. But I believe that is the person."

"I kilt most of the Pardee gang and Son's bunch up north and west of here."

"So we heard. It is a good thing you did. They were bad people."

"How many men does Sutherlin have with him?"

"Ten or twelve, at least."

Preacher did not ask how Kicking Bear and Runs Fast knew all this. The Indians had a grapevine that was both astonishing and very fast and accurate. When around whites, Indians usually said little and listened intently. The language of the Plains Indians varied with each tribe, but most Indians were multilingual and all could communicate thousands of words and thoughts with a few hundred signals by hand. The Arapaho were friends of nearly everyone—when convenient— but most did not like the Pawnee. Their sign for the Pawnee was the first two fingers of either hand held up in a V. No one knew why, it just was.

Preacher cocked an ear and listened. The birds were gone and the woods animals had ceased their playing. "I think we best head for them rocks. I don't think the Pawnee are gonna wait for dawn to hit us."

In two minutes flat, Preacher and the Arapaho were in the rocks and taking up positions.

Then, from all around their stone fort, came hoots of derision and taunting catcalls. "Arapaho shit!" a Pawnee called out. "You will not die well, I am thinking."

"You are incapable of thinking," Kicking Bear shouted. "Your mother was a buzzard and your father was a skunk."

The Arapaho warriors shouted insults for a time and then fell silent.

"They got their courage worked up now," Preacher remarked. "They been slippin' all around us for a few minutes. They'll be comin' at us pretty quick now."

No sooner had the words left his mouth when the Pawnee braves rushed the rocks, screaming war cries. Preacher blew a hole in one's chest with his Hawken, picked up his other Hawken, and almost blew the head off another. He jerked out one brace of pistols just as the charge broke off. Preacher and the two Arapaho had done some fearsome damage to the young Pawnee warriors. Six of them lay dead or dying around the rocks.

"They will quit now," Runs Fast said as he reloaded. "We have wiped out half of their band. Their medicine is no good."

The sounds of ponies galloping away reached them and Kicking Bear snorted in disgust. "They leave their dead behind. Filthy cowards."

Kicking Bear and Runs Fast took out their knives and went to work. First they scalped the dead, then cut off their hands, took out their eyes, and cut off their genitals. Now, in the World That Came After, the dead would not be able to see their way, find their enemies, or breed young to carry on the fight. Preacher watched them dispassionately. Unlike the missionaries, he seldom tried to change the Indians way of thinking or questioned their customs. He figured it just wasn't none of his damn business.

Which was one of the reasons he got along so well with most tribes.

When Runs Fast and Kicking Bear had finished, they held up their bloody trophies, grinned, and waved goodbye to Preacher. Preacher returned the smile, made the sign of thanks and farewell, and the two Arapaho rode off. Preacher packed up and got the hell gone from there.

Preacher found the trail of the Arapaho, followed it for a time to make sure they were not going to circle around back, and then cut north for a time. He wasn't in any hurry; had no place really to go and no timetable set for him. He wanted to meet up with this Sutherlin person, but didn't want to ride right into the post and start opening up. Also, one of the dead outlaws he'd left back on the trail had had him two pistols that Preacher had coveted something fierce almost immediately. Preacher had just now remembered that he'd picked up the broken guns and stashed them in his supplies. He wanted to find him a spot where he could work on the things.

The next afternoon, he made camp early and dug out the pistols. The pistols were complicated-looking things, each one of them having four barrels, over and under. He repaired the bullet-shattered butt of one with the brass butt plate from a spare of his own, then replaced the bent hammers on the second one with hammers taken from other spares he'd picked up from the dead and dying. They were the same caliber as his Hawken, so he loaded them up and taken them out to test-fire them. They were of a slightly shorter barrel than his other pistols, but gave him eight times the firepower. Once he got the hang of them, he was pleased, mighty pleased. Chuckling, he double-shotted two of the four barrels on each pistols and set about making holsters for them from a skin. Once that was done, he fashioned the holsters to his wide leather belt and went down to the creek to take a look at himself. He sure hadn't ever seen nothing like the image that reflected back up at him.

He looked like a . . . come to think of it, he didn't know what the hell he looked like. Then he had taken rawhide thongs, punched a hole in the bottom of each holster, and tied the holsters to his legs so's they wouldn't flop around so much.

Then he decided he'd see how fast he could get them out of the holsters and cock and fire them. First time he tried it he damned near blowed his foot off. Then he decided he'd try it with the pistols empty. He spent a week in his camp, practicing several hours each day. Each hour he got faster and more accurate.

"By God," he said to the cold winds. "I just might have me somethin' here. I don't know perxactly what, but it's something mighty important, I believe."

Only problem was, when he mounted up to do a little scouting around the camp, the damn pistols fell out of the holsters. Preacher sat down on a log and done a little head ruminatin'. Then he took some rawhide and fashioned some thongs at the top of each holster to loop over one hammer and that done the trick. To get in the habit, every time he dismounted, he slipped the thongs off the hammers to free his guns. Soon doing that became second nature to him.

Preacher would go down in history as being the first to do many things. Some had him as the first mountain man, but that was a lie. They was a lot of white men out in the wilderness long 'fore Preacher got there. What he didn't know, had no way of knowing, was that he would go down in history as being the first gunfighter to use the quick draw.

Preacher finally saddled up and packed up and pulled out, heading for the post on the Laramie in a roundabout way. Along the way, he met up with a disreputable-looking old reprobate of a mountain man called Natchez.

Natchez took one look at Preacher's rig slung around his lean waist and said, "What in the billy-hell has you got strapped around you, Preacher?"

"You know me, Natch. I'm always comin' up with something different."

"Looks plumb awkward to me. You be careful and don't get yourself kilt with them fool things."

"You been over yonder on the Laramie?"

"For a fact, I have. Man from back East is there, and a mighty quiet and secretive man he is, I say. He's got him ten or twelve brigands with him and they's tough enough, I reckon." The old man smiled. "Tough back East, that is. Out here, I 'spect they'll have to prove their mettle."

"This quiet man's name wouldn't be Sutherlin, would it now?"

"It would for a fact. You a friend of his'n?"

"No. Some Arapaho told me 'bout him back west of here a couple of weeks ago. I was also told he was up to no good."

"I don't take to him, for a fact. He's a tad on the sneaky side for me. Don't care for the look in his eyes. When he does bump his gums, you can tell he's a man with book larnin', but he talks down to people. I knowed if I stayed 'round there much longer I might have to shoot him."

"I do know the feelin'."

Natchez looked at the big four-barreled pistols slung in leather around Preacher's waist and shook his head. "Never seen nothin' like that in all my borned days. See you around, Preacher."

Preacher lifted a hand in farewell and the two men rode their separate ways. In the Ferris Mountains, Preacher found a cabin that had been built years back by a friend of his— long dead—and since the weather had turned bad, he decided to hole up for a time.

He cleaned out the sooted-up chimney and laid in wood and mudded up the chinks between the logs, making the cabin snug. He killed two deer and skinned and dressed them out, hanging the meat high from a limb. In a few hours the meat was froze solid. Preacher started work on the skins, for he needed new high-top moccasins and a shirt.

For a month he saw no sign of a human being and he was content. He killed several more deer, and when he was ready to leave the snug cabin, he was dressed in new buckskins from neck to feet. He had cut his hair and trimmed his beard close. He had practiced at least one hour a day, and had become incredibly fast and deadly accurate with his awesome pistols with the complicated hammer systems and four barrels each. He had taken skins and hardened them, making better holsters for his guns.

He wondered occasionally how the folks were getting on back at the mission during this hard winter . . . but he didn't dwell on it long. He knew that Windy and Rimrock and Caleb would not leave them in the lurch. And even if the mountain men did leave the mission to go their own way—they certainly were under no obligation to stay—the movers would make it; if they didn't, then to Preacher's way of thinking, they should have stayed to home.

Preacher wanted to have done with Sutherlin by early

spring, for that would give him several weeks to get back to the mission area to deal with what was left of the Pardees and their kind. Then he was through with movers and their damn wagon trains. He was going to head for the Southern Rockies; maybe go down on the Blue and get the hell away from wagon trains and movers and crazy women.

He got Hammer out of the little shelter and the big horse bucked and jumped and snorted and kicked and told Preacher in his own way that he was tired of being cooped up and let's get on the trail.

The day was pleasant, the sun warm and the snow melting—it would snow again, for winter was not over by a long shot—but the brief respite felt good. Preacher saddled up and pulled out.

"I'm gonna help these movers one more time, Sutherlin," he said to the warm winds as he headed east. "Then it's back to the mission, bury the Pardees, and I'm gone to the Big Lonesome down south."

Hammer shook his head and pranced in anticipation.

8

Preacher rode easy but in a distance-covering gait. He crossed the Shirley Mountains without incident and then got caught up in a blizzard near the southern curve of the North Laramie River. He forted up as best he could and he and Hammer and the packhorse sat it out. Finally the weather broke, the sun came out, the snows began to melt, and Preacher pushed on, reaching the post just as the first tentative touches of false spring were trying to shove winter aside.

He hadn't seen so damn many people all gathered together in years.

Indian tipis had been put up all around the post. Wagons were scattered here and there. A new corral had been built to handle the livestock and the post itself had been enlarged. Preacher sat his horse and stared in amazement.

"The push is on, Hammer," he said to his horse. "By May they'll be pilgrims all over the damn place. But if we have any luck a-tall, we'll be south of all this mess and bother. Let's go, Hammer, they's a whole feedbag of grain waitin' for you and my good packhorse."

Preacher wound his way through the tipis and movers'

tents and wagons and what have you, and rode into the post. He stabled his horses and gave the boy a coin to rub them down good and grain them. He saw no one he knew and no one called out his name, which was just fine with Preacher. He found him something to eat and then went to the store, which had a room that served as a saloon of sorts. Preacher got him a cup of whiskey and found a seat at a table in a darkened corner of the room. He figured that sooner or later Sutherlin would show up . . . and Preacher was a patient man.

After a time several men—eastern men, by their appearance—strolled in and bought them a jug. They were rough looking and heavily armed. The three men tried to peer through the gloom to see who it was sitting alone at the corner table, but finally gave up and contented themselves with talking in low murmurs, occasionally glancing toward Preacher.

"You there!" one of them called sharply and in a tone that rankled Preacher. "I ain't seen you around here 'fore."

"I got caught up in a blizzard west of here and it blowed me and my horses all the way over here. That was some wind, let me tell you. But it set us down gentle like about a mile from the post. Does that satisfy you?"

The burly, unwashed, and stinking lout stared at Preacher for a moment. "Were you borned with a smart-aleck mouth or did you come into it as you got butt-uglier over the years?"

Preacher smiled at the man. "You callin' me ugly is like a frog callin' a buzzard ugly. I bet your mamma had to tie some fatback around your neck to get the dogs to play with you."

The lout narrowed his eyes and sat his cup of whiskey down and stood up.

"That's Preacher," a man spoke from the archway leading from the store into the bar.

The burly man smiled, exposing a mouthful of bad teeth. "The famous Preacher, hey? I heared an awful lot about you, Preacher. Some folks has you meaner than a bear and quick as a panther and all man. But lookin' at you, I can see they was all lies. I think I'll just break you in two."

"It's been tried," Preacher said, then took a sip of his whiskey. He set the cup down on the table. "More'n oncest." He cut his eyes to the archway. A mountain man name of John Morris stood there. "John. You know this loudmouth?"

"I seen him around. He's a trouble hunter."

"He's found it," Preacher said quietly.

"Not in here, Preacher," the sutler said, stepping up to the archway.

"I come in here for a quiet drink," Preacher told him. "You know me, Hector. I ain't never started no trouble in your place. But I ain't takin' water from this ugly bastard."

"Sit down, Talbot," one of his friends urged him.

But Talbot wasn't having any of that. "You callin' me a bastard, Preacher?"

"Yeah."

"I'll break you in half."

"You ain't done nothin' yet 'ceptin' run your mouth."

"Your employer will certainly pay for the damages," Hector stated. "Or you all shall be barred from the post, and from any other post from here to the Oregon coast."

"I'll pay." Another voice was added.

Preacher looked over at the man. A cruel-faced man with little piggy eyes. But a massive brute of a man nonetheless. He stood well over six feet and weighed probably two hundred and thirty pounds. He had the look of a man who had fought some for money. Big hamlike hands and huge wrists. One ear was slightly cauliflowered and his nose had been busted a time or two. Scar tissue was over his eyes. Had to be Sutherlin. His clothing was either hand sewn or store-bought and tailored and very neat for the frontier.

Preacher had not risen from his chair. He drained his cup of whiskey and carefully placed the cup on the rough boards of the table.

"Fancy-pants," he said to Sutherlin, "you bes' tell your pet dog here to sit down and stop his barkin'. I just might decide to kill him."

"My name is Sutherlin. *Mister* Sutherlin, to you."

John Morris laughed at that and Sutherlin flushed under his clean-shaven face.

"Your name might be Sutherlin," Preacher said. "But it'll be a cold day in hell 'fore I call the likes of you mister."

Sutherlin's flush deepened and Talbot took a step toward Preacher, his hands balled into fists.

"I'll keep the others off of you, Preacher," John said, and pulled out two pistols.

"How do you want this, Talbot?" Preacher asked him. "Knives, fists, or guns?"

"Guns, Talbot. Let's be rid of him now."

Preacher stood up and all stared in confusion at the rig that hung around his waist.

"Guns it'll be," Preacher said. "Pull when you've a mind to, Talbot."

"We'll have a proper duel with seconds," Sutherlin said.

Preacher laughed at him. "This ain't New York, Sutherlin. You can forget all them *e*-laborate goin's-on. We like things simple out here. Now shut your flap and stand aside." He cut his eyes to Talbot. "Jerk and fire, you son of a bitch."

Talbot's hand flew to the butt of his pistol and that was as far as he got. Preacher pulled, cocked, and fired. One ball struck Talbot in the chest and the second ball tore a great, gaping hole in his throat. The thug was flung backward and died with his butt on the floor and his back to a wall. His pistol was still behind his belt.

Preacher holstered the awesome pistol and sat down in his chair.

"Damnest thing I ever seen," John Morris said. "I do believe you on to something, Preacher."

Sutherlin was visibly shaken by what had happened. His broad face was pale and his mouth was hanging open. While dueling was outlawed in most areas of the country, it was still practiced in secrecy in many areas. But no one had ever perfected the art of quick drawing, until now.

"Foul, I say." Sutherlin had found his voice. "That was not at all fair play."

"Gimme another drink of whiskey," Preacher said, tapping his cup on the table. "Shootin' makes me thirsty."

The men with Talbot had not moved, so shocked were they at the sudden events.

Hector brought a jug to Preacher's table and quickly backed away. Behind the plank bar, Hector pointed to the dead man. "Get him out of here and do it right now."

Sutherlin waved a hand at his men and they dragged the lifeless body of Talbot out of the room. He looked at Preacher. "We shall meet again."

"I'm countin' on it, fancy-pants," Preacher said, pouring a cup of whiskey.

Edward Sutherlin stared hard at Preacher, the knowledge hitting him suddenly that this rugged-looking and shaggy mountain man knew all about him. But *how?* No matter. He did. Sutherlin was sure of that. So this much was certain: Preacher had to die, and die quickly. Sutherlin had too much to lose for Preacher to stay alive and talk . . . and talk he would, Sutherlin was certain of that.

Sutherlin stepped from the room and went quickly to his quarters. His men would see to the burying of Talbot. The chief factor came to the saloon to briefly question Preacher and the matter was resolved and forgotten. Life was cheap in the wilderness. Staying alive was a day-to-day struggle that each man met in his own way.

In his quarters, Sutherlin sat down in a hide chair and pondered the situation. There had been no fear in Preacher— none; he had seen that. The man was totally unimpressed by either Sutherlin or his men. So in Sutherlin's mind, that made Preacher a fool.

Sutherlin would have liked to meet with Malachi Pardee and Son, but how? Communications were practically impossible out here in the wilderness, and for some reason as yet unknown to the man, his network of runners and riders had vanished. He did not know that Weasel Tail's braves had killed some of them and the others had fled for their lives, heading back across the Missouri into the safety of civilization . . . such as it was.

But no action could be taken against Preacher here at the fort. He was too well known and by now everyone would know that Sutherlin and Preacher had bad feelings between them. So Preacher must be watched at all times and Sutherlin and his men must be ready to leave at a moment's notice. He rose from the chair and walked outside to talk briefly with Lester, his second in command. Lester nodded his head and left to alert his men.

Preacher lounged in front of the store and watched the goings-on with a smile. He resupplied and toted the packages to the stable. There, he paid a man he knew very handsomely to sleep in the stall next to Hammer and report if anyone tried to tamper with his horses, supplies, or equipment. That taken care of, Preacher went outside the stockade walls and found him a Crow among the many Indians camped there. All Indians except Blackfeet were welcome at the post. He gave the Crow two of the pistols he'd taken from the dead, and a supply of shot and powder, to spy on Sutherlin and report back to him the man's every move. The Crow was known to Preacher and was a good man, friendly to the whites. Preacher had befriended the man several times, and the Crow was loyal to him.

Many at the fort eyeballed Preacher's guns and the way he wore them. Most shook their heads and dismissed the rig as being too cumbersome.

Before the dawning of the third day, Preacher was saddled up and ready to go. The Crow slipped into the stable.

"Piggy-face and his men are going to follow you, Preacher," the Crow told him.

"I'm countin' on it, Preacher replied. "You done good. I'll see you around."

The Crow nodded and slipped silently away into the predawn.

"What's with this Sutherlin feller?" the man Preacher had hired to stay with his gear asked, rising from the hay and brushing himself off.

"He's no-count. He's a murderer and worsen I aim to put out his lights."

"Power to you," the man said. "You want me to bring you some coffee?"

"Had my fill. You take care, Jeff. I'll see you next time around."

Preacher rode out of the main gate and headed west, conscious of being watched by Sutherlin's thugs.

"Come on, people," he muttered. "Follow ol' Preacher. I got some surprises for you."

Before leaving, Preacher gave Sutherlin's men the slip and had talked long with the factor of the post, telling him all he knew about Sutherlin and all that the people in the wagon trains knew about him. The man's frown had deepened the more Preacher talked.

"He has been under suspicion, Preacher," the man said. "I don't believe he is aware of it as yet, but if he leaves unorganized territory and heads back to the States, there are warrants for his arrest waiting for him." He handed Preacher a letter from the United States Federal Marshal's office.

Preacher read the letter and grunted. "He won't never go back. I'll see to that."

"And I'll pretend I didn't hear you say that."

Preacher headed for the Laramie Mountains and set a grueling pace. He wanted those behind him tuckered when he made his move. He crossed the Laramie River and plunged into the deep wilderness. Wilderness for them struggling along behind him; home territory for Preacher. As he rode, Preacher allowed himself to recall the tortured and mutilated

and raped and murdered bodies that he'd seen over the last
couple of years . . . all of them due to the cold-hearted treachery of Edward Sutherlin.

"Sutherlin," Preacher spoke to the cold winds of late winter in the Big Empty. "You'll not be responsible for another
death if I can help it. And I can help it."

At his camp that evening, in front of a small fire, Preacher
again inspected his strange and deadly pistols. Whoever had
made them had done so lovingly and with patient skill; they
were the work of someone who possessed a great knowledge
of firearms. Preacher had heard that firearms were in a state
of advancement, and that some were even experimenting
with some sort of revolving cylinder. He didn't see how anything like that would ever work, so he didn't dwell on it. But
these pistols, now, these pistols were a work of art. And they
gave him awesome firepower. Close in, he could damn near
wage a full-scale war with these beauties.

Something he certainly intended to do.

Sutherlin and his men sat close to the fire, for the nights
were still brutally cold. None of them had the foggiest idea
where they were, only that they were staying on the trail of
Preacher and they were heading west, in a roundabout manner. Sutherlin had heard back at the post that Malachi's gang
had been savaged by Preacher, the mountain man nearly destroying the gang. Sutherlin found that hard to believe and
felt the report was greatly exaggerated. No one man was capable of doing that.

Sutherlin knew little about the caliber of a person called
mountain man.

In their stinking, filthy lairs, Malachi and Dirk and Son
and what was left of their gangs brooded over their fires and
waited for the arrival of spring. They had spent the entire

winter nurturing the flames of hatred and now they could hardly contain themselves. To a man—even so far as Ansel, with all his goofiness—all they could think of was the killing of Preacher. And Ansel, at least in the minds of those near him, had gone completely around the bend. He mumbled and slobbered and grunted and had seemingly lost the ability to speak even semicoherently. Even Malachi had lost patience with him and now tried his best to ignore his brother. Couldn't nobody get any sense out of the fool. But they knew this: come the spring, they would hunt down and kill Preacher. They all agreed on that. Even Ansel, as far as anyone could tell. When asked, he would grunt and slobber and bob his head up and down.

"We kill Preacher come the spring," Kenrick said. "Even if we all die doin' it."

"Damn right," Son said.

Malachi nodded his head in agreement.

The men let their wild hatred fully consume them. They waited.

Preacher lay snug in his robes and slept. He didn't hate, he just knew what had to be done and he was going to do it.

At the mission, George Martin and Coretine, and Miles Cason and Betina were married by the missionaries.

9

Preacher had led the men deep into the wilderness. Now it was time to start the war. He struck the first blow between the Laramie and Medicine Bow mountains. Preacher was waiting on the west side of Muddy Creek when Sutherlin and his men stopped to rest and water their horses. He had Sutherlin all lined up in his sights, and just as he squeezed the trigger, a new man picked up back at the post made a very bad move by stepping in front of Sutherlin and took the ball directly in the center of his back. The big ball busted the man's spine, angled up and ripped out of his throat, and splattered Sutherlin with blood. Edward Sutherlin let out a scream of fright and shock, hit the rocky ground, and hugged it close as his men scattered out, seeking whatever cover they could find. The dead man fell directly on top of Sutherlin.

"Damn," Preacher said. He slipped back to his horses and pressed on westward, looking for another good ambush site. He consoled himself with the knowledge that at least there was one less to deal with.

Back at the creek, the outlaws dug a shallow grave and

dumped the dead man in it. They didn't even take the time to cover the mound with rocks. The dead man was known only as Peter. The outlaws rifled his saddlebags and pockets, took his boots, and rode off without a word of prayer. From this time on, Edward Sutherlin would ride in the center of the column and always have someone close beside him after dismounting.

"A thousand dollars to the man who kills Preacher," he told his men.

A thousand dollars was several years' wages. The men needed no further incentive.

"You got the money on you?" a man named Mueller asked, his voice heavily accented, a sly look in his eyes.

"Don't be foolish," Sutherlin told him. "So you'd better keep me alive."

"Accordin' to this map," Lester said, "which ain't worth a shit as far as I'm concerned, they's another creek about five miles ahead of us. Then they's a river of some sorts and then we hit more mountains."

"Is there any way around them?" Big Max asked.

"Yeah," Lester said sarcastically. "About five hundred miles south or five hundred miles north."

Just inside the Medicine Bow range, Preacher was waiting, his bow ready for a silent kill.

Sutherlin swung into the saddle. "Take the point, Meeker. Let's go."

Meeker, wanted for rape and murder in several states back East, nodded his head and took the lead.

Ward fell in behind him. Ward was wanted for killing his wife and children back in Vermont.

The third man in the rogues' column was Mueller, also a murderer and rapist . . . and those were his good points.

Next was Clubb, wanted for robbery, rape, murder, and numerous other infractions.

Doc Judd was a real doctor; unfortunately, he also got a

great deal of joy out of poisoning patients. Twelve of them before the law got wise back East and put him on the run.

Moffett was a con man, thief, and rapist.

Lester had done it all and was wanted in nearly every state in the Union for one thing or another. He was as ruthless as Sutherlin.

Big Max liked to beat people to death with his fist. And had, several times. Men, women, and children.

Beans Speer was a back shooter and would kill anyone for the right price.

Isaac was a knife man who liked to kill . . . slowly.

The other men Sutherlin had picked up along the way were Sharp and Bankston. Both murderers.

Thirteen brigands riding into the wilderness after one man. Each of them supremely confident he would be the one to kill Preacher and be a thousand dollars richer.

Had they had just one opportunity to take a look at what remained of the gangs of Malachi, Dirk, and Son, they might have changed their minds and ridden back East.

Bankston brought up the rear of the column, and Preacher waited until the others were around the bend in the trail and out of sight before he struck. From a distance of about twenty feet, he put an arrow all the way through the murderer. The arrow cut the spine and Bankston fell soundlessly from his saddle. Preacher jumped down from the rocks, grabbed the horse's reins, and calmed the jumpy animal, and then slung Bankston across the saddle. He led the horse into the rocks and waited, both hands filled with those deadly pistols.

But Sutherlin smelled something queer and refused to take the bait. Preacher could hear them talking and could pick out most of the conversation.

"Preacher got him," Lester said. "Listen to the boss and

don't go 'round that bend. Let's get the hell gone from here 'fore he picks off another one of us.

"I got an idea."

"What is it, Isaac?"

"We know he's here, so let's settle it now. Fan out and take him. We got him twelve to one. Some of us will get kilt, for sure, but we can take him out here and now."

Yes sirree, Preacher thought. You folks just come right on and do that little thing. I didn't figure on none of you bein' that damn ignorant.

Sutherlin thought about that for a moment, being careful to stand with his men all around him as human shields. Finally he nodded his head in agreement. "Lester, you and Beans and Clubb stay here with me. We'll get in those rocks over there. The rest of you men fan out and hunt this bastard down. Let's get it over and done with."

Preacher slipped back and into the brush, kneeling down and waiting. That he would soon be surrounded didn't bother him one whit. He'd been surrounded before, by men much more skilled in combat than this bunch of white trash.

Preacher had holstered his pistols and once more taken up his bow, notching an arrow. He was in good cover and blended in. He had noted days before that these men were not skilled in brush warfare. They might be experts in dark alleyways and the streets of towns, but they were careless in the wilderness. And that was gonna get them killed.

One of Sutherlin's bunch passed so close to Preacher that he could smell the body odor of the thug. Moving only his eyes, Preacher watched as the man vanished behind rocks. Ward slipped through the rocks and brush, trying to be quiet about it. He was no woodsman.

Preacher put an arrow into the man's chest. The instant the arrow flew, Preacher was moving, changing locations. Ward was kicking his legs as he lay on the ground, his mouth working with no sound coming out. But he was making quite a racket with his boots.

"Ward!" a man called. "Hush up all that damn noise. What the hell's the matter with you?"

Ward let out a fearful shriek, drummed his boot heels on the ground, and died.

"He's in amongst us!" Sharp cried out. "Be careful. Ward's down and dead."

Preacher let fly another arrow and Doc Judd turned just as it was loosed. The arrow missed and careened off a boulder, sending Doc belly down on the ground. "Over here!" Doc yelled. "Be careful. The man's a damn ghost."

Preacher stayed where he was, knowing movement attracted more attention than noise. Why none of the men hadn't found his horses was a mystery to him.

"This is no good!" Sutherlin shouted out. "Gather around and let's get out of here. Come on, men."

Preacher let them go. He had pressed his luck to the maximum this day and knew it. He remained motionless and listened to them ride off. The body of Ward lay where he had kicked out his last. Sutherlin and company had made no attempts to tend to the dead.

"Sorry bunch of bastards," Preacher muttered, standing up and walking over to the dead man. He looked down at him. It wasn't sympathy; he was trying to figure out how to best retrieve his arrow. It was a good arrow. Rolling the man over on one side, Preacher saw that when he fell, he had broken the arrow. Preacher dragged the man to a depression and kicked some dirt and rocks over him.

"You want him, Lord," Preacher briefly eulogized, "You got him. Here he is. Amen."

Now the chase was on and Preacher was at his best. He had them all running scared and knew it. He let them run for a full twenty-four hours before he made his next move. That night, he circled their camp, howling like a wolf, grunting like a bear, and coughing like a great panther. He was so convincing that a bear actually did come to investigate and Preacher damn near ruined his brand new longhandles when he turned around and the bear reared up not ten feet from him in the darkness.

Preacher hit the air and vacated the area. "Work, feet," he mumbled in a dead run, dodging trees and boulders and leaving the bear far behind. The bear had decided that Preacher was not worth the effort of pursuit—the camp held much more interesting smells.

"Holy shit!" Doc Judd screamed, catching sight of the great bear, a huge male grizzly. Doc lifted his rifle and the weapon misfired, momentarily blinding the man with powder burns. Doc threw the rifle at the bear and took off as the entire encampment went running in all directions. It scared the bear about as bad as the men and the griz took off in a lope, getting the hell away from that screaming wall of noise.

Sutherlin ran into a tree and knocked himself out. Lester ran right off the edge of an embankment and went rolling ass over elbows to the rocky ground below. Moffett climbed a tree. Mueller tried to climb the same tree and Moffett thought it was the bear and kicked the man in the head. Mueller hit the ground, unconscious.

A good mile away, Preacher stopped to catch his breath. The faint screaming of the badly frightened men drifted to him and he smiled. He made his way back to his horses and rode for a couple of miles before bedding down for the night.

Preacher trailed along behind the men for several miles, then popped up alongside them further along, but stayed well out of rifle range. He waved and shouted and made terribly obscene gestures toward the men, trying to get one of them to lose his temper and come after him. But no one would take the bait.

"Steady, men," Sutherlin cautioned his band of cutthroats and thugs. "Just ignore him. We'll have our chance."

Just before leaving the Medicine Bow range, Preacher pulled ahead of the men and cut north, taking them—if they chose to follow his trail—into the high country. Dutifully, they tagged along behind him, with Preacher thinking this just had to be some of the dumbest men he had ever encountered. And he had met some real dumbos in his time. He decided to find out just what the hell was going on.

That night he Injuned up to their camp and lay for a time, his eyes picking out the guards. The bunch had wised up right smart, and had taken to choosing their campsites with a lot more care. Preacher moved only several inches at a time. At the end of two hours, he was within hearing distance of the men. They were all gathered around a fire, which was definitely not smart at all. Look into the flames and it destroys a man's night vision. They were just real lucky there were no hostiles about. Or that no Indians had located their camp, Preacher corrected, for hostiles were always about.

"This is no good," Lester said, pouring himself another cup of coffee. "The man is just leading us wherever he wishes. He's making fools of us, boss."

"I don't like this country out here," Clubb said, a blanket wrapped around his shoulders against the chill of the night. "It's almost as if we have dropped off the edge of the world. It's so damn *empty!*"

"You would rather go back and face a hangman's noose, perhaps?" Mueller asked.

Clubb shook his head and had nothing else to say on the matter.

"Lester is right, of course," Sutherlin said. "But I am sure that this Preacher person knows all about us and our operation. If he lives, we will not be safe anywhere. I wish I knew where Malachi and his bunch were hiding out. Or if they're still alive. I fear that many are not. And I also think that there are new warrants out on all of us back in the States. So you see, gentlemen, Preacher has to die. For if he doesn't, we have no place left to run."

"I long to see California," Meeker said, "where it's warm all the time, and have soft-eyed Spanish women. I like to force myself on Spanish women. I'd love to hear them scream when I take them. I hate this damn country here. I would certainly not relish the thought of being buried here in this cold and inhospitable clime."

Worthless, no-count son of a bitch, Preacher thought. Then he lifted a pistol and put a ball right through the rapist's belly.

Meeker fell backward without a sound, screaming as his back touched the cold ground that he hated.

Preacher cocked the second hammer and blew a hole into Sharp's belly. Then, while the camp was in turmoil, Preacher slipped away into the darkness. The outlaws were firing at shadows, blasting away into the dead of night in their frightened panic. But Preacher had dropped into a natural depression in the earth and no bullets touched him as he ran back in the direction of his horses. He'd given the brigands quite enough to think on this evening.

When Preacher reached the camp the next morning, about an hour after dawn, the outlaws were gone and the ashes of their fires were cold.

Meeker lay on his back where he had fallen, and the gut-shot outlaw was not long for this world. His comrades had not even taken the time to dress his hideous wound. But they had taken the time to take his heavy coat and his boots. He watched Preacher through pain-filled eyes as the mountain man set about making a fire.

"Nice bunch of folks you took up with," Preacher remarked. "They sure cared a lot for you, didn't they?"

"Water seeks its own level," the wounded man said weakly.

"I reckon." Preacher tossed the man a rag of a blanket someone had left behind.

"Thank you."

"I'd do more for a wounded animal," Preacher said shortly. "You got a hole in your belly, but I 'spect a little coffee ain't gonna keep the dark angel waitin' too long for you to pass."

"I would appreciate that."

"You talk like you got some education."

"I have. I just took a wrong turn a long time ago and couldn't find the path."

"You *wouldn't* find the path," Preacher corrected. "Don't give me none of this 'couldn't' crap."

Meeker smiled faintly. "You also possess a fair amount of education, mountain man."

"I went to the fifth or sixth grades, I think. Mostly Ma taught me to home."

"That fire feels good."

"It do, for a fact, don't it? Where'd Sutherlin go this time?"

"I owe them nothing, so I'll tell you. They went hard to the ground. They're going to try to sit out the rest of the cold weather and then surface, heading west to the Oregon country to find Malachi and the others."

"They finally got smart, did they? Well, I doubt they'll lose me in this country, but it's been done afore, I have to allow." Preacher filled the coffee pot and put it on to boil, although he had doubts the man would live long enough to have him a taste of the brew.

"I have chicory root in my saddlebags over there," Meeker said. "If you like the added flavor."

"I do for a fact. It don't grow worth a damn out here, not this high up."

Preacher dumped the coffee into the boiling water, added some shaved chicory, and removed the pot from the fire to let the grounds settle.

"Does Sutherlin know they's federal warrants out for him?" Preacher asked the dying man.

"He suspects."

"The men ridin' with him?"

"They're all trash. Including me. They're riding away from a past that is filled with darkness and evil. You're doing the right thing."

Preacher glanced over at him. "Odd thing for a man like you to say."

"When one is dying, the truth is best, wouldn't you agree with that?"

Preacher nodded his head. "I 'spect."

"It's good to have someone near as the final moments grow closer."

Preacher looked at him. "What'd you do to turn bad?"

"I killed a man. Then another, then another. It reached the point where it simply did not matter."

Preacher noted that the man's voice was growing weaker. Now it was no more than a whisper. "I'll bury you proper."

"Thank you."

"Although I don't know why I should take the time," Preacher added.

Meeker smiled. "Because you are a man."

"Whatever that means." Preacher looked over at the outlaw. Meeker closed his eyes and died.

10

Preacher wrapped the man in the ragged blanket and buried him, piling rocks over the mound. He also buried Sharp, although not as deep or as well. He spoke no words over the graves. Preacher had his coffee and put out the fire, then swung into the saddle and began tracking the outlaws. They were heading for the high country, to the northwest, and they were doing their best to shake Preacher off their trail. The first creek they came to, they entered. They stayed with creeks until the water either played out or the creeks changed direction of flow. On the fourth day after Preacher buried Sharp and Meeker, it began snowing, and Preacher completely lost their trail.

"They holed up," he said to his horses. "They ain't far from here, but we lost 'em."

He knew to continue would be to no avail. He might wander for weeks and never cut their sign. He turned his horses west. Come the spring, and it was not far off, west was the only way open to the outlaws. That's the way they had to go, that's where Malachi and his pack of scum were hiding out, and if they still planned on striking the wagon train when it left the mission come true spring, that's where Preacher would be.

Or at least close by.

But winter was not yet ready to loosen its grasp on the high country. The snows continued to fall and the cold winds blew. It was still bitterly cold when Preacher came to within a couple days ride from the mission and rode into the camp of Windy and Rimrock. They'd been out hunting and had no luck at it. They looked up at him, nodded, and Windy pointed to the coffee pot.

"We done hunted this area out," Rimrock told Preacher, handing him a cup of coffee. "Been a lot of mouths to feed this winter. How you been, Preacher?"

"Tolerable. Seems to me like I done crisscrossed this country so many times over the past two years I begun namin' the trees and the rocks. Got some chicory root in my saddlebags."

"Where'd you come by that?" Windy asked.

"A dyin' outlaw give it to me."

"Dyin' on account of you?" Rimrock asked.

"I 'magine. Right nice feller there towards the end."

Preacher told them all that had transpired since he'd left the mission.

Windy and Rimrock exchanged glances and Preacher caught the quick looks. "Say it," he told them.

"Betina and Miles got married. So did George and Coretine," Rimrock said it quick.

"Good," Preacher replied. "That's a load off my mind. I 'spect I better not hang around the mission much, then. It might make them newlyweds nervous havin' me around. You say food is gettin' scarce?"

"They're just about out," Windy said. "And game has took to cover in all this snow and ice."

"Caleb and Carl is huntin' to the west," Rimrock added.

The men rested and talked and made another pot of coffee. When they were talked out and the coffee was gone,

Preacher stood up. "We best start foragin', then. I can't abide no thought of kids goin' hungry." He looked up at the sky. "I figure spring's a good three, four weeks off. We got our work ahead of us. I'll hunt towards the north and see you boys back at the mission when I get there."

Rimrock finally commented on the pistols belted around Preacher's waist. "That's the goddamnest rig I ever did see, Preacher. Where'd you come across them cumbersome-lookin' guns anyway?"

Preacher slowly removed the pistols from leather and handed one to each man. Windy whistled softly and Rimrock hefted the four-barrel and grinned.

"Fine, ain't they?" Preacher said.

"I'll say. Whoever made these had a love for firearms and knew what they was doin', for a fact," Windy said.

Preacher returned the guns to his holsters. "Let's go find some food for those hungry folks, boys."

Preacher hunted for two days and shot two deer, and mighty scrawny ones they was, for the winter had been hard. He skinned and dressed them and headed out for the mission, only a few hours ride away, for he had been working his way back with the first deer when he spotted the second one.

The three mountain men arrived at the mission within minutes of each other. Rimrock had killed a deer and so had Windy. But four deer wasn't going to last long with all these mouths to feed. Preacher swapped horses to give Hammer a much-needed rest and made ready to take out again when Miles approached him.

Preacher smiled and stuck out his hand for Miles to take, which he did, with a surprised look on his face. "Congratulations, boy," Preacher told him. "You lucked up and got yourself a fine woman, you did."

"I think so, Preacher. And I'm glad you approve. Aren't you going to rest before taking off again?"

"Rest when you're dead, Miles. Lots of hungry folks here whose bellies think their throat's been cut. I'm takin' a pack-horse to tote back the meat."

"If you can find any game to kill."

"I'll find it, Miles. I ain't got no choice in the matter. A body needs fat in the cold to survive. See you." He swung into the saddle and rode off, leading a packhorse.

A missionary walked up to stand for a moment beside Miles, both of them watching Preacher as he rode off. "They are hard-drinking, hard-living, and profane men, Miles. But most of them are good men. They have their scallywags among them, of course, but just think what might have happened to all these people here at the mission had not those men chosen to stay and help."

"And did you notice that Preacher is taking only a few supplies for his personal needs in order to bring back more meat?" Miles added.

"Their day is almost gone in the mountains," the missionary said, a genuine note of sadness in his voice. "Some are glad to see it gone, but I'm not. Tell you the truth, I'll really miss them. But don't tell Marcus that," he was quick to add with a smile. "Although he is much more fond of the men than he likes to admit."

Preacher didn't kid himself. This area had been hunted out for miles around, driving the animals further and further away. Now that false spring had come and gone, with mother nature coming in right behind it and dumping more snow and laying the heavy hand of cold all over the land, it was going to be difficult to find game.

But find it he and the others must.

At the end of his first full day out, Preacher hadn't even killed enough to feed himself. His supper was a skinny rabbit that he had almost had to fight a coyote over. But the next day he killed two big bucks that dressed out nicely, and he returned to the mission with the meat. Rimrock had killed a bear who had wandered out of hibernation, Windy brought in two nice deer, and Caleb and Carl each brought in a deer.

But there was no time to relax, for with so many people to feed, that meat wouldn't last two days.

Late and unexpected winter locked up the land cold and tight, and the mountain men where forced to spend every waking hour in the search for food. And the men of the wagon train did their part and more. They had become trail-tough and resourceful. They set snares for rabbits and other small game—anything to add to their meager diet.

By the time the first bits of greenery began poking out of the soil, Preacher and the other mountain men were just about wore down to a frazzle.

By the time game had once more begun coming out of shelter and moving around, and the men from the mission and the wagon train could take over the job of providing food, Preacher and his friends flopped on their beds in a crude cabin and relaxed for the first time in weeks.

"This past month has been enough to make a body swear off the human race," Caleb said. "Firs, warm winds that blow, I'm headin' for the Rockies."

"Me too," Windy and Rimrock said together.

Carl was taking the train on to the coast.

Nobody had to ask what Preacher was going to do. They looked at him, sitting on a bunk and carefully cleaning and oiling his guns. He had spent several days molding bullets.

"Snow's gone for this season," Preacher said. "Malachi and his bunch and Sutherlin and his pack of filth will be movin'. I'm thinkin' it would be best if you men stayed with the train to Oregon Territory. We got these movers this far. Be a shame to desert 'em for the human varmints this crost to where they want to settle."

"Mayhaps you be right, Preacher," Windy said. "The Rockies will be there for us."

Rimrock and Caleb nodded their heads in agreement. Caleb said, "When you takin' out, Preacher?"

"In about fifteen minutes. Malachi and his bunch are crost. I can smell 'em. And since trash seems to gather together, I 'spect Sutherlin and his gang will find them. If they ain't already done it." He stood up. "I'll see you boys at Fort Vancouver." He smiled. "I got me a pretty lady 'crost the mountains that I ain't seen in over a year. If she ain't done married up to some gospel-shouter, I might do me some sparkin' of my own." He slung his pistols around his waist and picked up his Hawken. "See you."

Preacher had been resting Hammer and the big horse was rarin' to hit the trail. Preacher got him settled down and saddled and was no more than a dot in the distance by the time the others at the mission realized he was gone.

Preacher began working in an ever-widening circle, scouring the still-cold ground for tracks. On his fifth day out, he found a hoofprint that looked familiar to him. He dismounted and more closely studied the depression in the dirt. He recognized the print as a horse belonging to one of Sutherlin's bunch. He walked the tracks for a time, memorizing the prints, and then swung into the saddle. The gang was heading as straight west as they could ride.

"Now we end it, Sutherlin," Preacher said. "You have run your race and you're about to lose."

Hammer snorted his agreement.

Preacher had him a hunch that once Malachi and Sutherlin linked up, they would ride due west and not attempt to strike the wagon train until it was about midway between the mission and The Dalles, smack in the middle of the Blue Mountains. It was a hard and backbreaking two hundred and fifty miles over the Cascades to the Willamette Valley. Sutherlin and the others would probably have plans to hit the train when the movers were exhausted.

If Preacher allowed them to do that. Which he most certainly would not.

Preacher figured Sutherlin had maybe ten men counting himself, and Malachi had about that many, maybe a few more. Say, twenty-five men all told. If Preacher could just figure out where Malachi and his pack of no-goods were hiding.

He linked up with a Yakima hunting party and ate and smoked and talked with them, slowly edging the conversation around to where he wanted it. Many Indians were notorious about not responding to direct questions, so a body had to work his way to that point little by little.

Preacher finally belched and wiped his hands on his buckskins and smiled at the subchief who was leading this hunting party. "Many bad white men live around here, so I was told."

The Yakima returned the smile. "Preacher walks all around what he has on his mind. Preacher is like us, one with the land and all things living on it. We are free people. Say what you wish, Preacher."

"Any white men livin' crost-by that you know of?"

The subchief opened and closed one hand three times. "That many live in old lodges that were abandoned. They are unclean people. Smell very bad. One of them is a child of the gods." That would be Ansel—crazy. "None of them wash properly. My people will not go near them for fear of catching some horrible disease." He pointed west. "Two days ride."

"You seen any other white men?"

The subchief nodded, his face grim. "Ten men ride one day ahead of you. Are more wagons coming, Preacher?" he asked abruptly changing the subject.

"Yes. And they will come always, each time bringing more people." Preacher was totally honest with Indians— just another reason he got along well with most of them. "Don't even think of stopping them. It would be impossible and the punishment would be harsh for your people."

"Little Hawk knows this. But he does not have to like the knowledge."

"I don't like it either," Preacher said.

"The whites come in and steal our land and we are supposed to behave as the Sanpoils?"

The Sanpoils were a small tribe who lived along about a one hundred miles stretch of the Columbia River. They were totally peaceful, and did not believe in warfare of any kind. They would not even revenge loss of life. Preacher doubted that any of the tribe would survive when the wagon trains really started moving through.

Preacher chose his words carefully before speaking. "I can't answer that, Little Hawk. Not an' give you no answer that would please everybody concerned."

"Whites are that many?"

"Oh, yes. More than ten of you could ever count in a lifetime. A hundred times over the number of buffalo that used to roam the land. A thousand times over. Makes my head hurt just thinkin' about it."

Little Hawk shook his head, his expression sad. "We are doomed, then."

"You will be if you fight them," Preacher said solemnly, thinking: And you damn sure will be if you don't fight them. Preacher knew that massive changes in everybody's lives was just around the corner. And he didn't like it any more than the Indians did. "You can't win by fighting them."

The Yakimas moved on, hunting game to feed their hungry camps, and Preacher moved on toward the west. He, too, was hunting game, so to speak.

Preacher was closing in on the gang fast, while still riding with caution. But even with all that going for him, he nearly got his head blowed off.

11

Preacher had just turned his head at movement off the faint trail when the rifle boomed. The slug tore a narrow furrow in Preacher's scalp and blew his hat off his head. Preacher hit the ground and lay still, his Hawken in hand. Slowly, he cocked the rifle and waited, motionless. His head throbbed with pain and he had no idea how bad hurt he was, but he suspected not too bad, for his vision was still good and he knew who he was.

He waited.

"I got him!" a man shouted. "By the Lord, Moffett. I kilt the bastard, I did."

"You watch yourself around him, Beans. He's tricky."

"He's *dead*, Moffett. I shot him right 'tween the eyes, I did. Blood all over the place."

Any fool knows that head wounds bleed like crazy for a few seconds, you igit! Preacher thought. *Now come on to me and let's settle this matter.*

"I reckon you right, Beans," Moffett said. "His head shore looks a mess to me."

Boot steps drew closer. Preacher's eyes were slitted and

he could see the man stop, laugh, and then twist to turn around. "He's shore deader than hell, Moffett." He laughed in a nasty way. "Why, I can practically feel that money in my hand. I'm agonna—"

"Die," Preacher said, coming to his knees and blowing a hole in Beans Speer. He lunged to the other side of the trail before Beans had hit the ground.

"Goddamn you!" Moffett screamed, and put a ball not half a foot from where Preacher lay.

Both men were then frantically trying to reload faster than the other, for the range was far too great for accurate pistol shooting. Like a fool, Moffett was standing in plain sight, in a clearing by the old trail.

Preacher swung the Hawken to his shoulder just as Moffett threw his rod to the ground. Preacher's Hawken roared and Moffett dropped his rifle and doubled over, the ball taking him in the belly. He screamed in pain and fell to his knees, both hands holding his burning belly.

Preacher took his time reloading and then jerked the powder horn from Beans. By its weight he could tell it was full. Even though Beans's rifle was of a different caliber than Preacher's rifle, he took the man's shot pouch, for the lead could be melted down and made into balls that would fit his Hawken.

He looked down at Beans. His ball had taken the man in the side at very nearly point-blank range and had torn through lungs and probably nicked the heart before exiting out the other side. Preacher walked up to where Moffett was kneeling on the ground. The man's face was pale and there was a ghastly look in his frightened eyes.

"You're a devil," Moffett said, looking at Preacher's bloody face. The dust from the trail had helped to stop the bleeding. Just as soon as Moffett passed, Preacher cleaned the wound proper and said, "I been called worse. Where's your buddies?"

"You go to hell, I say!"

Preacher turned to leave.

"Wait!" Moffett called, panic in his voice. Preacher turned around. "You're not going to leave me here to die alone, are you?"

"Why not? You ain't inclined to talk to me none."

"They're miles up the trail, man. I wouldn't lie to you moments from death."

"Maybe. Maybe not."

"I told you where they was," Moffett gasped out the words. "Don't leave me here to die alone. Please."

Preacher fetched his horses and picketed them on graze. Then he cleaned out the wound on his head, which started it bleeding again. He held a piece of cloth against the wound until the bleeding stopped. Moffett watched him in silence.

"I ain't no bad person," Moffett finally spoke.

Preacher looked at the man.

"I ain't," Moffett insisted, after fighting unsuccessfully to hold back a groan of pain. "I ain't. I was forced into this life."

"If you want me to stick around, you better pick another subject to bump your gums about. 'Cause I sure don't want to listen to this."

"I went to church as a boy."

"You should have paid more attention to what the minister had to say."

"We was poor."

"One more word and I'm gone." Preacher rose from the rock he was sitting on.

"Wait! Talk to me."

"I'm gonna drag your friend into the woods."

"You ain't gonna give him no Christian burial?"

"No. Shut up."

Preacher returned in a few minutes and looked at Moffett. "I was hopin' you'd passed by now."

"I ain' never seen no man as cold as you. You just ain't got no sympathy for them that's less fortunate."

Preacher laughed aloud. "You wastin' your time tryin' to convince me. You got your work cut out for you when you meet your Maker. And I wish you'd hurry up." Preacher looked at the man. It wouldn't be long now. For all his tough talk, he did not take death lightly. Preacher was just a very hard man in a land and a time that allowed few mistakes. He softened his tone when he again spoke. "You got any kin you want me to try to contact?"

"None that would give a damn."

"That is sad. Tell me about Sutherlin."

"I don't know much. He's cold, though, mighty cold. Nearabouts as cold as you."

"How many men do this leave him?"

"Seven, countin' himself." The man's voice was very weak.

"Where is Malachi Pardee hidin' out?"

"Just west of here. Some Red Injuns told us. Sutherlin knows exactly. I don't." He closed his eyes and began to weep.

Preacher tried to work up some sympathy for the man. He could not. It's hard to feel sorry for a man who just tried to kill you. "I'll bury you," Preacher finally said. "I can do that much, I reckon."

"Thank you. I'm sorry for the hard things I said about you. I'm sorry for the hurt I've caused other people. I'm . . ."

Whatever else he had to say stayed unsaid. Preacher found the men's horses, took their bedrolls, and wrapped both of them up in dirty blankets. He dug a shallow grave and planted both the dead outlaws, then stripped bridle and saddle from the horses and set them free.

Preacher stood by the grave for a moment, thinking that wherever good people go, bad people always follow. He reckoned it was the same all over the world. Preacher tried to think of some words to say. He couldn't think of a thing.

He stayed where he was for a time, letting his horses graze and water and roll. He built a small fire and had himself some coffee he'd taken from the outlaws' supplies. He didn't know where they'd gotten it, and didn't want to dwell on that for long.

Preacher was suddenly tired. Very, very tired. He figured a part of that came from his slight head wound, but most of it come from the fact that it had been a hard winter, and bein' constantly on the lookout for people tryin' to kill you was wearin' on a body. He carefully put out the fire and moved on for a couple of miles, until he found himself a good spot to camp. He was rolled up in his blankets before good dark and didn't wake up until near dawn. He figured he'd slept a good ten or eleven hours and he felt refreshed.

He chewed on jerky while the coffee water boiled and then he was in the saddle again, putting the careful miles behind him. He was grimly amused by the thought that when Moffett and Beans didn't show back up, Sutherlin would know that his gunmen had failed to kill Preacher and that he was on their trail. By this time, Sutherlin had probably linked up with the Pardee gang and they were planning their evil deeds.

Preacher looked up at the sun. Near noon. He would be getting close now. He couldn't make a plan 'cause he had no idea of the layout. Preacher reined up and stripped his horses of their burdens and picketed them, then he took his bow and quiver, and plenty of shot and powder for rifle and pistols. He started out on foot, staying off the trail and in the brush as much as possible, stopping often to listen and look and smell for smoke. Finally he caught a faint odor of smoke. Slipping through the brush, he pulled up short at the sight. An Indian family on the move had stopped to rest and eat. A man, his woman, and two kids about four and six, Preacher reckoned. Yakimas. Preacher called out in their language and stepped into the small clearing.

They eyed him suspiciously, noticing how heavily he was armed, but still waved him to the fire and pointed to the venison steaks that were cooking.

"I am sad that I have nothing to offer you," Preacher said, squatting down.

"That you come in peace is enough," the man said. "I thought for a moment that you were part of the bad white men who stayed the winter not far from here."

"I hunt them to kill them. I am called Preacher."

"Ahh!" the woman spoke. "White Wolf."

"Yes."

"Eat, eat," the man said. "We will talk."

"Has more white men joined the group?"

"Yes. Yesterday. We hid until they had all gone."

"They rode west?"

"Yes. A large band of them." He opened and closed one hand five times. "They are all very much afraid of White Wolf."

Preacher ate and thanked the Yakima man and wife and returned to his horses, quickly saddling up and pulling out. The Yakima had said he had slipped in close to the men and overheard the man who appeared to be in charge say something about The Dalles. He said the men all smelled very bad and he wondered why they did not wash themselves. Preacher did not ask why the man and his woman and kids were out alone from their tribe. It wasn't any of his business and wouldn't have been a polite thing to ask. They might have been traveling to visit relatives on one side of the family or another. That the wife had spoken Preacher's name before her husband did told him that she was probably the daughter of a tribal leader with some power.

Preacher rode on to where the brave had told him the Pardees had wintered and found the dugouts. Lord, did they stink. A buzzard would have a hard time staying in these things. Preacher quickly backed out, feeling like he was in desperate need of a bath.

The Yakima told him the gang was heading for The Dalles, or close to it. Fine. Preacher would be waiting for them.

* * *

Malachi and his gang, freshly reenforced by Sutherlin and what was left of his party, and now numbering nearly twenty-five rather odious men, rode west with confidence. For the first time this year Malachi felt like they just might beat Preacher and be rid of the man once and for all. And then things could get back to normal.

So he had lost a couple of men back down the trail. That wasn't the end of the world. Sutherlin still wasn't sure whether they had been killed or had just given up and fled from Preacher. He tended to believe the latter. But Sutherlin, like Malachi, did believe their luck was about to change for the better and Preacher's luck had run out.

What none of the men could know, and wouldn't have believed it had they been told, was that Preacher had rafted down the river, arrived several days before them, and was waiting for the outlaw gang to show up.

12

"They's a place just up ahead that'll be perfect," Malachi said to Sutherlin and Son. "The wagons got to stop there 'fore they tackle the hills. They'll be all tuckered out and will rest for a time; maybe spend the night. That's where we'll hit them."

"Lookie yonder," a thug named Ed Murphy said, pointing to the river. "A raft, and a big one, too."

"It's old," Clubb said. "Somebody used it and then abandoned it. See where some of the ropes has rotted and then somebody else come along and used thick vines to patch it up."

"I'll check it out," Mueller said.

"Why?" Clubb said.

"Because I want to," Mueller replied, as he walked down the slope to the river's edge.

"I'll go with you," Ed said.

Both men inspected the big raft, which was almost too big for one man to handle, and looked at each other.

"Vines is fresh," Mueller called back up to the trail.

"So what?" Lester returned the shout. "Some movers used it and then left it."

"I don't think so," Mueller muttered to Ed as both men stood up from their squat and started back up the slope.

"You think—?" Ed broke it off.

"Yeah. I think so."

A Hawken boomed and Ed went down, a huge hole in the center of his forehead. Mueller hit the ground, scrambling for cover as the gang scattered.

Preacher shifted positions and reloaded swiftly. He held the high ground in brush and rocks and was approachable only from the front. He was under no illusions that the fight would end here, but he could do some fearful damage to the gang before he pulled out.

Both Sutherlin and Malachi Pardee lay on the ground and cursed Preacher. They knew it wasn't Indians or another gang of outlaws. It was Preacher. Their constant and unforgiving adversary. For near 'bout a year now, the man had been on Malachi's back, very nearly destroying what had, at one time, been the most feared outlaw gang in all the West.

Now look at them. Malachi's thoughts were savage and tinged with bitterness.

Ansel jumped up and began shouting and grunting and waving his arms. Preacher held his fire. He did not want to shoot the fool, and he wouldn't shoot him except as a last resort.

Valiant jerked his brother down to the ground and pulled him back to the safety of cover.

Dirk lay on the ground and cussed Preacher until he was breathless. His eyes were wild and he was trembling with rage. The bastard had burned him out and hunted him like some sort of wild animal. No more, Dirk made up his mind. No more. He had taken all of this he was going to take. He rolled from cover and dashed to the timber, running in a zigzag movement.

Preacher held his fire and let him come on.

With Dirk running up one side of the hill, Lester decided to try the other side. Preacher ended those thoughts by putting a ball through Lester's brisket that doubled him over and sent him rolling back down the slope.

Damn! Sutherlin thought, just as Preacher started a huge rock rolling and crashing down the hill. The horses went into a panic and bolted, running in all directions. A man jumped up and tried to grab the reins of his horse. What he got was a hole in his side, the ball busting out the other side. The man dropped to the ground, dead.

Dirk chanced another short run and made it, closing the distance.

"Everybody stay down," Sutherlin called. "I do believe Dirk is going to make it."

Dirk didn't.

He got about fifty yards from Preacher and his boot hung on a loose rock and the man went rolling and tumbling down the grade, breaking bones on his trip down to the trail by the river. Dirk bounced once and then lay still on the rutted trail, unconscious, one arm and one leg broken badly. His scalp was torn open in several places and bleeding.

Malachi looked up at the sky and shook his head. Hell, it wasn't even midmorning. It was going to be a long day.

Preacher pulled out just about noon. But he left behind him a terrible scene. Five dead and Dirk out of commission. Preacher found several of the outlaws' horses and removed bridle and saddle, tossing them into the river. He found a full powder horn and kept that. Then he found him a good spot about a mile from the original ambush spot and waited.

"Let's pull out of here, Malachi," Valiant suggested. "You know Preacher is waitin' for us up the trail. And look over yonder." He pointed. "They's Injuns all up and down the ridges. They been watchin', enjoyin' the show. Preacher done whupped us, brother. We gotta admit that."

The Indians, from several tribes, hooted and laughed at the outlaws, but stayed well out of rifle range. They had heard that the outlaw gang was coming and that Preacher, the White Wolf, was going to kill them all. Indians enjoyed a good fight, for courage was what they respected the most. And this was going to be something fun to watch.

"Dirty, stinking savages," Sutherlin muttered darkly. "Up there ridiculing us."

"Why don't they attack?" Doc Judd asked.

What the outlaws couldn't know is that Preacher had recruited the Indians. He'd had plenty of time to do that, arriving several days before the outlaw gang.

Clubb had scouted back east of the ambush site and walked back to the main group, a grim look on his dirty, pale and frightened face. "Injuns has blocked the trail," he told the men, after pouring a cup of coffee. "One shouted out to me that we got to go on. They ain't gonna let us go back . . . even if we was of a mind to do that."

Kenrick Pardee sat down wearily on a log and sighed long. "That's it, then." His tone was deadlike. "Preacher's done gone and set up firm with the savages. Hell, he ain't no better than a savage hisself. We should have guessed he'd eventual do something like this. We ain't got no choice in the matter. We got to push on."

"What did the Injuns say they'd do if we was to try to head back?" Big Max asked.

Clubb looked at the man. "They said they believed that we would not die well."

Preacher made his coffee and chewed on a piece of jerky and waited. He knew the end was very near for the gang of cutthroats. He had them in a box they could not get out of. The Indians he'd talked with had said they would not attack the white outlaws. But they would certainly make them think they would. And Indians could be very convincing without saying a word.

Preacher put out his fire and took Hawken to hand. He walked up the trail a ways, threw back his head, and howled like a great gray timber wolf. The wild and savage call drifted down the banks of the river, faintly touching the band of outlaws. They looked at one another, fear in their eyes. Above them, on both sides of the river, Indians stood silently, watching them.

Malachi stood up and gripped his rifle. "I never took water from no man in my life. I'll die 'fore I do." He started walking up the trail. "Let's go, brothers," he called over his shoulder. "We got to accept the challenge and maintain the dignity of our good name. Never let it be said that no Pardee wasn't an honorable man."

Sutherlin looked at the man in amazement. He didn't believe he had ever before in his life heard such drivel. But picked up his rifle and waved what was left of his men forward.

"What happens if we kill Preacher?" Isaac asked. "I mean, with the savages?"

"They let us go," Clubb said. "So we better fight like we ain't never fit before. Or start makin' our peace with God."

A man called George was stumbling along with tears streaming and streaking his dirty face. "I jist don't wanna die. I don't wanna die."

"You should have thought of that 'fore you crossed the line from good to bad," Curtis told him.

"I didn't have no choice in the matter," George sobbed.

"Shit!" Curtis replied.

"We all have a choice," Sutherlin said in a firm voice. "It's balderdash that anyone thinks we don't. To a very large degree, we all control our destinies."

The men had left Dirk where he lay on the trail. His head busted open, limbs broken, and bleeding from internal injuries. They had left him without a second thought. Although a man called Jeff had taken the time to rip Dirk's watch from his dirty vest and stick it in his pocket. No point in leaving a good timepiece with a dying man.

"Why the hell did we even come out to this godforsaken

land?" Delbert asked, tossing the question out to anyone who might have an answer.

"I don't believe God forsake this land," Kenrick told him. "I think He don't even know it's *here!*"

Delbert opened his mouth to speak and a ball took him square in the chest and knocked him flat on the ground. The men left the trail and hunted for cover.

Preacher was pulling out all the stops now. He had loaded up three rifles and laid them out. He reloaded and waited, his eyes watching the suddenly deserted trail just below him.

"Did anybody see the smoke?" Kenrick called out hoarsely.

"Delbert damn shore didn't," Jeff replied, eyeballing the body of the outlaw. "I'd like to have them boots of his'n. Mine's plumb wore out."

"They ain't worth dyin' for," Valiant told him.

Sutherlin cut his eyes to the Pardee brother. We're all going to die right here, he thought. And I'm going to die with this trash if I don't start using my wits and think about getting out of here.

Sutherlin looked around him. He had chosen very good cover, on the river's side. He cut his eyes to Doc Judd, who had jumped into cover with him. "When the rest of them move out, we stay put," he whispered. "If we don't, we're going to be picked off one by one."

"What about the Indians?" Doc said, returning the whisper.

Sutherlin thought about that for a moment. "We'll just have to take our chances. Who would you rather face, them or Preacher?"

"That's easy. I'm with you."

Malachi and his followers began slipping up the trail, staying with the cover, now lush and green in full spring, vegetation blossoming everywhere. Sutherlin and Doc Judd stayed still and quiet. A silent tribute to the awesome fighting power of the mountain man called Preacher.

Something in Ansel's warped brain straightened out and a

voice in his head told him not to follow his brothers and to hunker down in some bushes and be quiet. Ansel slipped off the trail and slid down the riverbank. He crouched in brush and closed his eyes.

The Indians watching the men knew that Ansel was touched by the gods and they were wary of him. The actions of Sutherlin and Doc Judd had not escaped their eyes, either. Let the white men be afraid of them. Fear was sometimes a good thing.

Preacher lay in cover and watched the men slowly advance toward his position.

"You're a murderin' no-count. Preacher!" Malachi shouted. "I challenge you to step out here and fight me fair and square, man to man. How 'bout that, Preacher? You got the belly to face me eyeball to eyeball?"

Sure, Preacher thought. And as soon as I show myself I'll be shot full of holes.

"He's afeard of us, brother!" Valiant shouted. "We got him on the run." Valiant threw caution and good sense—the latter something he was woefully short of—to the wind and stepped out onto the trail.

Preacher sighted him in and the Hawken boomed, the ball dropping Valiant where he stood.

Kenrick looked at his brother, sprawled in death, and felt like puking. A wild rage seized the outlaw. He cursed Preacher, shouting out the black oaths from his cover.

Preacher waited.

"How come you doin' this to us, Preacher?" Malachi shouted. "We ain't done you no harm."

Preacher could no longer contain his tongue. "How many innocent people have you killed, Malachi?" he shouted. "How many children have you raped and sold into bondage? Answer me, you son of a bitch!"

"That ain't none of your affair, Preacher!" Malachi screamed. "Nobody made you the law out here. Git on out and leave us be. Ain't you done enough harm to my good family?"

"Not until I kill you all," Preacher told him.

Clubb left his cover and made a run for the rocks to the left of Preacher's position. Preacher knocked a leg out from under the man, the ball of lead shattering the man's knee. Clubb screamed and went rolling down the grade, losing his rifle along the way. He rolled across the trail and down the bank, landing in the river. The last anybody saw of him, he was caught up in the current and drifting downstream, screaming and flailing his arms.

"I can't swim!" he called out weakly. "Halp!" The current took him on and around a bend, then he was out of sight.

Ansel thought it was very funny and had to stifle his urge to giggle.

Sutherlin and Doc Judd looked at each other, both sharing the same thought: If they could somehow make the river, they'd swim for their lives.

Indians were sitting, squatting, and standing on both sides of the river, watching the show. This fight would provide them with many hours of talk around the fires. The one man who was called by many names, including Bloody Knife, fighting alone against many, was surely the bravest of the brave.

Mueller called out in a foreign tongue and leaped from cover, dashing to rocks below Preacher's position. Preacher fired too late and missed the man. Now his smoke was seen and the outlaws blasted at him, the lead howling and shrieking all around him. Preacher shifted locations, moving away from the river. Mueller panted up to the rocks and cursed when he saw that Preacher was gone.

The big man turned and felt a heavy blow strike his chest. The pain hit him a split second later. He looked down in amazement at the shaft of the arrow sticking out of his chest. Mueller fell backward, all sprawled out on top of the rocks.

He stretched out his arms, sighed once, and the murderer and rapist died, his face to the sky.

"Damn," Big Max whispered. Then he made up his mind. "Preacher!" he called. "Big Max Delvin here. I'm gone if you'll let me. I'll leave this country and you'll not see my face here no more. How about it?"

Malachi turned around and shot the man through the chest with a pistol. "It just don't pay to associate with trash," he told Kenrick. "Cain't trust 'em to have no honor."

13

This is not happening, Son thought, looking back up the bloody and body-littered trail. One man could not have caused all this havoc. But he knew that one man had done it. He silently cursed Preacher. Son looked around for any of his men. He could not find a one left.

Then the thought came to him: Where was Sutherlin and Doc Judd? He had not seen either man in a hour or so. He could see Malachi and Kenrick. There was Isaac. Jeff. Dill was over there. Good God, was this all that was left? Impossible. He looked all around. The Indians were gone. He blinked and looked again. They had vanished.

Sutherlin and Doc Judd had noticed that several minutes before Son. The two men had begun working their way back down the trail. They made their way slowly and cautiously, always keeping in the brush. Once they were out of rifle range of Preacher, they began to breathe easier. They found two saddled horses, swung into the saddle, and lit out down the trail.

Then they received yet another shock for that day.

Armed Indians blocked the trail. A lot of armed Indians.

Doc and Sutherlin reined up and stared. There was no way around the Indians.

One Indian rode his pony away from the others and pointed his rifle back up the trail. Doc and Sutherlin didn't need an interpreter. They got the message loud and clear.

"Can't we talk about this?" Sutherlin asked.

"No," the Yakima said.

"I have money."

"Don't want money."

"There are guns and powder and shot up ahead."

"From the dead. We will have those anyway." He smiled. "Yours, too. Ver' soon."

The two men cursed under their breath and slowly turned their horses around and rode back up the trail.

"Where's Ansel?" Malachi asked Kenrick.

"I ain't seen him. Maybe he broke and run and got clear, you reckon?"

"I hope. He's a good boy, that one is."

"Malachi?"

"Yeah, boy?"

"I guess we 'bout run our string out, ain't we?"

"Looks that way. But we've had us a time, ain't we?"

"We shore have. How many squallin' and kickin' and bitin' and scratchin' women and girls you reckon we've held down and humped, brother?"

"White women?"

"All of 'em."

"Oh . . . that'd be hard to say. I recollect the time over on the—"

His words were cut short by the crash of Preacher's Hawken. About fifty yards ahead of them, in a bend of the trail, Jeff slowly rolled out onto the trail, a large hole right between his eyes.

Malachi looked at the last of Sutherlin's men and shook his head. "Ansel," he called softly. "If you can hear me, listen to me. I want you to stay hid. Stay hid and don't move no matter what happens. Stay hid 'til come the dawnin' in the mornin'. Then you slip down to that raft we seen and get the hell gone from here. Good luck, boy."

"I'll be damned if he will!" Sutherlin spoke from the saddle, only a few yards behind the brothers. "I'll kill the goofy son of a bitch myself. Come out, you stupid oaf. Come out here and face me."

"Damn your eyes, you black-hearted bastard!" Malachi screamed at the man. He stood up, leveled his rifle, and blew Sutherlin out of the saddle before the man could protest.

Doc Judd's rifle crashed and Malachi went down to his knees, belly-shot.

Kenrick screamed curses and cocked a pistol and shot Doc Judd in the throat, almost tearing the man's head from his shoulders. Doc toppled backward from the saddle and Kenrick stood up from his crouch just as Sutherlin leveled a pistol and blew a large hole in Kenrick's head. Ansel roared and grunted and slobbered out of the brush, a pistol in each hand just as Son was running around the bend in the narrow road to see what in the hell was going on. He froze at the sight.

Ansel cocked and leveled his pistol at the dying Sutherlin and grunted and slobbered all down the front of his filthy shirt.

"You ignorant bastard," Sutherlin told him.

"No, Ansel!" Son shouted, waving his arms frantically. "No, boy. Don't do it. Don't shoot that man."

Ansel grinned at the man for a moment. Slowly he nodded his shaggy head. He grunted a time or two. "Aw rat," he said, and shot Son in the chest.

Son sat down hard in the rutted and bumpy trail. "Why, boy," he said. "I think you've killed me."

Ansel bobbed his head up and down and grinned.

"Git out of here, Ansel," Malachi groaned. "Run, boy."

"Go on, Ansel," Kenrick said. "Them Injuns around here

nor no other place ain't gonna bother you 'cause you're titched in the head. Run, boy. Git gone from this killin' place."

"Squirrelly bastard shot me," Son groaned. "Shot me. And I was always kinda partial to him, too."

"He liked you, Son," Malachi said. "He really did."

"Well . . . how come the son of a bitch *shot* me?"

"He ain't neither no son of a bitch!" Malachi said, then pondered on that for a few seconds. "Well . . . maybe."

Sutherlin cursed the addled Ansel and lifted another pistol to shoot Ansel and Ansel put his feet to work. He whooped and hollered once and then hopped over the side of the bank and disappeared.

Kenrick lifted a pistol and blew the top of Sutherlin's head slap off.

Preacher had left his cover and was squatting above the men, watching it all, his hands filled with pistols, shaking his head at the wild scene.

Ansel ran down the bank and to the raft. He untied the rope and jumped on, grabbing the pole and shoving off. He went floating merrily down the river, singing church songs at the top of his lungs.

The Indians watched him leave and all made the sign of a crazy person. Ansel would not be bothered by any Indian.

"There was two more of your gang got clear for a minute or two," Preacher spoke from above the dead and dying. "They jumped in the river and tried to swim clear. I don't think they made it."

"What happens to us?" Kenrick asked.

"I reckon you'll just lay there and expire," Preacher told him.

"I wish I'd never laid eyes on you, Preacher," Malachi said, his voice very weak.

"That's probably true."

"I hate you, Preacher," Son said.

"Man shouldn't ride off to his judgment day with no hate

in his heart," Preacher admonished the man. "That wouldn't set well with the Lord, I'm thinkin'."

"Who gives a damn what you think?" Kenrick said.

Preacher tried his best to look deeply hurt and extremely offended. He couldn't quite pull it off. "My dear sainted mommy did."

"You didn't have no mommy," Malachi said. "You was thrown up here on the earth from the hellfires."

"My daddy would have broke off a limb and wore your ass out if he heard you say that, Malachi. My daddy was strong on them thumb-sized branches, he was."

Several Indians had gathered around, picking up rifles and pistols and shot pouches and powder horns.

"Y'all can have their scalps if you've a mind to," Preacher told them. "But I'd appreciate it if you'd wait until they's all dead 'fore you jerked 'em off."

"Jesus Christ!" Son yelled.

"He make prayer to white man's God?" a Yakima questioned.

"Well . . . sort of," Preacher replied.

Kenrick laid his head down and rattled and died.

"My brother's daid!" Malachi wailed. "Oh, Lord!"

"He make prayer to God?" the Yakima asked.

"In a way," Preacher told him.

"White man pray funny."

"Some do. But if you think this is something, you should have seem them all-day singin's and shoutin's we used to have back in the hills. I got me enough religion in one day to last a whole lifetime. That gospel shouter damn near drowned me in that cold-ass creek that day I turned to the Lord."

"You?" Malachi sneered.

"Yeah, me. I been baptized."

"In what? A keg of gunpowder."

"You 'bout to make me mad, Malachi."

"Help me, goddamnit!" Son squalled.

"Help you do what?" Preacher asked. "You doin' a right good job of passin' without no help from me."

"Well, I was washed in the blood of the lamb myself!" Malachi said.

"You was washed in blood, all right," Preacher said. "But not of no lamb."

"I hate you," Malachi said.

"I'll see you in hell, Preacher!" Son yelled. Then he screamed. "Oh, God, it hurts, it hurts." He jerked a couple of times and bought the farm.

Preacher stood up and holstered his pistols.

"Don't leave me for the savages, Preacher!" Malachi whispered.

"You can't give me no good reason why I shouldn't."

"I'm a Christian."

Preacher spat on the ground. "Well, I'll just consider them Yakimas Romans then." He turned and walked away.

14

Ansel came up on a very waterlogged Clubb clinging to a log and dragged him on board the raft. A few miles further down, Isaac waved frantically from the north shore of the river at the men in the raft and Ansel somehow managed to get the raft over to the outlaw and get him on board.

"Just get us away from here," Isaac panted. "Get me away from that mountain man from Hell. I ain't never gonna go past the Mississippi again. I swear on the Good Book I ain't never gonna do it."

"What are you gonna do once we're safe?" Clubb asked with a groan, his shattered knee swollen and throbbing with pain.

"Farm," Isaac said. "Go to church and become a Christian. Find me a good woman and settle down. Never again will I raise a hand against a fellow man. Or woman," he added.

Ansel giggled.

Preacher pointed his horse's nose east, heading back to intercept the wagon train. He stopped briefly to look at Dirk. The Englishman lay dead by the trail. "You should have stayed in England," Preacher said, then lifted the reins and rode on.

A hundred yards further on, he came up on a gut-shot and dying man. "Who the hell are you?"

"Curt Morgan," the man gasped. "No, you didn't shoot me. Sutherlin stabbed while I was tryin' to get away from you. Him and that damn Doc Judd both stuck me."

Preacher stepped down and squatted by the man. Curt had been stabbed twice, once in the chest and once in the belly. There was nothing Preacher could do for him and told him so.

"I know it. I'm done for. I hooked up with this bunch about three weeks ago. Knew I was makin' a mistake when I done it. They all dead?"

"Near 'bouts."

Curt nodded his head. "A sorry lot they was, too. I tried to get shut of them, but them crazy damn Pardees said they'd shoot me if I tried. Stay with me. I ain't got long."

"I'll stay with you."

"I ain't never seen nobody like you in all my life, Preacher. Nobody in their right mind tackles twenty-odd men alone."

"Somebody had to," Preacher said simply. "What was left turned on each other. Damnest thing I ever seen."

"Don't let the savages get me, Preacher."

Preacher smiled. "These Yakimas are friendly. They was just runnin' a bluff like I asked them to. They wouldn't have hurt none of you had you tried to leave."

Morgan shook his head. "We was suckered."

"Right down the line."

"Well, I'll be damned." Morgan smiled for a second, then closed his eyes and died.

"Probably," Preacher said.

Days later, Preacher hooked up with the wagon train just as they were making camp for the night. He accepted a cup of coffee from Rimrock and sank wearily to the ground, stretching out with a sigh.

"Y'all ain't got nothin' to fight but the elements from

here on out," Preacher told them, as movers began gathering around. "The gang of brigands is gone. Three or four got clear, but I 'magine they're headin' east just as fast as they can."

He did not elaborate and nobody asked him to. The mountain men knew they would hear the story later from Indians. Preacher was already a legend in the Big Lonesome, and whatever he did was usually remembered by one tribe or another and talked and sung about.

"Where you bound for, Preacher?" Rimrock asked.

"The Rockies. I got me a cravin' to be alone for a time. I think I'll head way down deep in the mountains and just do nothin' for a while. I was goin' on to the Coast to see a little filly, but I changed my mind. I might get myself into a trap I couldn't get out of."

He drank his coffee and relaxed for the first time in days. He stayed by the fire as the wagon train pulled out early the next morning. The pioneers waved at him as they rode and walked past, and Preacher returned the farewells. A few moments later, the silence wrapped itself around Preacher.

While he had the safety of others around him, Preacher had taken a bath the past afternoon and washed his long-handles. He reckoned he'd gotten most of the fleas off him and discouraged what remained.

He lay back against his saddle and relaxed by the fire, a fresh pot of coffee on the rocks by the fire. His horses grazed nearby and it was a comforting sound. A pleasurable sound. What else does a man need? Preacher pondered. The Indians are right in a lot of ways, he thought. The white man worries about things that are not important. The Injun don't have no watches or clocks so he don't know whether it's nine o'clock in the mornin' or two o'clock in the afternoon and don't give a damn. Time takes care of itself.

A wolf pack loped up to scavenge amid what the movers had left behind in the garbage pile. They lowered their heads and looked at Preacher, sprawled by the fire.

"Go ahead," he told them. "I ain't gonna bother you."

Preacher had never been afraid of wolves and they had never bothered him. Unlike most men, Preacher had taken the time as a boy to understand their ways and pay heed to what he had learned, and to keep on learning about their ways. That was all it took—that and a bit of caution. Don't make no sudden moves around them, don't get between a male and his mate, and don't never try to make a pet out of one, for that was impossible. A wolf is a wild animal and one can't tame no wild animal. It wasn't fair to the animal to even try.

He'd known of men breeding dogs with wolves. He didn't approve of that. A dog is a dog and a wolf is a wolf. Problem was, when you done something like that, a body never knew which side was gonna be the dominant one. If it was the wolf, the animal might turn on you. If it was the dog, what the hell had you accomplished? It went agin the order of things. Nature knew what it was doin', and Preacher didn't believe in jackin' around with nature.

The wolves snarled and mock-fought and tussled over this and that and Preacher watched them and was content. They had some pups with them and the mother and father was teachin' them things they would need to survive.

The big male, and he was a big one, walked over to where Preacher lay, staying about twenty-five feet from the man. Preacher didn't look the wolf in the eyes, for that was a sign of challenge and he damn sure didn't want to challenge no one-hundred-and-fifty-pound timber wolf to nothin'. When the wolf understood that Preacher was subservient to him, and meant him no harm, he shook his big head and rejoined the pack. Occasionally he would glance over to where Preacher lay by the fire.

"Don't never trust no human, brother wolf," Preacher spoke to him. "That would be a big mistake. Stay clear of humans, for they're afraid of you, and whatever a human person is afeard of, they tend to kill instead of understandin'.

You run wild and free and wonderful like God intended you to do, and stay shut of humans."

After a time, the pack moved on and Preacher began packing up his gear. The wilderness lay all about him, clean and fresh, except for the pile of garbage the movers had left behind. And that irritated the mountain man. Why the hell can't people clean up after themselves and leave things as they found 'em? Why the hell do people think they have the right to come in and mess up whatever they touch? 'Fore long they'll be a goddamn garbage pile stretchin' from the Mississippi clear to the Pacific Ocean, Preacher thought sourly.

Why the hell can't we have a place that's left wild and free and untouched just like nature intended it to be?

He threw back his head and howled. In the distance, in the timber, a wolf answered his call, then another one joined in, and soon the pack was talking to him. Preacher grinned.

Felt good to be one with the wilderness.

15

Preacher headed southeast. He planned on taking his time and just enjoy being alone with no place in particular to go. Eventually he planned on lighting down around Bent's Fort, on the Arkansas in southeastern Colorado.

But that was subject to change, of course.

Preacher stopped often just to be doing nothing; but really he was doing something: he was *seeing* this land, all pure and untouched, for what could possibly be the last time. For once the movers started westward, there would be no stopping them. And it had started, and Preacher knew it.

Preacher rode across mountains, and sweated across desert country. But he knew where the water holes and the creeks were. He talked with friendly Indians and avoided those painted for war. In Nevada, one bunch did give him a run for it, but when three caught up with him and Preacher uncorked those fearsome pistols of his and left three braves shot all to hell and gone on the ground, the others wisely decided to let him be.

And there were cabins being built in the dampest places. Men were bringing their families out into the wilderness to live. Why, in one two-hundred-mile stretch, Preacher saw three brand-new cabins. He never heard of such a fool thing.

He just had to stop at the third one. Two kids and a woman run off into a cellar thing and slammed the door closed at the sight of him, whilst the man leveled a musket at him.

"Put that damn fool thing down, pilgrim," Preacher told him. "I didn't ride up here to do you no harm."

"What are you?" the man asked, not lowering the musket one inch.

"I'm a monkey from the Dark Continent. Hell's bells, what do you think I am?"

"I don't know. I ain't talked to no one 'ceptin' my wife and younguns for pert near a year." He lowered the musket. "I reckon you're human, for a fact."

"Thank you," Preacher said dryly. "Now can I get down and water my good horses and myself?"

"Oh, sure. You can see why we might be skittish about strangers, though, can't you?"

"Out here, it pays to be. You're in Ute country, mister. And them ain't the friendliest folks that ever lived." He lifted a gourd dipper from the bucket and looked at the man. "How in the hell did you get here?"

"Wagon most of the way. Then the wagon broke apart and we rode the mules."

An ungodly shriek came from the back of the cabin and Preacher damn near swallowed the gourd. "What the hell . . . ?"

"That's her brother, Simpson. He caught the fever on the way here and went out of his head. I'm afraid he'll never get any better."

"We have to keep him chained out back," the woman said, walking up with two kids, a boy and a girl, holding onto her skirts. "It's a shame, but what else can we do?"

"That's why the Utes ain't bothered you none. Injuns are fearful of crazy folks. Keep him alive and they'll never come near this place exceptin' to maybe leave some trinkets for the gods."

"I'm Otis and this is my wife, Shirley, and our two kids, Otis Tom and Mary."

"Pleased. They call me Preacher."

"*The* Preacher?" the man asked.

"I reckon. I'm the only one that I know of."

"We heard of you all the way back in Illinois," the woman said.

"What are y'all *doin'* out here?"

A sly look came into the man's eyes and he and his woman exchanged glances. Preacher knew then the answer to his question without having to ask again. Gold. Well, he was in the right country for it. "Forget I asked. I know. Luck to you in your diggin' and pannin'."

The man and woman and kids stood and stared at him, no hospitality in their gazes. There came no invite to stay for food and that didn't surprise Preacher. Preacher guessed the man had found him a little pocket of gold or silver and he might be thinking that Preacher was out to steal it. Preacher stepped into the saddle and lifted a hand in farewell.

"You folks take it easy," he said. "You get the hungries for someone to talk with, you got a neighbor about thirty miles to the northwest and another one 'bout thirty miles past that. I seen the cabins but didn't stop to visit none."

Neither man nor woman had anything to say about that. Preacher shook his head and rode away without looking back.

"Friendly folks," he said to Hammer. "Gold does strange things to people. He'd have fainted if I'd told him there was a pocket not two miles from his cabin. Just for meanness, I ought to go over there and dig it out."

But he rode on. He had him a little sack of nuggets tucked back for any emergencies that might arrive and knew where more was if need be. When he was a good eight or ten miles from the cabin, he got him a rabbit and then found him a nice spot to make camp and settled in. He was carefully rationing his coffee now, for he was just about out and Bent's Fort was still a long ways off.

Preacher was in the high-up country now, in the land that

he loved. All about him loomed the mountains, silent, snow-capped guardians of the wilderness. Preacher's hand closed on the butt of a pistol as his horses stopped their grazing and lifted their heads, ears pricked. He heard the sound of horses' hooves. Two of them, he guessed.

"Hello, the camp," the voice called. "It's Elmo Pike and I be friendly."

"Come on in, Elmo. Be nice to talk with someone friendly."

"Preacher," the burly mountain man said, seeing to his horses first off. "Ain't seen you in near 'bouts three years, I reckon. You ain't got no handsomer."

"I'd talk was I you, Elmo. You got any coffee?"

"A-plenty, and I'll share. I put Bent's place behind me some days ago and stocked up right whilst I was there. Place got too damn crowded to suit me."

"Still sells whiskey, don't he?"

"That they do." Elmo sat down and poured a cup of coffee. "Got a drink there now called a Hailstorm. Right tasty, it is. Whiskey and wild mint and ice."

"Ice?"

"Yes, sirree. Bent built him an icehouse, he did. How long's it been since you seen the place?"

"Several years."

"It's changed considerable. You'll see." He peered at Preacher from under the brim of his battered old hat. "You becomin' a famous man, Preacher. They's talk that a big-city man who makes books wants to do a story 'bout you."

Preacher grunted.

"Bent's got lodgin' for up to two hundred men now. It's a regular city when it's full. And got him a cook that'll fair make you hurt yourself come eatin' time. Name's Charlotte. She's a lady of color, she is, and can shore make a table groan with vittles."

Preacher refilled his cup and leaned back. "I spent time with Rimrock and Windy and Caleb and ol' Carl Lippett. They all done give up furrin'."

"Carl still afeard of bathwater?"

"Worse than ever."

Elmo shook his head. "He's a good boy to have around when they's trouble, but he can get powerful odious at times. They give up furrin'? What they doin'?"

"Helpin' a bunch of pilgrims move to the Coast."

"Like you done last year, I think it was."

"Yeah."

"Sad times."

"For a fact."

The two mountain men talked until well after dark and then turned in. They spoke of men whom they had known, men who prowled the high country and the great plains. Men such as Beckwourth and Bill Williams, Fitzpatrick and Carson, and others less well known but just as brave and knowledgeable of the country they helped blaze. And they spoke of men who had gone into the Big Lonesome and never come out. They lamented the fact that settlers were moving in and cussed progress and so-called civilization.

Elmo was gone at first light, but not before leaving a packet of coffee for Preacher.

Preacher wondered if he'd ever see the man again, for with the coming of pioneers, the Indians were getting all riled up and putting war paint on, and he really couldn't blame them for it.

Preacher pulled out, riding cautiously and always alert, for he was in the heart of Ute country, and the Utes were fierce fighters and did not particularly like the white man. Preacher took to making a fire only in the mornings for coffee, and it was a very small one. At night, his was a cold camp. This high up it was cold in more ways than one.

Just south of Cross Creek, he teamed up with a trapper called Batiste who was heading for Bent's Fort . . . mainly for the lack of anything better to do. Batiste was a French Canadian who had just recently been up in the Northwest.

"You played hell, my friend," he told Preacher. "Three men looking like something out of a nightmare stumbled into a camp on the Columbia telling wild stories about a devil they had fought near The Dalles. They said the devil was called Preacher."

Preacher smiled and Batiste's eyes twinkled.

"*Oui, mon ami.* It seems that these men had been part of a notorious gang. Now only the three of them are left. The Shoshoni camp I was in last week, I tink, they were singing songs about the man called Killing Ghost . . . among other names he has. What this gang do to make you so angry, Preacher?"

Preacher told him about the Pardees and Sutherlin.

Batiste shook his head. "You did right. But you beware, Preacher. Way I hear it, the Pardees have much cousins and such east of the Missouri, and they might come looking for you."

"I ain't hard to find. What happened to the three who rafted down the river?"

"The foolish one, way I hear it, he lef' the camp and wander around in the woods. The trappers trew the utters out and tol' them to get gone quickly. I have a thought that they were kill' in the woods by Indians."

"Good riddance."

Batiste laughed and the men rode on.

Bent's Fort, a huge place with adobe walls fourteen feet high and four feet thick, with two musketry towers—which housed a small cannon—and massive iron-sheathed front gates, was unsurpassed in size or importance anywhere west of the Mississippi. The fort was built in '33, by Mexican laborers, and could garrison more than two hundred men and about three hundred animals. The fort had a main dining hall, and blacksmith, tailor, and carpenter shops. The lodgings were built around a huge courtyard. From out of the fort, scouts and mountain men led the freight caravan wagons of the Bent brothers, which were loaded with everything from trinkets to axes. They would be traded to the Indians for buffalo hides. Inside the fort, Indians from a dozen tribes came to meet and trade in the main council room or on the grounds outside or in the courtyard. Hostilities were left outside the walls. The Indians came to swap for trinkets, knives, axes, and guns, powder, and shot—usually obtaining them for buffalo hides, for by 1839, the beaver trade just about finished.

A huge American flag flew atop the lookout post just above the front gates.

There was also a saloon and billiard room, which is where Preacher and Batiste went immediately upon seeing to their horses and gear.

"Easy you go, Preacher," a scout called Watson whispered to him just outside the room. "They's a man in yonder making war talk about you. He's big and ugly and mean lookin'."

"He got a name?"

"Kelly."

Preacher shrugged his shoulders. I don't know any Kelly right off . . ." He trailed that into silence. "Yeah, I do. Or did. Bum Kelly. I helped hang the no-count a year or so back. Him and three others."

"You done the world a favor. Mayhaps it's his brother. Man ain't old enough to be his daddy."

"Any in there with him?"

"Three others. Just as big and ugly and mean lookin'."

"Thanks. But I do want me a jug and I don't care if they's fifty in there makin' war talk, I'm gonna have me one of them new whiskey Hailstorms Batiste has told me about."

Watson grinned. "They some good. I think I'll join you."

"Both of you just stay out of the way when trouble starts. I stomp on my own snakes."

Both men eyeballed the guns Preacher was wearing about his waist and smiled. Watson said, "This ought to be fun."

Preacher opened the door and stepped inside. The men walked to the bar.

The big room was filled with pipe and cigar smoke. A few men were smoking tobacco rolled up tight in paper, a custom begun in Seville in the sixteenth century, when beggars shredded discarded cigar butts and rolled them in paper to smoke them. Roll-your-owns had not yet taken much of a hold in America and the unorganized territories.

"Give us all one of them Hailstorms," Preacher told the man behind the bar. "And put lots of mint in mine. I do like the taste of mint."

"Watch your back in here, Preacher," the man replied in a whisper. "The four men at the last billiard table are gunnin' for you."

"Thankee."

The trio drank their Hailstorms and smacked their lips. "Another round," Batiste said. "You got anything to eat?"

"Bread and cheese and a roast over yonder," the man replied, pointing. "The beef roast is good. I guarantee it. Charlotte cooked it."

"You want some, Preacher?" the French Canadian asked, not speaking his name loud enough for it to carry.

"No. I'll wait 'til this dance is over. I fight better on an empty stomach. Makes me meaner. You and Watson go on over there and fill your bellies. This spot here might turn plumb unhealthy in a few minutes."

Preacher sipped his Hailstorm and waited. He had turned as if watching his friends, but he was really looking over at the four men at the billiard table. They were everything that Watson had said they were. Big and mean-looking and as ugly a quartet as Preacher had ever laid eyes on. And he had seen some uglies in his day.

One of the men turned slightly and stared at Preacher. He said something in a low voice and the other three straightened up and all looked at Preacher.

"Here it comes," the man behind the bar whispered.

"I reckon," Preacher replied, holding his drink in his left hand. "You best get out of the way."

"My name's Kelly. You kilt my brother, Preacher!" one of the four man hollered, laying his cue stick on the felt.

"Son of a bitch needed killin'," Preacher calmly replied.

"Damn your eyes and your black heart," Kelly said, and jerked out a pistol.

16

Preacher stepped to one side and the ball smashed into an empty keg. Preacher drew and cocked his pistol and fired, the double-shotted barrel flinging out fire and smoke and lead. Both balls struck the man in the chest and knocked him off his feet, slamming him against the wall. He slid down to rest on his butt, his eyes wide and staring and dead.

The room was filled with smoke and shouts as Kelly's friends all drew their pistols and opened up. But Preacher had hit the floor and had both big hands filled with pistols. The shots from his would-be assassins hit the bar and the wall behind it while Preacher calmly pulled himself up to one knee, took aim, and placed his shots well.

Kelly was joined in death by two more. The fourth man, his pistols empty, dropped his pistols on the billiard table, threw his hands into the air and shouted, "I yield! Don't shoot no more."

Several trappers grabbed the man roughly and tossed him onto the floor, tying his hands behind his back with rawhide strips. Preacher calmly began reloading the empty pistols as other men gathered around, looking at the strange and deadly pistols.

"Look at them hammers," a trapper remarked. "The bottom pair's set forward of the top pair. Damnest thing I ever did see."

"Looks awkward to me," another said.

"Wasn't awkward to Preacher," a third man said, quieting the debate.

Preacher looked at the remaining member of the quartet. He had been jerked to his feet and was staring defiantly at Preacher. "What's your quarrel with me?" he asked.

"Bum was my cousin and you kilt him."

"I helped hang him for a fact," Preacher said, holstering his guns. "And no man ever deserved it more."

"Here, now," a man said, bursting into the smoky room. "Cease and desist immediately. This type of behavior is simply not allowed inside the fort."

"Tell them over yonder on the floor all that," Preacher told the man, obviously some sort of official with the Bent brothers. "Well, tell *him* that. It'd be kinda hard to get through to the others, I reckon."

"Preacher didn't start it," Watson stated.

Preacher's name brought the official up short. He stared at the mountain man for a moment. "There will have to be an inquiry, sir."

"Have at it. I ain't goin' nowheres no time soon."

The inquiry was held within the hour and Preacher was absolved of all blame. The lone survivor of Kelly's party was shown to the front gates of the fort and told not to come back. He was last seen heading east.

Preacher lounged around the fort for several days, until he got restless. Early one morning he saddled up and rode out, alone, heading northwest into the Rockies. There was a lot of summer left, and Preacher had him a craving to see some country that perhaps he hadn't seen before. He thought he might ride clear up into Canada . . . but he wasn't sure. Two weeks later, a rider hailed his lonely camp.

"You be Preacher?" the man said.

"I be. Light and set. The coffee's hot and strong."

"There's a wagon train gonna form up next spring in Missouri," the man said, sitting down on the ground.

"Good for them. Now that you told me that, I know I'm goin' to Canada and I might not come back."

"Fifty wagons."

"Why are you tellin' me this? I ain't interested not nary a bit."

"I missed you at the fort by only a couple of days. Batiste told me which direction you took."

"That Frenchy should have buttoned his lip."

"They'll be a minimum of two people to a wagon come the spring."

"I told you, I ain't interested. Mighty pretty afternoon, ain't it?"

"This is an American-government-sanctioned wagon train, Preacher."

"Then let the *Army* lead it. I love this time of year in the high-up country, don't you?"

"That is disputed territory out there, Preacher. Other governments might look with disfavor at the American Army leading a wagon train. There are a lot of lonesome men settling along the Coast and in the interior."

"Tell 'em to marry a squaw. They's lot of fine-lookin' Injun women. And they make good wives. Work hard." He looked at the government man. "What are you tryin' to tell me, mister?"

"This wagon train will be comprised of approximately one hundred and twenty-five women, Preacher."

"*Women!* Are you out of your goddamn mind? *Women!* Who's gonna be drivin' the wagons?"

"The women."

"You're crazy! Or somebody's crazy. Them women, for sure."

The man shrugged his shoulders. "The men out here want women, these women want husbands. They have elected to brave the trip. You know the way and you've taken wagons across."

Preacher sat speechless.

"You come highly recommended, Preacher."

"I'm a-fixin' to leave highly recommended, too. And if you try to follow me, I swear I'll shoot you."

"What I'm about to tell you must never be repeated, Preacher. The President of the United States is backing this plan. He wants you to take the wagons across. This land must be settled and it must be settled by Americans."

"It's already settled. Ask the Injuns."

"Sir . . ."

"Who is the President?"

"Mr. Martin Van Buren."

"Who the hell is he?"

"Of course, you would have to come to Missouri."

"I ain't goin' to Missouri. I ain't leadin' no damn wagon train of petticoats, neither."

"Can you read, sir?"

"Of course I can read. I ain't ignorant."

The man handed Preacher a wax-sealed envelope. Preacher broke the seal and stared at the words. He blinked and rubbed his eyes and read again.

The messenger smiled.

"Twenty-five hundred dollars!" Preacher shouted.

"Then may I take it that you are interested?"

"Twenty-five hundred dollars?"

"May I tell the President that you will be in Missouri no later than April the first of next year?"

"Twenty-five hundred dollars!" Preacher shook his head and stared at the man for a moment. "I probably am about to make the biggest mistake of my life."

"Oh, I think not, sir. You might even find you a good woman to marry."

Preacher glared at the man and shuddered at the thought. "How many women?"

"No less than one hundred and twenty-five, sir. Perhaps as many as a hundred and fifty. All the equipment will be brand new and you can hire some men to assist you."

Preacher shook his head at the awesomeness of it all. He didn't even know if something like this could be done. "I ain't never even *seen* that many fillies in one spot."

"I am thinking it will be a grand adventure, sir."

"I've heard that before." Preacher was thoughtful for a moment. Back in the States, twenty-five hundred dollars was near 'bout ten years' wages. But a hundred and twenty-five women all in one bunch?

Preacher looked at the man and made up his mind. "Where is it you want me to come next spring?"

The messenger smiled. "You'll not regret this decision, Preacher."

Somehow, Preacher doubted that.